CW00339831

LOST SOULS

HOTEL ST KILDA

LOST SOULS

For Francine

Well done for making it to the end!

MICHAEL KNAGGS

Copyright © 2016 Michael Knaggs

The moral right of the author has been asserted.

Apart from any fair dealing for the purposes of research or private study,
or criticism or review, as permitted under the Copyright, Designs and Patents
Act 1988, this publication may only be reproduced, stored or transmitted, in
any form or by any means, with the prior permission in writing of the
publishers, or in the case of reprographic reproduction in accordance with
the terms of licences issued by the Copyright Licensing Agency. Enquiries
concerning reproduction outside those terms should be sent to the publishers.

This is a work of fiction. Names, characters, businesses, places, events
and incidents are either the products of the author's imagination
or used in a fictitious manner. Any resemblance to actual persons,
living or dead is purely coincidental.

Matador
9 Priory Business Park,
Wistow Road, Kibworth Beauchamp,
Leicestershire. LE8 0RX
Tel: 0116 279 2299
Email: books@troubador.co.uk
Web: www.troubador.co.uk/matador
Twitter: @matadorbooks

ISBN 978 1785892 967

British Library Cataloguing in Publication Data.
A catalogue record for this book is available from the British Library.

Printed and bound in the UK by TJ International, Padstow, Cornwall
Typeset in 11pt Aldine401 BT by Troubador Publishing Ltd, Leicester, UK

Matador is an imprint of Troubador Publishing Ltd

For Carol

Also by Michael Knaggs

Catalyst
Heaven's Door

For a list of characters featuring in the three books of the *Hotel St Kilda* series, see the author's website:-

www.michaelknaggs.co.uk

What man of you, having a hundred sheep, if he lose one of them, doth not leave the ninety and nine in the wilderness, and go after that which is lost, until he find it?

Luke 15

'It is better to risk saving a guilty person than to condemn an innocent one.'

Voltaire

CHAPTER ONE

Friday; 28 August

"Just like in the movies," the young man said to himself.

He was of medium height and average build, with longish dark hair; and casually dressed in designer jeans, tee shirt and a tan leather jacket. He was seated on a bench, looking out across the nearly-deserted park at a shining lake where a mother and her small child pitched lumps of bread at a squabbling group of ducks in front of them. Until now, except for one elderly lady walking her border terrier a hundred yards or so away to his right, they had been the only visible signs of humanity in the tranquil grassy oasis close to the town centre.

He wondered how many times he'd watched this scene play out in spy films and TV dramas. The only thing that was missing was a rolled-up newspaper under the arm of the man who was approaching him. Instead, he was carrying a small day-pack, which he removed from his back and placed between them on the bench as he sat down.

The new arrival was tall, in his early thirties, with handsome chiselled features and short, dark hair. He was wearing an immaculate charcoal grey lounge suit, pale blue shirt and navy-and-grey striped tie. He also wore a pair of soft leather gloves.

"Sorry," the first man said, with a smile which was close to a sneer. "I've forgotten the password."

The newcomer fixed him with an intense stare from behind his dark-tinted glasses. The first man broke the uneasy silence.

"I mean, this is all a bit John le Carré isn't it?"

The stranger raised his eyebrows in surprise, still remaining silent.

1

"Some of us do read things other than the back page of *The Sun*, in case you're wondering. Anyway, why didn't the big guy come himself?"

His companion looked momentarily confused, and then smiled.

"You needn't concern yourself with the chain of command."

He nodded towards the bag. The first man unbuckled the single strap, lifted the flap and peered inside. He let out his breath.

"What if I say no?"

"Then there'll be five instead of four."

He closed the flap again, fastening the strap and slumping back on the bench, legs out-stretched in front of him.

The stranger raised his eyebrows again; this time with a question.

"Okay?"

The first man nodded, nervous now. It was a long time before he spoke again.

"When?"

"Down to you. But a week from today I'll expect to have read all about it. Then we meet again back here. I'll let you know when."

He got up from the bench, leaving the day-pack and walking away.

★

Jonathan Latiffe rose from his chair as his visitor was shown into his office. He reached across the desk to receive the Parliamentary Under-Secretary of State for Prisons with a firm handshake. The Under-Secretary was tall, with an upright posture and a mane of grey hair which accentuated his height. Even so, his physical presence was diminished by the huge figure of the senior man, who was two or three inches taller and with a considerable girth held in place by a mid-grey three-piece suit. His dark blue tie matched the colour of his twinkling eyes. A native Black South African in his mid-forties, his greying tight curls and neatly-trimmed full beard added a distinguished element to his imposing bulk.

"Good morning, Lawrence." He beamed at his colleague, waving him to sit down. "It must be the 28th August."

"Indeed it is, Minister, and they got underway right on schedule.

2

You'll want the names again, I presume." He placed a three-page document on the desk in front of Jonathan.

"Thank you." The Minister of Justice scanned the alphabetical list of prisoners' names, slowing to focus on a few in the middle, before skipping through to the end. "Anyone here I should recognise, be aware of, anything at all?"

"None that I know of, sir. A mix of street terrorists and dealers, mainly the former. This will take Alpha up to five hundred and ninety-eight – two less than plan because of the two deaths in the first group."

"Quite. And the hotel expansion? Any update on Beta? Are we still looking at second quarter next year?"

"That's right, sir." He paused as if choosing his words carefully. "But it's a tight schedule and, if I may be so bold, Minister, I think what we are missing right now is a Tom Brown to push from the highest level. I know the Prime Minister is determined that the new regime must manage itself without parliamentary interference, but the Home Secretary was so hands-on in getting the first platform completed. That high-level involvement is conspicuously absent, however hard the current team is pushing."

Jonathan sighed. "Well, I'm afraid there is – or, perhaps, *was* – only one Tom Brown and from what I hear, he's hardly in a fit state to manage himself right now, never mind anything else. I think the sooner the PM gets round to appointing a successor, the better – even though he or she won't have the same focus on the Exiles."

"Will it be you, if you don't mind my asking?"

Jonathan smiled. "When I checked this morning, I was still second favourite at five-to-two, well behind Hewlett at seven-to-four on."

"I'm really surprised she's emerged as the front runner – you know, after resigning from the shadow position."

"Well, remember that was in the aftermath of the abduction of her daughter, and it was nearly three years ago. But it's the Press that are pushing for the appointment. She won a lot of friends when she gave up the Shadow Cabinet role to concentrate on her own constituents – which was the *official* reason for her resignation. And our leader likes the Press on his side – God knows he's used them to good effect often enough in the past – so he might just go with popular opinion. You can bet he'll look at all the angles."

"And would it bother you if you didn't get it?"

Jonathan hesitated. "I guess it would in a way. Not for me personally, but it would send out such a powerful message if we had a black Home Secretary." He smiled. "It would be ironic, wouldn't it, if the Minister for Diversity prevented that happening by getting appointed herself?"

"I think the Press would love it," Lawrence chuckled. "In fact, that might be the very reason why they're pushing for it to happen."

Both men laughed.

"Anyway, we'll see," Jonathan said. He stood up to signal that the meeting was over and his colleague got to his feet. "Thank you, Lawrence. Just remind me when the next lot will be leaving."

"Four weeks from now, Minister, on the 24th September. And it will be the maiden voyage of PTV2 with two hundred on board. Then we wait for Beta."

★

Monday; 31 August

Delaware Street was alive with young people, mostly students, bustling in and out of the cafes, bars, takeaways and amusement arcades which, along with a few charity shops and estate agents, lined the pavements on both sides. They chatted and laughed in small groups, which spilled across the road almost blocking the thoroughfare to traffic. The man standing in one of the charity shop doorways looked – and felt – very conspicuous.

At a couple of weeks shy of his fifty-sixth birthday, David Gerrard was over twice the age of any of the people milling around him. Not only that, but he was dressed very conservatively in a dark blue blazer, white open-necked shirt, grey trousers and black lace-up shoes. It would not have been his chosen outfit for this venue had he not decided to go there directly from a pre-term meeting of staff at the local College of Higher Education close to where he lived in the small village fifty miles away.

He completely filled the doorway of the shop which, at 6.30 on a Monday evening, was closed. Its small entrance served to accentuate his huge two-metre-tall frame and massive shoulders and upper body. He felt very much like the proverbial sore thumb, even though, he had to concede, no-one seemed to be taking any notice of him.

It was the fourth time he'd been on this street, and on each occasion he had been looking for the same person. His second and third visits had been during the previous three days when his feeling of self-consciousness had been offset slightly by what he believed was more appropriate kit of tee shirt, jeans, leather jacket and trainers.

The first time had been exactly three months ago.

A small group of people burst noisily from one of the bars across the street. Two young men and a girl, all around twenty or so, were arguing with a man in his forties who looked as out of place there as David. He was clearly the worse for drink, his hair long and uncombed, his face a mass of stubble. But his clothes, though casual, looked expensive and fashionable. He was tall and slim and, apart from his unsteadiness, looked in good shape.

One of the two young men stepped right up to him so their faces were just inches apart.

"Look, just *fuck off!* We don't want you in there. Fucking whining and asking questions, trying to take over the place." He pushed the older man in the chest, causing him to stagger just a little, more from the effect of alcohol than the actual shove. He recovered quickly and stepped forward, pushing back hard. The young man went shooting backwards, falling heavily, his legs flying up in the air almost sending him over in a backward roll.

"Don't you *ever* put your hands on me!" the older man shouted at him.

He got to his feet, but chose to stay a safe distance away and say nothing more. A number of people had followed them out of the pub and were watching the action unfold. A few were shouting obscenities at the older man and some were taking photographs on their iPhones.

The girl stepped forward, putting a friendly arm around him. "Look, just go – please. No point in getting into any trouble. Sorry about all that…" She nodded towards his assailant, who hadn't moved or spoken. He shrugged himself free of the girl's arm and strode off down the street to a chorus of laughter and jeers. The girl watched him go and shook her head, her forehead creased in a frown.

David had seen the same man there last Friday and had barely recognised him at first. What he still didn't know was *why* he was there. He set off to follow him.

The pursuit did not last long. A black cab was disgorging a group of students further down the street. The man put on a spurt and stopped the cab just as it was about to pull away, slipping into the back. A few seconds later, it did a quick three-point turn and sped away.

★

The black cab pulled into Grindalls Road, stopping immediately in front of the beer garden of the Cross Keys public house. The rear nearside passenger door opened and Tom Brown almost fell onto the pavement. He steadied himself against the cab, fumbling with his wallet.

"Eleven pounds fifty," the driver said, without looking at him.

Tom pulled out a clutch of notes, looking for a five to go with one of the tens. He didn't have one. He reached into the pocket of his jeans, grabbing a fistful of change, all of which spilled out of his hand onto the ground. He watched glassy-eyed as the coins rolled in all directions.

"Fuck!" he said to himself. "Got any change?"

"No, sorry, mate."

"Well, what a surprise!" Tom said. He pulled out a twenty and threw it onto the seat next to the driver. The cab pulled away almost before Tom had extracted his hand.

"Bastard!" he yelled as it disappeared round the corner. He turned towards the pub ignoring the cash scattered around at his feet.

The beer garden was bathed in light from the low sun. It comprised a large area of decking, separated from the pavement by a low wooden picket fence, with twelve picnic style tables, each accommodating up to six people. All available seats were taken and everyone was looking at him. He raised both arms in the air.

"Good evening, everyone!" he shouted. "Please, treat me as an equal. No autographs, but you may touch my garments as I pass." He laughed and set off across the decking towards the open double-door entrance, colliding with a couple of tables on the way. Most of the drinkers continued to watch him with a sort of sad fascination; others looked away in disgust.

He blinked several times until his eyes became more accustomed to the relative darkness of the interior. There were less people inside with only a few of the tables occupied and a line of four young men on stools at the bar. One of a quartet of girls in the far corner seemed to recognise him and nudged the one opposite her whose back was towards the door. The second girl turned round and got to her feet.

"Oh, Mr Brown," she said. "You're here again."

Tom screwed up his eyes in the direction of the voice, eventually focussing on its source.

"Megan? Is that you, Megan?" he said, then shouted, "Wonderful to see you! How're you doing?"

"Not great, actually. What about you?"

"Not great either," he said, "but, hey, let me buy you girls a drink."

Megan's three companions had got to their feet. "We were just going, actually," said the girl who had first seen him, "but thanks all the same."

"One drink!" Tom's voice carried to all corners of the room. Two of the men at the bar got down from their stools and turned towards them. Tom gave the girls his best attempt at a friendly smile. "How often do you get an offer like that from an ex-Home Secretary?"

"It's really nice of you, but…"

"*No-one* leaves here without having a drink with me," Tom's voice carried genuine menace now.

"Are you sure about that?" One of the men at the bar shouted across to him. Tom spun round, a little too quickly for his own good and staggered a couple of paces to his left. Megan caught his arm.

"Mr Brown, I'd like to have a drink with you, but my friends have got to go. They were just about to leave when you came in."

Tom shook himself free of her hand and flopped on to a chair.

7

Megan nodded to her friends who left hurriedly. The men at the bar sat down again.

"I'll have an orange juice, please, Mr Brown. What about you?"

Tom looked at her for a long time. Megan was breathing fast, clearly very nervous.

"Malt whisky," he said, almost in a whisper, then very loudly. "A *large* malt whisky; in fact, a fucking *huge* malt whisky!"

"Okay, I'll go and get them. You just wait here."

She went to the bar, where the landlord was looking across at her companion, shaking his head.

"Jonnie, can I have...?"

"Yes, I heard," he said. "Are you okay?"

"Yes, I'm fine," Megan said.

Jonnie Denver scooped some ice into a glass and tipped two measures of Glenlivet onto it before pouring Megan's juice. She reached into her bag.

"It's his round, Megan," Jonnie said. "Or on the house if he doesn't offer."

"Thanks." She smiled at him and took the two glasses across to where Tom was sitting with his eyes closed and his head drooping on to his chest.

"There you go, Mr Brown."

She placed the whisky on the table in front of him. He opened his eyes with some effort and reached out in slow motion to grasp the glass. Then he lifted it up level with his eyes and glared at it.

"*Ice*! Did I say anything about ice? You don't drink malt whisky with *ice*! What sort of a fucking place *is* this?" He slammed the glass down on the table hard enough for some of the contents to spill out over his hand.

"Mr Brown, *please*!" Megan shouted at him, taking him by surprise. He turned towards her, seeing the tears running freely down her face. He froze, not moving a muscle for several seconds, then he reached out to her and they held on to each other. When they broke off the embrace, Tom's face was wet with his own tears as well as Megan's, and he was more calm and lucid.

"He wasn't guilty, was he?" she said in a small voice.

"No, of course, he wasn't," he said, in not much more than a whisper. "And I'll tell you what, Megan…" loud and angry now "… people are going to pay for what happened to Jack – *and* Jason. Not one single person is going to get away with what they did."

CHAPTER TWO

Craig Belmont was grateful to find that there was very little blood. The Detective Sergeant was of average height and build with a boyish face which made him look younger than his thirty-one years. If someone was going to die violently, he thought, he didn't feel any guilt about hoping they'd die quickly, so the heart didn't have time to pump them dry. Nothing wrong in thinking that, he told himself. A humane, Christian thought, and nothing to do with the fact that, after twelve years in the force, the sight of a lot of blood still impacted on his stomach every time, sometimes to the point of emptying it.

The man sitting in front of him on an upturned crate, holding a cigarette in a shaking hand, had just sobered up faster than he had ever done before in a decade of almost continuous drinking. Ten yards away, a technician was attaching a couple of free-standing spot lights to a portable generator, while the scene-of-crime officers were taping off the area around the body.

"Are you alright to talk now, Mr Tonkin?"

Lewis Tonkin drew hard and long on the cigarette then nodded his head. He was also in his early thirties, small and wiry, with lank, dark hair and a few days stubble. He wore a pair of blue jeans, a long-sleeved tee shirt and trainers. They were all of good quality but had seen better days.

The detective called across to his colleague who was chatting to one of the SOCOs. "Nat! Ready now."

Natalie Crusoe walked across to join them. She was the same height as her colleague, slim and athletic, with short, light-brown hair and a round, friendly face.

"Mr Tonkin, I'm Detective Sergeant Belmont and this is Detective Constable Crusoe. Let's start by you telling us why you were hanging around at the back of Cobham Station at one-thirty on a Thursday morning."

"I wasn't hanging around. I wanted a piss. Toilets on the platform were closed. So I just – you know. When you gotta go…"

"The point of the question, is why the station at that *time*, irrespective of what you were doing there?"

"Been out for a few beers with the lads in Lambeth. Got the last train back."

"Which gets in at about half past midnight. Am I right?"

"I was pretty rat-arsed. I fell asleep on the train and nearly missed the stop. I must have fallen asleep again on the platform."

"So where had you been – with the lads – in Lambeth? Can you remember?"

"Not all the places. White Hart, Crown, Scooters, Slug and Lettuce." He paused, frowning, deep in thought. "No that's all. Can't remember the others."

The two detectives exchanged glances. "That's a pretty impressive haul without the others," Natalie said. "When did all this take place?"

"Started around five; got the last train back, as I said. Leaves Waterloo at about ten to twelve."

"And there are people who will confirm this – that you were with them during that period in those places?"

Lewis smiled and took another drag on the cigarette. "Landlord at the Slug certainly will; he had to ask us to leave. We were being a bit – you know – noisy." The smile disappeared. "Hey, just a minute, you don't think *I* did the bloke in?"

"We didn't say that," Craig said.

"Then why do I have to account for where I was? If I'd done him, I wouldn't be calling the police to report it, would I?"

"Not unless you were trying to be clever. No, we don't think at this moment that you did it, but we do have to eliminate you from our enquiries, don't we? So, if the time of death turns out to be sometime when you were with your friends, then that's you off the hook. Okay? But right now you're the only one we can definitely place at the scene of the crime. So tell us how you found him."

11

"Well, just as I'd finished – pissing, I mean – this car went past on the road behind the station and the headlights sort of swung round through the bushes and lit up the alley, just for a second or so. That's when I saw it. I thought it was a pile of clothes. Some people throw some great gear away, you know." He lifted up his right foot. "I found these trainers in a waste bin just up the road, can you believe? Anyway, it wasn't a pile of clothes… was it?" He drew on the cigarette and his hand began to shake again.

"So what did you do then?" Craig said.

"I phoned you lot, didn't I?"

"Did you check whether he was dead? Did you touch the body?"

"No, I…"

"Why not? How could you know he was dead?"

"Well it was fucking obvious. There was blood on the ground under his head."

"How was he lying? On his front or on his back?"

"On his back like he is now. Look, I've told you I never touched him!"

"Okay, if you say so, Mr Tonkin," Natalie said. "We have to be sure, you see." She nodded towards where the SOCOs were working. "Because if you did, those guys will be able to tell, and, of course, if we find out from them that you *did* touch him now you've denied it, we'll wonder why you haven't told the truth. You do understand, don't you?"

Lewis was looking from one to the other, his eyes wide and anxious.

"Also," Natalie, went on, "They'll know how he was lying when he died; whether it was face-down or not. Okay? We're just making you aware of what we'll find out in the next few minutes, so you have the chance to remember exactly how you found him and what you did."

Lewis's body sagged and he dropped the spent cigarette onto the ground.

"Okay," he said. "He was lying face down. I turned him over."

"Why did you do that?"

"Well… just to see if I knew who he was."

"So why didn't you tell us that?" Craig asked. "Why did you lie?"

Lewis shrugged. "Thought I'd get into trouble. You know – interfering with a crime scene or something."

"Or was it because you turned him over to check his pockets?" Natalie said. "And before you answer, they can tell if anything you have on your person right now has been removed from the body."

Craig shot her a quick glance, smiling to himself. Lewis sighed and reached into the back pocket of his jeans, removing a small wad of notes. He tossed them onto the ground in front of him without speaking.

"Not doing very well so far, are we, Mr Tonkin?" Natalie continued. "Do you want to tell us now why you killed him and save us a lot of trouble?"

Lewis held his head in his hands and was silent for a long time.

"Look, I didn't kill him. I saw the body – it scared the shit out of me, by the way – and I turned him over and checked his pockets. He had forty quid in his wallet – three tens and two fives." He nodded at the notes in front of him. "That's all. I thought, well, it's no use to him any more, is it? I didn't take anything else."

Craig's mobile rang and he walked out of earshot to take the call.

"Hi, Alice."

"Hi, Sarge. Your man checks out okay. A couple of drunk and disorderlies and one threatening behaviour *whilst* drunk and disorderly. Nothing else."

"Okay. Seems he's got a good alibi, anyway. We'll get a few names you can check with just to rule him out officially."

He stepped back to rejoin them.

"Apparently Mr Tonkin is *not* a psychopathic killer after all," he said to his colleague. "So no more lies, eh, Mr Tonkin. Let's see if you can get your story straight before our boss arrives. Okay?"

Lewis nodded.

"Do you recognise the man?"

"I've seen him on the train a few times. Don't know his name."

"Always on the train?"

"Yes, but only a few times, as I said. Probably once every couple of weeks at the most."

"Sergeant!" A tallish, sturdily built woman wearing a white hooded all-in-one called them over.

"Stay here," Craig told Lewis. The two detectives went over to where Doctor Amy White was ducking out of the taped-off area, pulling off her surgical gloves.

"Where's the DI?" she asked

"On his way," Craig said. "Been at a mason's dinner in Kensington; was supposed to be staying overnight. He'll be in a great mood. So, what have we got, Doc?"

"Single shot, back of the head from very close range. Fell forward – his face is smashed up a bit – so someone turned him over afterwards. Your guy?" Craig nodded. "Clean exit wound so the bullet will have carried God knows how far along the alley. Very little chance of finding it tonight. And I'd say, with the amount of rubbish lying around on the ground, it's hard to imagine the killer could have crept up on him without making a noise, so I reckon they probably walked down the alley together – one behind the other, perhaps."

"For what, I wonder – sex, drugs…?"

"Rock'n'roll?" Natalie offered. The others snorted a laugh.

"We've found a bit of billy on him," Amy said, "but nothing much. Wallet contains benefits card, weekly rail ticket, Visa debit card, but no cash."

"The cash was removed," said Craig nodding across to Lewis. "We'll get the SOCOs to bag it, and we'll need to fingerprint our lying little friend there. So we have an ID – from the cards?"

"Yes, your stiff is one Lawrence Harvey Newhouse of The Nook, Ivygreen Avenue, here in Cobham."

★

Saturday; 5 September

The young man stepped through the double front doors of his home, pausing to look anxiously up and down the street. It was a habit he thought he'd kicked some time ago, but which he'd slipped back into during the past few days. Mickey Kadawe was tall, dark-skinned – from a Black South African father and Indian mother – well-dressed and good-looking; and twenty years old.

He walked down the steps and across the street. His black

BMW Series 3 Coupe was waiting for him where the other car had been parked, three months ago, on the day Sammo Sampson had come bursting into Manston Grange with a rambling story about a guy who'd brought him round to see Mickey.

"So *why* has he brought you round?" he had asked Sammo.

"Well, he was *sent* to bring me here," Sammo said.

"Sent by who?"

"By you."

"So let me get this right. This guy met you and said I'd sent him to bring you here. Is that what you're telling me?"

"That's right."

"Why the fuck would I do that? You've got a phone haven't you? Why wouldn't I just call you?"

"Well, I…"

"And he's out there now?"

Mickey had gone straight out into the street, pushing Sammo ahead of him through the doors and down the steps. Sammo had pointed out the huge man sitting in the car holding a camera. There were three quick flashes and the car had pulled away, turning the corner onto Grindalls Road with a screech of tyres.

There had been no sign of the man since then at or near the house, and the passage of time had all but erased him from Mickey's memory; until the last few days. Sammo had somehow dropped off the edge of the world. It was a week ago from last Thursday when he had last seen him. It was Saturday today, so that was nine days. And right now he needed to know that things were okay.

He checked his watch. Just after midday. There was somewhere he needed to be – in fact, he was late. At least that would take his mind off it for a while. He opened the car door and slipped behind the wheel.

★

The Sweet Rock Hall was part of one of the huge leisure complexes that had been the main feature of Phase Two of Gerald Portman's Urban Redevelopment Initiative during his final year as Home Secretary in the previous government. In recognition of his enterprise, the complex had been named Portman Palace

15

and boasted four cinemas, two gymnasia, an outdoor training centre with a twenty metre high climbing wall, an Olympic-size swimming pool, eight fast food café/restaurants and the concert venue itself.

Inside the Hall, for the third time that day, the girl, with a brief apology, walked off the stage to seek the refuge of her dressing room. Technicians, musicians and stage hands sighed and fidgeted with frustration.

"What the fuck's wrong with her?" The stage director stormed up from his seat in the front row and kicked over one of the mike stands. "She might as well fuck off home if she's going to be like this all day!"

"Fuck off yourself, Malc! There must be something wrong; she's not usually like this."

Dagger-Zee, lead guitarist of Abattoir Ratts, leaped to her defence. Malc backed off.

"Yes, okay, Dags, you're right," he said. "It's not like her, but, we'll be right in the shit if his royal fucking highness…"

The door at the back of the auditorium swing noisily open and both men looked round.

"Oh, fuck! Speak of the devil. That's all we need," Malc said, half to himself.

The new arrival strode down the aisle to the stage.

"Don't let me interrupt," he said, looking round. "I trust the rehearsal's going well. Where is it, incidentally? I thought it was here."

"She's not well," Dagger said. "Not herself at all. I'll go and tell her you're here."

"No you won't," the man said. "Is she in her room?"

They nodded.

"How far have we got?"

Dags and Malc looked at each other.

"*Simply the Best*," Malc said. "Just polishing it up then…"

"*Simply the Best*! Correct me if I'm wrong, but isn't that the opening fucking number?"

He set off towards the dressing room area, then stopped and turned back.

"Has anybody seen Sammo?" he shouted.

Everyone shook their heads.

"Fuck!" He disappeared from the stage.

★

The girl leant with her hands on the table in front of the mirror, staring far beyond her own reflected image, as if looking for a solution to her dilemma. Every instinct pointed her in one direction, but the feeling of self-preservation had blocked the way so far.

The door crashed open behind her as if it had been kicked in from outside. She jerked upright with a start as his angry reflection appeared in the mirror.

"Sorry. Didn't hear you knock, Mickey, or I'd have shouted 'Come in.' She spoke without turning to face him.

"What the fuck's going on? What's wrong with you, for Christ's sake?"

"Just not feeling great. Thank you for your concern," she said. "Got a lot on my mind, right now. A lot to think about."

His expression changed. He spoke quietly and slowly, with more than a hint of menace.

"Oh, yes. Such as what? Anything to do with me, by any chance?"

She hesitated, regretting what she had said.

"Well, let's have it?" his voice was rising. He repeated, "Anything to do with me?"

"Not unless you shagged me when I wasn't looking," the girl said.

"What?"

"No, nothing to do with you," she said. "I think I might be pregnant, that's all."

He stared at her in silence for a long time. "That's *all*. Oh, what great news. Congratulations. I'm sure you'll make a wonderful mother – or, should I say, *would* have made a wonderful mother." He walked up behind her, his icy look holding her eyes in the mirror, and placed his hands on her shoulders close to her neck.

"The only problem is," he continued, "it doesn't exactly fit with our plans, does it?" His fingers reached forwards and upwards, tilting back her head and stroking her throat. "What with the three-

17

month tour I've just taken a fuck-load of trouble setting up starting in, let me think now, four weeks' time. And they'll be expecting to see all this exactly as it is now, right?"

As he spoke he ran his hands down the front of her body, touching her breasts on the way and pinning back her arms against her sides. His left hand caressed her bare midriff, gently fingering her navel, whilst his other hand reached further to just inside the top of her leggings.

"And we want all those thousands of guys out there imagining they're right here doing this to you, don't we? All part of the ticket price, after all."

He moved his left hand up inside her skimpy top, bending to kiss the back of her neck and lick the lobe of her ear. In spite of her fighting against it, she felt her body responding to his touch. She pushed back against him, seeking evidence of his own arousal. There was none – no reaction at all – confirmation of his sexual indifference to her. She knew why, of course.

"And they're not going to get a stalk on for a big lump and swollen tits, are they?" He was whispering in her ear. "That's *definitely* not what they're paying for."

He swung her round to face him. The anger blazed in his eyes.

"So here's the deal," he almost spat into her face. "If you *are* pregnant, you either get rid of it in time for the first date, or I'll replace you with someone else. Right? You're not that fucking special! Oh, and by the way, I'll see to it that you *never* get another chance. Okay? And while you're turning that over in your tiny mind, get out there onto that fucking stage! I've got more important things to think about right now than useless little prima-donnas!"

He turned and stormed from the room.

"Thanks for your concern!" she shouted after him.

A few moments later her anger subsided and she smiled to herself, pleased with the spontaneous lie about her suspected pregnancy. Easy to reverse – she would simply say she had been mistaken – and difficult for anyone to challenge her behaviour in the meantime. More to the point, she seemed to have deflected his suspicions from her real issue.

★

DI Harry Waters checked his watch – 11.27 pm. The fine rain was making a ruined evening seem even worse. This time he was the one waiting for his colleague to arrive, having dragged her away from a birthday dinner with friends. At least it wasn't *her* birthday, he thought. He'd mention that if she started complaining.

Members of the Crime Scene Investigation Unit had taped off both ends of the alley which ran between the back gardens of the two rows of detached houses on adjacent streets close to Woking rail station. Police cars were parked across both ends of each street and uniform officers were already knocking on doors asking residents if they had seen or heard anything unusual during the past hour or so. So far, no-one had, except the person who had phoned the police.

Harry heard the quiet purring of a large engine and looked round to see Amy White's 700 series BMW glide to a stop alongside one of the police cars. She gave Harry a little wave as she got out of the passenger seat before opening the boot to remove her bag and folded overall. One of the SOCOs held up a large umbrella for her as she sacrificed her dignity and hitched up her tight-fitting party dress to wriggle awkwardly into the suit, before pulling on her surgical gloves.

"Is this revenge for Wednesday night, Detective Inspector – for interrupting your booze-up in Kensington?"

"If you're inferring that I killed him just to get back at you, then no. And I do apologise…"

"Don't mention it, Harry. You did me a favour. I could never stand the birthday boy anyway. Just a business associate of my husband. Only attending out of duty."

They ducked under the tape and walked down the alley. Security lights operating on sensors at the end of most of the gardens shed enough brightness to illuminate the scene and cameras were flashing all round. The body was lying face down, arms stretched forward and one leg crooked to the side.

"Shot in the back of the head," Harry said, "like a carbon copy of the other night in Cobham, except we didn't have a kleptomaniac turning him over before we got here this time. Not touched him at all yet, so if you can find some ID as soon as, that would be helpful."

"Okay," Amy said. She nodded to Craig Belmont before walking across to the senior SOCO. "So here we are again, Rory. We can't go on meeting like this."

"You won't catch me complaining, Doc."

Amy laughed. "What have we got so far?"

Harry and Craig left them to it and walked on through the alley to where the uniformed sergeant was talking to a couple of his officers.

"Any luck, Mac?" Harry said.

Sergeant Bruce McDonald shook his head. "Nothing more, sir. No-one saw or heard anything. The guy who phoned us – Mr Gus Walton – had let his dog into the garden for a pee – better than taking it for a walk in this, I suppose. The dog went straight to the end of the garden and went mad, according to Mr Walton, barking and jumping about. He walked down to see what was wrong and – you know. But he said he hadn't heard anything before that."

"Right. Keep knocking and asking, Mac. Gets us a time of death quicker if someone did."

They set off back down the alley. Craig's iPhone rang. He stopped to take the call while Harry went across to where Amy was checking the body.

"Anything yet, Doc?"

Amy held up a wallet. Harry slipped on his surgical gloves and took it from her.

"Winston Grimes, according to his credit card. Same MO as Newhouse on Wednesday. Be interesting to see if it's the same gun – that's if we can find the bullet. Might not be tonight."

Craig walked up to join them.

"That was the desk at HQ, sir. We've got another. Behind some wheelie bins on a retail park. Couple of uniforms there already; seems he was shot from behind like this one."

"Christ! Where are we – bloody Tombstone? Looks like you won't be getting back to your party very soon, Doc."

"Well, at least that's one good thing. Where next then, Sergeant?"

"About three streets away. We could probably walk."

CHAPTER THREE

Sunday; 6 September

The prime minister's inner sanctum at 10 Downing Street was comfortable, functional, quiet and his preferred place of work when not on official duties in the building. And 'official' by his own definition was any formal meeting or gathering in what he regarded as the museum which comprised the remainder of the famous address.

This relatively secret office featured an antique wooden desk with red leather inlay covered by a glass top, with a well-upholstered swivel chair of similar vintage behind it and a pair of wing chairs in front. A huge sideboard occupied one side of the room and floor-to-ceiling book shelves the other, in front of which was a low, circular glass-topped table between two armchairs. The functionality was reflected in the scratches, stains and other marks on all the furniture and the untidiness of the horizontal surfaces, which played host to scattered documents, files and folders.

In spite of the informality of his surroundings, and the fact that it was Sunday morning, Andrew Donald wore an expensive pin-striped Italian suit, white shirt and Eton Old Boys tie, held in place with a pin which matched his cufflinks. He was a couple of inches over six feet, with dark hair combed to the side from a ruler-straight parting, above a round, boyish face.

Standing just inside the door when he entered the office was his chief aide, Marcus Henshaw.

"Good morning, Prime Minister."

"Good morning, Marcus. What have we here?"

The Sunday newspapers were stacked on the side-board in three neat piles as usual, but today one had been opened at a particular page and placed on his desk.

"Comment in *The Mail on Sunday*, sir. Peter Bridgley, page 25. I think you may want to read that first. Your tray is on its way. Anything more, Prime Minister?"

"No, that's all," Andrew said, absently, as he took his seat at the desk, already frowning at the headline, '*A Change of Heart and Mind?*' The door closed as he picked up the paper and began to read.

> '*How times have changed. Not long ago, never a day passed without Tom Brown, the then Home Secretary, giving at least a couple of interviews, charming us all with his smiling wit and convincing words. And whereas it is not possible for him to formally comment these days, that doesn't mean he doesn't have a lot to say. But what he does say bears little resemblance to his reassuring messages from the past.*
>
> *The national and international audience that he used to attract has been replaced by a somewhat narrower cross section of humanity, and the channels of communication made available to him by the media have been substituted by a louder voice and stronger language. But he remains as committed to his beliefs as ever. It's just that those beliefs are not only different to the ones he held before; they are diametrically opposite.*
>
> *For those who have only recently emerged from a coma, Tom Brown was the architect of the New Justice Regime which includes, among its provisions, expulsion – the permanent banishment from our society of anyone over the age of eighteen who misbehaves himself (no provisions for 'herself' at the moment) enough to be regarded as a nuisance. Mr Brown was so pleased with this popular – though brutal – way of dealing with high-spirited senior adolescents, that he began to extend it to other crimes earlier this year – the first on his list being Class A drug dealing. Against considerable opposition, even within his own party, he pushed this through, only to discover that his own son was, himself, a drug dealer.*
>
> *What subsequently happened to his son is something that no parent should have to endure, and we continue to extend to him our deepest sympathy for his loss. It has clearly had a devastating impact*

on his personal life as well as precipitating the end of his political career. However, Mr Brown still retains his clarity of thought. Only now he seems to think that expulsion is a bad idea.

In a series of impromptu speeches in bars and clubs in Central London and similar venues south of the Capital, he has been energetically sharing his U-turn with – it has to be said – an unwilling audience. Unwilling in the sense that they didn't go to that particular place on that particular day to hear a former politician attempting to discharge his guilt in a torrent of slurred clichés while they sipped their drinks. What is clear, however, is that strong support (sympathy?) for Tom Brown is still out there. He undoubtedly retains the ability to take large numbers – perhaps even a majority *– of people along with his opinions and beliefs.*

While he was around defending the contentious issue of expulsion, it was always likely to survive. It's just as likely to collapse with his opposing it. And, along with it, perhaps the whole NJR.

Over to you, Mr Donald!'

Andrew was prevented from tearing the paper to pieces by the knock on the door which signalled the arrival of his breakfast tray. By the time it had been placed on his desk, the plunger of the cafetiere depressed, and the junior aide had left the room, he was thinking more constructively.

He reached instinctively for the white phone on the desk in front of him and picked up the handset; then paused. He checked his watch – 9.15 am. Six hours difference – that would make it 3.15 am. He replaced the handset and took his mobile from his side pocket, scrolling through his contacts until he found the number he wanted.

"I need you here, now. It won't wait. Where are you? … Right, twenty minutes, then."

He ended the call.

*

The detective sergeant opened the rear door of the black Mondeo to greet the new arrival.

"Hi, Craig. Jesus, what a weekend," Harry said as he eased out of the car.

"Evening, sir. Sorry you had to turn out at this time on a Sunday, but we seem to have been hit by some sort of epidemic."

"That's okay, Craig. It's my wife you need to apologise to; she now has to listen on her own to the latest episode in the saga of her parents' dodgy central heating. She begged me to bring her along."

DS Belmont laughed. "You could always call her and ask for back-up, sir."

"No, as long as I'm out of it. So what have we got?"

"Same again, I'm afraid, sir."

Craig led the way across to the taped-off area at the end of the narrow cul-de-sac. The street was part of a small industrial estate behind the railway station, normally dark and deserted at this time on a Sunday evening but currently alive with police and SOCOs and brightly illuminated by the portable spot lamps, camera flashes and searching torchlights.

They stopped at the barrier while Harry pulled on the white overshoes and surgical gloves, then Craig lifted the tape and they ducked under it. A couple of the SOCOs glanced across at them and did a double-take. For once, DI Waters was not wearing his hallmark faded grey suit, but sported a pale blue cashmere sweater and black jeans under a navy soft-shell jacket.

"Been out clubbing, sir?" one of the officers asked.

"I'll be clubbing you in a minute, Jarvis. Tell me what you've got."

"Doc reckons same MO, sir. Head shot from behind. Probably dead before he hit the deck. Got the bullet already, so we should get a match tonight."

"Or no match," the DI said.

"Or no match; but if I was a betting man…"

"Yes, I'm sure you're right. ID?"

"Elliot Simms," Craig said. "Known to the police, but only as a drug user. Prosecution before the amnesty for use of crack but, as far as we know, soft stuff only for some years now."

"So what's all this about? No criminal background worthy of note, so who would want him dead? There has to be some link between these people. They're just too similar to be random targets."

"Except the first one, sir," Craig said. "Newhouse had previous, including two custodial."

"Yes, but they were some time ago. Recently, he's been pretty much the same as this one and the two last night." He turned to Rory Jarvis, nodding across to the figure in the white all-in-one kneeling over the body. "Any idea of time of death yet?"

Amy White stood up and turned to them as if she had sensed the nod in her direction.

"Hi, Harry. Don't tell me they've dragged you out of church."

Harry smiled. "Believe it or not, Amy, I went this morning."

"I *don't* believe it. Anyway, it seems like we have a bit of a rampage going on in Woking at the moment."

"It would seem so. Time of death?"

"Guesstimate for now, I'd say three to five hours ago. That would put it between five-thirty and seven-thirty. I'll be able to get closer when we get him to the morgue."

"Who found him?" The DI turned again to his sergeant.

"Phone call from a mobile about an hour ago. Desk said it sounded like kids. No reason why they should be round here unless they were up to mischief, so I guess they didn't want to stick around and get involved answering awkward questions. We'll be able to pinpoint the phone close enough to ask the right people some questions, but they couldn't have been any part of it. Unless they waited at least two hours before reporting it, which I very much doubt."

"No sign of them coming back to check out the scene? When I was a kid, I wouldn't have been able to stay away."

"There was a group of about six kids on bikes rode past the end just after we got here, but they disappeared when we approached them and we've not seen anybody since."

"Okay, well let's see if we can find them." He turned back to the pathologist. "How soon before you finish here, Amy?"

"CSI unit will be here for a while yet, but once you've checked over the late Mr Simms, we can get him to the lab right away. So we'll be there, let's say, thirty minutes after you sign his pass-out."

"Right, let's take a look-see."

★

Tom stared up at the unfamiliar ceiling, at the ornate chandelier with its sculptured rose; the decorative cornice; the picture rail. His mind was struggling to combine a confusion of disparate thoughts into some sort of reasoned picture. Vague calculations of timescales floundered for tangible results.

Eleven weeks – or thereabouts – since his close encounter with the River Thames on the central arch of Vauxhall Bridge. Or was it really a close encounter? A cry for help – that's what people say when you look like you're going to end it all and then you don't. If it was a cry for help, he had no idea who he was supposed to be crying out to. Anyway, he had changed his mind. Katey had been responsible for that – even though she wasn't there on the bridge. Except she was, of course. In his mind; in his heart. She'd made the difference.

So, eleven weeks back to then. And it was three weeks prior to *that* when his son had done what he, himself, had only pretended he was going to do.

Fourteen weeks, then, during which his world had descended into an unstructured procession of lost nights and half-remembered days. As a consequence, waking up as he just had, at a little before noon, with a severe headache and a wretched taste in his mouth, he was not at all surprised to discover that he had no idea where he was.

He was lying on a bed. That was a good start – he'd woken up in a lot worse places recently. He forced himself to move, pulling himself into a sitting position and swinging his legs round to touch the floor. The effort took its immediate toll and he fell back onto the bed clutching his temples and groaning. At least he didn't feel sick this time. In fact, he didn't feel anything. Except, that is, sadness, regret, shame… Come to think of it, he felt a lot of things, and most of all loss – his son – irretrievably; his wife; his daughter; Jason; and – very soon – his best friend… again…

He tried once more to sit up, then succumbed to the way of least resistance and went back to sleep.

When he woke again, he felt worse. His body now ached all over from being in an unnatural position for… how long? He checked his watch again, which his unknown host had removed from his wrist and placed on the bedside table next to him. It was 1.45 pm, nearly two hours since his last attempt to rise. What was the point in getting up, anyway? He had nothing planned for the rest of the day – or the rest of his life, for that matter.

Then he thought of Katey again and was swamped by a wave of guilt and shame. She deserved better from him than this. She had been a shining light for him and Mags through the darkest passage of their life, supporting them through the pain of her own double loss of a brother and a lover.

"For fuck's sake, get yourself together!" He shouted the words out loud at the chandelier, slowly sitting up again.

He looked around the room for some clue as to where he had landed. It was large and high-ceilinged and furnished in a regency style with a white marble fireplace and other period features. The luxurious patterned rug left about two feet of polished oak floor visible around the perimeter of the room. The mint condition of the furniture and features gave away the fact that it was a modern replica of the period, but the whole had a lavish and authentic feel about it.

He rose to his feet, noticing for the first time that he was wearing only his boxer shorts. He felt a sudden wave of panic, wondering whether he had been compromised in some way. Then he laughed out loud – such thoughts were part of another life. In this one he had nothing more to lose in terms of status and self-esteem. He took a few seconds to steady himself before walking over to open the large white-panelled door.

"Hello! Anyone there?" he shouted along the short corridor outside the room towards what looked like an open plan living area. There was no answer, not that he expected one. He could feel that the place was empty.

He turned back into the bedroom and went over to the window, pulling up the Roman blind to look outside and blinking in the brightness of the light. Immediately in front of him was the four-horse chariot of the Quadriga crowning Wellington Arch, and across to his right the main residence of the reigning monarch. From the buildings around him, he reckoned he must be on about the fourth floor. How the hell had he got there? He had no memory whatsoever of his movements over the past twenty-four hours… forty-eight hours… longer than that. In fact, the total recall of his recent past seemed to be distilled into a composite image of a bar interior assembled from vague recollections of the insides of numerous pubs he must have visited.

He looked round the room for his clothes, not remembering what he had been wearing and hoping he'd recognise them. They were on a large wicker chair on the far side of the king-size bed he had been occupying; polo shirt folded neatly on the seat and chinos draped, just as neatly, over the back. His loafers were under the chair, one rolled-up sock in each, cream linen sports jacket on a hanger hooked onto the picture rail behind the chair.

The sleeves and front of the jacket were damp. His keeper, whoever he – or she – was, had found the need to sponge something off. He groaned inwardly at the thought, and checked the other items. The shirt was okay, but the fronts of both trouser legs were also wet and one knee was torn.

Jesus, what have I been doing?

He heard a door open and close somewhere in the apartment; footsteps in the corridor outside. He rushed to put on his chinos and shirt, just before the bedroom door opened and a familiar face peered round it into the room.

★

Detective Inspector Joannita Cottrell was leaning forward in her chair, resting her elbows on the L-shaped desk. She was of medium height, with an attractive, shapely figure, and was from dual White British and Caribbean ancestry – 'three quarters West Indian', as she described herself. Her black curls with their blonde highlights hung loosely down around her face; her large dark eyes stared down at her hands clasped in front of her. She had been sitting in that position for twenty minutes, since arriving at the station at just after two o'clock.

The desk itself was completely devoid of any signs of activity – no papers, files, journals, not even a cup of coffee. The PC on the short leg of the 'L' at her left-hand side showed a blank screen. The knock on the door brought her out of her trance. She looked up.

"Come in!"

DC Natalie Crusoe entered the room clutching a single A4 sheet of paper. "Can I have a word, ma'am?"

"Of course, Nat. Sit down."

"How were things up in Leicester? Are they trying to entice you away from us again?"

"No, just had to attend court about the case I was working on – for about five minutes – before I got called back. Actually, that's how long I was at the courthouse before they told me I wouldn't be needed."

"So, a wasted journey?" Natalie said, eyes wide and innocent.

"Oh, I wouldn't say that," Jo said, smiling. "There was other stuff down there to occupy me over the weekend."

"So how is DS Carter?"

"He's fine, thank you. As big and as fit as ever. And yet… just as gentle."

Natalie fanned herself with the sheet of paper.

"Enough, enough! This isn't doing me any good at all."

Jo laughed. "Okay, so down to business then. You wanted a word?"

"Well, I'm not sure how all this fits together. Probably no mystery at all."

"Go on, I'm fascinated."

"We've had four fatal shootings over the past five days. No apparent motive, small-time victims, same MO – back-of-the-head shot – 9mm – same gun for each hit. One yesterday evening – we think around seven o'clock – two the night before – all three of those in Woking – and one last Wednesday night in Cobham."

"Gang reprisals, do we think?"

"Almost certainly not. These were loners – the only link they have to each other is how they died and the weapon that killed them. Plus… one other…" She paused.

"Yes?"

"The records show that you *personally* accessed all their files a few months ago."

Jo reached across the desk and took the piece of paper out of Natalie's hand. She looked at the four names.

"Jesus!"

"Ma'am?"

"One other link," Jo said. "These are all customers of a street trader called Sammo Sampson."

"I know Sammo – know him well. Trades in Woking, doesn't he? He's an arrogant little shit, can be violent as well, but I'm not sure he's capable of murder."

"I don't know, Nat, but he's the common denominator, or *one* common denominator. I think you need to speak to him." She paused to think for a moment. "And if he's *not* capable and he *didn't* do it, then our little shit might be in deep shit himself. Either way, we need to get him off the streets, quick!"

Natalie stood up. "I'll get him picked up right away." She started to leave and then stopped in the doorway. "So do you know any reason why they should all be dead?"

Jo remained silent for a while before answering.

"Yes, I think I might. Get the hunt for Sammo started then come back in here."

"Okay."

Jo took out her mobile and wondered which one of three people to call. It took her less than five seconds to choose; and to decide she needed to see him rather than phone; and see him before Natalie came back.

★

Tom went through into the living area feeling much better mentally and physically after a long, hot shower. The sight of the full cafetiere in the middle of the dining table made him feel better still. His host lifted it up as Tom sat down.

"Shall I be mother?"

"Yes, please," Tom said.

Tony Dobson pressed down the plunger and filled two mugs. Tony was a youthful thirty-two, average height, slim and with a pleasant, friendly face. As a young reporter learning his trade, he had been one of Tom's fiercest critics, but over recent years their growing mutual respect had turned into genuine friendship.

"And talking about you being mother, I'm dreading to hear how you've been looking after me for the past – how many hours – days?"

"Well, if you're *absolutely* sure you want to hear," Tony said, giving him a grim smile. "Just how much do you remember? Last night you only just about recognised me."

Tom shook his head. "If you assume I can't remember anything, that will be exactly right. In fact, at this moment, I have no recollection of where I've been for God knows how long. Who was it who said 'a couple of weeks ago I went onto a whisky diet and I've already lost three days'? I used to think that was funny."

Tony snorted a laugh. "Bad as that?"

Tom looked round at the open-plan surroundings. In contrast to the bedroom, they were ultra modern. The eat-in kitchen was large and square with plain white gloss cabinet doors and black granite worktops round three sides. In the middle, where they were seated, was a chrome, tubular-frame, glass-topped dining table with six matching chairs. The fourth side of the room was open and led through to an enormous living area where three black leather sofas and a rectangular coffee table of a similar chrome-and-glass design were positioned in front of a modern tiled fireplace. The rest of the room was filled with other clusters of easy chairs and tables and modern standard lamps. The ceiling was as high as that of the bedroom, but instead of a chandelier, the kitchen and seating areas were served by a series of spotlights angled out of suspended horizontal chrome tubes.

"Well you can start by telling me *exactly* where I am now," Tom said. "And how you can afford a place like this."

Tony smiled. "You are currently in one of the most expensive apartments in the Capital, in Grosvenor Crescent, Belgravia. You were in the third bedroom, by the way; the other two are about twice the size and have a view of Hyde Park. And the answer to your second question is I *can't* afford a place like this. It belongs to an Arab friend of mine; someone I did an article about last year which made *Times* magazine and described his role in a recent business issue rather more sympathetically – and accurately – than had been the case to date. It opened quite a few doors for him in the West and he has since shown his gratitude by allowing me to use this place whenever he's away. Which, I'm shamelessly happy to say, is most of the time."

"Well, it's very impressive, although a little inconsistent with its décor. What period – or periods – is it meant to be?"

31

Tony laughed. "I think of it as a time machine. You live all day in the twenty-first century then go to sleep two hundred years ago."

"Well, whatever, I'm very glad to be here *and* very grateful. So what happened? I guess I'll have to find out sooner or later."

"I got a call last night around nine o'clock from a guy I know. He'd found you asleep on a bench in Woking railway station. He didn't know what to do so he called me, knowing that you and I are friends. I suggested he put you on a train and I'd meet you at Waterloo, but he didn't think you'd be able to find your way to where I suggested we should meet. In the end he stayed with you until I picked you up in Woking. I brought you back and – well, here we are."

Tom leaned his elbows on the table and put his head in his hands. "Jesus, Tony, I'm really sorry. Woking? What the hell was I doing in Woking? What possible reason would I have for going there?"

"Well, that's where Jack used to spend a lot of his time."

"Yes, but why would *I*...?"

Tony held up his hand to stop him. "It's not the only time you've been there, Tom. I've heard of sightings on Delaware and at the Cross Keys. Both places where Jack used to hang out. Both in the past week."

"Sightings? Are you having me watched?"

"No, but I might do for your own good after what's just happened. There are always guys around taking pictures. Most end up on YouTube or Facebook, but some of them aim higher and try to get into the official press. I'm always getting offered stuff to use, and probably *would* have used it five years or so ago before I became respectable – thanks in part, to you, of course. I've been contacted a few times with reports and pictures of you."

"So I've been hanging round Woking this past week? What was I doing?"

"Not exactly winning lots of friends. Bit of a fracas on Delaware, but not really your fault, according to my source. A bit aggressive with some girls in the Cross Keys but, again, nothing major. In fact, one of them was Jack's girlfriend – Meg, is it?"

"Megan. Oh, God! What have I been saying to her?"

"Well, apparently, you had a friendly chat with her but only after you'd scared away a bunch of her friends. No harm done, so nothing to worry about *except,* of course, that you can't remember any of it. That should *really* worry you."

Tom was silent for a long time before speaking. "Listen, Tony, I'm really grateful. God knows what could have happened…" His voice broke.

"Well, you've survived so far. But, as your temporary mother-substitute, I'm telling you that you're grounded for tonight. You can stay here until tomorrow and remind yourself what it's like to wake up without a hangover. You just might like it."

"Don't know about that," Tom said with a weak smile. "Was it the same guy who said 'I feel sorry for people who don't drink…'"

"'Because when they wake up in the morning that's the best they're going to feel all day'. Yes, I've heard it before and it *is* a joke, remember. It's not real life."

"Okay… Mum… I'll do what you say. And I must get in touch with your friend to thank him."

Tony sighed and shook his head. "Well, before you go gushing all over him, I have to tell you he's not so much a friend as an associate."

Tom frowned. "Meaning?"

"A member of the Press. You might as well see these now as later." He pushed a couple of morning papers across the table to Tom. "The *Mail* and *Mirror* must have been on their toes to get this into their first editions."

The *Mirror*'s second story at the bottom of the front page had the headline *'Then and Now'* above two pictures of Tom. The *'Then'* picture was a reproduction of the image of him making his statement to the Press shortly after his resignation as Home Secretary and Member of Parliament for Princes and Marlburgh, which made the front page of all the dailies the following day. It showed him dishevelled and unkempt, his eyes struggling for focus, gripping a lectern with one hand to steady himself, and wagging a limp finger at the camera. The *'Now'* image was of a man seated on a bench on a railway platform, leaning forward with his elbows resting on his knees and his head in his hands. His hair was uncombed and his clothes creased. It was not obviously him because the man's face was not visible, but Tom recognised his own clothes and had no reason to believe it was other than who the story claimed it was. Under a brief description of the two pictures were the words *'What Next?'*

The *Mail's* message was similar although it only featured the latest picture in the railway station.

"I'm sorry, Tom. He did warn me he was going to use the picture and I tried my best to talk him out of it. But I can understand his point of view. It's going to sell papers, and that's his job. What he did point out, though, was that when that first picture was published, it generated a wave of sympathy. And he's right about that. This is more likely to do the same than to damage you in any way."

Tom's initial flash of anger changed rapidly through despair to indifference. He looked up into his friend's sad eyes with a blank expression.

"To be honest, Tony, I don't really care. It couldn't get any worse, that's for sure."

★

Chief Superintendent John Mackay listened tight-lipped from behind his oak desk. He was a large man, and still relatively fit for his fifty-two years, although now he carried a little too much weight around his middle. His arms were stretched out in front of him, hands gripping the edge of the desk, bracing his ample frame against the back of his chair. He was drumming with his fingers on the desktop as if he was playing a key-board.

"And this means exactly what, Jo? How does it fit with anything that's gone before?"

Jo Cottrell looked surprised at the question. "Well, there's very clearly a common denominator here, isn't there? Going back to what we discussed some weeks ago…"

"And *dismissed* some weeks ago."

"Yes, but this puts a new spin on it surely, sir?"

"Okay, tell me then, what *is* this very clear common denominator?"

"Well, Mickey Kadawe, of course. What or who else could it possibly be?"

John sighed. "Okay. Explain to me how and why he is involved with the deaths of four nobodies in Woking and Cobham."

"Well, isn't it obvious?" Jo spread her hands in exasperation.

John shot forward, leaning a long way across the desk, taking Jo by surprise.

"It's not obvious to *me*, Detective Inspector," he growled, "or I wouldn't be asking you to explain it."

"No, sir. Sorry, sir. The four deaths were all users whose main source was Randall Sampson – known as Sammo. He was the one who led David Gerrard to Mickey Kadawe. Kadawe is Sammo's supplier." Jo opened her eyes wide and shrugged, as if she had just explained everything.

"And why would Mr Kadawe, who we believe has a shrewd business head on his shoulders, choose to start bumping off his own clients? Or his client's clients, anyway."

"Well, because of their links to Jack. Each of these users approached Jack on Delaware."

"Along with four others who, as far as I am aware, are still alive."

"Yes, sir – as far as we know. But they could be next."

John shook his head. He leaned back again.

"Let's just go back to that discussion a few weeks ago and recap on what we concluded. Please, stop me if I go wrong, Detective Inspector, because it seems my recollection of it may not agree with yours. In fact, let's go back even further."

He got to his feet and began pacing back and forth behind his desk, an action which, by design or otherwise, always made Jo feel she was being disciplined.

"Jack Tomlinson-Brown and Jason Midanda were found guilty of peddling Class A drugs based on the following evidence." He began counting on his fingers. "*One,* a total of seven people phoned the police about some dodgy crack they'd received from two local dealers, their descriptions of whom matched those of Jack and Jason. Four of the seven subsequently came forward and positively identified them from photographs as the two dealers. How am I doing so far?"

"Look, sir, I know all this stuff and I don't think it's necessary to…"

"Oh, this is for *my* benefit, DI Cottrell, because I can't help feeling that I must have missed something along the way or perhaps just forgotten it. So, *two,* one of the users said he'd been to Jack's home and thrown a bag of the stuff over the perimeter wall exactly where a bag was later found when the grounds were searched. A bag which had that user's prints on it.

"*Three*, direct police surveillance and CCTV picked out Jack on twelve occasions being approached by eight different users on Delaware, all of whom were known at some time to be into Class A drugs. And just to be absolutely fair and objective about this, so you know that I *have* been listening to you, four of those eight were the four recently shot to death in Woking and Cobham, *including* the one approached by David Gerrard at your request. Right?"

"Not exactly, sir. It was David's suggestion and..."

"You tried to talk him out of it?"

"Well... no."

"Then, as far as I'm concerned, it's no different to it being at your request. Agreed?"

Jo said nothing and John continued.

"So, *four* – and the absolute clincher – following an anonymous tip-off, Jack's and Jason's houses were subjected to raids led by you and DI Waters, respectively. At each location Class A drugs were found, along with surgical gloves and mobile phones whose numbers matched those given by the seven users who originally contacted the police." He paused and stopped pacing, leaning on the back of his chair looking down at Jo. "Have I missed anything?"

"Only the party at Jack's and the break-in at Jason's. To be *absolutely* objective...sir. When it was just possible – as Harry admitted at the trial – that the drugs could have been planted."

"At the break-in, yes, according to Harry," John said. "*Not* the party. That was just an unsubstantiated suggestion by the Defence." John sat down again. "So," he continued. "That, as I remember it, is the evidence upon which a guilty verdict was reached. *Not* the verdict that you or I – or any of the investigating team, for that matter – wanted, but one which I understood we had both accepted as correct. And which, unless you can come up with something better than you have today, I *still* accept as correct."

There was a long pause before Jo broke the silence.

"So we just ignore what's happened?"

"*Ignore!*" John thundered. "Of course we don't *ignore* what's happened. Harry's team will be working flat out to track down the

36

bastard who killed four sad, but harmless, young men and I've no doubt along the way, they'll establish *why* he – or she – or they – did it. If – and it's a massive 'if' – the reason links in any way to Jack and Jason's case, then I'll be the first one racing to knock on your office door to let you know. But until then, leave it alone and let Harry get on with his job."

Jo remained silent for a long time again before speaking.

"Just one thing, sir; when I get back to my office, DC Crusoe may be waiting for me and I'm going to have to tell her why I was checking out those guys. Given that it was sort of unofficial, I don't know what to tell her. Harry's going to go ballistic if he finds out I've been checking up on his case without him knowing. I just wondered whether you *did* tell him at the time and, if not, whether you want me to put off seeing Nat until you have."

John leaned back in his chair. "That's a very good point, Jo," he said. "No I didn't tell him. Do you know if he's in right now?"

"I believe so, sir. He'll be holding his briefing at four and I think he'll expect Nat to have an answer from me before then."

John picked up his desk phone and pressed the intercom button. "Sir?"

"Janice, can you ask DI Waters to come up here right away, please."

"Yes, sir."

Jo got up to leave.

"No, stay there, Jo. I want you here when I tell Harry. If there *is* going to be an issue I want it out in the open now so we can sort it between us."

★

Total silence was not the reaction Jo expected or wanted. The quiet simmering rage was apparent, but not the angry, resentful outburst she had been preparing to meet head-on with her own energetic display of righteous indignation. Harry Waters *was* clearly displeased, but his dignified calmness was to be admired, Jo conceded, once she had got over the anti-climax of not having a battle to fight and win.

"I don't have to tell you, Harry," John Mackay was saying, "that it had nothing to do with my having any doubts over your handling of the case *or* your integrity in objectively cooperating with any further examination of any aspect of it." John raised his eyebrows inviting a response, which was not forthcoming. He continued, "I personally felt – and *still do* – that there were no grounds for further investigation. However, in the light of Jo's continuing concerns, I sanctioned her to go back through the records to satisfy *herself* there were no underlying links between seemingly unconnected parties involved in the case."

Harry finally spoke, in a quiet voice filled with rancour. "And all this was as a result of DI Cottrell's bully-boy catching and threatening one of the innocent guys caught on camera? A guy who wasn't even *questioned* in court."

"Because the investigating team couldn't *find* him!" snapped Jo, "That's why!"

"And a guy who is now dead," Harry went on. "And who's to say whether or not as a direct consequence of…"

John's hand came crashing down on his desktop, taking them both by surprise

"Enough! Angry words and accusations are not what are needed here. If anyone is to blame for a lack of communication it's me, and I'm not about to resign, so we're stuck with each other. *I* sanctioned Jo, at her request, to check through the records – making it very clear that I had absolutely no intention of officially re-opening the case. And *I* chose not to inform you, Harry, because I was – and still am – convinced it wasn't going anywhere; that nothing significant would come to light. And…" he turned to Jo, "… nothing has. Right, DI Cottrell?"

Jo sighed and nodded.

"So let's all get back to work and catch the person who is probably Woking's first ever serial killer. There you go, Harry – a chance to get into the records books. And it could be, of course, that their common trader *is* a relevant link; that Mr Sampson just might be an important lead."

Harry turned to Jo. "So what are you planning to tell Natalie now that she believes you've virtually solved the case?"

Jo shrugged with exaggerated indifference. "Whatever you want me to tell her."

John got to his feet with a wide smile. "Well, I'm sure you don't need me for this, or my office to discuss it in. Two DIs should be enough to decide what to tell one detective constable. Meeting closed. Thank you, both."

CHAPTER FOUR

The white BMW M6 Coupe pulled to a stop at the entrance of the apartment building on Vauxhall Bridge Road in SW1. The driver nudged his sleeping passenger, who blinked himself awake.

"We're here."

"God, that was quick."

"It's only just over a mile, Tom. I'm amazed you had time to go to sleep."

"Are you coming in?"

"No, thanks; got to get on. Some of us still have jobs, you know?"

Tom smiled. "The last person who said that to me was Grace Goody, the day before my calamitous meeting with the press."

"Well, I'm sure it was more memorable coming from her. Where is she, anyway? I thought perhaps, you know, you and her … She might be what you need to keep you out of trouble."

"Not sure where she is. I think she's still in the US. And there certainly isn't any 'you and her' as you put it. One day – off the record – I'll tell you all about it. Perhaps *not* off the record."

"I can't wait. Just let me know when. And in the meantime, if you're going to pass out somewhere, can you make it a bit nearer than Woking?"

"It's a promise." He shook Tony's hand, holding onto it. "Thanks again, my friend. I really do appreciate all you've done."

"I know. You take care."

Tom waved as Tony pulled out into the traffic then let himself in the main entrance by tapping the four-digit code into the security key pad. He tried to remember the last time he'd been there. It couldn't have been long ago; there was no build-up of mail behind the door of the apartment; and only a couple of messages unchecked on the answer phone. Neither from Katey, he noted sadly. Not that he expected they would be.

He tossed his jacket onto the bed in the master bedroom before walking through into the huge living area with its floor-to-ceiling windows in a wide half-circle overlooking the Thames. He opened the drinks cabinet and took out a glass and a half-full bottle of Jack Daniels and flopped onto one of the large black leather sofas. Before he had time to pour himself a drink, there was a knock on the door.

It took him a few seconds to realise what the sound was. His apartment at Balmaha in SW1 comprised half of the top floor of the building. A large ornate landing separated it from a second property, which had remained unoccupied for four years. It was a situation which had suited him perfectly, to the extent that he had considered acquiring it himself, as both an investment and to maintain his practical isolation. The only visitors he had ever received up to that moment had always rung his doorbell from outside the building at street level.

The man standing on the landing was tall and dark and in his early thirties. He was also strikingly good-looking behind the pair of heavy-framed spectacles which seemed to be at odds with the designer jeans and tight-fitting tee shirt.

"Hi. Just heard you arrive and thought it polite to introduce myself. Oscar Strange – your new neighbour." He extended his hand which Tom took.

"Hi, Oscar. Tom Brown." He frowned. "How long have you been here – I mean, living here?"

"Only since yesterday; still moving in. I'd invite you over for coffee but I've hardly got anything in there yet. Nowhere to sit, for a start. And anyway, I'm afraid I've got nothing stronger."

He smiled and nodded at the bottle and glass Tom was still holding.

Tom gave a hollow laugh. "Just tidying up," he said. "Why don't *you* come in and have a coffee, seeing as you're half way here."

He stepped back and the young man was past him and heading for the living room before he had time to move again. Oscar sat down in the exact place Tom had just vacated, leaning back, crossing his legs and stretching out his arms along the back of the sofa. Then he sprang to his feet and walked over to the window.

"Wow, what a view. I'm facing the other way, of course. Still good, but nothing like this. Don't want to swap, I suppose." He laughed.

"You suppose right," said Tom. "Would *you* like something stronger than coffee?"

"No, thanks." He was looking round the room, rather intrusively, Tom thought. "In fact, I won't stay this time, if you don't mind. Got a load of stuff still to do."

He turned and strode out of the room and down the short corridor towards the door. "Great to meet you. See you soon, no doubt." He let himself out before Tom had time to speak.

★

The office door opened a fraction. Harry's head poked round.

"Can I come in?"

"Be my guest."

"What are you doing right now? Have you got a few minutes to spare?"

"Oh, yes please," said Jo. She moved the curser on the screen in front of her and closed the document. "The boss has got me surfing the bloody net for any information that could be linked to a gun-running set-up down in Brighton. Guess where I'll be going next."

"Well, we do like to be beside the seaside, don't we? Although I guess it does take you quite a bit further away from Leicester."

"Is there anyone in this station who doesn't know about my love-life?"

"No, nobody. Which is why my next question may be a bit unexpected. How do you fancy seeing a movie?"

Jo frowned. "This is all a bit sudden, Harry. When exactly?"

"Well, I thought right now – hence the question about whether you had time to spare."

"Now? At midday on a Tuesday? Exactly where did you have in mind?"

"My office; and attendance is mandatory. Shall I send out for some popcorn?"

Jo could hear the sound of moving equipment in the background as the person answered the phone.

"DI Cottrell, what a pleasant surprise."

"How are you, David? What's that noise?"

"You always phone when I'm at the gym halfway through an exercise? Right now, I'm on the cross-trainer. You must think I spend all my time here."

"Oh, no I don't," Jo said. "In fact, you'd be surprised how much I know about how you spend your time."

There was a pause before he replied.

"Meaning what, exactly?"

"Meaning I need to see you; *officially*. So it won't be the Olde London or the Dog this time, I'm afraid. Can you come to Guildford?"

Another pause.

"I'm fascinated. It can't be for fiddling my expenses because you didn't pay me any. We're not going to fall out of friends are we? Seb's not told you to stop seeing me?"

"God, I'm fed up of people going on about Seb. No, of course we're not going to fall out of friends, David, but I'd really like you to come in without any further questions. I suggest we meet somewhere away from the office and then we'll come in together. Okay?"

"You mean so it will look like you've caught and arrested me. I don't suppose there's any chance of you wrestling me to the ground is there?"

Jo laughed. "How is it you always do that?"

"Do what?"

"Make me laugh when I'm trying to be serious. But I do need you to come in, David. If you do, I'll ignore the sexual connotations of that last remark and not charge you with harassment."

"I really don't know what you mean, but of course I'll come to Guildford if you need me to. Can I finish on the cross-trainer first? Only a couple of minutes to go."

She laughed again. "It will keep until tomorrow. It's not that desperately urgent."

"Just tell me when and where. And are you going to tell me what and why as well?"

"No, but you'll work it out. You used to be a detective, after all."

★

Wednesday; 9 September

Tom rolled over and nearly off the bed at the sound of the banging. He checked the digital clock on the bedside table, moving the empty Jack Daniels bottle out of the way so he could see the display. The large red numbers said '10:45' and the smaller letters and digits underneath told him it was 'WED 9 SEPT'. How fortunate, he thought, to have a clock that tells you what day it is.

He sat up and swung his legs out of bed, reaching down for the short bathrobe that had found its way onto the floor. He got to his feet, pulling on the robe and wondering why he didn't feel worse than he did. Perhaps the answer was the empty bottle – he seemed to remember it had only been half full when he got it from the cabinet... when... twenty-four hours ago? That was a long time for it to last. Perhaps he had finished a second bottle and still didn't feel half bad. That really would be worrying.

The noise, whatever it was, had stopped. Perhaps it had been nothing at all; perhaps he'd dreamt it. No, there it was again; his heart sank. It was someone knocking at the apartment door, and it could only be one person. As if to confirm the worst, this time it was followed by the sound of a voice.

"Tom! Mr Brown! Are you okay?"

The words seemed very loud and clear for someone shouting from the landing. He moved across to the bedroom door and listened. He could hear the muted sound of carefully-placed footsteps in the corridor outside. He looked round for a possible weapon and, seeing nothing suitable, grasped the handle of the door and pulled it open, stepping out.

Oscar Strange took a small step backwards but recovered quickly, lunging forward and grabbing the lapels of Tom's robe, pushing him against the wall. He released his hold immediately and stepped back again before Tom could react.

44

"Sorry, Tom. Jesus, you scared the shit out of me," he said. "Are you okay? The apartment door wasn't properly closed and I thought there must be an intruder in here. I've been knocking and shouting for about five minutes."

Tom straightened his robe very deliberately and stepped up close to the younger man.

"Look... *Oscar*! I'm not sure how you got in..."

"I just told you – the door wasn't properly closed. I stood outside knocking and shouting... I didn't know whether you were okay or what. Check the door; I haven't smashed it in or anything."

"Okay, okay!" Tom held up his hands "However you did it, I don't want you in here uninvited. Right?"

"Well, shit! What if you *hadn't* been okay? What if somebody *had* got in?"

"I've lived here for four years, quite happily and securely without a neighbour, I don't need looking after, thank you."

"Well, I'm not sure about that, Mr Brown. I did see Monday's papers, you know. And that's why I was worried. I'm sorry I bothered."

He turned to leave. Tom reached across and grabbed his arm to stop him.

"You're right, Oscar. *I'm* sorry. You didn't deserve any of that. I guess just because I don't like myself at the moment, doesn't give me the right to dislike everyone else." He smiled. "As you can see, I'm alright, but thanks for your concern."

"That's okay, and I'm sorry I said that about the papers. I guess you've every right to drown your sorrows after what you've been through. Not sure that I could deal with something like that." He held out his hand. "Can we be friends?"

Tom shook his hand. "Of course. Look I'd invite you for that coffee again, but I need to get a shower and..."

"That's okay. I've got stuff to do. Got to catch up at work. I've taken quite a bit of time off to move in the past couple of days. Perhaps sometime later?"

Tom walked him to the door and closed it behind him. He turned to go for his shower, then stopped and turned back. Opening the door a few inches, he released it and watched it close with a decisive clunk. He checked it had locked, and then opened it again.

This time he rested it as gently as he could against the jamb, so the spring mechanism could not generate any momentum. Even so, it closed smoothly and locked.

He shrugged and went to get his shower.

★

Jo's door opened a fraction and half of DI Water's face appeared.

"Hi, Harry."

"Hi. You might want to see this news feed, just for information. Putting out a misper appeal on all channels for Sammo. On in a couple of minutes."

"Okay, thanks. A bit soon, isn't it?'"

"Better safe. We absolutely saturated Sammo's patch yesterday after your meeting with Nat and no-one has seen him for nearly two weeks, including his family – parents, siblings. Not been home or anything. Anyway, it's just coming on."

She stepped out of the office into the MIT room where a group of detectives from the team covering the murders were gathered round the large TV screen angled high across one corner of the room. One of the *Morning is Breaking* presenters was announcing the half-hourly local news bulletin.

"And now it's just coming up to eleven-thirty and time to look at the news where you are."

The two national news presenters were replaced on the screen by an almost identical couple seated on a similar curved sofa. The missing person announcement was the second item covered. A full facial and a profile of Sammo were shown side-by-side.

"Police are looking for a local drugs trader by the name of Randall Sampson – know as Sammo – in connection with the recent deaths of four users in the Cobham and Woking areas. Mr Sampson, who is listed on the Police Register of Licensed Street Traders, is not a suspect in the case, but police are concerned about his safety, given his close association with the four victims, and ask that he go to the nearest police station and make himself known. Mr Sampson, who has not been seen for nearly two weeks, is five-foot eight to five foot ten inches tall – that's between 1.75 and 1.8 metres – slim build, with longish dark hair and a Mediterranean complexion. He is not

46

thought to be dangerous, but the police advise members of the public who see him not to approach him but to contact them immediately on one of the three numbers shown at the bottom of the screen."

★

The Ministerial Director of Justice reached sleepily for her mobile, thinking it was its alarm waking her. She pressed the 'OK' key a couple of times to no effect before realising it was an incoming call.

"This is Goody," she said, putting on her glasses.

"Good morning, darling."

"Oh, good morning." She yawned.

"I guess I probably woke you up. What time is it in Chicago? Six am?"

"Five-fifty to be exact."

"I'm sorry about that, but it means that while we're talking I can picture you lying there in bed in a hot hotel room in minimal nightwear – perhaps none at all – and vulnerably disorientated by your sudden awakening."

"And in this fantasy of yours, am I on my own?"

"Well, as it's *my* fantasy, then, yes, you're on your own. So tell me, how close am I?"

"Well, you can forget the hot hotel room. It's freezing in here with the air conditioning. So, what's new over there?"

"Did Uncle Don call you?"

"Yes, he told me about his new job. Sounds interesting."

"Right. Well as far as the rest is concerned, I'm counting the minutes to your coming home, of course. Everything's ready for you. Rubbish has been cleared out – except the article you wanted keeping. Update on the drug issue is on your desk awaiting your return, and the appropriate items deleted as requested. Look, do we have to talk about work. Can't we say how much we've missed each other and stuff like that. You know, like normal people."

Grace laughed. "I've never really thought of you as being normal. There'll be time for that very soon. But thanks for the call; must get some clothes on – you know how it is?"

"Okay. But just for now, then. Bye. Love you."

"Love you, too."

She ended the call, pulled on a dressing gown and walked over to the balcony of her twenty-fifth-floor suite. She opened the French windows and stepped outside to where the temperature had already climbed to a comfortable twenty degrees. The phone sounded again. This time it was the alarm and she let it run its course while she scanned the panorama in front of her. Beyond the imposing bulk of the Sears Tower – just two blocks away – she looked out across Lake Michigan, the heat haze blending its horizon seamlessly with the early morning sky.

Leaving the windows open she went back inside to prepare for the final day of her extended visit, which would include attending lunch with the US President and a closing address from his Chief of Staff. She was pleased to be leaving. It wasn't that she hadn't enjoyed the assignment and, in particular, the time away from Andrew; not to mention the close and charming attention the President himself had paid her. She wondered how many of his security people would have listened in to the carefully guarded and coded phone call she'd just had with her associate back in the UK. CIA? FBI? Perhaps even Homeland Security. She hoped it had sounded innocent enough for it not to get back to the President himself. They seemed to have established a close personal bond, and she didn't want that spoiled by his believing she had a lover back home.

However, she needed to get back. There were things to do that only she could manage; and the personal issue of Tom Brown to take care of, one way or another.

*

They hugged for a long time on the pavement outside Costa in the small pedestrian precinct close to Guildford New Station. As always, the embrace had a comic element to it; David was just over a foot taller than Jo and, to save arching her back, her face always ended up nestled against his chest.

"You look great," she said, placing the tray of coffees and cakes on the corner table where David had settled himself.

"And you look wonderful, too," David said. "Same as last time. Which was only four weeks ago, come to think of it, so you wouldn't expect too much degeneration since then."

She laughed. "And how's the new job at the college? Not frightening them too much, I hope. Do you wear your street-cred action man disguise?"

"No, the college closes before the nine o'clock watershed, so I'm not allowed. This is only my second week, but it's going okay, though I wouldn't really call it a job."

"So, what would you call it?"

"Well, its official title is part-time lecturer on Local Government Management at Cullen Field College of Higher Education. Two days a week; two forty-minute lectures each day; one in the afternoon, one in the evening. Total working time – one hundred and sixty minutes; less than three hours a week. So it doesn't *seem* much like a job. Anyway, most of the questions I get asked are about how I got to be so big, how someone as old as me manages to keep in shape and stuff about when I played rugby."

"Well, that's pretty flattering isn't it?" Jo said, with a sly smile. "There can't be that many pensioners attracting comments like that from a bunch of teens and twenties. You'd better watch you don't get a reputation."

"It's just as well they don't ask me questions about the actual subject, because I tell them everything I know up front in the lectures."

Jo laughed again. "And let me guess. The days you work are Tuesday and Thursday. Right?"

David nodded. "And you know that because I'm here today and last Friday and Monday, I was appearing on reality television. You said I'd work it out, and you were right."

Jo became serious. "Have you heard about Laser?"

David shook his head. "What about him?"

"We've had four killings over the past week – one in Cobham, three in Woking. The first was Laser, in Cobham, late last Wednesday."

"Shit! How? Why?"

"All shot. One link between the four deaths is Sammo Sampson. They were all his customers *and* four of the people seen approaching Jack. We've been looking for Sammo for the past twenty-four hours and nobody – I mean *nobody* – has seen him in nearly two weeks. They even asked Kadawe if he knew where he was. This morning they put out a misper on local TV and radio. And, as you'd expect, they checked CCTV in all the places he might be, the most likely of which being…"

"Delaware Street," put in David.

"Correct. And that's where they picked you out on camera. In the very same place where they'd normally expect to see Sammo. Harry Waters – remember him? CIO on Jack and Jason's case – wants to talk to you. This is his case, not mine."

"Does he know we're meeting beforehand?"

"Yes. I asked him and he okayed it. Johnny Mac told him the other day, for the first time, that I'd been looking into the Jack and Jason case *after* the convictions. He had to tell him why, of course, so your part in it had to come out. And to be fair to Harry, he's been okay about it; a lot more reasonable than I would have been. But less than twenty-four hours after he heard about you and been told you were no longer involved, up you pop on TV. So I'm afraid you're not DI Waters' favourite person right now. And I had to tell him that I had no idea what you were doing there. I'm sorry, I felt like I was letting you down, but… well, I *didn't* know…"

David held up his hand. "Hey, it's me who should be sorry – *am* sorry. You made it very clear that it was job done as far as I was concerned. Laid off, I think you called it. It's just that when we met last month, I felt you were still unsure, that it was still preying on your mind. And I still regret missing the opportunity to get more out of Sammo when I had the chance instead of charging after the Duke. If I *had* talked to him about Laser – and the others – well, perhaps you wouldn't be in this state."

"I wouldn't say I'm in a state, David."

"Okay, wrong choice of words. Still haunted, then. How's that? And if I'm honest, I actually enjoyed tracking down Laser and Sammo and Mickey Kadawe. That's what I'm good at; not preaching to a bunch of kids who are just counting down the minutes until they can go home. So I thought I'd try to find him again and put it all to bed. Naturally, I started back at the place where I found him last time."

Jo was silent for a while, then she reached across the table and placed her hand on his. "Thanks, David. You're always looking out for me, aren't you? And you're right; I haven't let it go, although I'd told myself I had. I didn't fool you, though, did I? And if I convinced

Johnny Mac, then I've just *un*convinced him by charging into his office telling him the killings prove I was right – which they don't, of course."

Neither spoke for a long time. David took the opportunity to demolish his cake.

"There's something you need to know," he said, "unless you've already spotted him on camera as well. On two of the nights I was on Delaware – Friday and Monday – Tom Brown was there as well. Same place, more or less the same time each day – six-thirty-ish – right opposite where I was standing. First time, he was going into a pub and hadn't come out by the time I'd left. Second time he got into an altercation with some young guy outside the same pub. Then he got into a cab and left. And you must have seen these." He reached into his pocket and pulled out a couple of folded sheets of newsprint, spreading out the front pages of Monday's *Mail* and *Mirror* on the table.

Jo nodded. "Yes," she said. "Terribly sad, don't you think?"

David nodded. They sat in silence for a while.

"So," David said, eventually. "What happens now?"

"We'll go in and I'll introduce you to Harry. He wants to see you immediately after his four o'clock team meeting. You're not a suspect, but, obviously, he needs to ask you some questions, given that you were looking for the same guy that we are – a guy now possibly linked to a number of deaths. My guess is it will be fairly informal – no recording, for example, although he's likely to have Detective Sergeant Belmont with him. He'll probably warn you off, and it would be better for both our sakes if you heeded that warning, David. Although I really *am* grateful – honestly."

David smiled. "Okay. And what about afterwards? Are you going to take me for dinner? One coffee and two pieces of cake aren't going to keep me going until I get home."

"*Two* pieces of cake?"

"Well, you haven't touched yours. I just thought…"

★

The interview room was small but not unfriendly, with a pale-brown woven carpet and four comfortably upholstered chairs

51

placed two either side of a rectangular beech-top table. It was well-lit by spotlights set in a cream tiled ceiling, the same colour as the walls. Harry Waters and David Gerrard faced each other across the table with Craig Belmont on Harry's left. In the middle of the table was a tray containing three mugs of coffee. Craig had a small notebook open and ready in front of him.

"Thank you for coming in, Mr Gerrard. I'm Detective Inspector Waters and this is Detective Sergeant Belmont. I believe you have already met with DI Cottrell and she will have told you why we need to speak to you. She may have also mentioned that this will be an informal meeting, *if* what you tell us is what we expect. You are *not* a suspect. We value DI Cottrell's judgement far too much to believe she would be friends with a serial killer." He smiled and David gave a little laugh. "Okay, Mr Gerrard?"

"Okay. But please call me David?"

"That's fine with us, David, but we do need answers to some questions. And, before we get to those, I think it's only fair to tell you I am not impressed with the fact that you accosted a number of people on my patch a few months ago in pursuit of proving that I had failed to do my job in the Tomlinson-Brown case." He held up his hand as David leaned forward to speak. "However, I do understand *why* you did it and I have enough respect for Jo Cottrell to put that on one side. I just wanted to get that said and out of the way. Okay?"

"Okay. But let *me* say that DI Cottrell never questioned the integrity and efficiency of the investigation. Her concern was with the issue of fast-tracking under the new regime, and the pressure that puts on officers to, perhaps, accept things more readily than they would otherwise."

Harry nodded. "So, on the subject of DI Cottrell's concern, can you start by telling us in your own words why *you* were pursuing Lawrence Newhouse and Randall Sampson in the first place?"

Harry leaned back and Craig reached for his note pad. David paused to collect his thoughts before answering.

"Jo Cottrell has the best instincts of any police officer I have ever worked with. You have to appreciate that to put into context what I did. I understand she was not involved in the case you mentioned except to lead the raid on Etherington Place, and that she was chosen to do that because she was new and because Tom Brown and his family had some very close friends in the senior police ranks at Guildford. It suited the needs of the case to use someone with no previous history with the target. Right?" Harry nodded; David continued, "So when she carried out the raid and found the drugs, she was meeting the family – or the three that were there – for the first time. She had no knowledge or preconceived ideas as to what they were like and how they would react in that situation."

"I understand all that, Mr Gerrard – David, but what is your point?"

"That her assessment of Jack's reaction was one hundred percent objective, uncluttered by any expectations. And she was *convinced* that he had no idea that the drugs were in his room."

"And because of that belief, she chose to ignore all the rest of the evidence which pointed towards his being a dealer?"

"Absolutely not, but you know how it is with instincts and, as I said, Jo Cottrell's are the best."

Harry got up from his chair and paced back and forth in the limited space available.

"You know, I've thought a lot about the case since then, David. Especially because of what happened to Jack and the devastating effect it had on the family of a man I couldn't have admired more. We all wanted to be wrong. You talk about accepting things too readily, but we dissected every bit of evidence that we got to support our case, pulling it apart to try to find something unreliable about it. I've never known anything like it; the police working as hard as they could to avoid making an arrest and then a conviction. But everything – I mean *everything* – pointed the way we didn't want to go."

He stopped pacing and stared at the wall, deep in his own thoughts.

"But let's get back to the original question," he said, sitting down again. "Tell us how you got involved."

"Jo shared her concerns with me. She wasn't sleeping; couldn't leave it alone; kept going back in her mind to Jack's reaction. She mentioned the fact that none of the guys caught on camera had been questioned, thought that was unusual – that was her point about fast-tracking – wouldn't have happened in the olden days before NJR, she said. So…"

"And what about you? What did you think?"

"I told her the police didn't need to call them in for questioning, that they – you – had enough witnesses to support the case. I felt she was most likely wrong – still do."

"So why, when she asked you to look for Laser…"

"She didn't ask me. I offered, and at first she said no. I told her to think about it and she changed her mind."

"Okay then, why did you offer when you believed she was wrong?"

"Two reasons. Firstly, Jo's instincts – as I already mentioned. In my experience, except on one occasion only, Jo's feel for a situation has been spot-on every time, so if she felt that way it was worth a look. And secondly, I wanted to help her put it behind her. I believed she would come round to thinking she'd been wrong this time as well. That was the main reason."

"And I heard you had a very productive day's hunting. First Laser, then Sammo, then 'The Duke' who turns out to be Kadawe. Quite impressive for a few hours work. So, take us through what happened that day. In fact, start with how you planned it with DI Cottrell."

"I thought Jo had told you."

"She has, but I need to hear it from you. Let's say so we can *officially* eliminate you from our enquiries into a multiple murder and a missing person."

David smiled and nodded. "Well, as I said, I offered to do a bit of digging on her behalf if it would settle her mind. Jo said no thanks, then phoned me saying she'd changed her mind. We met at my place and she brought copies of some stills from the CCTV tapes on Delaware. They showed Jack and Laser – Lawrence Newhouse – and, on one, Sammo was in the background. She also gave me Laser's address – which is actually his Auntie's address – in Cobham."

"So these were the stills used as evidence by the Prosecution in Jack and Jason's case?"

"Copies of the stills."

Harry shook his head. "Go on."

"Day one, I showed his picture around a few of his known haunts. No-one had seen him – or so they said. Day two, I waited outside the house and got lucky. I saw him go in, waited a while longer, he came out and I picked him up. We... chatted... and he told me how Sammo had put him up to approaching Jack, but said not to tell Jack he'd sent him. He also said that when he asked Jack about the stuff, Jack acted as if he didn't know what he was talking about."

"And then he took you to Sammo?"

"No, he showed me where I could find him and told me when he was likely to be there. He also mentioned 'The Duke'. Said that he was the big guy and that Sammo was scared stiff of him."

"So you waited for Sammo...?"

"That's right – same day, on Delaware where I got caught on camera this time. He turned up and – long story short – I persuaded him to take me to 'The Duke' who turned out to be Kadawe."

"When you say 'persuaded him'...?"

"Tricked him, I guess. I said Mickey had contacted me and told me to pick him – Sammo – up and take him to Mickey's place."

"And when you got there – to Manston Grange – what happened then?"

"Not a lot. I dropped Sammo off, he went inside and I waited in the car. A few minutes later, Sammo came out of the house, Mickey right behind yelling at him. I took a few quick photos of him and drove off."

"And Jo ID'd Mickey from the photos?"

"From the address, actually, before I got chance to show her the pictures. The name of the house is above the front door."

Harry sighed and shook his head again. Then he shrugged.

"Water under the bridge, I guess. So what did it prove?"

"It didn't *prove* anything; just flagged a couple of questions."

"Which were?"

"Well firstly why did Sammo make sure Laser approached Jack where the CCTV cameras couldn't fail to pick him up and identify him? And, secondly, why didn't he want Jack to know he had sent Laser to speak to him? And if I was Jo, I'd been flagging the link – or 'loop' as she calls it – which connects Jack to Laser, Laser to Sammo, Sammo to Kadawe, the circle being closed by Kadawe's close friendship with Jack."

"Christ! It's not at all complicated, is it?" Harry said. "If Jack was a dealer, of course they'd all know each other, wouldn't they? Not so much a loop, more of a… matrix."

"I totally agree," David said. "And I told her that."

"But Jo didn't buy it?"

"Well I didn't get chance to say that until after she'd been to see Chief Superintendent Mackay, and by then he'd already said pretty much the same, and probably more succinctly."

"And it's clear the chief believed she'd let it go, perhaps not straight away, but certainly by now."

"I thought she had as well. Then the last time we met – about a month ago – she started talking about it again. It didn't seem to be bothering her all that much, to be honest, but I always regretted not pressing Sammo more about why he chose that exact spot and why he didn't want Jack to know he'd put Laser on to him. So I went and waited in the same place, which is where you picked me up on camera. Jo had absolutely no idea what I was doing, by the way. In fact, I'd decided that if I didn't succeed in speaking to Sammo, I wasn't going to tell her I tried."

"And I take it you didn't succeed?"

"No, I didn't."

Harry shook his head and sighed. Then he smiled.

"By the way, you might be interested to know that, in *our* search for Sammo over the last twenty-four hours, we asked Mickey Kadawe if he knew where he might be, and he described someone who he felt might be responsible for his disappearance. Someone who sounded remarkably like you – except this guy had a shaved head, tattoos and an earring."

David stretched his neck and pulled open his shirt at the collar, turning his head from side-to-side.

"Well, as you can see, no pierced ear and no tattoos."

"I didn't say *where* this guy was tattooed."

David laughed and raised his hands in surrender. "Okay, guilty as charged – for the tattoos, not Sammo's disappearance."

"So, did you ask around on Delaware; ask anybody if they'd seen him; knew where he was?"

"No."

"Did anyone approach you? Anybody ask what you were doing there; what you were after?"

"No, nobody."

"Challenge you in any way?"

"No."

Harry smiled. "Can't say I'm surprised. Did you see anyone acting suspiciously?"

"Before I answer that, can I ask if *you* saw anyone else of interest when you picked me out on camera?"

Harry furrowed his brow and leaned forward, clasping his hands together on the table in front of him.

"Go on."

"Can I show you on the CCTV recording?"

★

The street lights along the road behind the boundary wall of the park, halfway into their full glow, reflected in the smooth water of the small lake. This time, in the gathering dusk at a little after seven in the evening, there were no duck-feeders, no dog-walkers; just the same two men occupying the same bench with the same day-pack between them.

"So what happens now?" asked the smaller of the two men.

"Job done," his companion said. "You give me the bag, I give you this." He took a stuffed brown envelope from the side pocket of his cashmere pea coat. "Then we shake hands and go our separate ways. Great doing business with you."

He handed over the package and picked up the bag, opening the flap and checking inside. His companion looked at the thick wads of fifties and pushed the envelope inside his bomber jacket, tucking it into the top of his jeans. They stood up and shook hands. The taller man was wearing the same leather gloves.

"Just one more thing," he said. "We need to get rid of this." He held up the bag. "We'll do it now so we're both happy with where it's going."

"We can't do it here." His companion looked around the park.

"Other side of the pond. Found the perfect place. Looks like some sort of burrow in the bank. We can get rid of it for good. Come on, we do this together, then I promise, it's all over."

They walked over to where the ducks were languishing in a silent group under an overhanging willow. At the men's approach they swam purposefully across, eager for any food that might be forthcoming, and paddled along the water's edge close to them as they walked round the perimeter of the lake. Between the back of the lake and the high boundary wall of the park the trees and undergrowth were thick and untended. They picked their way carefully, the taller man leading, through a mass of brambles, nettles and dead branches. He stopped at the back edge where the ground was less overgrown on a narrow grassy bank overhanging the water. In front of them more branches hung low over the lake blocking any view of the park itself.

"It's down there," he said. "If you reach under you'll feel where the hole is."

"If *I* reach under. Why do *I* have to reach under?"

"Oh, come on," said the other man, smiling. "You're more dressed for it than I am. You get down and I'll pass you the bag. Mind you don't fall in or drop the money."

The smaller man carefully knelt down and shuffled to the edge. He leaned forward, bending his arm round under the bank.

"Can't find a hole," he said, straightening back up again.

"Not a problem."

The muffled shot was loud enough to send the ducks flying up off the lake.

*

David pressed the answer button on the steering wheel as Classic FM was interrupted by the ring tone of his phone.

"Hi."

"Hi. Where are you?"

"I'm just coming off the M25 at Junction 30; nearly home. By the way, what you can hear in the background isn't traffic noise, it's my stomach rumbling."

"I'm really sorry. I assume you got my message from Tina. Johnny Mac had some guys up from Brighton for a meeting. It's where I'm probably going next."

"Not back to Leicester, then?"

"No, not yet. And don't you dare mention anything about being further away from Seb. I've had that already."

"Never crossed my mind."

"How did you get on with Uncle Harry? He's alright, isn't he?"

"Yes, it went okay I think. You were right about me not being his favourite person, but he's clearly got a lot of time for you. And we watched a movie together, just like you did. I'm surprised no-one had spotted Mr Brown. I think DI Waters was a little embarrassed when I pointed him out."

"It's this knack you have of stealing every scene, David."

"I was just going to say that, but it sounds better coming from you. So what about dinner? Do I get to see you again soon?"

"Of course, that's the main reason I was phoning. I was thinking maybe lunch though – on Saturday? We can do the Dog and Duck or Ye Olde London, or somewhere halfway between us off the M25. What do you think? Sevenoaks, perhaps."

"To be honest, I've had enough of the ring road today to last me for a long time. Can we do the London again; just both jump on a train. Shall we say midday?"

"Great, see you there."

CHAPTER FIVE

Thursday; 10 September

The half dozen conversations filling the major incident team room with noise died away quickly as the two detective inspectors stepped out of one of the side offices. Harry Waters checked his watch.

"Morning everybody. Eight-fifteen; let's get started. I've asked DI Cottrell to join us this morning as she was the one who put us onto Sammo. It will keep her in the loop without me having to remember to pass anything on."

He turned to Jo. "Before we start, Detective Inspector, could you bring the group up to speed on the Sammo connection?"

"Yes, of course. Natalie asked me on Monday why I had been checking all four victims' files a couple of months or so ago. The reason was that the Chief Super had asked me to tick a few boxes for his final report on the Jack and Jason case and the four people concerned were among the eight who were observed on Delaware approaching Jack. When Nat showed me the names, I remembered they were all customers of Sammo Sampson."

There were some puzzled looks and furrowed brows.

"You're not suggesting, ma'am, that these deaths are in any way connected with that case?" Craig Belmont asked.

"Highly unlikely," Harry jumped in before Jo could respond. "But DI Cottrell may have provided a valuable link between the victims. And certainly she was right to point out the importance of finding Sammo as soon as possible. So many thanks for that." He smiled at Jo before turning back to Craig. "Sergeant, do you want to kick us off?"

"Yes, sir. DC Crusoe has been coordinating the calls coming in from the misper appeal. Nat ..."

Natalie Crusoe was seated at a table in the centre of the room. She clicked on an icon on the laptop display in front of her and four columns of words and numbers filled the large screen at one end of the room.

"We've had fifty-seven reported sightings," she said. "These are twenty of them; the other thirty-seven are on separate pages. The list shows the name and address of the caller; place, time and date of the reported sighting. We've given each sighting a number and you can see on the maps where they were." She pointed to four maps attached to the wall, two on either side of the projection screen. "Each of the red stickers on the maps has the corresponding number on it. There's another column to the list, not shown on here, with the details of each sighting, but I can talk you through a few of interest. The full document's on e-file and I'll leave hard copies for reference.

"We can probably ignore the other pages. They're all on file but they're the usual nuisance calls, hoaxes and our regulars who see *everyone* we put out a misper appeal for. But there's one exception in that last category which I've shown here."

She zoomed in on one of the entries and there were some muted groans around the room as the name became more prominent.

"Mrs Lois Dearing was walking her border terrier..."

"Jacky," one of the officers said. Natalie gave a little laugh.

"Yes... her border terrier, Jacky, on Middleton Green near Woking town centre a couple of weeks ago. She can't remember exactly which day it was, but I think we can establish that. She said she saw our man sitting on a park bench. He appeared to be waiting for someone – she thought – because he kept looking round all the time, but not at anything in particular."

She paused as a number of muttered conversations started up.

"Let's have some quiet, please," Harry said. "Go on, Nat."

"That on its own might not be of interest except for..." she moved to another name on the list and zoomed in again "... Louise Thornbury. She was in the park on the same day with her daughter, Ellie, feeding the ducks and she says she saw our man on the park bench. She mentioned that there was also an elderly lady there walking her dog. But after the lady left, Mrs Thornbury began to feel a bit uncomfortable with just her and Ellie alone with the man who seemed agitated and kept looking round and across at her and her daughter. She said she wasn't sure whether he was looking around because he was expecting someone or to check that there was no-one else about. So she decided to leave just as another man arrived and sat next to him."

"Did she describe the second man?" Harry asked.

"Yes, she said he looked totally different to the first one and completely out of place in the park. He was much taller, good-looking and dressed very smartly in a suit, like a bank manager or something. He had dark glasses and she seemed to remember he was wearing gloves, although looking back she thought it unusual at that time of day in August."

"When in August?"

"Friday 28th, sir, at around three in the afternoon. Mrs Thornbury is certain of the time and the date because Ellie had an appointment that day at the doctor's which is right next to the park. So it's nearly two weeks ago, but it's the last corroborated sighting we've got – if it was him, of course."

"Did she say how old the second man was?"

"She wasn't sure; could have been anywhere between thirty and forty. She was leaving as he arrived, so saw him only briefly."

"So she didn't see what they did – whether they sat and talked, got up and left together... whatever?"

"No, sir."

"Okay, thanks, Nat. Carry on."

"As I say, that's the only corroborated sighting, but there are eight individual reports of Sammo being seen around Woking railway station during last week and three at Cobham station, including one late evening on Wednesday 2nd September. That's the place and date of the first murder. The man who reported seeing him on that occasion said he couldn't be sure because his hair was different. The other seven sightings were all in different places." She scrolled down the list.

"Known associates?"

"That's the *really* interesting thing, sir. No-one claiming to know Sammo has contacted us. Either there's some sort of conspiracy out there, or he's managed to stay clear of *everyone* who knows him personally."

"Okay, thank you, detective. Any questions for Natalie? No? Right, I want the twenty people on that list questioned up close and personal so we can expand the information we already have. And any more we get that Nat puts on her front page. Before that, get the image guys to give Sammo a haircut – a few haircuts, in fact – and get them all to look them over, especially Mr Undecided of Cobham. And let's put the new images on the website along with the existing ones and the phone numbers. Good stuff."

He looked round the room, his eyes alighting on a young officer in jeans, tee shirt and a blue linen sports jacket.

"Mr Bradley, CCTV?"

Natalie closed the document on the screen and DC Owen Bradley replaced her at the table in front of the laptop.

"Just before we continue," Harry said, "you've all seen the images of Tom Brown on Delaware that we *missed* when we checked earlier?" Everyone either nodded or muttered a 'yes'. "A bit embarrassing to say the least having him pointed out to me by someone I'd brought in for questioning because he had appeared on the *same* image stream. Please let's do better next time, okay? Bradley."

The detective constable opened a folder on the screen which yielded a list of about twenty files, each titled with a date and the initial 'C' or 'W'.

"These are out-takes from CCTV streams in and around Cobham and Woking stations on the three days from a few hours before to a few hours after the times of the murders. Problem is, of course, apart from Sammo Sampson, who isn't at this stage linked with the actual murders – only with the victims – we don't know who we're looking for. However, following on from what you just said, sir, just take a look at this."

He selected one of the 'W's and brought up a still image showing people apparently waiting for a train on a station platform. A click on the small arrow and the picture moved.

"This is just after five-thirty last Sunday evening. Waterloo train just coming in to Woking station. You'll see someone get off the train ... there! Watch him now."

The man in the picture – tall, forty-something, in dark chinos and a light jacket – stepped over to the side of the platform and stood with his back to the wall studying the crowd of fellow passengers bustling out of the station while the people waiting climbed aboard. He remained, motionless, until the platform was almost empty before walking off camera.

"Recognise him?" DC Bradley asked.

"Tom Brown," Harry said, half to himself.

"The very same. Not that it's a surprise his being there, because he was photographed in the station later that same evening and his picture appeared in the morning papers. But he looks okay on the platform here; whereas later he looked decidedly *not* okay. In some distress, in fact."

Harry furrowed his brow. "Your point being what, exactly?"

"Well, something had happened to change him in the time between five thirty-five pm and when the photo was taken."

"But he'd clearly been drinking, hadn't he?" Jo put in. "Everyone is aware, aren't they, that it's pretty much *all* he does these days."

"Go on, Bradley," Harry said.

"You're right, of course, ma'am, but we also have images of him at Woking station the previous night – Saturday – and – this is more interesting – at Cobham station on Wednesday, late afternoon."

"Sorry to interrupt again," Jo said, "but no-one seriously believes that Tom Brown could be involved in these murders, do they? Surely that's unlikely enough to be dismissed even as a remote possibility."

Owen Bradley shrugged. "About as unlikely as his son being a drug dealer, do you mean?"

Harry glanced across at Jo to stall any response. "Who knows how a mind in that much turmoil works," he said. "But I agree with DI Cottrell. I can't see that at all. I've no idea why Mr Brown would take himself off to Cobham, but Jack *did* spend a lot of time in and around Woking, so let's follow up by checking out a few of Jack's regular haunts to see if he's been there and, if so, why. We could, of course, just ask the man himself – or get the chief to ask him, for that matter. But I don't want to do that; not yet, anyway. I don't want him to feel like we're challenging him or anything. So let's go softly-softly. Perhaps a couple of you could do it undercover – you know, no badges, just pub chat, that sort of thing. And if we can find out why he's hanging around Woking, it might also explain why he was in Cobham. And let's be clear, we're doing this in order to *eliminate* Mr Brown from our enquiries. Okay? Good spot, Bradley. Anything else?"

Owen clicked on another file.

"This is Wednesday around half-past midnight – actually, early Thursday morning." The picture showed a different station, deserted except for a couple seated on a bench and one man standing at the edge of the platform looking down the line. "Cobham – close to the scene of the first murder and close to the time, as well. That guy there could pass for Sammo, with a new hair style."

He paused the image and enlarged it; the man was almost face-on to the camera. Owen moved the image to one side on the screen and brought up next to it the picture of Sammo released through the missing person appeal.

"Not conclusive, but pretty close, we think," he said.

There was silence for a while as the group studied the two images.

"Agree it's not conclusive," said a large, balding man in a grey suit which was in need of pressing. "Not sure I agree it's close."

A few more opinions were offered, everyone speaking at once. Harry held up his hand for quiet.

"I think it's a good spot, whoever picked it out." He looked round the room. The petite, blonde-pigtailed figure of DC Elizabeth Gordon raised a hand. "I think Beth might have something. Let's get his hair cut and make the comparison again. Any more?"

Owen closed the misper image and the CCTV picture filled the screen again.

"If we continued with this we'd see the guy – Sammo or not – get on the train that comes in a couple of minutes later – that would be the eleven-fifty from Waterloo – and our friend Lewis Tonkin get off and go to sleep on one of the benches, just like he said he did. Then he wakes up and goes round the back of the station – presumably for his pee – at one-twenty-six am. So his story checks out one hundred percent.

"At this and the other sites, in addition to the immediate proximity, we've checked all cameras within a four-hundred metre radius of the death sites from an hour before the earliest to an hour after the latest ETDs. Given that the death sites are close to busy railway stations, that covers one hell of a lot of people charging about, even late evening, making it difficult to follow individuals from camera to camera. So, other than the Tom Brown and the possible Sammo sightings, there's nothing more, I'm afraid."

"Okay. So, what next, do you think?"

"Well, as far as Sammo's concerned," Owen continued, "we could check the camera records around the places and times on Nat's list." There were loud groans from all parts of the room. "But if we do decide to do it, sir, I'm afraid I won't be able to help because I'm volunteering to go undercover with DC Gordon."

The team whooped and jeered as Beth opened her eyes wide in mock horror.

Harry smiled. "Joking apart, that might be what we need to do next if we don't get anything else. But let's wait until we've spoken to all of Nat's top twenty. That way we may find we can be more selective before we resort to CCTV again. Has anyone got anything else?" There was a general shaking of heads. "Are the local uniforms still showing mug shots of the victims and Sammo around the two stations?"

Craig Belmont answered. "They are, sir, but not for much longer, I don't think. 'Not a productive use of resources' – I quote. We've had quite a number of people recognising them but nothing of any use in the way of information. We've done the same on Delaware and in and around all stations on the line as far north as, and including, Waterloo. I think certainly the Cobham trail's getting a bit cold; over a week now."

"Agreed, but let them carry on looking until they actually *do* pull out. Don't let them off the hook yet." He turned to speak to the man in the grey suit. "George, I know it's early days, but how are we getting on with finding the rest of Sammo's clients?"

"Unfortunately, PROLIST was down on Tuesday, guv, so we only had yesterday. Not found any of them yet and to be honest, I'm not sure what we say to them when we do. 'Watch out, you're next' doesn't sound very helpful somehow." There were a few snorted laughs. "What *are* we supposed to tell them?"

"Well, use a bit of judgement," said Harry. "We're simply

making them aware of a connection between the killings and the fact that the same connection applies to them. That's *all* we can tell them. What they do with the information is up to them. We can't give them all police protection, that *is* a fact. Anyone else got any thoughts on that? DI Cottrell?"

"I think, as you say, they *must* be told, but further than that we can't advise them what to do. It's been, what, four days since the last killing, but there were three days between the first and second, so no reason to believe our killer plans to stop at four, unless, of course, the four had something in common which doesn't apply to anyone else." She looked at Harry and shrugged.

"Any other thoughts?" he said. "No? Okay let's carry on looking. We've still got two separate searches – one for Sammo and one for the killer. And, in spite of his possible sighting and CCTV catch at Cobham, as far as we know at this stage, those are two different people."

★

The consultant's voice on the end of the phone was flat and impassive.

"Mr Brown, just to let you know, Mr Deverall is well enough at present to receive visitors and has asked to see you and your wife together as soon as possible. We've informed Mrs Tomlinson-Brown and we're expecting her to arrive around one-thirty. Could you make it for that time? I think it's very important that you try."

"Yes, of course. Is he… any better?"

"I'm afraid we're very near the end now, Mr Brown. I think you need to treat any opportunity to see him as being very probably your last. So I do advise that you…"

"Yes, yes, I'll come. I just wondered…"

"To be honest, I am amazed he is still with us. He's been on borrowed time for the last few months."

Tom ended the call and slumped onto the sofa, dropping his head into his hands. The doctor was right, Jad was supposed to die back in June – three months ago. That's what they'd all been told at the time – 'just a matter of days'. How he wished that had been the case. Following each subsequent visit to his friend it had taken him longer to reconstruct his chosen image of the brave, dashing hero of their time together with the Special Forces – and before; the picture he wanted to keep in his memory for ever. He had no wish to be wrenched back to reality by another painful meeting with a man he barely recognised.

He checked his watch – just after 12.15 pm. He couldn't remember the last time he had seen his car keys. Actually, he *could* remember – it was on the morning of the Press conference. He recalled having them in his hand, then dropping them, then... well, who knows? But that was – what – eleven, twelve weeks ago? Surely he must have had them since then?

It was academic, anyway. At no time during that period had he been in a fit state to drive. Perhaps it was better that he didn't find them too soon. So, another taxi-ride then. He calculated the time, working backwards – arrive at St Bart's at one-thirty; fifteen minutes in the cab – one-fifteen; five to find a cab – one-ten. That gave him just under an hour to transform himself into something approaching a suitable escort for a beautiful woman.

★

Mags was already seated, alone, in the small waiting area along the corridor from Jad's room. When Tom entered, she looked up briefly from the magazine she was reading, and then dropped her eyes again, as if he had been a complete stranger walking in. She looked, as always, stunningly beautiful, this time in a cream knitted cardigan worn over a knee-length floral dress. Her golden-blonde hair was swept back from her face in a long pony-tail. He sat down on the chair next to her. She shifted her position to put as much distance between them as possible without actually changing her seat.

It was a further ten minutes, during which time not a word passed between them, before the door opened and the nurse entered.

"Mr Deverall can see you now, but you won't be able to stay more than a few minutes. He loses his strength very quickly. I'm sorry, but I'm sure you understand."

They followed her along the corridor to Jad's room and as

she opened the door to admit them, Mags took a deep breath and grabbed Tom's hand. It was unexpected and momentarily exhilarating until he realised it was simply a gesture of solidarity for the sake of the patient. Even with their palms touching, Tom could feel the cold, gaping void between them.

Jad, lying in bed, propped up with pillows, seemed to sense it as well. His initial smile disappeared quickly as he looked from one to the other, as if he could see the discomfort and pain in their eyes. Mags went over and knelt at his bedside, taking one of his hands in both of hers and kissing him on the cheek. Tom reached down and grasped his other hand. Jad was pale and drawn, but not any worse, they thought, than they had seen him at other times.

"Thanks for coming," he said.

Their shock at the weakness of his voice made them both grip his hands more firmly, as if to prevent him slipping away from them at that moment.

"Don't talk, Jad," Mags said, her own voice wavering. "Keep your strength for…"

"Oh, I have to talk, Maggie. That's why you're both here – to listen." He continued looking from one to the other. "I can't stop thinking about Jack," he said, finally, tears welling in his eyes as he spoke the words. "I'm so sorry."

Mags's head dropped forward so that it rested on her hands, which still held tightly on to his. Jad looked across at Tom, raising his eyebrows with an unspoken question. Tom shook his head.

"Ironic that I kept that piece of Heaven's door as a reminder of the good times," he said. He had long since decided that there was no point in Mags knowing their friend's involvement in Jack's death.

Jad nodded his understanding, his tears spilling over in a combination of relief and sorrow. Mags sat back up again, the lines of her own tears showing on her cheeks.

"You mustn't leave us again, Jad. You must fight…"

"And *you* must fight, Maggie." He turned to Tom. "Both of you. I know this must have ripped you apart, but you need each other, you really do. You've each meant more to me than any other person in my entire life. More even than Alma, and I found out too late how much that was. A dying man always gets a last request – and this is it. I want you to promise me that you'll stay together, because I know you'll be lost without each other – and I won't be around to save you next time, Tom."

He managed a chuckle which changed immediately into a fit of coughing. Mags hugged him until it subsided.

"I don't know, Jad," she said. "There are some things…"

Jad seemed to sink into his pillows. His eyes closed and he forced out his words.

"Dying man… last request… please, Maggie… Tom…"

His eyes opened again, no more than slits.

"Maggie, Tom…?" He could barely whisper.

"Okay, Jad," Tom said, putting his hand on Mags's shoulder. "For you, for all of us."

He felt Mags stiffen when he touched her, but she did not pull away. Instead, she placed her hand on his.

"Okay, Jad, we promise," she said.

"Thank you," Jad said as his eyes closed again.

The nurse came into the room from where she had been watching through the glass partition of the adjoining anteroom.

"That's enough for now. Thank you for coming."

Tom leaned over to embrace his friend. "See you soon," he said, his voice hoarse with emotion.

"You bet, old pal o' mine."

Tom turned and followed the nurse out of the room.

★

Mags felt Jad's grip on her hand tighten, preventing her from leaving with the others.

"Something just for you, Maggie," he said, "no-one else, not even Tom, okay?" His voice was soft but seemed stronger. "Remember, what seemed to happen to me once before turned out not to be true."

"I don't understand…"

"I think you will," he said.

In the doorway, she looked back at him. He smiled a big smile, his eyes now wide open.

Tom was speaking to the nurse when she joined them.

"How long?" he asked.

"Not long at all, I'm afraid. A few days; a week. I know we've been saying this for what seems like a long time now. But I can't see him lasting more than, say, two weeks at the most. I'm so sorry."

"Thank you," Tom said.

They walked out of the building and stood together briefly on the pavement outside.

"Have we nothing to say to each other?" he said. "We just promised Jad…"

She began to walk away, and then stopped and turned back to him.

"Just one thing. Next time you decide to make the front pages, just think of Katey before you choose how you're going to do it."

★

The front door of the neat little mid-terraced house opened almost before they had rung the bell. The young woman in front of them was average height, slim, with spiky red hair and a pleasant freckled face. She was wearing a light fleece jacket.

"Mrs Louise Thornbury?"

"Yes."

The two plain-clothed officers showed their badges.

"I'm Detective Constable Crusoe and this is Detective Constable Clancy. We're just following up your call to the police yesterday about the missing person."

The woman looked anxious. "I didn't realise I'd have to get involved. I mean I've got a young daughter – she's only five – there's just the two of us now – I don't want…"

"That's okay, Mrs Thornbury," Natalie said. "This is very informal. We just want to check in case you've remembered anything else since you called in. We're really grateful for your help. Is now a good time?"

"Well, I was just leaving as you arrived. Got to pick up Ellie from school."

"Is that far away?" George Clancy asked.

"No, just a couple of hundred yards – at the end of the road." She checked her watch. "I'll have to go; they let the reception class out at three o'clock so they don't get trampled by the rest of the school."

She gave a nervous smile.

"Do you mind if we wait, Mrs Thornbury?" Natalie asked. "Are you bringing Ellie straight home?"

"Yes, but I don't want her upset with talk of murder and that sort of thing."

"Of course not, but the man you saw is not a suspect as such. We just think he might have some information which could help us. But you go and get Ellie – we don't want to make you late. We'll just wait here."

"Very well," Louise said.

She was back within ten minutes. The two officers both said 'Hi' to Ellie who seemed to enjoy the attention of her new friends.

"Just a few minutes, Mrs Thornbury and we'll be out of your way."

"Okay, come in then."

Seated at the table in the dining room, DC Clancy spread out the photos of Sammo in front of Louise while Ellie brought a procession of toys and drawings to show Natalie.

"These are the pictures of Mr Sampson you saw on the television," George said, "and based on descriptions from other sightings, these are examples of how he may look now. Which of these are most like the man you saw?"

"The television ones," Louise replied without hesitation. "What I remembered most was the length of his hair – plus his dark complexion."

"And seeing the pictures again, can you be reasonably certain this was the man?"

"More than reasonably, I'd say. I'm very good at remembering faces and I looked across at this man quite a few times." She dropped her voice to nearly a whisper. "I was a little concerned about being there with Ellie and just him."

George nodded. "You also gave us a good description of the second man. Can you remember any more about him? And what the two men did once they had met?"

"No, I told the person who I spoke to on the phone, by that time I'd decided to go and he arrived just as I was leaving."

George gathered up the photos then took a card from his wallet and placed it on the table. "That's been really helpful, Mrs Thornbury, but if you do think of anything else, please call me on that number. And now I'll try to prise my colleague away from the attentions of your daughter. I'm sure she'd much rather stay here and play."

They all laughed.

"You're absolutely right there," Natalie said, trying hard to fit a saddle on to a little pink pony. "Can we just ask you one small favour, please, Mrs Thornbury? Could you and Ellie show us the bench where the two men met? It would mean we could check where the nearest CCTV cameras are. The park is only a few minutes drive away, I believe. Perhaps Ellie could show me the ducks you were feeding."

★

George and Louise stood by the park bench while Ellie and Natalie fed and counted the small animated flotilla on the lake.

"The lady with the dog was over there, the first man was sitting here. Then the lady went away and after about five minutes or so, the second man came from that direction and sat down."

"And at that time you were on the point of leaving?"

"That's right."

"Let's go to where you were standing with Ellie and check the scene from there. It might just jog your memory."

They walked down to join the others at the water's edge.

"It was just here," said Louise. She paused for a few moments looking at the bench and to the left and right of it. "Oh, one other thing," she added. "I seem to remember the second man was carrying a bag – on his back. He put it down on the seat when he sat down. Yes, that's right – a small rucksack."

"Was he giving it to the other man, do you think?" asked George.

"I don't know. I guess he'd have to take it off to sit down anyway – it being a backpack. But I didn't see; that's when I was leaving."

George looked around the park.

"Is it always this quiet? It's a lovely little spot, right in the middle of town."

"We hardly ever come here, to be honest, even though it is so close. Only when we go to the doctor's or the clinic. In fact, we'll probably be coming again on Saturday morning – Ellie's got an appointment for a check-up. But there's only the ducks to feed, no swings or anything."

The ducks had eaten everything Ellie had thrown for them and paddled off to the back of the lake, disappearing from sight under the overhanging branches, from where they set up a cacophony of sound with quacking voices and flapping wings.

"They seem very agitated today," said Louise. "Usually they follow us almost out of the park on the off chance of one final crust. Not sure what the attraction is over there. Anyway, young lady, time to go."

"Yes, thank you, Mrs Thornbury – and Ellie," said Natalie. "Let's get you back to those little ponies. They'll be ready for grooming and feeding by now."

★

DC Bradley clicked on the screen to change the view of Grindalls Road from map to satellite.

"That's the Cross Keys, on the corner," Owen said. "Landlord, Jonathan – known as Jonnie – Denver, one of the character witnesses called by the Defence to testify on behalf of Jack and Jason. And that…" he pointed to a large house further along and just off the same road "… is Manston Grange, home of Mickey Kadawe and *second* home of Jack and Jason. So I reckon that's got to have been their local watering hole and, after Delaware, the next obvious place to check. Okay?"

"Makes sense," Beth said. She smiled at Owen. "So, what are we going as?"

"I thought perhaps young lovers who can't keep their hands off each other."

"What about brother and sister?"

"Okay then, college friends of Jack. I mean you look a bit long in the tooth, but I could pass for twenty, easily."

"Until you open your mouth and then they'll think you're half that age."

Owen laughed. "Touché! But college friends will be easy to carry off. You know – 'Jack always talked about this place and we just wanted to check it out and mix with other guys who knew him' – that sort of thing."

"Okay, sounds good. But I'll need to change into something tacky so we look like we're together."

Owen laughed again and checked his watch. "It's nearly four now. When should we start, do you think?"

"Let's aim to get to Delaware for around six-thirty. Our man's been seen there a few times recently at about that time, hasn't he? We can call at my place on the way so I can get changed."

"Okay, but I'm not coming in for coffee. Not on a first date."

"At least we're agreed on that."

★

Tom awoke to the Westminster chimes of the wall clock heralding the quarter-hour just a metre away from him, above and behind the sofa. It was 4.15 pm – he'd been asleep for just over an hour.

He reflected on an afternoon that had been every bit as bad as he'd feared it would be. He may well have seen his friend alive for the last time. He realised that he was accepting this for the *first* time. Jad had all but left him again, and at a time when he needed a close friend more than ever before. He had one, of course. Tony had proved himself in that quarter more than he, Tom, had deserved over the past few months. But he could never take Jad's place. There could never be the same strength of camaraderie between him and another human being as existed with Jad.

It was Jad who had saved him so miraculously at Shah e Kot when he had been nearly fatally wounded. The miracle was as much to do with Jad finding him at all as it was to his carrying him barely conscious under fire across his shoulders for over a mile to safety. 'Out of the jaws of hell' the US general had described it when he had later presented Jad with a Presidential Citation along with the Congressional Medal of Honour for saving an American soldier in the same operation.

Even after the incident, when the two men had been kept apart by diverging career paths, he had always felt close to him spiritually and with no reason to believe such feelings were not reciprocated. He remembered his and Mags's desolation at hearing of Jad's death, and the euphoria of his dramatic return in the witness box at the Old Bailey, when his true identity was revealed following his sentencing for the killing of the Bradys. He smiled in wonder at the memories, marvelling at the sheer thrill of knowing John Deverall.

The great sadness was that his *final* memory should be so harrowing. The terminal fragility of the bravest man he had ever known; the skeletal remains of greatness struggling to whisper his last request. And the concluding act Jad had performed for him – providing the lethal capsule which he had passed on to Jack at their traumatic final meeting.

Now, in his waking moments, that melancholy was replaced by something he could handle much better.

Anger.

This feeling towards Mags took him by surprise. Earlier he had been filled with regret over their separation, but not now, not at this moment. She could not possibly be hurting more than he was, and yet there was *nothing* coming his way in terms of sympathy, understanding, forgiveness. The way she'd behaved earlier, and in front of Jad, too, like she was the only one suffering; pathetically wallowing in her own self-righteousness. Okay, he'd lost her, but it was *her* fault, not his.

And then there was Grace Goody. It was true that recently he'd had serious concerns over where her loyalties lay. But that was *his* fault, not hers. He had let Grace down big-time, hadn't he, even though she had never, *ever*, wavered in her support for him. Whereas Mags – typical only child – always used to getting her own way – couldn't stand *anyone* disagreeing with her. He owed Grace a lot and what had he done? Reacted with indifference when she confessed her feelings for him. Made her look foolish; robbed her of her self-respect. Well, he'd put that right when she got back from the US. He'd make it like it used to be.

But right now, he needed something to take his mind off *everything*.

Half an hour later, showered, shaved, totally refreshed, and with a new resolve, Tom stepped out of his apartment door onto the landing. Oscar Strange was standing, feet apart, hands on hips, with his back to the floor-to-ceiling stained-glass window opposite the entrance to the stairwell. The sun streamed in behind him, throwing a multicoloured pattern onto the tiled floor and silhouetting his frame against the light.

"Christ, Oscar, are you living in the apartment or on the fucking landing?"

Oscar gave a little laugh. "Just admiring the décor."

"Well, I'm... going out," Tom said. He turned back to his apartment door, absently checking that it had closed properly, before striding off down the stairs.

★

They parked on Grindalls Road a hundred or so yards past the pub and walked back to the beer garden. Owen wore his usual casual work clothes and Beth had changed into skinny jeans, high heels and a loose, wide-necked top that hung off one shoulder. Her colleague decided he had been wrong – she looked about ten fewer than her twenty-nine years.

"What the hell!" He stopped, taking in the scene in front of them.

The beer garden was full of people most of whom were standing and looking towards the pub itself. Others were peering in through the windows and the open double doors. There were raised voices inside and a crash of breaking glass. Owen started forward. Beth grabbed his arm.

"We're undercover, remember," she said. "Let's go in quietly. It's probably nothing. Softly-softly, the boss said."

"Yes, but..."

"If there's a *real* problem, then... that's different. Come on."

She took his hand and they weaved their way through the crowd to the doors. Inside, two men were being wrestled away from each other by an excited group including a number of girls. The younger of the two men, a thick-set early-twenty-something with a shaven head and heavy stubble, was bleeding profusely from the nose and was holding the neck of a broken bottle, reaching forward to point its jagged remains at the other man. His adversary was around twice his age, tall, slim and muscular with handsome features, and dressed in casual designer gear. There was blood on the knuckles of his right hand. He looked quite relaxed, but at the same time primed for more action.

Two powerfully built men in tight black tee shirts and jeans had intervened and were standing between the two combatants to deter any further engagement. The landlord stepped up to the younger man and took the bottle from his hand.

"Right, Floyd. You're barred. Get out, *now!*"

"*I'm* barred! What about this geriatric wanker here? He's the one who's causing the fucking problem."

"Yeah, come on, Jonnie. That's not right," one of the men holding Floyd put in, and several others voiced their support. Jonnie relented.

"Okay, barred just for tonight. I want you out of here and away – not hanging about outside. But the next time you do something like that…" he held up the bottle close to Floyd's face "… it's for good. Okay?"

The young man stormed out of the pub, pushing the watchers, including Beth and Owen, roughly aside as he left. Jonnie, turned to the other man, then spoke to the two people holding his arms.

"Take him over there and sit him down." He nodded towards the corner of the room furthest away from the door.

Owen and Beth edged their way into the pub, both noting that the steely composure the man had shown in the face of the action had dissolved in its aftermath to reveal his true, intoxicated condition. It was all the two girls who were supporting him could do just to get him to walk to the corner table.

The detectives gently elbowed their way to the bar, Beth easing herself onto a stool and Owen standing next to her. The people peering in at the window had returned to their tables and inside the tension subsided. One of the barmen caught Beth's eye.

"Can I get you guys anything?"

"Large white wine," Beth said.

"LA beer, please. What was all that about?"

The barman paused before replying. "Old guy over there comes in regular. He's an MP. *Was* an MP, I mean. His son used to come in here a lot." He placed the drinks on the bar in front of them. "Seven-fifty, please."

Owen passed him a ten. "One for yourself," he said. "Yes, I know who he is, but what was all that about?"

The barman gave Owen two pound coins. "Thanks for the drink. You'd best ask the landlord about Mr Brown." He nodded along the bar to where Jonnie Denver was watching them.

"What's going on, Duane?" he asked, walking across, not taking his eyes off Beth and Owen.

"They're just asking about Mr Brown."

Duane went to serve another customer and the landlord leaned across the bar. His face was very close to theirs. Jonnie Denver was no more than average height and wiry, but his hard features reflected the toughness gained from a working lifetime in lively bars like the Cross Keys.

"So why the interest? Reporters, are you?"

Beth and Owen looked at each other and laughed.

"Absolutely not!" Beth said. "Why on Earth...?"

"Because there's a lot of people trying to make Mr Brown look bad, and anyone planning to do that is not welcome here. So if that's what you're after, then you can have your money back and leave."

"We are *not* reporters," Beth said, "we are college friends of Jack, and we came here because he used to talk about this place a lot and we know he had a lot of friends here. That's all. Okay?"

"And we know that's his father over there," Owen said, "so what *was* all that about?"

Jonnie looked from one to the other again, then relaxed and sighed.

"If I'm honest, he's getting to be a bit of a liability. He has a habit of winding people up – not deliberately, but just droning on about how bad things are for him, like he's the victim in the whole affair with Jack and Jay. That's the third time he's got into a fight in the last couple of weeks along with a few heated arguments as well. Floyd's right, it should be Mr Brown I'm barring."

"So what's the problem?" Beth asked. "I would have thought he'd get a lot of sympathy here, because of Jack. In fact, isn't that why he comes?"

"I don't know why he comes – you can't get any sense out of him when you ask. But Jack was real popular here and a lot of guys blame his dad for what happened to him. And remember this is the age group that's most targeted by the new laws. Not these actual people – there are no drug dealers or – what did Tom Brown call them? – 'domestic terrorists' in here – but they can still identify with the ones who are getting shipped out."

While they were talking one of the girls who had been sitting with Tom had come up to the bar. They could hear her in conversation with Duane.

"Just one more, Duane, and then he promises to go. He's given me the number to ring for a taxi for him."

"God, Megan, don't you think he's had enough. Can't you persuade him to go now?"

Jonnie leaned across. "Give him just a single, Duane. And let Duane have the number, Megan; he'll phone for the cab. Where's he going?"

"Back to the station. God knows how he'll get home from there on his own." She handed the barman a piece of paper. "Thanks, Duane."

The landlord nodded to the two men in black jeans and tee shirts who were standing just inside the door. They nodded back. Beth and Owen exchanged a quick glance.

"This could go either way," Jonnie said, "when Megan turns up with a small whisky. Just playing it safe. I would not like to get on the wrong side of this guy in a fight – not one-on-one – thank you. He was in here last week mouthing off about how he was going to get all the people who had been involved in Jack's conviction. It was a bit chilling listening to him, to say the least."

"When was that?" Owen asked.

Beth glared at him. "What's that got to do with anything?" she snapped.

Owen looked suitably chastised. "Nothing," he said. "Just wondered. What with seeing him in the paper…"

The landlord glanced from one to the other, the suspicious look returning. He walked away to where Duane had just ended his call.

"Taxi in ten minutes," the barman said. They looked across to the corner. The single whisky was untouched. Tom Brown had passed out with his head on the table, arms hanging straight down so that his bloodied knuckles touched the floor.

80

CHAPTER SIX

Friday; 11 September

Kim Lacey showed Grace into the Minister's office just before 8.00 am and returned three minutes later with two china mugs and a cafetiere on a silver tray, which she placed on the desk. Grace wore a navy suit with a short, straight skirt, and a cream shirt with a striped silk scarf in both colours loosely tied around her neck. Her eyes were soft and friendly behind her light metal-framed glasses. They shook hands with genuine warmth.

"Well, should I say congratulations or commiserations?"

"A bit of both, I guess," Jonathan said. "I must admit I would have liked the Home Secretary position, but at least Andrew's taken Justice out of the Home Office again so, obviously, I'm pleased to get full cabinet ministerial status. And I'm pleased for Jackie – she'll do a good job, I'm sure."

Grace gave a little scowl. "I'm not convinced I'm afraid. But, we'll see. I was hoping it would be you."

"Well, thank you, Grace. Over here, I think." The room was large and high with a desk and chair suitably proportioned for its substantial occupant. At the side away from the window was a square conference table with eight chairs upholstered in green leather round it. In front of the floor-to-ceiling window itself were two wing chairs, one at either side of a small circular table. He waved a hand towards them, picking up the tray and placing it on the table as they settled themselves into the chairs.

"So, how was the assignment? I've missed you." Jonathan's wide smile was returned in kind.

"Why, Jonathan, what a lovely thing to say."

They both laughed.

"It was fine," Grace said. "I'll get the full report to you by close of business today, but there's nothing in it to surprise you. There was a lot of interest on the impact of the NJR, of course, and – sadly – Tom's situation as well. He was virtually a cult figure over there, as you know, so his demise has left a lot of people sad and confused."

"That just about sums up my feelings as well," Jonathan said. "I don't know whether you've been following his exploits while you've been over there, but he seems to be self-destructing, plunging new depths every day. I've had reports through Eddie Mills of his brawling in the street and in a couple of pubs in Woking. He's been picked up on three occasions by the police and taken home – when they should probably have charged him with something – and on each occasion he had no idea where he'd been or what he'd been doing – at least, that's what he said." He shook his head and sighed. "I just wonder where it's all going; how it's going to end."

"Has he said any more about wanting to repeal the sentencing law for drug dealers?"

"I'm not aware that he's said anything specifically about that. I guess the idea must have died with Jack."

"But there's still Jason. Not that there's a chance that Andrew would ever agree to it, even if Tom was still in office – unless he was persuaded by his Minister of Justice, of course?"

Grace raised her eyebrows to turn it into a question. Jonathan shrugged and gave a brief smile.

"It's kind of you to suggest that the Prime Minister would listen to my opinion on the subject. No, I think the deed is done and should be left alone. I supported Tom when he proposed it – in the face of a lot of opposition – and I see no reason to reverse it."

"You did more than just support him, Jonathan; you virtually carried the meeting *and* the proposal according to Andrew."

Jonathan was silent for a moment. "Most of the time I try to forget that. Because if I *hadn't* supported him, it might not have got through. And if it *hadn't* got through, his son would have been alive today and Tom wouldn't be heading for what I believe will be a calamity – if not a tragedy."

"You really mustn't think of it that way, Jonathan. Your loyalty to Tom is legend – the way you accepted *and* embraced a second tier position in his department, when everyone expected you to get full ministerial responsibility – which you deserved. Whatever has happened since, it would have been much *worse* without you around looking out for him."

"Thank you, Grace." Jonathan smiled. "I guess I know that, but it helps when someone reminds me."

They sipped their coffee in silence for a few moments.

"I guess when I mentioned Jason," Grace said, "I was thinking that if Tom had pursued his objective to reverse that decision, it would have given him some sort of focus and perhaps saved him from this… freefall. So what, if anything, *has* he been saying to people on these wild adventures?"

"Well mostly the rantings of a soul in distress, I think. He's been going on about how expulsion is a really bad idea – not just for drug dealers – which is a bit of a worry."

"Yes, I heard about that."

"*And*, it seems he's going to spring Jason somehow, and at the same time wreak revenge on everyone involved in the case against Jack."

"Is he now?" Grace said, her eyes glazing over in thought. "How very interesting…"

★

The officers were standing around in small groups, some chatting, some watching the morning news on the TV screen, when Harry stepped out of his office into the major incident team room, inhaling the appealing fragrance of coffee, bacon and hotdogs. Someone switched off the set and they all turned to the detective inspector.

"I've been working this out," he said. "If we can get the bacon butty wagon to set up outside at a *quarter* to eight, we could start these meetings on the hour, saving fifteen minutes a day; that's one-and-a-half hours a week, including Saturdays. Times twenty people, that's thirty person-hours a week. We could let one of you go and not notice the difference."

There was booing and hissing all round.

"Alternatively," he went on, "you could take it in turns to bring

83

me a bacon sandwich every morning and we'll say no more about it. Why don't you start it off on Monday, Bradley? Crispy, no fat – okay?"

The booing changed to laughter as Harry turned to face the collective mastication of his team.

"Right, let's get to it. No talking with your mouths full. Who's going to start? George?"

DC Clancy swallowed hard before speaking. "Yesterday afternoon Nat and I called in on Lois Dearing and then Louise Thornbury about the Middleton Green sighting. Nothing new from the interviews, except that Mrs Thornbury remembered the second man had a small rucksack with him which he put down on the bench when he joined the first man. Also, she was certain that the man she saw *was* Sammo based on the original photo on the misper appeal, and that his hair was long at the time. We showed her the new images but if he *has* changed his appearance, it seems that it must have been after that date. That's all, I think. Nat?"

DC Crusoe nodded.

"Could she tell whether the second man was giving the rucksack to him?" Harry asked.

"We asked her that, guv, but she couldn't say. At that point she was leaving the park."

"Okay, thanks, you two. You can finish your hotdog now, George." He turned to DS Belmont who was seated at the table in front of the PC. "Any progress with the haircuts, sergeant?"

"Yes. This is the CCTV image from last Wednesday at Cobham station. We think this looks pretty conclusive."

He moved the cursor and opened a file, projecting onto the screen the still from the camera recording alongside one of the updated images of Sammo with shorter hair. There was a clear likeness, acknowledged by nodding heads and muttered agreement.

"So, well done, Beth, for spotting that in the first place. Also, DC Grantham took the new pictures to the guy who reported the possible sighting, *also* last Wednesday at Cobham station. Alice?"

"The guy who phoned in was a Mr Dave Emerson." The speaker was a tall, slim woman with a mass of brown curls framing an attractive ebony face. "We showed him the new images of Sammo and he seemed pretty sure that it was him that he saw. He remembered him because they accidentally bumped into each other and Mr Emerson said the other guy seemed really uptight and aggressive."

"Thanks, Alice. Has anyone spoken to any of the other callers yet with the new pictures?" There was a general shaking of heads. "Okay, but let's do it as soon as." He paused as if to gather his thoughts. "Right," he went on. "So we now have two independent pieces of information placing Sammo at Cobham station at the approximate time of the first murder. Interesting. Give us a recap on what we know about Sammo, Nat."

"Initially into hard drugs – using *and* dealing – but that was eight years ago – in his early twenties. Four convictions, including one custodial of nine months – five years ago – and since then he's been a good boy and stuck to peddling the soft stuff. Applied for registration as a licensed street trader after the amnesty and got his license straight away. No recent history of violence, but just after he was released from prison, he was one of a group of five arrested on suspicion of killing a dealer. A man and a woman were subsequently convicted, but the other three, including Sammo, were released without charge."

"You say no *recent* history of violence. Does that mean he does have some in the past?"

"The custodial was a GBH in a fight involving rival gangs in Lambeth. The dealer who was later killed was from the other gang, which was why Sammo was initially in the frame, particularly as it happened just after his release."

"So no previous with firearms?"

"No, sir – although the dealer who was killed was shot to death. But – obviously – not by Sammo."

"Okay," Harry said, "so we have Sammo meeting someone who – possibly – passes him a rucksack. Sometime in the next few days, he has a haircut – perhaps he just feels he needs one or he does it deliberately to change his appearance. Then he turns up with his new look at Cobham station where he is seen around the time that one of his clients is murdered."

Harry spread his arms and raised his eyebrows, inviting any comment.

"Sammo's a licensed trader, sir," Craig Belmont said, "so the most likely explanation for his meeting in the park would be to get supplies. Lawrence Newhouse was one of his customers, so that would explain why they were both at Cobham station at the same time."

"That's true," Harry said, "but – for whatever reason – during the past ten days, he has not been seen by anyone who knows him or in any of the places where he can usually be found *and* has not responded to a request for him to come forward."

"Perhaps he's doing the hard stuff again," George Clancy said, "so he's gone underground."

"Or perhaps," Natalie suggested, "he's number five and we just haven't found him yet."

"Or maybe," DC Bradley said, "there's absolutely no connection between Sammo and the murders, and he's away on holiday."

There was a long silence before Harry spoke again.

"Three very good points, all real possibilities; which means we need to keep a very open mind at this stage. Greg, what about ATMs and bank withdrawals – any joy?"

The stocky, bespectacled, and suited figure of DC Gregory Branwell consulted his notebook. "No withdrawals, sir, at cash machines or over the counter since well before the sighting in the park. No deposits either. A total of four direct debits paid over the past week – usual stuff – and no standing orders. Other than the DDs, he seems to work exclusively with cash – like all traders."

Harry shook his head. "Can we check any posts or tweets during the same period – I assume he's on Facebook and Twitter. Also Instagram. Perhaps…"

"Already checked, sir," Greg said. "Nothing in the last ten days and nothing out of the ordinary before that."

"Mobile phone?"

"Found in his apartment in Byfleet. This is the one included on his PROLIST file. Last calls made and received on that were over a month ago. So he must have a new one he hasn't registered yet – for whatever reason."

The DI sighed. "We're running on empty here. To Owen's point, let's check flights and ferries and tunnel passengers during, let's say, the past four weeks. Also hospitals, walk-in centres – he just might have checked in or been taken in and given a false name. And let's have some ideas and scenarios for the four o'clock meeting."

He looked across to Beth and Owen. "Well, Bonnie and Clyde, any luck tracking Mr Brown?"

"Well, we *did* get lucky, in fact," Beth said. "We started off on Delaware at the Bear Pit where Chief Inspector Gerrard had seen him a couple of times recently. We got there around six-thirty and stayed until just before eight. Didn't get much out of anybody except a universal feeling that he's an effing nuisance. After that we went to the Cross Keys on Grindalls, very close to Mickey Kadawe's house where Jack and Jason seemed to spend most of their time. Turns out they spent a lot of time in the Cross Keys as well, particularly Jack. Anyway, when we arrived – guess what – Tom Brown was actually there, pissed as a newt and causing quite a disturbance. He'd just been in a fight with another guy and had come off rather the better of the two. The other guy got thrown out and Mr Brown calmed down, but passed out soon afterwards. They put him in a taxi at… it would have been around quarter to nine, I guess." She looked at Owen for confirmation and he nodded.

"Did you get where he was going?" It was DS Belmont asking the question.

"To Woking station, apparently," Owen said. "We stayed at the pub for a bit after he left, chatted to a few people, then we drove to the station ourselves, just to see if he was still there and okay. But by then there was no sign of him, so we assume he managed to get on a train for home – or wherever he was going. I wouldn't mind checking the station tapes for last night just to see how he coped when he got there."

"So what did you find out at the pub?" Harry asked.

"Well, for a start he spends quite a bit of time there," Beth said, "and, to use the landlord's words, 'is getting to be a bit of a liability'. Gets into arguments and fights quite frequently. But one very interesting piece of information; sometime last week – although we don't know exactly when – he was threatening to sort out all the people who were involved in the case against Jack and Jason."

Muttered comments and knowing looks passed between some of those present. Harry cut off the debate.

"Now let's not try to fly before we can crawl. Here's a guy who has recently had to deal with incredible despair and guilt, was presumably – as Beth put it so genteelly – 'pissed as a newt', mouthing off to whoever would listen, and who, quite probably, wouldn't even remember *what* he said the next day. And these guys – the victims – were *not* involved in the case. Not directly, anyway. They could hardly be described as legitimate targets for retribution. So let's not pretend, in the absence of anything else, that this is some sort of meaningful lead. Okay?"

The statement was greeted with blank faces and a few shaking heads. After a long pause, Owen Bradley seemed to capture the general mood.

"With respect, sir, this feels a bit like déjà vu. I think I speak for everyone in this room when I say no-one wants to believe Tom Brown has sunk low enough to be exacting this sort of revenge on innocent people. It's a depressing thought. But if there is evidence to support that as a possibility, however unlikely, surely we can't dismiss it? This must come under your heading of 'very open mind'. And when I say déjà vu, I mean, of course, the case against Jack and Jason – Jack, in particular – when we were desperate to disbelieve the evidence of our own eyes and ears."

He looked around and noted a good few nodding heads.

"Tom Brown is – or was – a trained killer," he continued, "just like his friend, John Deverall, who took *his* revenge on people he believed had been responsible for the death of his mother. You know what they say – 'they teach these guys how to kill, but when they de-enlist, no-one teaches them how to stop'."

Harry was looking at the wall behind the hushed group, stone-faced with the muscles in his jaw tensed and set. After a long time his eyes dropped to look directly at Owen Bradley.

"I hear what you're saying, Owen." His voice was quiet and calm. "And it *needed* saying, not just because it seems to reflect the views of the people in this room, but also because you are right. We must pursue *all* lines of enquiry, with equal energy and objectivity, and without fear as to where they might lead us."

★

Tom's face was wet and sticky and his sight through one eye was blurred. His mouth was open and he gagged on the appalling taste and stench. It took him almost a minute to realise he was lying face down in his own vomit. He pushed himself up onto one elbow, supporting his head inches from the floor with his hand. Screwing up his eyes to ease the pain, he looked along the hallway towards the living room, then, sensing someone behind him, he tried to turn his head to see. The challenge proved to be too great and his head fell forward again into the foul mess on the carpet. Feet approached from the hall and stopped a yard or so behind him.

"Jesus Christ, Tom. How is it possible for anybody to get that bad in such a short time?"

He felt hands under his armpits lifting him into an unsteady kneeling position. The hands moved down and strong arms clutched him from behind round the waist, lifting him upright. Tom leaned back against his rescuer, unable to stand. His eyes cleared enough to notice that he was halfway between the outer door of the apartment and the living room door at the end of the narrow hall.

"It's Oscar," the voice said. "You know, the guy you told to fuck off a couple of days ago because you could look after yourself."

Oscar walked him into the main bedroom, still supporting him and using his own legs to move Tom's, like a macabre music hall act. When they got to the bed, he turned Tom around, lowered him gently onto it and let him fall backwards before lifting up his feet to lay him down.

"Oscar, what the fuck?" Tom's words came out as a whispered moan. He rolled onto his side.

"You need to come round and get yourself cleaned up. Right now, you don't look a lot like someone who doesn't need any help. Where have you been, for God's sake? What have you been doing? And how did you get the blood on your shirt?"

"Don't know... Don't know... Don't know." Tom gave a muffled laugh, then closed his eyes and seemed to drift off to sleep again. Oscar shook him hard, making him cough until he threw up again onto the bed. Oscar disappeared. Tom heard the sound of running water and Oscar returned with a wet towel.

"Here, wipe yourself with this."

Tom rubbed the towel over his face and round his neck, then he struggled into a sitting position and his eyes cleared a little. He shuffled sideways away from the pool of vomit next to him on the bed and recovered enough to glare at his uninvited guest.

"So, how did you get in this time?" His strength just about lasted to the end of the question.

"Dead easy. Same game. You didn't close the door properly again."

Tom snorted a feeble laugh. "Really?"

"Yes, *really*. I just found you now – as I was going out." He looked at his watch. "And I'm late. This may surprise you, but I've got better things to do than to keep checking your apartment to see whether you're still alive. Now, do you want me to help clean up all this mess, or what?"

"No, but you could get me some water before you leave."

Oscar disappeared into the bathroom again and brought out a full glass. He handed it to Tom.

"You might want this, as well," he said, reaching into his pocket. He handed Tom a mobile phone. "Yours, I think. I found it on the grass outside the main entrance. You'll probably need it to phone for an ambulance one day very soon."

Tom stared at the phone, trying to remember when he last used it. Oscar walked from the room, turning back in the doorway. "Oh, that's quite alright, don't mention it; that's what good neighbours are for, after all."

Tom listened as he left, hearing the apartment door close with the same solid clunk.

★

Saturday; 12 September

A few minutes before noon; George Clancy stood glassy-eyed on the concourse of the small shopping arcade, both arms straining to hold heavy bags of groceries. His wife, a couple of yards away, just inside a shop entrance, was working her way along the 50%-off end-of-season bargain rail. His mobile phone sounded, causing him to inwardly whoop with joy at the break in the monotony. By the time he had balanced the bags on the tiled floor, and retrieved the phone from his pocket, the caller had rung off. George checked the missed call – a landline number he didn't recognise. He called back.

"Louise Thornbury."

"Oh, hello, Mrs Thornbury. You just phoned. Sorry, I missed the call."

"Detective Clancy. Well, actually I rang off. I don't think this will have anything to do with you, but you gave me your card and … It's a bit silly, really."

"Then, I'm definitely your man," George said. "I get all the silly jobs. Is it to do with Thursday?"

"Yes, but… Well, you know when we were at the park, Ellie and your colleague were feeding the ducks and they were really excited – the ducks, I mean." She gave a little laugh.

"*And* my colleague," George said. "Yes, I do remember, they didn't follow you like they usually do and they were flapping and making a real racket under the trees."

"That's right. Well, I think I told you, we had an appointment today at the clinic and we went to the park afterwards. This time when we tried to feed them they didn't come out at all, they just stayed under the overhanging tree and they were… Well, they seemed frantic about something." She paused. "Now I feel *really* stupid. It can't *possibly* be anything to do with you. Perhaps you could tell me who to call. You see I do think something is wrong there. There's a funny smell, for a start."

George looked down at the bags of shopping and across to his wife, not yet halfway along the rail. It was an easy decision.

"No, that's okay, Mrs Thornbury. I'll get down there right away and have a look."

★

The police car pulled up on the road next to Middleton Green and two uniformed officers got out and walked down to the side of the lake. They were each carrying a pair of rubber wading trousers.

"Hi, guys," George said. He pointed across to the overhanging branches. "Behind there. I think there's something in the water. If you get down and look from over here." He walked a little way round the lake and crouched down where it was possible to look through a gap behind the branches. He pointed to where the ducks were flapping over and around something in the water.

"Looks like a bag of something," one of the officers said. "Shouldn't we be phoning the council – Environmental and Waste Department or something?"

"Possibly, but the ducks seem to think it's something exciting."

"A bag of *bread*, then. It can't take much to get them excited, can it? When you think of what they do all day." He turned to his colleague. "Okay, let's take a look. Get your tights on, Tommy."

They pulled on the waders, crossing the straps over their shoulders, and paddled across towards the area of water hidden by the trees. Tommy turned back briefly as they got closer.

"Christ, what a smell!" he shouted. "If it is bread, it's way past it's sell-by date."

They pushed aside the branches and disappeared behind them. Thirty seconds later they reappeared, looking pale and shocked.

"SOCOs I think, George."

★

The trill of his work mobile was the death knell of Harry's relaxing afternoon in front of the rugby on TV. Swinging his feet down from the sofa and hitting the mute button on the remote control, he reached for the phone and checked the name on the display before answering.

"This had better be good, George. They've only just kicked off, for God's sake." There was silence at the other end. "England and the All Blacks. Don't you have another life, DC Clancy?"

"Of course I do, guv. Saturdays I have a job as a pack mule. It's good steady work…"

Harry snorted a laugh. "So what is it, detective?"

"We've found Sammo. In the park where Mrs Thornbury saw him two weeks ago."

"That's great! What was he doing, feeding the ducks?"

"I guess you could say that."

★

By the time Harry arrived, after making the usual calls, the whole of the park had been cordoned off with blue-and-white plastic crime tape, and pedestrians were being diverted to the pavement on the other side of the road which ran alongside the Green. A police crew was in the process of screening off the lake itself with two-metre-high boards hooked onto metal poles held securely in place by guy-ropes. One of the boards had been left to swing open like a door in order to give access to the crime scene. As he walked across from his car, a white overalled figure emerged from behind the screens.

"Hi, Amy."

"Hi, Harry," said Dr White. "This is a bit of a turn-up, isn't it? A bunch of ducks beating you to finding Sammo. Will they be giving a press statement or are you planning to claim the credit?"

Harry smiled. "Not decided yet. How long has he been here, do you think?"

"I would say a couple, maybe three, days at most. So he must have come back. Plenty of damage to soft tissue from whatever's feeding in the lake, but not enough to suggest he's been here very long."

"So what happened to him?"

"Same as the others – back-of-the-head shot – this time I'd say a contact shot, judging from the wound and the burns around it. He – and his killer – went round to the back of the lake through the undergrowth near the wall. I'll show you."

She led Harry through the loose panel and round the side of the lake to where DC Clancy was watching proceedings.

"Afternoon, guv. Sorry about the rugby."

"Hi, George. No problem – we're probably going to lose anyway."

Amy pointed to a long, narrow boardwalk which had been positioned to create a walkway from the bank over the water and through the overhanging branches.

"You can see the body from this. They went through there." She pointed further along the lake edge. "The vegetation's been trampled recently and the team have found fabric and fibres on the thorns and brambles where they must have passed."

Amy led Harry along the walkway which wobbled on the uneven bed of the lake. She pushed aside the branches and they looked across at the remains of Randall Sampson, most of which lay below the surface of the water. Just the back of his jacket showed above, along with the bottom half of his legs, which were still resting on the bank. Four SOCOs were searching the grassy area around him.

"We're sure it's Sammo?" Harry asked.

"We've lifted him once. Can't confirm from facial recognition – you'll see why soon enough – but we removed a wallet from the jacket. It's definitely Sammo's wallet, so unless this is someone who stole it from him, then yes, it's your man."

"Is it too soon to decide why he's in that position – I mean, with his legs still on the bank?"

Amy called across to one of the team. "Rory, can you tell how he came to be lying like that?"

Rory Jarvis got to his feet.

"Still checking, Doc, but it looks like he knelt down here," he pointed to some indentations in the soft ground about half a metre from the edge, "and shuffled forward. So I'd say he was kneeling down when he was shot. That would explain why his legs aren't in the water – you know, if he'd just fallen forward from that position."

"Like an execution, you mean?" Harry asked.

"Possibly, I suppose."

"A bit chilling, don't you think?" Amy said. "Forcing him to walk through all those thorns just to kill him. You'd think he'd take his chances and make a break for it."

"Not if he didn't know what was going to happen," Harry said.

"But why else would he think they were struggling through this lot; and why would he kneel down at the edge like that?"

Harry shrugged and called across to the SOCO.

"What are the chances of finding the bullet, Jarvis? Or is that a silly question?"

"Not necessarily, sir. It depends how he was kneeling when he was shot. If he was leaning forward and the angle of the shot was more or less straight downwards, then virtually no chance at all. It would be buried deep in the mud at whatever depth. If he was kneeling upright and the shot was close to the horizontal – say, just slightly downwards – then it would have been slowed as it entered the water and could be just nestling on the bottom. That way we might have a chance."

"Okay, thanks."

Harry and Amy turned round carefully as the boardwalk rocked a little and stepped slowly back to dry land. George had been joined by DS Belmont and DC Crusoe.

"Hi, you two," said Harry. "I guess you won first prize, Nat." Natalie frowned. "Number five and we just haven't found him yet," Harry quoted.

"Oh, yes. Not that I wanted to be right. Same MO, sir?"

"Looks like it. Might have a hard time confirming whether or not it's the same gun. Search for the bullet's not going to be easy."

"Sir!" One of the SOCOs near the front of the lake called across to them. "You're not going to believe this."

★

The courtyard of the Ye Olde London public house on Ludgate Hill was bathed in warm sunshine. The tables were filling rapidly and many of the diners wore shorts and light tops or vests, lending a mid-summer feel to an end-of-summer day. Jo wore a short, yellow, off-the-shoulder dress and David a cream lightweight linen suit over a pale blue tee shirt.

"Do you remember the first time we came here?" she asked him.

"You ask me that *every* time we come here," David said.

"Yes but I've no way of knowing if your memory's gone yet, have I? It's just a health check."

"Well I *do* remember. It was the day before Mr Deverall was given his life sentence three years ago. I seem to remember you saying you were going to visit him in prison in the hope that he'd take you out when he was released."

"That's right, and you said he probably *would* take me out because after eight years inside he'd be desperate enough for anything – or something equally complimentary."

David chuckled. "So why haven't you visited him? Or have you?"

"Well, I'm afraid our avenging hero is terminally ill in St Bart's. I think I told you some time ago. It's not been in the Press in case he's still a target for some sort of retribution – or even a vigilante rescue attempt."

"You told me he'd been moved, but not that he was terminally ill."

"Well, he is, I'm afraid. Great shame – and *not* just because I won't get to go out with him, in case you're wondering."

David smiled. "Never crossed my mind. Shall we order?"

They called the waiter across.

"A plate of your famous fish and chips for me," Jo said.

"And for me," David said, "and same again for drinks, please."

The waiter hurried away, flashing a smile at Jo. She smiled back at him then leaned across the table towards David.

"So, any thoughts at all about the killings?"

"Uncle Harry made it quite clear I wasn't *allowed* to think about them. But I can understand *you* putting two and two together and getting the same answer you always get – irrespective of the actual calculation."

Jo leaned back and away from him, frowning and pouting. "That is *so* unfair, David. I am never anything but totally objective. But, really, don't you believe there just might be a connection with Jack and Jason's case?"

David thought for a moment. "There *might* be – but there probably isn't. There's a fine line between being focused and being blinkered, you know. I accept that it's a bit of a coincidence that four of the guys who were seen talking to Jack are the same four who have been shot. But it makes no sense to me, in the context of the other case, *why* they should be targeted. So, you tell me."

"Well," Jo leaned forward again, "now the deed is done – Jack and Jason have been successfully framed – and the dust has settled, whoever framed them can start to cover their tracks."

"By getting rid of everybody who provided evidence – directly or indirectly – against Jack and/or Jason at the trial."

"That's right. The guys who came forward after the phone calls are still under police protection – for another month at least, I think – so he's hitting the soft targets first."

"After which, he'll go after the ones who phoned in?"

"Right again."

"So, in this theory of yours, how far is he – or they – likely to go? *You* gave evidence for the Prosecution – are *you* a target?"

"Of course not." Jo shuffled, impatiently. "I was set up as well, along with Harry, Johnny Mac, Doctor what's-his-name and the other legitimate prosecution witnesses. We were deceived into believing stuff that led to the convictions."

"Your hypothesis, then, is that the perpetrator of this deception is in the process of eliminating anyone who might *change* their story and, as a result, raise a doubt."

"Correct."

"But these guys who have been murdered don't have a story to change. They have never given evidence – never been asked to."

"Not so far, but they could have provided *new* evidence if they'd been questioned; if we'd got round to asking them like you asked Laser, then..." Jo stopped.

David sighed and looked down at his hands resting on the table.

"You're reading my mind," he said. "*If* you are correct about who is behind all this, then if I hadn't grabbed Laser, then Sammo, and forced him to take me to Manston Grange, Mickey Kadawe might never have felt threatened, and four ordinary, harmless people would still be alive today. Quite frankly, Jo, I don't *want* to believe there is anything in this other than a coincidence. I don't want my dreams haunted by Laser's expression of wide-eyed hopelessness and the knowledge that my exploitation of that hopelessness led directly to his death."

Jo placed both her hands on his. "David, I'm sorry."

David looked up into her eyes. "Right now, it's okay because I believe you're wrong and that there is no link, and I'm not anxious for you to prove otherwise. Okay?" Neither spoke for a few moments until David broke the uneasy silence. "And here are a couple of thoughts which I probably *am* allowed to have. Firstly, if Kadawe *is* behind these killings, it's more likely to be to avenge his friends. Certainly it's way outside street protocol to contact the police with complaints against dealers. That sort of thing *will* get you shot, and if Mickey *is* lashing out, he might just see the guys who approached Jack on camera as legitimate targets.

"And, secondly, on the subject of revenge, here's another thought you are definitely *not* going to like. What about Tom Brown? A trained killer, off the rails, distraught with despair and anger, and almost certainly with access to all the details of the case including names, addresses, background of those involved. And, if he believes Jack to be innocent, then he *would* see the guys who approached him on Delaware as part of the frame and, as such, people deserving of retribution. Right?"

"I really can't believe that – and even Harry…"

"So it's already been raised as a possibility?"

"More accurately *dismissed* as a possibility – by Harry at a meeting with his MIT."

"Anyway," David continued, "neither of the revenge scenarios – be it Mickey or Tom – points to a wrong verdict. Just a powerful person getting back at the people who helped put Jack and Jason away."

The waiter appeared at the table with their meals and two bottles of lager.

"Thank you," they said, in unison, as he withdrew. He gave Jo his special smile again, returned with less enthusiasm this time. They sat in silence for a few moments, staring at their plates.

"So," Jo said, "it seems that if *I'm* right you will be forever haunted by a feeling of guilt, and if *you're* right, the former Home Secretary may be heading for prison. Let's hope we're both wrong."

David reached for his lager. "I'll drink to that." Jo clinked her bottle against his.

The sky clouded over as they ate and a seasonal chill in the air sent them inside for their coffee and a large Jack Daniels each. Police work was deleted from the agenda and David had just started teasing Jo about her toy-boy sergeant when her mobile sounded. She frowned at the name on the display.

"Hello, Harry."

"Hi, Jo. Just wanted to let you know, we've found Sammo – dead – shot in the head like the others. I'm scrambling some of the team, but this is just for your information. Seems you were right about the connection."

"Where?"

"In the park where he was seen two weeks ago, but that's not when he was killed. Doc White says two or three days ago." Jo remained silent, and Harry continued. "Jo, I can hear those cogs turning from here. Trust me, this doesn't mean *anything* in relation to the other case – no more than the first four did. So have a good weekend and I'll see you Monday."

"Okay, Harry. Thanks for letting me know."

She ended the call and looked wide-eyed across at David.

"Sammo?" he said.

"I'm afraid so. Same MO, it appears." David's face clouded over. "But Harry said this doesn't mean anything," Jo continued. "No links to the other case."

They sat in silence for a few moments. Jo checked her watch.

"Look, I'm sorry, David. Got a train to catch. You started asking me about Seb; well I'm seeing him tonight – in Leicester. He can't get away, so it's just this evening – and overnight. Then I'm seeing Maggie Tomlinson-Brown tomorrow afternoon. Not looking forward to it, to be honest. I'll now have this Tom Brown thing at the back of my mind all the time – I just know it. But it's been arranged for some time and I don't like to cancel. I suppose you could say we've become good friends – amazingly, given the only thing I ever did for her was take her son away."

She got to her feet and David stood up.

"Walk me to the station?"

"Actually," David said, "if you don't mind, I think I'll stay and have another."

Jo's eyes widened a little with surprise. "Okay," she said. "Good idea." She put her arms around him and they held on to each other for a long time. "Bye for now," she said, pulling away. "And *please*, sleep well. I'm the one who should be having the nightmares."

He remained standing as she left, turning briefly in the doorway to give him a little wave, then he walked over to stand at the bar.

CHAPTER SEVEN

Sunday; 13 September

The three huge buildings which comprise the Home Office are joined together by the 'Street', a four-storey bridge connecting the first, second, third and fourth floors of each building. The vast ultra-modern structure is spacious and bright inside with a predominantly open-plan arrangement of work areas throughout, designed to encourage cooperation and community.

The new office of the Ministerial Director of Justice, on the eighth floor of Seacole Building, was large and rectangular, and included two floor-to-ceiling windows furnished with vertical blinds which were currently pulled aside to allow the sun to cast a warm glow into the room. The large mahogany desk, along with the antique tilt-and-swivel behind it and a half-circle of four leather-upholstered wing chairs in front, faced the oak-panelled door and occupied one half of the room. The other half comprised a lounge area with three two-seater, brown-fabric sofas positioned around a square, glass-topped coffee table in front of a black marble fireplace. The walls and ceiling were painted white, giving the room a bright and airy feel, in contrast to the compact wood-panelled office in her suite of rooms at the Headquarters of the Ministry of Defence.

Grace Goody was standing in front of the window behind the desk, looking out across the Thames at the chimneys and turrets of Lambeth Palace. Right now, mid-morning on Sunday, there were very few people in the building above the level of the Street, and she welcomed the quiet and the opportunity to collect her thoughts as she shook off the last lingering effects of jet-lag.

At exactly 11.00 am there was a light knock on the door and Georgia Compton, Grace's PA, poked her curly head into the room.

"Mr Walcott's here, Miss Goody."

"Thanks, Georgia," she said,

Georgia's head disappeared and Grace's visitor stepped into the room. He waited until the door had closed before speaking.

"Hello, darling. Long time, no see." Grace whirled round to face him. "Oh, please don't move," he continued. "Stay exactly where you are."

Grace looked down, realising that the bright sunlight shining in through the window was making her thin silk top completely transparent. Her undercut bra would leave little to his imagination. She stepped to one side, instantly annoyed with herself for reacting so quickly.

"Too late," the man said. "Captured forever in my memory and filed away with all the other images that keep me awake at night. Not that I waste the time – you know – while I'm awake at night…"

"You really don't have to work so hard to disgust me, Jamie. Your just being here does it quite effectively."

"I love it when you tease me like that. For the record, did you have any clothes on when we spoke on Wednesday? Just so I don't file away the wrong image. I like my fantasies to be as real as possible."

Grace sat down at her desk. "You could achieve that by just excluding me from them."

"I'm not sure that's true, darling. I know I make you feel uncomfortable, but I think I could make you do a lot of other things if I really wanted."

Grace looked at him for a long time. "I think you greatly overestimate your importance, Mr Walcott, and severely *underestimate* your vulnerability. And as far as you're concerned, I am 'Miss Goody' or 'ma'am'. I am not your 'darling' – except when I have to be – or 'Grace' at any other time. Your proximity within a five metre radius is repugnant to me and any pathetic attempt at innuendo relating to intimacy makes me feel physically sick. Do we understand each other?"

The man smiled and leaned over the desk towards her. "Perfectly, *ma'am*. I just can't help myself sometimes. I've always had this insatiable appetite for much older women."

He pulled himself up straight before dropping into one of the wing chairs. He was breathing heavily and Grace noticed clear signs of his arousal as he fidgeted in his seat to get comfortable. She also observed, not for the first time, what an attractive man he would be if his behaviour matched his looks. Tall, dark and athletic, with handsome features and sparkling blue eyes. Perhaps it was better that he *was* like he was. In the end, it would make what was inevitable that much easier.

"There's been a change of plan," Grace said.

The man started a little and leaned forward in his chair. "But everything's been done…"

"Okay, let's call it an extension, then."

★

The two women were seated at a table in a quiet corner of the café area in Avocet Hide at the nature reserve. The viewing platform, which was about six feet deep and four steps up from the café floor, ran the full length of the room, and the low bench seats, in front of the long windows with their shutters raised and secured, were all occupied.

"Interesting part of the year, this," Mags said. "It'll be like Chicago O'Hare out there for the next few weeks, with all the birds arriving and the others leaving. I will never get over the enormity of what they achieve – *every* year, just as a matter of routine. How they have the strength to make the journeys, how they know where to go and – most amazing of all – how they find their way back to exactly the same place – often the same *nest*."

Jo Cottrell looked round the room, with its square-section wooden pillars, picnic-style tables and exposed beams in the arched ceiling. "This is a really special place," she said. "And you were responsible for it – you and your group?"

"Well I was the chair of the Kings Leyburn Redevelopment Committee which raised the money for the project, but we left the design of the site and the Visitors' Centre to the experts, of course. It's now an official RSPB reserve, which is what we hoped for when we started. Actually, I chose the name for this hide. I've always had a fascination for avocets – it's always struck me that they've got their beaks on upside-down – so when they asked me to name this hide … Tom was always teasing me about…"

Her voice tailed off and she looked away. When she turned back, she was smiling but her eyes were full of tears.

"Sorry, Jo." She nodded towards the viewing area. "Let's see if we can find a gap in the line of watchers."

Jo reached across and placed her hand on Mags's hand. "Look, if you want to talk about *anything*, then that's part of why I'm here – as your friend. I'm so sorry I let you down with the case…"

Mags gave a little sob, but the smile stayed in place.

"You didn't let me down, Jo. Don't ever think that. You did much more than I could have expected, going out on a limb like that. You and your friend. You took a risk and did your best." She paused, breathing deeply. "But I haven't stopped believing Jack was innocent – *and* Jason. And I never will. Something will surface soon to prove I'm right, I just know it."

The two sat in silence for a few moments. Jo withdrew her hand.

"Look, this is none of my business, Maggie, but I wouldn't be your friend if I didn't tell you. Tom has been picked up by the police a few times recently, and got into a few fights."

Mags's eyes flashed. "You're right, Jo, it *is* none of your business…"

Jo held up her hands. "I'm sorry. As I said, I just wanted to let you know, not tell you what to do."

"No, *I'm* sorry. God knows I need a friend right now. A *proper* friend who will say what I need to hear. Not someone pussy-footing around my sensitivities. So tell me; what's he been up to, other than making the front page of the nationals?"

"Just what I said. He's been wandering around, drinking heavily, and he's got into a few fights and arguments. Our guys have picked him up and taken him home a few times – not charged him or anything. Just looking after him."

Mags's eyes flashed again. "Because I'm *not*? Is that what you mean?"

Jo looked back at her. "I can pussy-foot if you like, Maggie. If that's what you'd prefer."

Mags smiled this time. "Point taken. Put it down to my being an only child, Jo. Always got my own way – never any competition. That's something else Tom was always pointing out." She paused for a long time, deep in thought. When she spoke again, it was in a hushed voice, full of emotion. "In my more rational moments, I worry like mad that something bad is going to happen to him. I can even understand why he did what he did – you know, gave Jack the capsule." Her voice broke a little. "But I can't take him back. Probably not ever. It would be like – you know – backing down. And I'm not sure I can do that. I can't ever remember having had to do that. In a way, what's happened to me is what happened to Jack. I've been tipped out of a cushioned existence where I've never had to worry about anything into a situation I'm totally unequipped to deal with. The fact is, Jo, I simply don't know *what* to do."

The tears ran freely now. Mags bowed her head to save her embarrassment and they clasped each other's hands in the middle of the table. It occurred to Jo that Mags was crying for Tom this time – or for herself *and* Tom as an entity – and not for Jack. That had to be a good thing, she thought. They stayed like that for a long time. Mags recovered her composure and smiled across at Jo.

"I think I needed that," she said.

Jo nodded. "I'll tell you what I think you ought to do right now?"

Mags opened her eyes wide in anticipation.

"There's a family moving out," Jo continued, looking up at the viewing area. "I think you should lead the way up there so we can both give those avocets a good looking at."

*

Monday; 14 September

There was more of a buzz than usual in the MIT room. The hotdogs, bacon sandwiches and coffee were all in evidence as normal, but today, instead of small groups of detectives spread around the room, they were clustered together, ready for the briefing, with all eyes focused on the DI's office door. Harry eventually made his entrance with Amy White to murmurs of anticipation.

"Morning, everybody. You all know Dr White. I've asked

her along to cover the autopsy details arising from the latest developments." Amy smiled and nodded to the group. "As you know," Harry continued, "on Saturday our ace detective Sherlock Clancy, with the help of some ducks, finally found our missing trader, Randall Sampson." There was some applause and cheering from the team. "Well done, George. Saturday afternoon I got some of the team together and we started looking at a way forward, and yesterday we got the Doc's initial report. So just for the benefit of those of you who skived off for the full weekend, George, can you briefly run through the events for us. Then I'll ask the Doc to give us feedback from the autopsy."

George stepped to the front and turned to face the group.

"Much as I'm tempted to take the credit, I have to say, the person we should be thanking is Louise Thornbury. She's the lady who spotted Sammo with the tall guy two weeks ago and it was her noticing the ducks' behaviour on Saturday that led us to the scene. I got a call from her around midday and went to the park to investigate. I guess you know the rest from the guv's phone calls and the local news, and the Doc will fill in the details. But just to recap, we found Sammo at the back of the lake, face-down in the water with his feet still on the bank, but out of sight of anyone in the park itself. Right now the park is still closed and the lake cordoned off.

"Mrs Thornbury came in yesterday to work with the image guys and we've got an e-fit for Mister Tall-dark-and-handsome. Here he is." He held up a sheet of A4. "Pretty, isn't he? We're already showing this around the area close to Middleton Green, and we'll be checking the CCTV footage again at the stations on the nights of the murders right after this meeting."

DC Branwell raised an arm.

"Yes, Greg?"

"Didn't you say that Mrs Thornbury only got a brief look at this man?" He checked his notebook. "She was leaving the park at the time and only glanced at him a couple of times. Isn't that right?"

"True, and I put that to her, but she says she's very good at remembering faces. She works part-time as a receptionist for a firm of lawyers in Leatherhead, and she says she got the job after a three-month trial, mainly because of her ability to remember clients' names and faces. It seems it makes them feel important if they're welcomed by name each time they visit the company."

"Okay," Harry said. "Good point though, Greg. Any other questions for George?"

Owen Bradley raised his arm. "Just one, sir. Could DC Clancy share with the group the special skills he used in order to quack the case?"

Harry held up his arms to silence the jeers and groans. "I would have thought, with over thirty-six hours to prepare, you could have come up with something better than that, Bradley. And another thing – where's my bacon butty?"

"I fed it to the ducks, sir. I thought they deserved it."

This time Harry joined in the laughter.

"Okay, okay, enough," he said. "Let's remember why we're here." He turned to Amy. "Over to you, Doc."

Amy stepped to the front.

"Good morning, everybody. I'll run through the points quickly – not in any order of importance – and answer any questions as we go along." She opened her notebook. "We established the body ID from fingerprint records. There was no chance of a facial match but just about enough left of his finger ends to get prints off them. He'd been shot in the back of the head – like the other four. The only difference – we're sure this was a contact shot from the burns around the point of entry. At this stage we estimate the time of death was between fifty and eighty hours before he was found on Saturday; so that would be sometime from four am Wednesday to ten am Thursday last week. We should be able to narrow that down with further testing, but that could take a day or two."

She turned to Harry.

"Shall I carry on with the CSIU report?"

Harry nodded.

"From an examination of the ground near the body, it seems likely that the victim knelt down close to the lake and then shuffled forward right up to the edge of the bank. It's certain that he was shot whilst in that position, which would explain why his feet were still on the bank.

"The two men – assuming the killer *is* a man, even though it may not be the one the mother saw – must have pushed their way through the thick undergrowth at the back of the lake to get there. But here's an interesting thing – it appears that the killer led the way. Our initial assumption was that he must have forced the victim to walk in front before getting him to kneel down to shoot him. But fibres and bits of fabric caught on the thorns along where they had passed indicate otherwise. In three places, bits from both the victim's jacket and a cashmere coat were caught on the same thorn, but with the cashmere underneath."

Amy paused as if to allow time for the enormity of the revelation to sink in. She was greeted with a collective expression of mute confusion.

"That was my reaction at first," Harry said, "until Rory Jarvis explained. If you get two pieces of fabric on the same thorn, one very clearly under the other, the one on top will be from the second person passing that way."

"Any questions so far?" Amy said.

Greg raised his hand. "Is it possible the victim had the gun initially and forced the other guy to walk in front – like he was going to kill him? Then the cashmere guy somehow managed to get the gun off him?"

"Possible," Harry put in, "but unlikely. There was no sign of a struggle anywhere along where they walked." He looked round the group. "Any other questions for George or Doc White? No? Right, now for the big finish. Take it away, Amy."

"As Rory Jarvis told DI Waters at the scene, normally the chances of finding the bullet would have been small. But we reckoned without the ducks again. Another one of the team found a dead duck, totally submerged, close to the front of the lake. The duck had a bullet in its side – a 9mm from the same gun that killed the four users in Woking and Cobham. I think we can assume it was the bullet that killed Sammo. The duck would have died instantly where it was hit, so, assuming it hadn't been moved, and from the angle between the entry and exit wounds in the victim's head, it's possible to establish Sammo's exact position when he was shot. He was kneeling down, but in an upright position – not leaning forward."

The group erupted into a babble of conversations and some laughter.

"And, if *that* wasn't a lucky break..." Harry said.

"Not for the duck; poor little thing." DC Gordon's comment was loud enough for all to hear and made with such genuine, heartfelt sadness that the room became instantly hushed, many looking embarrassed and awkward. Harry broke the uneasy silence.

"Quite right, Beth. But if it helps us get this bastard then it won't have died in vain. Let's make sure it didn't." He looked round at the circle of serious faces. "So what next? Thoughts, anyone?"

"Well I guess we can safely delete Sammo from our list of suspects," George said.

"I thought Sammo *was* our list of suspects," Alice Grantham said.

"Not so," Harry jumped in. "We were clear that until proved otherwise, Sammo and the killer were two different people. This has just confirmed that hypothesis, so we're no further back or – unfortunately – further forward. Any other ideas?"

"Well, do we think the guy who met Sammo before is the one who killed him?" It was DC Crusoe putting the question. "Like the sarge said, their meeting could just have been Sammo picking up supplies."

"Although, from Mrs T's description, he did sound like a cashmere sort of person," said Owen, looking across at Amy.

"I believe the material is top quality stuff," she said. "Not the usual gear you wear for picking blackberries or similar. He should be easy to pick up on CCTV if there are any cameras near the park."

"There aren't, unfortunately," said George. "The park itself and the road alongside is a real surveillance blind spot. We could look for cars parked in the nearby streets on the day of the first sighting and on Wednesday and Thursday last week. It could yield some registrations to check."

"Let's do that," Harry said, "and see if we can spot Mr Cashmere getting in or out of one. Right," he continued, pacing up and down in front of the team, "we start over again, I'm afraid, showing people pictures – this time of our mysterious park attendant. Let's trawl the CCTV footage around the stations again, like George said, and in the streets near Middleton Green. And, of course, see if we can match him to anyone we've already got on file. I'm making a statement about Sammo on local TV at eleven-thirty at which time I'll also be sharing this same picture with viewers.

"Then we wait for Lois Dearing to call."

★

The first thought that struck the duty sergeant, seated behind his security window looking onto the reception area at Guildford New Station, was how little the girl standing in front of him was wearing. Her purple shorts were not much more than bikini bottoms and her strapless white lace top was high and brief enough to give a tantalising view of both the top and bottom of her small but well-rounded breasts. Her only other visible item of clothing was a pair of purple leather lace-up wedge boots. Her delicate features, in a heart-shaped face below a mass of spiky purple-and-white streaked hair, were devoid of make-up and close to perfection.

Her voice was a gentle tingle when she spoke.

"I'd like to see Chief Superintendent John Mackay, please."

The two young male constables seated at desks behind the sergeant looked up and across at the visitor. Both were quickly on their feet and crowding round him.

"Okay, Sarge," said one, his eyes fixed on the girl, "must be time for your break. I'll take over from here."

"Hold on," said the other. "I've done sod-all this morning. Leave this to me. Time I got my finger out…"

"You'll both sit down," the sergeant said, to no effect. He turned back to the girl.

"Sorry about that. Your name please?"

"Catrina Thompson."

"And you say you want to see…"

"But that's not your *real* name, is it?" the first PC said.

"Yes, that's my real name."

"Okay, then. I mean, that's not your *only* name?"

The girl sighed.

"Look, what's going on?" the sergeant said. "Stay out of this Bradshaw – and you, Simpkiss. I am sure this young lady knows her own name…"

"Lilli Bo-Peep. Right?" Bradshaw said.

The girl sighed again, but smiled this time.

"I'm Catrina Thompson. I'm only Lilli Bo-Peep about two percent of the time – I worked it out."

"Look, would somebody mind telling me…" the sergeant asked.

"Sarge, this young lady is a singer – a *great* singer, in my opinion," Simpkiss said. "And when she's on stage – and apparently *only* when she's on stage – she's Lilli Bo-Peep."

"He's right, sergeant," she said, "and thank you for the compliment." She nodded to Simpkiss. "But, as I said, I'm Catrina Thompson right now and I really need to see Mr Mackay."

The other people waiting in reception were now all showing an interest in the new arrival and her unveiled identity. The sergeant turned to Bradshaw.

"Okay, you've got your wish; take over the desk. Miss Thompson, would you like to go through there." He indicated a door leading off the area then disappeared for a few moments to open it from the other side letting her through into a small room with four upholstered dining-style chairs arranged two on each side of a rectangular table.

"Now, Miss Thompson," he said, when they were seated, facing each other across the table, "I'm Sergeant Gerry Masters; I'm afraid the Chief Superintendent isn't at the station today until later, and anyway, he wouldn't normally be the first person you would get to see. Even for a celebrity like you." He gave her a big smile. "Lilli Bo-Peep, eh. Well, assuming you're not here to report some lost sheep, if you tell me what it's about, I'll get someone else to see you."

She smiled, then hesitated, looking down and twisting her hands together. The sergeant picked up on her nervousness.

"Look, take your time; there's no hurry."

She looked up and into his eyes, as if assessing whether she could trust him with her information.

"It's just that… Well, if what I say gets back to a certain person…" her voice broke a little as the fear surfaced, "… it would be really bad for me. It could be anyway, but…"

"So could you just tell me what it's about without mentioning this person's name?"

She paused for a moment.

"It's to do with Jack Tomlinson-Brown."

The sergeant's eyes opened wide in surprise.

"About his death, do you mean?"

"No, about his conviction. Something was missed. It might not be important, but..."

Gerry held up his hand to call a halt for now.

"I think I'd better get someone else for you to speak to," he said. "I'll only be a few minutes, but I'm going to ask Constable Simpkiss to sit with you and get you a drink if you want one. Are you okay with that? I'll tell him not to drool too much, but it seems he's a big fan."

She laughed. "No that's fine. He can tell me how good I am again."

★

Jo picked up the phone.

"Ma'am, DC Grantham here. I've got Sergeant Masters on the line wanting to speak to you."

"Okay, thanks, Alice – put him through. Hi, Gerry. What's new?"

"Well, ma'am, I've got a young lady here – Catrina Thompson. She says she's got information about the Tomlinson-Brown kid's conviction. About something that was missed."

Jo's stomach gave a little flip. "She needs to speak to Harry Waters."

"I know that, ma'am. That's who I was trying to contact, but I believe he's talking to the Press and won't be available for a while."

"Can you ask her to wait?"

"I could, but she seems very nervous – frightened even. I'm just concerned that if she can't see someone right away, she might change her mind about telling us anything."

"Okay, Gerry. It should really be somebody from Harry's team, but DS Belmont's not here either."

"The thing is she's asked to see the chief. No disrespect to the DCs but – again – she might change her mind if it isn't a senior officer."

Jo thought for a moment. "Okay, I'll come along and bring DC Grantham with me. Where is she?"

"Interview Room A off reception."

"Are there recorders in there?"

"There will be by the time you get there."

★

They found Catrina and Liam Simpkiss drinking coffee and clearly enjoying each others' company. Gerry set up the recorders then he and Liam left, the latter with a backward glance and a wide smile to the singer. Jo introduced herself and DC Grantham, telling the singer how much of a fan she was and asking about future dates. Catrina mentioned the forthcoming tour and by the time they got down to business, she seemed relaxed and talkative.

"I'm afraid Detective Inspector Harry Waters, who was the investigating officer on Jack and Jason's case, is not available," Jo told her, "but DC Grantham was part of his team. Would you mind if we recorded this so that DI Waters can pick up on what you have to tell us?"

"Of course not, no problem," Catrina answered, smiling. "I'm used to making recordings."

"Just as long as we don't have any copyright issues when we've finished," Jo smiled. "Right, let's make a start; you just say what you came to say; and we'll chip in if we need to."

"Okay."

Jo switched on the two recorders.

"Recording of an interview in Room A, GNS Reception, on Monday, 14th September. Present, Miss Catrina Thompson, DI Jo Cottrell and DC Alice Grantham. For the record, Miss Thompson came in voluntarily at her own instigation with information relating to the case of Jack Tomlinson-Brown and Jason Midanda. Interview started at eleven-oh-five am."

She nodded for Catrina to proceed.

"I'm not sure whether this is relevant or not, and I've not only *just* thought about it but – well – I've only recently got up the courage to tell someone. My manager – agent – call him what you like – is a guy called Mickey Kadawe." Jo felt another flip. "He arranged for me – and The Rams – that's my backing group – they're called Abattoir Ratts when they play on their own – play completely different stuff. Rams one minute, Ratts the next. They take a load of shit from the other heavies for that..."

"I can imagine..."

"Sorry, I'm wandering..."

"No, that's okay," Jo said. "Go on."

"Well, he'd arranged for us to provide the music at Jack and Katey's party. On the night, everybody was checked in through the gates by the on-site security guys when they arrived. They took everyone's name, description, time they arrived and such. Except for Mickey; he was in the back of one of our vans hidden under the equipment. He swore us to secrecy and threatened us with God knows what if we gave him away – then or afterwards. He's a real vicious bastard – I tell you, if he ever finds out I came here I don't know what..."

Her voice broke as the fear returned.

"Go on, Catrina. It'll be okay." Jo was almost beside herself with anticipation. "Presumably he told you why he was doing this?"

"Yes, he said he suspected Jack was dealing drugs – you know, the hard stuff. And Mickey was worried that would put the heat on his place – given that Jack spent a lot of time there. He said he was going to check out the house and grounds. So while we were setting up, he sneaked off to look around – and we didn't see him again that night. I guess that in itself isn't surprising; I mean, he wasn't supposed to be there."

"What do you think Mickey meant about putting the heat on his place?"

"I *know* what he meant. Mickey's a legit trader now, but he does other stuff as well. Some of the bad shit he reckoned Jack was doing. Can I say something off the record?" She pointed with her two index fingers to the recorders.

"Sure," Jo said. "Recording interrupted at eleven-fifteen am." She paused the machines.

"He gets that stuff for me from time-to-time, and for the rest of his artists. It's a way to keep us quiet and – well – loyal to him, I suppose. We couldn't get it anywhere else at what he charges us for it and we get a regular supply and pay for it through a cut in our earnings."

"Right," Jo said. "Actually, we'd have been okay to record that, Catrina. *Using* the stuff isn't illegal any more. You're not breaking any law."

"I know, but I don't want the wrong publicity. I'm the squeaky-clean, innocent, little nursery-rhyme girl. I'm supposed to be different. And I *am*… most of the time, but I just need a little boost every so often."

"Sure, I understand. So, are we ready to go again?" She placed her fingers over the pause buttons. Catrina nodded. Jo started the recorders.

"Recording re-commenced at eleven-nineteen. Catrina, why are you telling us this now?"

"Well," Catrina said, shifting on her chair. "I thought you should know…"

"Oh, I agree," Jo said, "but what I mean is why *now*? Why not earlier, when it could have made a difference?"

"Look, you don't know what he's like," she answered. "You have *no idea* what he's like, what I've gone through to get here today. I am *shit scared!*" Her voice was rising, showing signs of her losing control.

Jo held up her hands.

"Hey, Catrina, if that came out like a criticism; it wasn't meant to. But we *are* interested, of course, in what has changed to make you prepared to risk coming forward now. I didn't mean to upset you. Please go on."

Catrina took some deep breaths, struggling to become calm again before continuing.

"Well," she said, "when the stuff was found and Jack was arrested, I thought it just proved Mickey was right. I mean, there *were* drugs in the house. So it seemed – well – justified – what he did."

"Did he say anything to you afterwards? I mean, after he'd searched the house."

"Not to me. He told Dags he hadn't found anything…"

"Dags?"

"Dagger-Zee – lead guitarist. He was driving the van with just him and me in it – plus Mickey in the back. We were the only two who knew what he'd done. Still are, I guess."

"Okay. Go on."

"Well, as I said, when Jack was caught, it all seemed to fit – at first."

"So, I have to ask again, why now? What's changed to make you suddenly think that it *doesn't* fit?"

Catrina didn't speak for a long time.

"Okay, if you must know, it was hearing about Sammo yesterday on the news. The fact that he'd been found dead – shot."

"So why would that prompt you to tell us about Mickey?"

"Well, some weeks ago, Mickey and Sammo fell out big-time. Apparently some guy had tricked Sammo into taking him to Manston Grange, I don't know who the guy was, but he's obviously got Mickey worried. He's never shown up again and Mickey's watching his back all the time. He had a real go at Sammo when it happened and he's been at him ever since, threatening him with all sorts."

"Is – was – Sammo a friend of yours?"

Catrina squirmed on her chair. "Christ, no! Obnoxious little shit, gave me the creeps. Had a really violent temper as well. But Mickey just fucks around with people's lives, and I just think he ought to be stopped."

"Are you saying you think Mickey Kadawe killed Sammo?" Alice asked.

"I don't know, but I believe he's capable of it."

Alice leaned forward, elbows on the table. "Do you really think that Sammo revealing Mickey's address is a strong enough motive for murder?"

Catrina paused before answering.

"Look, I don't know – and that's not what I came to talk about. You asked me why I chose *now* to tell you about the night of the party. Sammo's murder just started me thinking what Mickey's like and how he treats people. And… I'd already been thinking a lot recently about Jack." She gave a little sob. "I liked him. I mean, I *really* liked him. I know he had a girlfriend, but I don't think he was all that serious about her. I sort of hoped that him and me… you know. And since he… died… It's been going round in my mind. I just can't believe he was into that sort of thing. He was so laid-back, pleasant… and funny. He made everyone laugh – all the time. Drug dealers aren't like that – nothing like that."

She was gently crying now. She reached into her shoulder bag and took out a tissue, dabbing her eyes.

"So I thought what if Mickey actually took the stuff into the house that night. I mean, planted it there, for someone to find. *That* could be why he sneaked in, He had a rucksack with him, and I thought it probably had tools in it – you know screw-drivers, crow-bars and such – for searching. But it could have had drugs in it, I suppose. The stuff that was found. The more I think about it... Oh, God! If he did do that, then I helped him frame Jack. This is all my fault..."

The tears came freely, her body shaking with the sobs.

Jo switched off the recorders and went round the table to comfort her. She crouched beside the chair and put an arm round her shoulders, making a 'drink' sign with her free hand to Alice, who left the room to fetch more coffee.

"I'll let you into a secret, Catrina," Jo said. "Well, it's no secret, actually, but it might be news to you. I'm the one who found the drugs in Jack's house, in his room. So if you're right about a set-up, we can both feel bad together."

★

They sat in silence for a long time, all staring at the recorder on the Chief Superintendent's desk as if the machine itself was responsible for what they had just heard. The two men sat tight-lipped and serious; Jo struggled to suppress her simmering excitement.

"Just step us through the timing again, Jo," John Mackay said.

"Yes, sir. Catrina Thompson arrived here at ten-forty-two. Sergeant Masters phoned for Harry ten minutes later at ten-fifty-two – DC Grantham took the call. Harry wasn't contactable and Gerry was concerned that Miss Thompson might change her mind and leave if she was asked to wait or if she couldn't speak to a senior officer. So DC Grantham and I talked to her and recorded the interview, starting at eleven-oh-five. The meeting finally ended at eleven-forty-eight and I pointed out as she left that Harry, as the CIO on the case, may want to speak to her separately."

John looked at Harry and raised his eyebrows with the unspoken question.

"All fine with me," said Harry, shrugging.

They were silent again for a while, then John got to his feet and began pacing back and forth behind his desk.

"Okay," he said, "this clearly *is* a cause for concern. If we had known about Kadawe's foray into the grounds on the night of the party, it would have opened up a new line of questioning for the Defence. Even so, as I see it, there are a couple of real biggies in the way of this making a difference to the outcome.

"One; Mickey's explanation about *why* he was there – to check whether Jack *did* have drugs in his possession – which, to be honest, rings true to me. And, if it *is* true, then, as Miss Thompson initially concluded, he was subsequently proved right. And, two – the *real* biggy – the mass of other evidence that points the way the verdicts went. As I've said to you before, Jo, we had enough to bring a case *before* the drugs were found."

"I understand that, sir, but what we know for certain now is that Mickey lied in court."

"No he didn't; not in court. He was never *asked* at the trial whether he was at Etherington Place on the night of the party. Why would he be asked? He was up there on the stand as a character witness trying to get them off. If he did that with the knowledge that at least one of them *was* dealing, then the worst you can accuse him of is misplaced loyalty. He's more likely to end up a hero than a villain." He turned to the other officer. "Harry, thoughts?"

Harry took his time in answering.

"There's no doubt the Defence would have developed that piece of information, so – of course – we can't just dismiss it. I just worry that, if the end verdicts were correct, it would be dangerous – and pointless – to raise this to public awareness and discredit an investigation carried out with so much care and sympathy on behalf of the defendants. I see no benefit – at this stage – to risk undermining people's confidence in the police – *and* the system."

"Absolutely agree," said John. "And I don't want you deflected from the current investigation, Harry, so I'm going to put you onto this, Jo, and…"

Harry jumped to his feet. "With respect, sir…"

John held up his hands. "I want this as low profile as possible,

Harry – like you said yourself just now. If I drag you off these five murders there's no way we'll be able to achieve that. So you go full steam ahead with what you're doing." He turned to Jo. "Let's move really quickly on this, Jo. Get a small team together right away – include DS Ramirez as your number two – she was on Harry's team on the J and J case and she can provide the link. Then I'd like to speak to them before you do anything else. But I'm going to position this as our tying up loose ends. I don't want rumours circulating that there's a chance we screwed up, because I don't believe for one minute that we did. Miss Thompson was almost certainly correct in her first conclusion – that Mickey suspected Jack was dealing, and that he was right."

Jo was shaking her head, without realising it.

"Please don't take that dismissive attitude with me, Detective Inspector!" said John. "I know you feel very strongly about this, but the truth will not be best served if you pitch in with a blinkered intention to achieve your preferred result."

It was Jo's turn to bristle.

"With respect, sir, I hope you're not suggesting that I have some vested interest in the outcome. I have opinions that may differ from yours and DI Waters', but if you think I'm not capable of an objective approach to this, then I would rather you got someone else to lead the investigation. I don't feel I'd be able to give it my best if I thought someone was looking over my shoulder checking what I was doing all of the time."

John leaned on his knuckles across the desk, still angry. "No, *you* will lead the investigation, Jo. And *just* you – there's no job for your superhero this time. David Gerrard is very definitely off-limits – okay? And before you do anything else, get this Dagger-Zee in to confirm her story,"

"Okay, sir, but I can't see there being any doubt that it's true. Even if he chooses not to corroborate it, then I'd still believe her. She has nothing to gain and everything to lose by fingering Mickey if she's made it all up."

"Very well, but talk to him anyway. Right now you need to get out there and gather the troops." He looked at his watch. "It's one-thirty. I'll expect them to be ready for me by three. Okay? And in the meantime, I'm going to have to flag this with the Chief Constable."

He turned to Harry. "I feel like I'm back in the movie again; at the centre of the earth waiting for that bloody volcano."

★

This time it was the more familiar sound of the bell that disturbed his sleep. Tom checked the display on the clock at the side of the bed – *15.15, MON 14 SEPT.* A quarter past three! Christ, he'd been out for a full day! He remembered watching England v the All-Blacks highlights early on Sunday afternoon and after that… nothing!

He pulled on his dressing gown and staggered to the front door of the apartment, hitting both sides of the door jamb as he left the bedroom. He squinted at the display on the monitor and saw a man in a suit. Tom pressed the speaker button.

"Dan?"

"Hi, Tom. We need to talk."

"What about? The trial's not for another three months."

"Less than two months. Look, are you going to let me in or do I have to discuss it with you in a loud voice from down here?"

"I wish you'd phoned first."

"I did – *many* times. The phone must be off the hook and your mobile switched off."

Tom felt his stomach preparing to relinquish its contents. "Okay, come on up."

He activated the lock on the street door and fled into the bathroom to throw up. He splashed water onto his face and went back to let his visitor into the apartment.

Daniel Hastings, Senior Partner at Hastings and Medforth Associates Ltd looked the same as always; handsome, smart, relaxed and distinguished; today in a grey pinstripe suit, cream shirt and dark red silk tie, and carrying a traditional calfskin briefcase. He looked Tom up and down before speaking.

"Well it's reassuring to see you're taking good care of yourself."

"Very amusing," said his host, blinking his eyes into focus. "Coffee?"

"Yes, please. I'll wait through here," Dan said, heading for the living room.

"God, sorry," Tom said, a few minutes later, glancing round the room as he placed two steaming cups on the edge of a coffee table. Dan had seated himself at the end of one of the black leather sofas in the only place free of discarded clothes and scattered papers. Tom knew his guest could not have failed to detect the smell of stale sweat and whisky. "I don't get many visitors these days."

"Can't think why," said Daniel. "I see you've got a neighbour, though."

"Was he camped out on the landing again?"

"No, but I could see the door was ajar when I came up. Wedged open with something, I think."

"Well, he's getting on my nerves at the moment; like he's lying in wait for me all the time." He took a sip of his coffee and winced at the taste. "Anyway, what's the great urgency? I'm going to plead guilty, aren't I? The plea of not guilty to the magistrate was to enable me to recede from public life with dignity, wasn't it? Well I certainly fucked that up."

"Yes, you did rather. We could plead *not* guilty to the charge of helping a prisoner take his own life on the basis that you believed it was not his intention at the time; that the capsule was provided as insurance for the future *if* necessary. That's the truth, in fact, isn't it? But you're guilty of something, that's for certain."

Tom's head dropped forward on to his chest.

"I'm sorry, Tom. I didn't mean that to sound so detached and dispassionate, and you're right, there's no great urgency. If you want the truth, I came today as a friend to check how you were and to encourage you to get yourself together. It's around seven weeks to the trial and now's a good time to start getting in shape for it. Maggie must be really worried about you, seeing your picture…"

"Did she send you?" Tom looked up, taking Daniel by surprise. "That's why you're here. Mags asked you to check up on me because it would be – like – *giving in* if she were to come herself."

"That's not how it was, Tom. Maggie *did* call me – yesterday evening – to ask if I'd seen you and when we'd be starting to prepare for the trial. But she didn't ask me to check up on you. *I* decided that. To be honest I feel a bit guilty not getting in touch earlier – as your friend, not your solicitor."

"Well now you know…"

"Yes, now I know. You're a mess and you're *not* looking after yourself. You're going to look really bad at trial if you don't pull yourself together. Okay? So – how can I help?"

Tom thought for a few moments.

"You can't," he said. "It's down to me. But you're right. I *do* need to get myself together, because there's some unfinished business I have to take care of."

CHAPTER EIGHT

Jo Cottrell and Christina Ramirez sat, deep in thought, across the table from each other in the vacant office off the major incident team room. The sergeant was similar to Jo in size and shape – five-and-a-half feet tall, quite slim, with a round, pretty face and hair cut just short of shoulder length. Otherwise, she was just as pale as Jo was dark, her blonde hair and fair complexion giving her a distinctly Scandinavian look, rather than the Mediterranean or Latin American tone her name suggested.

There was a light tap on the door and DC Alice Grantham poked her head into the room. She opened her eyes wide in an expression of mock horror.

"Your visitor's here," she said.

The man who stepped into the room certainly did have an initial aura of menace about him. Standing well over six feet – assisted by a pair of high-heeled, tan-leather cowboy boots – he was thin almost to the point of emaciation. His faded blue jeans were torn horizontally across both knees and in several places above; he wore a grey tee shirt sporting the band's logo under a padded black gilet. His dyed-black hair was long and flowed over his shoulders; he had a good many days' stubble, and five metal studs around each ear. In spite of all this, Jo observed a sensitive face with soft blue eyes and a worried, hunted expression. Her overall impression was of a chosen image that failed to hide the caring, empathetic individual behind it.

The two officers got to their feet as he entered and Tina stepped round the table to stand beside Jo.

"Thank you for coming in… Do we call you Mr Zee… or what?" Jo smiled at him as she extended her hand. "I'm Detective Inspector Cottrell, and this is Detective Sergeant Ramirez. Seriously, what do you prefer to be called?"

"Dagger's fine." He reached forward to shake hands, limply, without making eye contact with either of them.

"Please sit down, Dagger," Jo said, as she and Tina took their seats. "We appreciate you coming in like this. We would have been happy to come and meet you…"

The man, who had remained standing, drew in his breath.

"Don't even think of it," he said. "Please don't come anywhere near where we're working." His voice was also gentle, though anxious, and unexpectedly deep for his lean frame. Jo and Tina exchanged a puzzled look.

"Why do you say that, Dagger, we only…"

"Look, this is really awkward," he said, still standing but leaning on the back of the chair Tina had vacated. "Before we go anywhere with this, I need to tell you that Cat is retracting her story."

Jo raised her eyebrows. "And why would she want to do that, Dagger?"

"She… just does."

"Is it not true what she told us? Was she just deliberately wasting police time?"

"She's changed her mind."

Jo leaned across the table. "Changed her mind about *what?*" All pretence at calmness put aside, her voice was angry. "She can't change her mind about *telling* us, because she already has. So, I ask you again – was it all a pack of lies? Has she changed her mind about what happened at Jack's party?" He hung his head like a scolded child. "And for God's sake, Dagger, *sit down!*"

He slipped onto the chair, sitting with his knees together, and with the palms of his hands resting on them, head still bowed. Jo wondered for a moment whether he was actually going to cry. But when he looked up his eyes were angry.

"Cat should never have come to you. God knows what she was thinking about. All she's done is put herself in danger. Kadawe would *kill* her if he found out – both of us, probably. So you can't use what she told you. She'll deny everything…"

"She can't deny it now, Dagger. We've got it on tape."

"I mean she'll say it wasn't true, that she was just getting at Mickey because she's pissed off with him – the way he treats her. She'll say the party thing was just a load of crap she made up."

"This is what *you've* told her to say, right?" said Jo, narrowing her eyes. "But the truth is *exactly* what Catrina told us yesterday, isn't that also right?"

Dagger raised his head but avoided looking at them, moving it rapidly from side to side.

"Isn't that right?" Jo was almost shouting now. She took a deep breath. "Look, Dagger, no recorders, just us three here. So tell me – isn't what Catrina told us exactly what happened?"

"Yes," he looked her in the eye, "but it makes no difference. She'll deny it. It's simply a matter of life and death – nothing else."

★

Jo was leaning back in her chair, side-on to the desk, staring at the blank wall of her office. She barely heard the tap on the door, only waking from her trance when Tina stepped into the room. The sergeant laid a sheet of paper on the desk and sat down.

"Address in Dorking for the four under police protection – the ones who phoned in then agreed to be interviewed. It's a small combo the Witness Protection guys use from time-to-time. Part of a complex of thirty-four apartments, with its own swimming pool, sauna and stuff. They're on a corner block of four. Looks good, I wouldn't mind being a protected witness if I could live there free of charge."

"And how much longer will they be there, basking in the lap of luxury? I take it they won't be applying to be released early for good behaviour."

"It should be until the end of October but they could be released early for *bad* behaviour. The other residents aren't very happy with them. The deal, as always, is that they behave themselves and keep a low profile. I think filling the communal pool with empty lager cans and urinating into it falls outside those terms and conditions."

"I take it there won't be any ludicrous red tape crap to get through before we can speak to them?"

Tina smiled. "Don't be too sure. The guy in charge said he'd have to check whether no further questioning by the police was part of the contract."

"Oh, for Christ's sake! He might also want to check whether permission to piss in the pool was in the small print."

"I think we'll be okay. I've worked with him before. Any more thoughts on Dagger's speech?

"I've thought of nothing else for…" she checked her watch "… three hours. What about you?"

"Well, looking at the glass half-full, we *know* what happened, don't we? I've been thinking it's like getting an anonymous letter or phone call. One that we've no reason to disbelieve. So, how would we move forward from something like that?"

"Go on."

"Well, we wouldn't spend a lot of time trying to find who sent it – or made it – would we? Our main push would be to verify the information through other sources – in this case, for example, getting Mickey to give himself away – somehow – and/or check other stuff – CCTV at the party, get forensics in the van, question other guests. Somebody just *might* have seen Mickey there, but wouldn't know he hadn't checked in properly."

"I doubt that. Jack and Katey were sure that he hadn't attended the party, and he'd make certain no-one would see him – or at least *recognise* him – or he'd have some explaining to do later. Why didn't we check if he had an alibi on the night?"

"Because he didn't *need* an alibi – he wasn't accused of anything – or even suspected of anything. He was asked where he was – as much out of curiosity as anything. He explained he'd taken a friend to Heathrow who was returning to Jo'burg, and that was that. His attendance or non-attendance on the night was never an issue."

They were both silent for a while, Jo drumming her fingers on the desk, a habit she had picked up from her boss.

"You're right, Tina. Let's put Catrina and Dagger on one side for now and work with what we know. CCTV seems like a good place to start. Let's get the team looking at the tapes from the party – please God, we still have them. Particularly the cameras covering where the vans were parked. And get the full list of guests just in case we need to go down that route. Let's do that first before we visit the Dorking Four."

Tina stood up to leave just as Jo's desk phone sounded. She lifted the receiver.

"This is DI Cottrell." She looked across at Tina, her eyes wide. "Hi, Catrina. Just hold on a second, do you mind if I put you on the speaker, I've got a colleague with me here. The one who spoke to Dagger with me earlier. Thank you." Jo pressed a button on the phone and replaced the handset. Catrina's tinkling voice filled the room.

"Listen, I'm sorry about Dags. He's only looking out for me and what he said was right. Mickey would kill us both if he found out – or get someone else to do it, I mean. He'd never risk doing it himself. What I told you was true, but having thought about it I don't want it ever to come out that you found out from me."

"I understand that you're frightened, Catrina, and all the more credit to you for coming forward. But other officers are already aware of our conversation yesterday. So what do you expect us to do now? Just pretend it didn't happen like that?"

"No, but if Mickey were to *admit* he'd been there on the night, you wouldn't need to use me, would you?"

"No, I guess not, but…"

"Well, I've got an idea."

★

Wednesday; 16 September

One of the first meetings the new Home Secretary attended was an informal one with the person she had just defeated in the unofficial race for the position. They took their seats in a quiet corner of the vast atrium which is the ground floor of Portcullis House, with its predominance of glass and flora providing a real essence of the outdoors.

"I feel I should start with a sort of apology, if that doesn't sound patronising."

Jonathan laughed. "Not necessary, Jackie – as I'm sure you know. I've got a promotion and you've got a sideways move – albeit one with a very steep gradient – so why should I be anything but pleased. And I'm really looking forward to working with you – I mean that very sincerely."

Jackie Hewlett smiled. "You're too good to be true, at times, Jonathan. Although," she continued with a shake of the head, "I'd rather be getting this under different circumstances. I mean, not by replacing Tom. You know I feel really bad – I haven't been in touch with him for weeks. We were such good friends – *are* such good friends – and it seems he really needs help right now. The problem is, of course, the longer you leave it without contacting someone, the harder it is to do it. Have you seen him recently?"

"No, I've not been in touch either. I probably know a bit more of what he's doing because I'm getting reports from the police that, thankfully, *aren't* making the papers. I've not shared any of these with Andrew – although I mentioned it to Grace recently. They were really close as well, of course, and I know she's very concerned about his welfare."

Jackie's face clouded over.

"Sorry, Jackie, did I say something wrong?"

"To be honest, Grace was the main reason why I wanted to meet with you like this – I mean, unofficially."

Jonathan raised his eyebrows. "Sounds fascinating. Do go on."

Jackie paused.

"I don't think it's a secret that Grace has a very close relationship with Andrew – I mean close in the professional sense. Nothing wrong in that – it goes back a long way, though no-one seems to know in what capacity. But I get the impression that she feeds back stuff to Andrew *all* the time – alerting him to what people are doing or thinking, just so he can keep on top of them." She smiled, a little embarrassed. "I'm not explaining it very well, but I shared this with Tom when I went to visit him shortly after he handed in his resignation, and I think it started him wondering along the same lines. We never got to discuss it because – ironically – Grace turned up at his apartment."

Jonathan frowned and shook his head. "So what exactly are you suggesting we do, Jackie? I have to say, my relationship with Grace is very good at the moment. I don't get the feeling that she's spying on me, if that's what you mean."

Jackie shifted on her seat. "I'm not suggesting we *do* anything. But I thought it only right that I shared my concerns with you. If I'm wrong, then all to the good. Perhaps this was not a good subject for a first meeting between two senior ministers."

★

"So the chief actually sanctioned this?" Tina couldn't hide her surprise.

"Absolutely, albeit with less than gushing enthusiasm, and with the proviso that any arrest at this stage must not be related in any way to perversion of justice. I had to point out to him that, depending on how it went, we might have to step in at some point."

"Well, you can't fault our Little Polly Flinders for courage. When is she due here?"

Jo checked her watch. "She said around six-thirty, so any minute now. I've asked the desk to contact me so you can bring her up. She'll never get through the team room if any of the guys get to her first."

"Yes, I did notice the fever of excitement out there."

The desk phone rang. "This could be her," Jo said, reaching for it.

★

At 7.00 pm, Jo stepped out of her office into the MIT room. With her was Catrina Thompson, the focus of seven pairs of male eyes and an unwelcome, albeit innocent, distraction from Jo's critical final briefing of her surveillance team. At 8.00 pm, the group dispersed, leaving Jo to oversee the fitting and testing of the tiny transmitter/receiver Catrina would be carrying the following day. Danny, the surveillance technician, had commented on – though not complained about – the lack of options for concealing the device, given her minimal amount of clothing. In the end, with little chance of hiding it, he had placed it in full view, as part of a pair of large earrings designed specifically for the job.

"Okay," he said. "The really important thing is to make sure you switch off the receiver when I tell you. The equipment is virtually impossible to detect visually, so as long as you remember that, there'll be no problem. Okay?"

"Okay."

"You'll still be able to receive the warning pulses, but no-one else will be able to hear them – that's a promise." He beamed and received a nervous smile in return.

"So let's do one last check on the pulsed signals. Turn off the receiver, I'll pulse you and you tell me what the signal means. Okay?"

"Okay," Catrina said, briefly touching her left earring and turning away from Danny.

"Here goes," he said.

★

The two men speaking together in hushed voices near the line of cars in the reserved spaces in front of the building watched her leave. They stopped talking as she passed, then resumed again as soon as she was out of earshot.

"'Undercover' is hardly an appropriate description, is it?" Chief Constable Eddie Mills said, leering at the girl's token outfit. "'Uncovered' would be more accurate. Just about enough material to prevent her own arrest for indecent exposure."

John Mackay gave a quick smile.

"I'm dreading the fall-out from this…"

"What fall-out?" Eddie jumped in. "There'll be no fall-out. There's no reason to believe Kadawe put the stuff there. His explanation hangs together. And if he was complicit in sending these guys to approach Jack, then that would be consistent with him checking him out. You know, to see if he's dealing the stuff. When he gets no joy, he searches the place. He finds the stuff, has to leave it because he gets disturbed or something. Then we find it. There's nothing so far that the girl's told us, and Kadawe's told *her*, that doesn't fit with the Brown kid being guilty. So that's why we need the news black-out, John, because this perversion of justice business has to be made to go away. As I said – there will be no fall-out."

"That's fine with me, but DI Cottrell is in no doubt. She found the stuff in the house and saw Jack's reaction. And her instincts are exceptional, according to Rayburn; in addition to which she's like a dog with a bone. Short of calling her off..."

"Yes, well, just think about that. Your little terrier might have a hard lesson coming her way."

"Lesson?" John said. "What lesson?"

"The principle of the greater good," Eddie replied. "That some actions and decisions which appear to lack reason and integrity when appraised on a stand-alone basis are totally justified in the wider context. And that's a direct quote from our ex-Home Secretary, because it's that very principle which justifies the NJR's permanent and brutal banishment of senior adolescents. So it won't be completely new to our Jo, will it?"

"Well, no, but..."

"This whole fucking thing has gone too far, John. We should have cut her off at the knees as soon as we knew she'd gone it alone with Gerrard – and hit him with a fucking harassment charge or something. Instead she gets carte blanche to do what she likes..."

"Hold on!" John interrupted, getting angry himself. "And what about the singer? Should we have cut her off as well? Charged her with wasting police time? Perhaps the best thing to do would be to get rid of Kadawe. That would just about solve everything, wouldn't it?"

Eddie glared back at him for several seconds.

"Just hold that thought," he said.

He turned and got into his black Jaguar Coupe, leaving the Chief Superintendent to ponder the meaning of his last remark as he drove away.

*

Thursday; 17 September

The two-person surveillance team in the white van with the blue 'CountryNet' lettering was already in place, parked at the rear of the Sweet Rock Hall concert venue, well before Lilli Bo-Peep was due to arrive by taxi at 10.00 am for her rehearsal with the Rams an hour later.

"I'm here." They picked up her voice in the van at just after five past the hour.

"That's great, Catrina," Jo said. "You're loud and clear. Let's test the pulsed signals again."

Danny sent the three pre-arranged signals – each one a number of beeps – directly into her ear through a carbon fibre half the thickness of a human hair attached to her earring.

"Did you get those, Cat?" Danny this time.

"Yes, got them all."

"Okay," Jo said. "De-activating voice transmitter now. Switch off the receiver your end. Good luck, Catrina, and don't worry; remember we're right here for you. But please be careful."

"Okay, thanks."

Danny switched it off. Jo radioed the two unmarked police cars – three plain-clothes officers in each – both on post within fifty yards and between them covering the main and side entrances.

Everyone settled down to await the target.

★

At 10.35, Mickey Kadawe burst into the hall in the same way he had done two weeks earlier, and with the same scowling impatience. The band was tuning up and carrying out sound checks.

"Can we get going, for fuck's sake? All this was supposed to be done last night. Where's Cat?"

"In her room," Dagger said. "And we're not due to start until eleven."

Mickey rounded on him.

"And it would be terrible if someone started work a fucking minute before they had to, wouldn't it?"

Mickey didn't burst into her room straight away this time but hammered on the door.

"Cat! You ready?"

"Not yet. We've got another…"

Mickey opened the door and walked in. Cat jumped up from the chair and turned to face him.

"I wish you wouldn't do that. I could be standing here…"

"Naked?" Mickey sneered. "That can be arranged right now. It wouldn't take much, would it?"

He moved towards her. Cat picked up the chair and held it up between them. Mickey laughed.

"Don't worry, Cat. I'm not into skinny little girls."

"I know that, Mickey. You like tall, statuesque, rich ones, don't you? I guess she's all yours now. Now you've got rid of the opposition."

Mickey stiffened.

"Meaning what, exactly?"

"Oh, nothing," the girl replied.

"No, come on," Mickey shouted. "What the fuck did you mean by that?"

Cat thrust her face forward.

"I mean Katey. It's just worked out so well, hasn't it? Jason out of the way for good; and Jack. Now she's all yours – or you hope so."

"And what the fuck's wrong with that? Don't you think she'll need some support? Her world's fallen apart, hasn't it, you selfish little cow?"

"Oh, come on, Mickey. Did it really fall or was it *pulled* apart?"

She was still holding the chair in front of her. Mickey lunged forward and swept it aside. It crashed against the wall.

★

They picked up the noise in the van.

"Jesus, what now? Beep her, Danny."

Danny sent a two-beep pulse; their signal for 'back off." Jo spoke into her police radio. "Stand by."

"Yay-okay," from both cars.

★

"What the fuck are you talking about?"

"Nothing, nothing," Cat said. "But I've been thinking. When you went to the house that night..."

"Go on. This had better be good."

★

"She's going too fast," Jo said. "Beep her again."

Danny sent the same signal.

★

"You said you were searching for drugs, right?"

No response.

"But you wouldn't have had a chance of finding them, would you? Not in a place that big, with people just about everywhere. I didn't think before, but where would you start? You could only look where there was no-one around and, as I say, that was nowhere."

"And your point being what, exactly?"

"You didn't go there to search for drugs at all, did you?"

Mickey remained silent for a long time.

"No, I didn't," he said, sounding calm and relaxed. "Not to search, exactly."

"So what?"

"Because I knew where the stuff was. Jack had let it slip when he was pissed one night. Said something about there being much more valuable stuff in his wardrobe than designer clothes. So I went straight there…"

"To his bedroom?"

"That's right. And there it was…"

"So what was in the rucksack?"

"Rucksack? What rucksack?"

"The one you were carrying when you left us."

"I don't know. I can't remember…"

"You were carrying a rucksack and you don't know what was in it? There wasn't a load of crack in it, was there? And you didn't happen to leave it in Jack's wardrobe?"

There was an even longer silence. Mickey was staring into Catrina's eyes. She could feel herself starting to tremble. But when he spoke, it was with the same quiet control.

"So that's it. You think I set him up. That I took the stuff in with me and put it in his wardrobe. Well, that is the most fucking stupid thing I have ever heard… Why the fuck would I do that?"

"To get rid of Jack."

"And – same question – why the fuck would I do that? He was

133

just about my best mate. I nearly got myself arrested standing up for him in court. So come on, *why?*"

"Okay, Jason, then. To get rid of Jason."

"I put eighty-K's worth of drugs in Jack's wardrobe to get rid of *Jason?* Have you any idea how fucking ridiculous that sounds?"

"Okay, what was in the sack, then?" she asked.

"Nothing. Well, a few tools. In fact, depending on how much of the stuff was there and if I'd had the time, I was going to take it. And you know why, don't you, because I told you. I'm a legit trader now…" he raised his eyebrows in a gesture of innocence "… and I couldn't have someone that close – best friend or not – putting the heat on me. Right?"

"And what were you going to do with the stuff?"

"I never got that far. There was just too little time; people milling around all over, like you said. I had to leave it and get away quick. So I honestly don't know. Dump it I guess…"

"You told Dags you didn't find anything."

"I know. He didn't need to know, did he? I wanted to keep Jack as clean as possible until I decided what to do."

"And what about Jack? What were you going to do with him?"

"Again, not sure. Tell him what I'd done. Warn him off, perhaps. Possibly nothing; let him think someone at the party had found it and taken it – which would have been true, wouldn't it? I was still wondering about that afterwards when he got arrested."

★

"Send her terminate," Jo said, with a sigh of resignation. "I reckon we've got as much as we're going to get."

Danny sent a single sustained beep.

★

Cat felt a rush of relief.

"Then I guess I owe you an apology, Mickey. It all makes sense now."

She turned to retrieve the chair as calmly as she could and placed it back near the dressing table. Mickey didn't respond. He stared at her, tense and unmoving.

"It's hard to accept, though, isn't it?" she continued. "Just like you said in court, you can't really imagine Jack being involved in anything like that. Jason, just maybe – at a stretch – but not Jack. I mean…"

"Is it Jack's kid?" Mickey asked.

"What do you mean?"

"Was it Jack who got you pregnant?"

"Oh, that. No… I was mistaken. I'm not pregnant. False alarm." She paused, before adding, "And it couldn't have been Jack's, anyway, could it? I'd be at least six months by now…" She laughed, nervously.

Mickey continued to stare at her.

"Have you told this to anyone else?"

"What, about being pregnant?"

"No, about you believing I set Jack up."

"No, of course not." Cat could feel her face reddening. "It only came to me this morning. I don't know why. I was thinking about Jack – as I do every day – pretty much all the time, in fact – and trying to make sense of it. I guess I'll just have to accept that he was guilty. But it's hard. I liked him a lot. I really did." She dropped down onto the chair and began to cry.

"Because if you did," Mickey said, grabbing her by the arms and pulling her to her feet again, "then you'd better go and fucking *un*tell them while you've still got the breath left to do it."

Cat was sobbing now. All the courage had flowed out of her.

"I haven't, Mickey. I swear. Honestly. You're hurting me!"

★

"Still standing by?" Jo.

"Yay-okay."

Both cars responded together.

★

Mickey pushed her back onto the chair and glared down at her for a long time.

"I have nowhere near finished with you yet."

135

He slammed the door as he left the room. After a couple of minutes Cat spoke to the surveillance team.

"Switching on the receiver now," she whispered. "Sorry, I guess that didn't go as well as we wanted."

Jo nodded to Danny to turn on the voice transmitter.

"No that was fine, Catrina. You were brilliant."

"I don't think he believed me." Cat's voice was trembling.

"Believed you?"

"I mean, believed that I believe him; about that night. The way he looked at me. I'm scared, Jo. I don't know what he'll do…"

"Don't worry; we'll be watching him every minute. He can't do you any harm now. Okay?"

"*He* won't do anything himself. He'll get someone else to do it. There are people who are so shit scared of him they'll do anything he tells them to. It just takes a phone call… Fuck, I wish I'd never got into this."

She started to cry again.

"Right, Catrina, here's what we'll do. We'll pick him up as he leaves; before he can make any calls or anything. Okay?"

There was silence for a few seconds. "Okay." Her reply was barely audible.

"Good girl. The best thing you could do now, I reckon, is to get on to that stage. Oh, and switch off your transmitter. Otherwise you might get some weird effects from the sound system. But if you need to speak to us or alert us about anything, switch it back on; we'll still be listening. And if you can let us know somehow when he's about to leave that would be great. But don't take any risks. Okay?"

"Okay."

"Honestly, Catrina, you did great. We've got him in the house on the night of the party, and in the very room where we found the drugs. That's a massive step forward. More than we could have hoped for."

"Right; if you say so." Cat sounded unconvinced. "Speak later."

"Oh, just before you go," Jo said. "That thing about Mickey and Katey. Is that right? Is it a big thing with Mickey?"

"You bet it is. Worst kept secret at the Grange. I think only Jason, Jack and Katey didn't know about it. Some time ago Mickey got some of his thugs to warn Jason off. Jay didn't know it was Mickey's doing, of course. Anyway, that's when Jack came on the scene. Stepped in to save Jason and Mickey called them off. It's like he's just been biding his time ever since."

"I heard about that, but I didn't know Mickey had set them on to Jason in the first place. Anyway, thanks again, Catrina. As I said, you did really great."

★

The contact was broken and Jo turned to Danny, shrugging in answer to his querulous look.

"What else could I say?"

Danny shrugged back without speaking.

"Anyway, let's move." She picked up the radio. "Victor Delta Nine to front entrance; joining you there."

"Yay-okay."

"Whisky Bravo Two stay in position."

"Yay-okay."

As she opened the rear door of the vehicle to get out, they heard Cat's voice again.

"Bye, Mickey. See you later." Then, in a whisper, "Just leaving; main entrance."

Jo set off at a run round to the front of the building, speaking into the radio as she went.

"Both cars, immediately to strike, main entrance!"

★

Mags answered within three seconds, as always. Jo could imagine her seeing the name on the display and thinking perhaps *this* time it would be the news she'd been waiting for – some progress towards proving her son's innocence. If that was the case, she was about to let her down again.

"Hi, Jo."

"Hi, Maggie. Just to let you know that we arrested Mickey Kadawe today on suspicion of dealing Class A drugs. This has nothing to do with Jack and Jason's case, so I wanted to make sure you got the information from me rather than be wondering what was going on. I'm sure rumours will be rife at Manston Grange."

"Okay, thanks, Jo."

★

Katey left immediately for Manston Grange when she heard the news from her mother. She found the place swarming with police officers, including the one who had invaded their home, with such devastating consequences, on that Tuesday morning five months ago, and who now – quite probably – was the main person behind removing Mickey.

Megan saw Katey arrive and rushed over to embrace her; they held each other, without speaking, for a long time.

"What's happening, Megs? What are they looking for?"

"A bag or something. A rucksack, somebody said. I don't know what Mickey will make of this. He'll go ballistic when he finds out. He's been at the Hall this morning with Cat and the band, but they reckon he left there not long after eleven. We've been trying to contact him but he's not answering his phone. I don't suppose you know where he is, do you?"

Katey took a deep breath. "He's been arrested," she said. "Just this morning."

"Christ! What for?"

"Not a clue," Katey lied. "Tax evasion, perhaps. I really don't know. Where's Cat right now? She might know something."

"As I said, she was at the Hall earlier, but I don't know whether she's still there."

"I need to go," Katey said, hugging Megan again.

"Come back again soon. Please."

"I will. I promise."

She got Catrina's mobile number from a chart pinned up in the large entrance hall, noting with sadness that Jack's and Jason's own contact details were still on the list.

"Hi, Cat, it's Katey."

"Katey?"

"Yes. Jack's sister… Katey Tomlinson-Brown."

"Oh. What do you want?"

138

Katey was surprised by the coldness in her voice.

"Nothing. Just wondered if you knew any more about Mickey."

"What about him?"

"Are you alright, Cat? You sound sort of... anxious, I guess."

"Look, I don't know anything, right? I have to go."

"I think you do, Cat," Katey said. "And if you really don't, well, perhaps you'd like to hear what *I* know."

"What do you mean? What do you know? Tell me."

"Can't talk now, Cat. Not over the phone. Let's meet up somewhere."

There was a long silence.

"Okay. But I can't today. Phone me tomorrow."

She ended the call.

Katey phoned her back straight away, but Catrina wasn't answering.

★

A figure appeared behind the frosted glass of Jo's office door, hand raised about to knock.

"Come in!" Jo shouted. Tina stepped into the office.

"I've just had Denny Crosland of Witness Protection on the phone, ma'am. He says the four guys will be together at the combo in Dorking from six o'clock – about an hour from now. We could see them all today and save a few journeys. I know you said to check the party CCTV first, but..."

"I did, but only because I thought we'd have to wait for days before we could meet with them. Shit! I've got a meeting with the chief in half an hour. He wants an update on the fruitless search of Manston Grange – although he doesn't know it was fruitless yet." She paused for just a moment. "Tell you what; I'll leave a message with Janice. I was surprised he agreed to us questioning these guys at all, so let's do it before he changes his mind."

★

Tina's mobile trilled as they crawled forward in the heavy traffic along the A25. She pressed the green button on the steering wheel.

"DS Ramirez."

"H, Tina. This is Denny Crosland. I'm going to have to leave you to it, I'm afraid. I was planning to stay to make introductions and such, but I've just been called back to base."

"That's okay. Looks like we could be a bit late anyway with this traffic. I assume they're expecting us?"

"Yes, they are. You know your way to the combo, don't you? It's set out around three sides of a square with parking in the middle. They're in North Turret – right-hand corner block, you can't miss it, there's a name plaque on the wall. They're in Apartments 21 to 24. They've got a buzzer each on a speaker panel outside at ground level, but I'll text you the four-digit building access code just in case they decide to fool around. I understand you want to see them individually, so you have a choice of their own apartment or there are some small communal rooms on the ground floor – nearly always empty. Sorry I won't be there."

"That's okay, Denny. And thanks for moving so quickly on this. We thought it would take a lot longer to clear."

"So did I, to be honest. The powers that be chose to fast-track the request. Good luck."

★

It was 6.15 pm when they eventually arrived, the slow traffic having come to a complete stop for ten minutes due to an accident on the new by-pass, ironically named The Fastway. "Tempting providence, calling it that" had been Jo's assessment.

The combo was designed like a fort with one side missing. Four square three-storey blocks, one at each corner – the 'Turrets' – were joined together on three sides by two-storey rows of apartments. The missing side gave access to a central parking area surrounded by neat lawns and well-tended flower beds. The swimming pool, they assumed, must be at the rear of the complex. They parked in one of the residents' reserved spaces in front of North Turret, facing the ground floor entrance just a few yards away.

They pushed open the car doors.

Then came the blinding flash, along with a deafening boom and the tinkling crash of a hundred shattering windows. The half-opened car doors slammed shut as the vehicle shot backwards a few feet. The windscreen was transformed into a dense web of fractured glass, but held together except for a few shards which dropped onto the dashboard.

Jo, temporarily blinded and deafened, fumbled for her door handle as the temperature inside the vehicle increased.

It wouldn't open.

Throwing herself against it in panic, she forced it loose and rolled out of the vehicle onto the smoking tarmac.

She felt her way round the back of the car to the driver's side as her eyes began to clear. She tore at the hot handle, ignoring the pain in her hands, and managed to wrench open the driver's door.

Tina was barely conscious, her forehead bleeding from the impact of the door closing against it.

"Tina, I have to get you out." Jo shouted at her.

Tina's head lolled towards her and she opened her eyes. They came into focus, wide with confusion and terror. "Yes," she whispered. "Please."

"Can you move everything – legs, arms?"

"Yes."

"Right, lean over to me."

Jo felt rather than heard the running feet behind her, the anxious voices, the shouts and screams. She eased Tina from the car, willing hands helping to support her as they lifted her clear of the vehicle. Flames were finding their way into the foot well beneath the dashboard and flickering out from underneath the car around the front wheels.

They half-carried, half-supported Tina, her legs barely touching the ground, as they retreated from the now burning car. Jo turned back to watch, her eyes wide in disbelief.

North Turret had ceased to exist. The two rows of apartments, which a minute ago were joined to it, now ended abruptly in jagged projections of smouldering masonry. Where the corner block had been, a pile of rubble spouted huge flames and dense smoke. The three-storey building had collapsed into itself when the explosion blew away the ground floor.

Jo began to shake. In spite of the intense heat all around her, she felt herself go cold at the thought that, had they arrived on time, right now she and Tina would be lying dead underneath all that. She turned away, noticing for the first time the thin young man standing a couple of yards to her right, staring wide-eyed in horror at the scene of devastation in front of them.

She'd seen him before – a few months ago – sitting outside a courtroom.

CHAPTER NINE

Friday; 18 September

"*Officially*, we're still examining the site for clues as to the cause of the explosion," the Chief Superintendent was saying. "As far as the public – and the Press – is concerned, we suspect a gas explosion, and that fits – very fortunately – with the fact that they've been working on a gas leak two streets away for the last couple of days. However, it's hardly fair on National Utilities to spread that concern when we know that's not the truth. Especially in the case of fatalities."

The other two people in the private room off the main A & E ward nodded their agreement. Tina was sitting up in bed, having been kept in overnight for observation, but was looking fresh and alert, in spite of the heavy dressing around her head. Jo was sitting at the side of the bed, with both her hands bandaged, facing John Mackay on the other side.

"The truth being," Jo said, "that this was a targeted attack designed to kill the four witnesses in the block."

"Or," Tina said, "to kill all *six* people who were expected to be in the building at that time. I mean, if we hadn't been delayed..." She gave a shudder.

"Thank God for The Fastway," Jo said. "Even so, I can't see how anybody could have set this up to include the two of us as well. The only person who knew we were going at that time and who was there in the building beforehand was Denny Croswell." She looked at the sergeant. "You know him, don't you, Tina? What do you think?"

"I would say there's absolutely no chance it was Denny. He's not a personal friend but I've had quite a few dealings with him.

He's a quiet, helpful... administrator. It's unthinkable he'd get involved in anything like this."

"You get the feeling though, don't you," John said, "that when we do get to the bottom of all this, *whatever's* gone on is going to seem unthinkable?"

No-one spoke for a few moments. John Mackay broke the silence with a loud sigh.

"Look, I accept that this latest incident could be linked to the five recent killings in Cobham and Woking. It would be ridiculous not to seriously consider that a possibility – and also that the obvious link is the Jack and Jason case. It seems there may well be a vendetta against the people whose evidence – or simply whose actions – led to their conviction. The question is who and why ... You're shaking your head again, DI Cottrell. You must try to get out of that habit."

"I'm sorry, sir. It's just that..."

"Detective Sergeant, what do you think?" John turned to Tina. She paused to gather her thoughts.

"Well, sir. It's hard to believe it's the same person who's done this even if there is a link. The circumstances are so different. It would be fairly easy to take out four – five, including Sammo – unsuspecting people who are out on the streets a lot of the time, and mostly alone. But even *we* didn't know where these four guys were holed up until Tuesday – less than three days ago, so that information must be limited to relatively few people."

"An excellent point, DS Ramirez," John said, "but that assumes *they* haven't told anyone about where they're staying. From what I hear, they've not exactly been keeping their heads down. It may be general knowledge out on the streets. So it's quite possible that the people who had easy access to the first five victims knew exactly where to find these four. The most likely scenario is that someone is sending out a clear warning to anyone considering cooperating with the police against their own."

"You're assuming Jack and Jason *were* part of 'their own' as you put it, sir?" Jo said.

"I *am* assuming that until we have reason to assume otherwise. DI Waters will pick up these murders as part of his current ongoing investigation. I expect you to confer with him – obviously – but *your* task, DI Cottrell and DS Ramirez, is to check out what Mickey

Kadawe did – and why – at Etherington Place on the night of the party. That's all. So is everyone clear on that?"

"Good," he said, acknowledging the nods of ascent, and standing up ready to leave. "You two take it slowly for now. You've had a hell of a shock on top of your actual injuries. But if you think *you* had a lucky escape, what about Billy Wade? When you hadn't arrived at six o'clock, he waited for ten minutes then popped out for cigarettes. Smoking didn't kill *him*, did it?"

The two women laughed.

"Where is he now, sir?" Jo asked.

"They've moved all the residents, including Wade, from the combo to a Premier Inn, apart from three who are still in hospital with cuts and minor burns. Billy's got a guard on him twenty-four-seven now. What about Mr Kadawe? Is he settling in? We've had him for – what – nearly twenty-four hours now."

"Not spoken to him yet, sir. He refused to talk to us without his lawyer when we first brought him in. And since then… we've been a bit tied up." She raised her hands. "Well, bandaged up, anyway."

John snorted a laugh. "That'll teach you to stand me up for a meeting."

After he had left, Jo and Tina sat in silence for a long time with their separate thoughts.

"One thing that puzzles me," Tina said.

"*One* thing?"

"Okay, *one* of the things that puzzles me…"

"Go on."

"If these guys were under police protection for their own safety, why would they *not* keep a low profile? Why – if the chief is right – would they let people know where they were?"

Jo paused for a moment. "Why do you think?"

Tina shrugged. "Because, in spite of what they'd done, they didn't believe they were in any danger."

★

Saturday; 19 September

Grace picked up her desk phone, checking the time on the display – 10.45 am.

"Your visitor is here. Shall I ask him to wait?"

He was fifteen minutes early, a reflection, she hoped, of how much he was looking forward to their meeting.

"Two minutes, Georgia. Then please ask him to come in."

She got up from her chair and made a final assessment of herself in the long mirror on the wall next to her desk, twisting her body to the right and left. She opened another button on her thin silk top and hitched her tight-fitting skirt up just a fraction more at the waist before walking over to stand in front of the window.

The door opened and Georgia stepped inside the room. "The Under-Secretary, ma'am."

Lawrence Harding was wearing a light grey lounge suit, navy shirt and pale blue tie. Grace always thought that he wore his steel grey hair just a little too long, but otherwise she couldn't really find any fault with his appearance. He was clearly appreciative of Grace's efforts, too. She remained at the window just long enough to see his eyes open slightly wider as they dropped to appraise her breasts in the back-light. She turned briefly on the spot to give him the benefit of their profile before waving him to a seat. They both stepped over to the desk and shook hands, Grace holding on long enough to make something more of the customary gesture.

"I really appreciate your giving up your time to see me, Lawrence. It's very kind of you."

"It's my pleasure," he said. "As always."

He seated himself in one of the wing chairs and Grace perched on the front edge of the desk close to him. She crossed her legs and leaned back supporting herself with her palms flat on the desktop.

"I hope what I'm going to ask isn't going to make it hard for you," she said, with the slightest flash of her eyes, "but I need you to do something with me that must stay between just the two of us."

She squirmed a little as she spoke aware of Lawrence's struggle to keep his eyes on hers.

"I think transparency is very important, don't you?" she continued, seeing his gaze drop just a fraction as he considered the question. "But, goodness me! Where are my manners? I trust you'd like some coffee – yes? This might take some time – if that's okay with you?" She opened her eyes wide as she spoke.

"Oh, yes," he said. "To the coffee and the time."

"Excellent."

She twisted where she sat and rocked back to pick up the desk phone, her legs lifting and parting slightly as she did so.

"Georgia, could you bring us some coffee, please and – wait just a moment." She looked at Lawrence with the same wide eyes. "Would you like something to nibble on?"

"Yes again."

"And some cakes and biscuits as well, please, Georgia."

She repeated the manoeuvre to replace the phone and turned back to him. "That's sorted, then. Let's get down to it."

★

Sunday; 20 September

Catrina entered her code into the pad at the entrance to the small apartment block in Leatherhead. Dagger was standing behind her, looking nervously around as she opened the door. As they were about to step inside, a black Porsche Boxter pulled to a halt in front of the building, the driver's dark-tinted window descending as it stopped.

"Cat!"

They almost leapt into the air as they turned to where the shout had come from. The occupant stepped out of the car and walked towards them.

"Jeez, Katey!" Dagger shouted. "What the fuck are you trying to do – scare us to death?"

"Sorry, Dags," Katey said. "Didn't mean to startle you. But I've been trying to speak to Cat for three days now." She turned to the singer. "If you'd just answer your phone... What're you so scared of, anyway? And where have you been?"

"Staying with Dags," Cat said, now looking around herself. "How did you know where to find me?"

Katey followed her eyes, wondering what she expected to see. There was nothing and no-one.

"Well, you live here, don't you? Sort of. I've been round half-a-dozen times since Thursday. I didn't realise you'd moved out." She looked from one to the other of them. "And that you and Dags were..."

"We're not. Dags is just looking after me for a while."

Dagger nodded, looking disappointed.

"What do you want, anyway?" Cat went on.

"You know what I want. To talk about Mickey. Can we go inside?"

Cat and Dagger looked at each other. Cat pushed open the door and the three of them stepped through into the small hallway then up the stairs to the apartment which occupied the whole of the second floor.

"Do you want a drink, Katey," Dagger asked. "A brew, I mean."

"Thanks. Coffee would be great."

He went in to the kitchen. Cat waved Katey through into a large lounge, with low black leather sofas and whitewood coffee tables. The cream thick-pile rugs, positioned perfectly between and around the furniture on the light oak floor, gave the place a feel of luxury. Katey spent a couple of minutes walking round the room, taking in the colourful abstract paintings on all the walls. She smiled her appreciation at Cat and they sat down, on different sofas, at right-angles to each other.

"So… what exactly?" Cat started to ask.

Katey leaned forward.

"Mickey has been arrested, as I am *sure* you know. In fact, I got the distinct impression when I spoke to you on Thursday that you knew quite a bit about it. I don't know how and what you know, but I want to understand what happened. And why that fucking police bitch seems determined to get rid of everybody who means anything to me." Her voice had risen with the last comment as her anger took over. "So what's the score, Cat? I want to know!"

Dagger walked in at that point, carrying a tray with three coffee mugs, which he placed on one of the tables.

"You'd better be sure you want to know," he said to Katey. "And don't start having a go at Cat. You've no idea what she has to put up with from that bastard."

Katey frowned and looked from one to the other.

"Which bastard? The police woman?"

"No. Mickey," Cat said. "Mister-fucking-wonderful!"

Katey looked shocked.

"Mickey? Why, what's he ever done to you, except get you all this?" She looked round the apartment.

Katey could see the fury in Cat's face as she rose from the sofa and began to pace the room.

"Oh, and I guess Cat's done fuck-all," Dagger snarled. "She's a crap singer, after all; no presence on stage, face like a fruit bat. Yes, Kadawe's a fucking genius helping her succeed with all that shit to deal with!"

Katey jumped to her feet.

"I'm sorry, Cat. Dags is right; that was out of order." She went over and gave her a hug. "I was just a bit surprised that's all. I really don't understand. Mickey's been great with me. He calls me every day just to see…"

"Of course he's great with you!" Dagger snapped. "He's planning on fucking you, isn't he?"

"Dags, *please*," Cat said. "Katey, come and sit down again… here."

Cat returned to her seat and patted the space next to her. Katey sat down beside her.

"That just isn't right," she said, speaking to herself. She was lost in thought.

"It's true, I'm afraid, Katey." Cat took both her hands in hers. "I'll tell you everything I know, *and* what I believe. But it's going to hurt. Please don't hate me; I'm just the messenger."

★

Jo looked at the closed door of her office. The major incident team room beyond it was empty, its lights switched off, making the place feel unfamiliar without the voices and bustle accompanying the usual shadowy shapes thrown against the frosted glass of the door panel.

She checked her watch – 7.15 pm. She'd been there for eight-and-a-half hours preparing – or, more accurately, *failing* to prepare – for the next interview with Mickey Kadawe. Sifting through records of Jack and Jason's trial, and replaying recordings of Mickey's conversation with Cat and the three stumbling hour-long interviews they'd already had with him over the past couple of days.

It made for embarrassing listening. They'd been going nowhere; Mickey had been quick to realise and had thoroughly enjoyed exploiting their lack of a game plan.

She was also aware that none of this was going down at all well with Harry, and right now she needed his help. She gritted her teeth and phoned him on his work mobile.

"Harry, sorry to call at this hour on a Sunday, but I need your help."

There was a long silence.

"Harry, are you there?"

"Must be a bad line; can you repeat that?"

"Technically, it's not a line at all," Jo said. "It's mobile to mobile and…"

"Crap signal, then. Just repeat what you said."

Jo sighed.

"I need your help, Harry. Please."

"Help with what, exactly? Hairdryer packed in? Need a light-bulb changing?"

"What's all this about, Harry?"

"Well, it's Sunday night, Jo. It can't be police work, surely. Unless you've just solved my case as well as yours."

"Look, I know you're pissed off with me about this Mickey Kadawe thing…"

"Just a bit. Anyway, are you okay? I hear you got your fingers burnt. I was expecting it, but not like that."

Jo laughed. "Yes, it was a bit scary. What's even more frightening is the thought of what *could* have happened."

"You're not kidding. Is Tina okay?"

"She's fine, thanks."

"So this help you need?"

"I'd like you to listen to a CD with me, if you wouldn't mind."

"Is this in return for me inviting you to the movies? What is it, this CD? Soft music? Shall I bring a bottle round?"

"You can if you like, but I think I ought to tell you a couple of things first. One, it's not soft music; it's a recording of the conversation between Kadawe and the singer just before we picked him up. I'd like you to listen for anything in there that leaps out at you. And two, I'm in my office?"

"At the station?"

"The very place."

"What the hell are you doing there, trying to beat Monday's rush hour?"

"No, I'm failing to get a break-through with this investigation. No doubt that piece of information will make your weekend."

"You don't mean you want me to listen to it now... this evening, do you?"

"No, of course not. In the morning."

"Okay, what time?"

"Seven o'clock okay? Give us plenty of time before your meeting?"

"Jeez! Monday morning, as well. Yes, okay."

"Thanks again, Harry. Night."

"Night, Jo. And go home, for Christ's sake."

★

Mags grabbed her mobile off the table at her side, breathing a sigh of relief at the name on the display.

"Hi. Everything okay?"

"Hi, Mum. Sorry it's so late..."

"It's only nine-fifteen, Katey, so not really late enough for an apology."

"I know you're just saying that. I've always been home well before this since..." Her voice tailed off. "So I know you'll have been worrying. You're always telling me that's part of your job as a mum, remember?"

Mags gave a little laugh. "Well, I suppose I did wonder."

There was a long pause and a catch in Katey's voice when she spoke again.

"Look, Mum, is it okay if I stay over at a friend's tonight? Just for tonight."

"Yes, of course, but is something wrong, darling? Are you sure you're alright?"

"Yes, I'm sure. We've just been talking about Jack. I got a bit emotional, that's all. Will you be okay on your own? If not, I'll come right back. Just say."

"I'll be fine."

"I wish dad was there with you."

"I'm fine. Really. Please take care."

"Love you, mum."

"Love you."

They ended the call.

CHAPTER TEN

Monday, 21 September

Harry Waters arrived in Jo's office five minutes early at 6.55 am. She waved him to sit down and poured coffee from a cafetiere.

"So how's the search for the killer – or killers – going?" she asked. "Any leads?"

"Going down the road to nowhere at the moment. No new leads, which means – unless we pin our hopes on the mystery man in the park – no leads at all. You know the really sad thing, Jo; nobody cares. We don't have parents or siblings coming forward offering to make tearful appeals to the public for information. No push at all to solve the case apart from us, of course. Not even the Press demanding action and results. I get the impression if we just said, oh, sod it, no-one would bother. How can precious lives become so cheap and meaningless?"

"Christ, Harry, you're going to have me crying in a minute."

"Me, too. So show me what you've got to take my mind off it."

"Okay. I do appreciate this, you know."

"No problem. Take it away."

Jo pressed the Play button and they sat back in their chairs, Harry with an open notebook in one hand and a pen in the other. They listened without speaking to Mickey's noisy entrance into Cat's dressing room and the ensuing conversation. Harry's eyes widened as Mickey revealed he had been in Jack's bedroom on the night of the party and from that point he leaned forward in his seat, his brow creased in concentration. Jo let the recording run to the end to capture Cat's concerns after Mickey's departure.

"So," she said, pressing Stop, then Rewind, "did anything leap out at you?"

Harry frowned. "There was *something*. Can't put my finger on it. Run it again."

Jo pressed Play again and sat back. Harry remained leaning forward, almost hunched over the machine.

"Just stop it there," he said, "and skip back thirty seconds."

Jo pressed Stop and the reverse arrow twice. Harry was poised with notepad and pen.

Kadawe's voice sounded as Jo restarted the CD.

"...think I set him up. That I took the stuff in with me and put it in his wardrobe. Well, that is the most fucking stupid thing I have ever heard... Why the fuck would I do that?"

"To get rid of Jack..."

"And – same question – why the fuck would I do that? He was just about my best mate. I nearly got myself arrested standing up for him in court. So come on, *why?*"

"Okay, Jason, then. To get rid of Jason."

"I put eighty-k's worth of drugs in Jack's wardrobe to get rid of *Jason?* Have you any idea..."

"Stop there!" Harry said, scribbling something on his pad as Jo hit the Pause button. He turned to Jo, holding up the pad with '80 K' written on it.

"Where did he get the eighty-k from?" he asked.

Jo frowned.

"Not sure I understand. He wouldn't have needed to get the cash up front..."

"No!" Harry almost shouted. "I don't mean..."

And then Jo did understand.

"You mean the *figure* of eighty thousand!?" she said.

"Exactly! That's the first time I've heard that number quoted. We've had 'a six-figure number', 'well over a hundred thousand', 'getting on for a quarter of a million'... The *Express* quoted 'almost half a million' – God knows where that came from. They were all guesses anyway, but I'm certain there's been nothing as low or specific as eighty thousand."

"And I guess the only means of establishing the real value is through the deal that's done at the point of sale. And he seems to know *exactly* how much the stuff in that wardrobe was worth. Now how would he know that?"

Harry shrugged. Jo got to her feet and opened the door.

"Tina! In here, please."

DS Ramirez entered the room.

"Tina, I'd like you and the guys to dig for every last reference to the value of the drugs found in Jack's wardrobe. Statements, transcripts of interviews, what was said in court, newspaper reports, and TV and radio news quotes. And anything on the stuff at Jason's as well. We need to know whether a figure of eighty thousand has ever been mentioned. Or, if not, something implying that amount – say – 'over seventy', 'nearly a hundred'. Okay?"

Tina's eyes widened.

"Will do, ma-am," she said. "Can I assume, though, that you believe such a figure has *never* been mentioned?"

"That's right."

"In which case, I'm not sure how we'll know when to stop looking."

Jo thought for a moment.

"Neither am I, Tina," she said, holding up her hands. "Just look *everywhere*. And this has priority until further notice over everything else, so the guys can drop what they're doing now until – well – midday, at least. We'll waive the eight o'clock meeting, but I'd like an update at noon from you, in here – unless you find something before then, of course. Then if we need to go on after that, we'll get a further heads-up at the daily meet at four. Okay?"

"Yes, ma'am," Tina said. "May I ask…?"

"Kadawe quoted that amount to Catrina and we need to check where he could have got it from, because if…"

"Yes, I've worked *that* out, ma'am." Tina interrupted, with a twinkle in her eye. "After all, I *am* a detective. But I was going to ask that, if you two are working together, is it okay if we all make friends again out here as well?"

Jo scowled and turned to Harry.

"I'm sure I don't know what she's talking about, do you, Detective Inspector?"

"Not a clue," Harry said.

Tina gave a sly smile.

"Our mistake, then. Thank you, ma'am… sir."

She left the room and they both gave a brief laugh.

"I guess my being pissed off must have been showing a little," Harry said.

"Possibly," Jo smiled. "Anyway, Harry, good spot, that eighty-k. I can't believe I missed it."

"Well, let's not get ahead of ourselves. We're just the police, don't forget. We know next to nothing. Eighty-k might be an open secret on the streets."

They sat in silence drinking their coffee for a full minute before Harry spoke again.

"Tell you what, Jo. *If* – and I still think it's a very big if – but *if* there is something in this theory of yours, I reckon right now would be a good time to talk to Billy Wade. He must be feeling just a little scared and vulnerable after what happened on Friday. And with your permission – and your presence, of course – *I'd* like to interview the little shit again."

"Should we perhaps wait until Tina's done some digging?"

"Your call, Jo. You decide. You've got three days left to square this, and if you want to use up one of them just waiting around, then I suppose…"

"Okay. Let's go get him," Jo said.

★

If William Torstein Wade was feeling scared and vulnerable after his close encounter with death, he wasn't showing it. He seemed relaxed and confident, seated in the interview room looking from one to the other across the table, with just the hint of a smirk on his face.

"You don't mind if we record this, do you, Billy?" Jo asked.

"Feel free."

Jo switched on the twin recorders. "Recording of an interview on Monday 21st September. Present Billy Wade, DI Harry Waters and DI Jo Cottrell. Interview commenced eleven-thirty-two am." She turned to Harry.

"So we meet again, Billy," he said. "We talked a short time ago, right? And quite a few times before that."

Billy nodded.

"So first, let's go over what we talked about last time. You claimed you'd bought some crack off Jack Tomlinson-Brown…"

"I *did* buy it. You make it sound like I was lying."

"Okay, you *did* buy some crack which you claimed made you ill…"

"It *did* make me ill. Look what is this? I thought I was fucking dying for about a week. The stuff was absolute shit – other guys got ill as well."

"So you phoned the police. Why?"

"Well, it's not right, is it? He took my money and handed over this… I'm not even sure what it was. All I know is it nearly killed me."

"Who are you, Billy, the *Wimpy Kid*? That's not how real men settle their differences, is it? Running to the police?"

"Well, I didn't do that right away. I followed him home to have it out with him. I was going to make him take the stuff – see how he liked it. But when I got to his house, there were these security guys all over it. They must have been fucking good at their job, mustn't they…" he gave a little laugh, "… letting all that crack into the house? Anyway, I just got mad and chucked the stuff over the wall. *Then* I decided to call you. Couldn't think of any other way to get back at him."

"And after that, you came to New Station and we had our little chat, right?"

"That's right."

Harry leaned forward.

"Listen, Wade," he hissed. "You've made me look a right pillock; and I just *hate* it when that happens."

"Hey, just a…"

"What you told me," Harry shouted, "was a pack of lies, wasn't it?"

"No it wasn't. It was exactly…"

Harry leapt to his feet, sending his chair crashing to the floor behind him and leaning with his knuckles on the table, his face inches from Billy's.

"You lying little toe-rag!"

Billy almost fell off the chair with surprise.

"I want a lawyer," he said.

"Well you can't have one!" Harry yelled, glaring wild-eyed at him.

"I know my rights…"

"You're not being charged with anything yet, Billy," Jo said. "There'll be plenty of time for lawyers later when you are."

"Charged?" he said. "Charged with what?"

Jo pulled Harry gently away from him. He turned and picked up his chair, lowering himself slowly onto it.

"The thing is, Billy," Jo said, "we now know for a fact that Jack didn't do drugs – take them or deal them. Just listen to the exact words: *we… know… for… a… fact…*" She paused. "Do you understand? Because you are going to have to tell us the truth now to save your own neck. You see, Jack Tomlinson-Brown is dead as a direct result of being found guilty of dealing crack. *Now* we know he was *not* guilty. He was set up. The people who set him up are directly responsible for his death. Obviously, it's not murder as such, but certainly whoever planned this will be put away for – I'd say – fifteen to twenty years; perhaps get out in ten to twelve… What do you think, DI Waters?"

"If they're lucky." Harry spat out the words.

Jo paused, staring at Billy.

"So, what do you say? Are you going to help us nail the guy who set him up, or are we going to nail *you* for the job?"

Billy looked from one to the other again, clearly struggling to recover his poise.

"Look," he said, his voice steady and calm again, "I told you the truth. I got this shit off him and then…"

"You really *don't* understand, do you?" Jo said. She turned to Harry. "DI Waters, it seems I'm getting nowhere. You tell him."

Harry got noisily to his feet again, breathing hard and walking backwards and forwards behind Jo for a while in a show of wrestling with his temper. He circled round behind Billy, who hunched his shoulders and screwed up his face as if anticipating a blow to the back of the head. Instead, Harry crouched beside his chair and spoke into his ear, his voice little more than a whisper.

"You see, Wade, someone really clever set this up. I mean, it fooled me, and I'm bloody brilliant. Someone arranged for seven guys to phone the police, eight more to tap Jack up for crack where he'd be caught on camera; he set up a network of mobile phones and lists of callers, put a supply of drugs in two different houses, one of which is slightly more secure than Fort bleeding Knox; tipped off the police about them, told all those so-called witnesses exactly what to say in court... I tell you, I admire this person, I really do. I just wish he was on our side!"

Harry stood up and started pacing the room again.

"And that's definitely not *you*. But I'll tell you something for certain, Wade. Someone's going down for this – someone has to – and it might as well be you if we can't find the right guy. It won't give us a lot of satisfaction putting the *wrong* guy away; except, I suppose, it's another major junkie off the streets. By the way, you still doing the hard stuff, Billy? Keeping the dealers in designer clothes and fast cars?"

"Don't do that any more," Billy said, seeming more relaxed now the shouting had ceased. "Just the fun stuff now."

"Really," Harry said, lightening up and flashing a glance at Jo. "When did that change? When did you start being a good boy?"

"Ages ago," Billy said. "When they legalised the soft shit. Made it safer to stay with that."

"That would be... let's see... well over two years ago. That about right?" Harry asked.

Billy nodded.

"Well, I'm impressed, Billy." He squeezed his shoulder. "Credit where it's due. And you've never gone back to a bit of the old crack or brown in all that time? Come on," Harry chuckled. "I don't believe you. There's nothing illegal about *taking* the stuff, you know."

"I know that, don't I?" Billy said. "But it's true, honestly." He smiled. "Just a bit of billy for Billy these days."

Harry laughed and took his seat again beside Jo. He turned to her.

"So what do you make of that, DI Cottrell?"

Jo smiled across at Billy.

"I think he's telling the truth, DI Waters. I don't think he does do the hard shit any more, and I reckon I believe him when he says he hasn't for over two years. It seems this young man has cleaned up his life."

Billy snorted a laugh of satisfaction.

"You bet," he said. The smug expression had returned.

"Okay, Billy," Jo said. She reached forward to switch off the recorders, and then paused over the buttons. "Oh, before we finish, just clear up one thing for me, would you? If you've not done crack for over two years, what were you doing throwing a bag of it over Jack Tomlinson-Brown's wall less than six months ago? And what was all that about him being your regular supplier?"

Billy's expression changed, the smirk replaced by wide-eyed panic.

"Well... I... I ..."

"I can't wait to hear this," Harry said, rubbing his hands.

Billy started breathing fast.

"Well, that was a... sort of... one-off. Yes, just a one-off, that's it. Now I remember..."

"Really?"

"Yes, really."

Jo shuffled the papers in front of her, still looking across at Billy before lowering her eyes to read from the top sheet.

"These were questions put to you by Detective Inspector Harry Waters in the presence of Detective Constable Alice Grantham when you came to talk to the police some time after you made the initial phone call. The interview was recorded, by the way. DI Waters: 'Mr Wade, approximately how long has Mr Tomlinson-Brown been supplying you with drugs?' Answer: – this is you, Billy – 'Over twelve months.' Question: 'And what sort of drugs were they – amphetamines, marihuana?' Answer: 'No, heroine and crack.' Question: 'By crack, do you mean crack cocaine?' Answer: 'Yes'."

Jo looked up at Billy again, moving the sheet to one side, and then looking down at the next one.

"At the trial itself, under cross examination by Council for the Defence: 'Mr Wade, how long are you claiming that Mr Tomlinson-Brown has been supplying you with drugs?' Answer: 'About a year – perhaps a bit more.'"

Jo looked hard into his eyes.

"More than twelve months, Billy? That's a hell of a one-off."

Billy seemed unable to speak, gulping in mouthfuls of air as if he was hyperventilating. Harry leant across to him again.

"Well, Wade. Your turn, I believe. Let's hear it."

Billy didn't speak for a long time, twitching and fidgeting as if a battle was raging inside him. Jo and Harry waited him out.

"Look, everything I told you previously was true." He spoke as if he had been rehearsing the statement. "I do use crack all the time, and I was lying just now when I said I hadn't touched it for years. Until he was arrested, Jack Tomlinson-Brown – or 'Jake' as I knew him – was my regular supplier and had been for at least twelve months. That's all I'm going to say, and I expect you to let me go, or arrest me and let me speak to a lawyer."

Harry took a noisy intake of breath, but Jo spoke before he could say anything.

"Clearly you haven't thought this through properly, Mr Wade, because just let me repeat what I said. We *know* you are lying. Jack Tomlinson-Brown did *not* sell drugs or even take them. You are free to go – for now – but please make sure you are available if – or should I say, when – we want to speak to you again. That is, of course, if you're still alive. It's more than likely that whoever wants you dead won't miss next time. But just in case you get lucky, I suggest you start working on your next carefully-worded statement which you'll need very shortly to explain why you lied through your teeth on three separate occasions – when you first approached the police, under oath in court, and today."

"Interview ended at twelve-ten."

They both got to their feet and left the room.

★

"That could have gone a whole lot better." Jo watched from her office window as Billy Wade was driven away in an unmarked police car to his latest desirable residence. "At least we know he lied about taking crack. It's clear now that he's on the soft stuff, so he certainly wouldn't have been asking Jack for…"

"Hang on, Jo," Harry cut in. "You need to take a step back from this. All that about him being off the hard stuff – I just led him into thinking that's what we wanted to hear. He would have said that to take the pressure off. He's told us three times that he *does* do crack. Why would you think he lied three times and told the truth just once? Unless Johnny Mac was right, of course, and you *do* have a preferred outcome. There's a big difference between being focussed and being blinkered…"

"Oh really," Jo snapped, "I thought it was a fine line!"

"Look, I've never had any trouble breaking Billy Wade before. He's a pushover. If he's not changing his story with me spitting threats into his face, then it's probably the truth. And as far as the eighty-k is concerned – as I said before – that might be word-on-the-street knowledge; the value of what was left of the stuff that killed the Johnson kid. General feeling out there is it was the same stuff. Kadawe could easily know about that without having any involvement with it."

Jo looked away from him into the corner of the room.

"And another thing," Harry went on, "For whatever reason, Wade's just missed being killed. If that was because of something he's lied about in the past, that big bang in Dorking would surely have persuaded him to tell the truth now. Why not own up to save his own neck, as you put it?"

Jo took a long time to answer.

"I think that just reflects how scared of Mickey Kadawe he is. And I can believe it after looking into his eyes when I was cautioning him outside the Sweet Rock Hall. I'm not sure I wouldn't be doing exactly what our Billy's doing in his situation."

"Either that or… he's telling the truth." Harry got to his feet. "At least think about it, Jo," he said, as he closed her office door behind him.

Jo continued to stare into space. The knock on the door broke the spell.

"Come in, Tina." She waved her to a chair. "Your immediate job, Detective Sergeant, is to cheer me up, starting… *now!*"

"Well, we've found no reference to eighty thousand or anything close or implying that amount. I guess that counts as good news, doesn't it?"

"As far as it goes, I suppose. We got nothing out of Wade," Jo said. "Not a thing. I think if DI Waters had torn his arms off, he still wouldn't have changed his story. So, conclusions?"

Tina furrowed her brow as if in deep thought.

"He's telling the truth," she offered.

"No," Jo said.

"He's shit-scared of somebody."

"Got it in two. At least, that's what I think."

Jo looked thoughtful for a moment.

"Tell me, Tina, do you believe in what we're doing? I mean, you were on the team that secured the convictions. Do you believe there could have been a miscarriage of justice?"

Tina frowned. "Miscarriage of justice, ma'am? I thought the Chief Super said we were just tying up loose ends." She smiled. "To be honest, I guess I don't *want* there to be. But if you're convinced, then we're committed to get to the truth."

Jo smiled. "Thanks, Tina. Not quite a 'yes', but I'll take it. What we need is a rock solid, material link between the drugs in Jack's room – forget those at Jason's for now – and Mickey Kadawe…"

"Agreed."

"And the only material link, as I see it, is…"

"The rucksack," Tina said.

Jo opened her eyes wide.

"Very good, Tina."

"Well, as I said; I am, after all…"

"A detective," Jo finished. "Yes, I know; it's just that it was that very thing I was thinking about."

"Well, I've been thinking about it as well and doing a bit of digging – well, quite a lot of digging. It's something I was going to raise with you first thing this morning until we got started into the hunt for the eighty grand."

"Go on."

"Okay. Mickey was in the grounds with the rucksack. Little Miss Muffet told us that and Mickey is on record confirming it. In fact, he goes so far as to admitting being in Jack's room where the drugs were found. Right?"

"Right."

"He says he found the stuff, but was disturbed before he could take it and had to – I think his words were – 'leave it and get away quick'."

Jo nodded.

"And yet, it seems he had time to put everything back exactly as it was – replace the bottom panel of the wardrobe, restack

163

the magazines, put back anything else he'd disturbed, close the wardrobe. Surely it would have been a lot quicker just to stuff the lot into the bag and run away."

"But perhaps he really did have to get away very quickly and had to leave everything out. Maybe Jack put it all back afterwards."

"But it's certain that Jack wouldn't have just put it back in the same place knowing someone knew it was there. He would have moved it somewhere else or even got rid of it completely."

Jo smiled. "Keep going, Tina. I'm getting more cheered up by the minute."

"Well, we virtually demolished the Grange and the bag clearly isn't there, which kind of supports the idea that it was incriminating and so he got rid of it. It would be dead easy; stick it in a wheelie bin on the way home from the party. Virtually no chance of us finding it again even if we'd known about it immediately after the drugs were found. On the face of it, then, we might as well forget it."

"Yes, but…" Jo started to interrupt, but Tina waved her arms to stop her.

"That's if he *did* leave the party with the rucksack," she continued. "But could you really imagine him doing that? Risking going through a security check with a bag that had contained drugs – or even a bag with just a set of tools in it."

"Probably not," Jo said. "Go on."

"And he didn't leave the same way he got in because no-one else saw him again that night. Right?"

"Right."

"On Saturday, we ran a check on the security records for that night, including, firstly, the full CCTV coverage at the main gates – seven hours of it, from eight o'clock onwards. Anyway, there was any number of people arriving and leaving with various bags, including day-packs and larger sacks. So no real clues there – not yet. So we went through the computer records of people checked in and out. Everybody arriving was searched and listed on a register through a hand-held link to the computer in the Monitoring Centre a mile away. Then, as people left, they gave their name and were checked out against the 'in' list – to make sure everyone had left, except – I suppose – those who'd been invited to stay – Jack's girlfriend for example. In fact, I think she was the only one. The guys did a really good job under the circumstances – everyone accounted for in and out – except for one very minor blip. Or it seemed very minor at the time.

"One guy appeared to leave twice – a guy called Davis Winkler. He was checked in like the rest, with a brief description of him included on the record, as for everybody. Davis, in spite of his name, is actually a Somali – tall, slim, good-looking, twenty years old – ring any bells? Anyway, according to the records, he appeared to check out at eleven-twenty-three pm, along with a few others at the same time. Later – much later – at two-seventeen Saturday morning, his name was given by someone else leaving the grounds. The security guys walked him back to the party where a number of people confirmed that he was, in fact, Davis Winkler. So it was just assumed that the guy checking people out earlier had made a mistake or that someone was having a joke.

"Anyway, we went back and checked the CCTV through the period ten minutes either side of eleven-twenty. It was early for party leaving, so there was just this group of seven heading out during that time. Not possible to identify people individually because of hoods and hats, but one thing was very clear; none of them was carrying a bag of any kind. And it had to be one of those seven people who claimed to be Davis Winkler and who was *not* Davis Winkler."

"So you think one of them could have been Kadawe?"

"Quite possibly, although the camera was positioned primarily to catch people arriving. But one of the seven didn't seem to be part of the group. They all left at the same time, but this guy seemed to be sort of tagging along behind them. Perhaps you need to see it to know what I mean."

"And could *he* have been Kadawe?"

"Well, he was sort of hunched over, round-shouldered. But I guess he would be trying not to look like he usually does..."

"Just one thing," Jo put in. "Would Mickey know, or know of, this Davis Winkler?"

"They both live at Manston Grange." Tina paused for effect. "So he would either know Winkler was going, or he could have seen him there while he was prowling round."

"Wow!" said Jo, feeling herself trembling – rather unprofessionally – with excitement. "So, conclusions?"

Tina shrugged.

"Well, if he was part of that group – which seems possible – even *probable* – then he ditched the bag somewhere in the grounds."

"Or back in the van," Jo offered. "We did a search of the grounds at the time of Jack's arrest. Though we could have missed it."

"Yes, or the van, I suppose," Tina said.

The two women smiled at each other across the desk.

"So, what next?" Tina asked. "Back to the number hunt?"

Jo looked at her watch. 1.50 pm.

"Oh, I don't think so, do you? We've got around five hours of daylight left. We can number-hunt inside with the lights on later if we have to. Let's get the guys and dogs out. You chase down the vans they used that night. I'll let Johnny Mac know and set up the search of the grounds; then I've got to meet with the lady of the house.

"And, Tina; bloody great work, by the way."

★

Jo had only just arrived at Etherington Place and taken a seat in the front sitting room when the screech of tyres sounded on the gravel outside followed by running footsteps in the hall. Katey Tomlinson-Brown burst into the room.

"What's that woman doing here?" she demanded, as Jo rose to her feet. "Why is she in Dad's chair? And what are that lot doing outside?"

Mags turned to her, shocked at her manner.

"This is Detective Inspector Cottrell."

"Yes, I know who she is. I just want to know why she's bothering you."

"Now that's enough!" Mags said. "The Inspector has been working…" She turned to Jo. "Is it alright to tell Katey?"

Jo nodded.

"After Jack and Jason were convicted, I asked DI Cottrell to look into the case as a favour to me. She took a big risk in doing that without the official approval of her superiors. She went out on a limb for us. So I think she deserves a little better than to be snapped at, don't you? And DI Cottrell is in that chair because that's where I invited her to sit."

Katey continued to stare at Jo, but the muscles in her face relaxed.

"She's here to ask permission to search the grounds for a rucksack in connection with another case, the one against Mickey Kadawe. That's right, isn't it, Jo?"

"That's correct." Jo looked across at Katey. "I saw you, didn't I, when we were searching Manston Grange? For the same rucksack, as it happens."

Katey nodded.

"What were you doing there exactly? That would have been just after you'd heard from your mum about Mickey's arrest."

"Well, a short while after. I went to see if I could find out any more. I thought…"

"Did you tell anyone that he'd been arrested?"

"Well, it was common knowledge…"

"No it wasn't," Jo said. "Certainly none of the officers searching told anyone. And up to the time you arrived there, people kept asking us where Mickey was. After you left, everyone seemed to know he'd been arrested."

"Really, Jo," Mags intervened, "you can't expect to keep that sort of thing…"

"No you can't," Jo said, without taking her eyes off Katey, "because there's always someone who speaks out of turn."

"Look, I…" Katey started.

"Did you tell them *why* he'd been arrested?"

"No, definitely not," Katey said. "I said it was probably tax evasion."

Jo could not suppress a smile.

"Well, if it's good enough for Al Capone…" Mags added.

There were a few moments of silence.

"Please," Mags said, waving for Jo to sit down again. Jo resumed her seat. Katey sat next to Mags on the sofa.

"Okay, I'm sorry," she said. "But why are you here? I thought Kadawe had been arrested for dealing."

"That's right," Jo said. "Technically, on *suspicion* of dealing. Something's come up which leads us to believe that the rucksack may have been left here after the party."

"Who by? And what something?"

"I can't answer either of those questions at the moment," Jo said, rising again from the chair. "If we can get started, Maggie," she added.

"Of course. And let me know if you and your team need a drink of something." She looked out of the window at the officers disembarking outside. "I think we've got enough mugs to go round."

Jo smiled. "I hope we won't need to be here very long."

As Jo left the house to get the search under way, her mobile trilled.

"Hi Tina. Ready to go here. What about you?"

"We've got it," Tina said.

"What?"

"We've found it. Easy peasy. Stuffed into the tool compartment with the wheel-brace and jack under the floor of one of the vans. And it gets much better. It was one of the dogs that found it, so there must be traces of something in there."

"God, that's brilliant. Let's get Catrina to ID it. I'll phone her and pick her up on the way. Where are you?"

"At the SRH. It's cordoned off as a crime scene; SOCOs on the way."

"Be right there. Call the lab and tell them it might be a late night."

She went back to tell Mags the news. As she left again, Katey followed her down the steps.

"Can I have a word, please?"

"We need to go, Miss Tomlinson…"

"Katey… please. Look, I'm sorry I behaved like a spoilt little girl just now. Although, in my defence, that's exactly what I am."

Jo smiled.

"That's okay Miss… Katey. But I really have to…"

"Just one minute."

"Quickly then."

"I just want to tell you that I met with Cat Thompson yesterday. She told me everything she told you."

Jo frowned. "She wasn't supposed to do that."

"My fault again. I went to see her especially to find out as much as I could. She also told me that Mickey had the hots for me – if you can believe that."

168

"Yes, Katey, I find that very easy to believe. She mentioned it to me as well."

"And she's right. I didn't believe her at first. Didn't want to believe her. But then I thought back, and there were times – quite a lot of times…"

"You mean he actually… propositioned you?"

"I'm not sure what that means," said Katey, making Jo feel about ninety, "but if you mean did he try to hit on me, then no, not exactly. It was just suggestive little comments and touches. I just took them as his little jokes at the time but, thinking back, it was always when Jason wasn't there. In fact, always when we were alone."

"Okay, Katey, thank you for that, and now…"

"Look, can I tell mum about this? All that stuff about Mickey being arrested for dealing, it's just a cover, isn't it? I think you're looking at this in the context of Jason and Jack."

Jo did not respond straight away. It was strange, she thought, hearing Jason mentioned ahead of Jack. But Jason was actually more important now.

"I can't comment on that right now, Katey. But I do understand why you want to talk to your mum as soon as possible. Look, I'd like you to hold off for twenty-four hours. Let's say until tomorrow evening, and then I'll talk to both of you. Will you to do that?"

"Well, if I have to, I guess…"

"You don't *have* to, Katey. I'm just asking you if you will. I believe it will be better for your mum to wait another day for what will most probably be a much fuller picture."

"Okay. Sorry. SKS again, I'm afraid."

"SKS?"

"Spoilt kid syndrome – it appears to be untreatable."

Jo laughed this time.

"Don't despair, Katey. I've seen a lot worse cases. See you tomorrow. Let your mum know; I'll phone her with a time beforehand."

She got into the front passenger seat and, as the car pulled away, took her mobile from her pocket to make the second call to her boss in the space of two hours.

★

169

If John Mackay's office was large, then his boss's was palatial. It resembled a set in a period drama, with carved-panelled walls, pictures of hunting scenes and pastoral landscapes, floor-to-ceiling book shelves packed with leather-bound volumes, a range of antique furniture and a pair of chandeliers, shedding a soft glow over everything. The occupant seemed somewhat out of place in the midst of all this splendour. Edwin Mills was of average height and stocky, with the rugged face of a prize-fighter under greying, close-cropped hair.

His reaction to the news was exactly what John had expected.

"So you gave the go-ahead to search for the rucksack?" He glared across the desk at the Chief Superintendent.

"Well, of course I did. Kadawe went into the grounds with it and came out without it. What else would you expect me to do, for God's sake?"

"So what happens next?"

"Well, she's taking the Thompson girl to formally ID the rucksack, then it will go to forensics – as always. Then I guess early tomorrow we'll have an idea if it's…"

"*Shit!* Look, we need more time; this is moving too fast, I have to go higher with everything we do on this." He looked hard across at John. "You *do* understand, don't you? You *can* see the bigger picture? Expulsion is the symbolic flagship of the NJR. If the process is discredited by a wrongful conviction, it could shake the foundation of the whole structure!"

"Come on, Eddie. It would just be seen as an unfortunate mistake. Collateral victims – as Tom Brown himself would point out. People voted for the NJR knowing this could happen."

"No they didn't, John! That's where you're wrong! They voted for getting rid of known domestic terrorists. It was only a few months ago that the possibility of shipping an innocent abroad came up. It was only *then* that the concept of accepting collateral damage was raised, at that TV interview with Sylvie Hanker the day after the announcement." He got up from his chair and started stalking round the room. "And this is what pisses me off; all this is that arrogant bastard's own fault! Expulsion was never designed for criminals found guilty of a specific offence. It was a new environment created for individuals who had serially rejected this one. *That* made sense. Wonder Boy himself said – or rather endorsed Deverall saying – the choice is 'better or not' as opposed to 'guilty or not guilty?' 'Would it be better without these people?', rather than, 'are they guilty of a crime?' That was the whole fucking point! If he hadn't railroaded his drug dealing thing through, there could never have been such a thing as a miscarriage of justice with Exiles."

"Well," John said, "in less than forty-eight hours we have to release Kadawe or charge him. Assuming we get something from the rucksack, we can't release him. Cottrell's team is in celebration mode already. What do we tell them? Forget it, it's too embarrassing? I understand even Harry Waters has been helping them."

"Waters? Doesn't he realise what *he*'s got to lose? The world's gone fucking mad."

He sat down again, trying to compose himself.

"Okay, John, here's what you do – or what you tell your little terrier bitch to do. Charge him with dealing, ostensibly to give us longer to fully investigate the perversion case. That will give us all time to line up what we do next. Okay?"

"I don't think Cottrell will like…"

Eddie banged his fist down on the desk, half-standing and leaning over to shout in John's face. "I don't give a shit what she likes or doesn't like. Last time I checked, you out-ranked her by some considerable distance. If you'd like it to remain that way, then do your job and go and *tell* her what her Chief Constable has decided."

John sprang to his feet.

"I don't like being threatened or yelled at," he shouted back. "We may have convicted two innocent men, resulting in a tragic death, and all the powers that be are worried about is how it's going to look. How *they're* going to look. Well, for one thing, they're still alive. That must be some consolation!"

Eddie dropped back into his chair again. John remained on his feet for a while longer before sitting down.

"The big picture, John. You're *still* missing the big picture – like you frequently do." Eddie's voice was quiet now. "It's nothing to do with how people – individuals – are going to look; it's about public confidence in the justice system. Now whether you believe that or not, please go and tell DI Cottrell that – for now, at least – the charge has to be dealing. And tell her not to charge him until, at the earliest, the day after tomorrow – Wednesday. That will give us a bit more time. Then we'll move forward at a pace we can manage in order to avoid any fall-out from this. If she doesn't like it, send her to see me, and I'm sure I can convince her we're all on the same side."

John rose to his feet to leave.

"I doubt that, Chief Constable. You've certainly not convinced me. But don't worry, she's an excellent officer and she'll do as she's told. I only hope we have enough on the dealing charge for the magistrate to commit."

★

Jo parked her car a short distance away from the police vehicles and she and Cat walked across to where Tina was standing near the van in which the bag had been discovered. It was still in its hiding place, squeezed in amongst the tools under the floor at the rear of the vehicle. Cables and amplifiers from the back of the van were stacked close by and were also being examined.

Cat identified the rucksack straight away

"Not found anything else yet," Tina said, "But we've got what we came for."

Jo waved the senior SOCO over.

"We can move this now, Rory," she said, indicating the rucksack, "and recover the van. Let's get the bag to the lab right away." She looked across at Tina.

"They're expecting it any time," the sergeant said.

Jo turned to Cat.

"Great. I guess that's it. Thanks again. I'll drive you back to Dagger's. See you at the station, Tina."

★

Cat didn't speak at all during the short journey to Dagger's place. When they arrived, Jo went in with her.

"Well, Catrina," she said, when they were all seated together

172

at his dining table. "There's a good chance that we'll be charging Mickey with perversion. You know what that means, don't you?"

"You'll be accusing him of setting up Jack and Jason."

"That's right."

"He's going to assume I've fingered him, isn't he?"

"Not necessarily. Once we get him to admit he was at the party, we'll be throwing other stuff at him as well. From what you've told us, he's more likely to think it was something to do with the big guy who's been worrying him these last few months. Or he might not have been telling you the truth when he said you two were the only ones who knew he was at the party. Whatever happens, we'll keep your name – and Dagger's – out of it. That was the deal as far as I'm concerned."

There was a long, uneasy silence. Dagger was frowning, deep in thought.

"I'd really like to believe that," he said. "Look, he's been arrested for dealing, right?"

"Suspicion of dealing…"

Dags dismissed the technicality with a roll of his eyes. "And if he was to be found guilty of *that*, he'd be dumped at sea, right?"

Jo nodded.

"In which case, Cat would be safe. But instead you're going for perversion of justice, which means what, exactly? He'll do time and then be out again? And in the meantime, I suppose, he'll be able to contact all his cronies – all the guys who are so shit-scared of him they'll do anything he tells them. So where does that leave Cat? Right in the fucking firing line, that's where! Cat's taken this massive risk…"

"Hold on, Dags." Cat smiled across at him and took hold of his hand. "My hero. What have I ever done to deserve you? But remember, it was my idea. It was my decision to tell the police about Mickey being at the party. Nobody asked me to. And DI Cottrell made it very clear about the risks of confronting Mickey when I offered to do that. But I was happy to do it. If Mickey set up Jack and Jason, I want to help make things as bad as possible for him."

They sat in silence for a while before Dagger spoke again with the trace of tears in his eyes.

"Yes, but, Cat, I couldn't stand it if something were to happen to you."

Cat squeezed his hand.

"I'll be safe with you," she said.

"Look," said Jo. "We'll make sure that neither of you will be on your own while this gets resolved. Then perhaps you can drop out of sight for a while until…"

"Drop out of sight!" Dags shouted. "Fucking hell! We go on tour in just under two weeks. This is everything we've worked towards. Our first headlining tour! We can't just drop out. There are contracts already signed. We'd never work again. If you ask me, Cat's only going to be safe if Mickey Kadawe is either exiled or dead."

CHAPTER ELEVEN

It was 2.40 am when Jo and Tina finally met with Doctor Donovan Menzies, Head of O-SFS – On-Site Forensic Services – to review the information yielded by the rucksack. Jo had sent the rest of the team home at around 8.00 pm when it became obvious there would be a long wait for the analysis, with instructions to be in at 7.00 am the following morning. As the evening dragged itself into the night, Jo started to wonder when – or if – she and Tina were going to get any sleep themselves.

Their host wore the regulation white lab coat of his trade, and with his unruly mass of thinning hair, beaky nose and wire-rimmed glasses – currently pushed up high on his forehead – he looked every inch the quintessential mad professor. He was, in fact, one of the very best of his kind in the country.

"The right-hand side pocket of the bag," he was saying, "contained two screw-drivers, a wood-chisel and a small hammer. There were no prints on these, but we did find traces of powder. Let's leave those for now and come back to them a little later.

"We've tested the two surgical gloves found in the main compartment of the bag, and got good skin samples from inside, and product samples on the outside. Skin will be easy to match – though, even pulling a few strings, it could take up to twenty-four hours from when we get something to match it *with*. External powder traces are consistent with drugs found at Etherington Place and Copley Road. However, even if DNA testing shows Kadawe wore them, from what you say, that won't prove anything. It would be common sense to use gloves in the circumstances he described, and he's admitted finding the stuff and would probably say he'd handled it. All that would do on its own is substantiate his story.

"However, the bag itself contains a significant amount of the same substance as that found on the gloves. And when I say significant, I mean there is far more than can be explained away as coming off the gloves themselves. In fact, it is all over the interior of the bag – the bottom, the sides, even on the inside of the top flap. I'd say the rucksack has been full of the stuff at some time or other."

"So would you be able to stand up in court and say the stuff found in Jack Tomlinson-Brown's wardrobe had previously been in the rucksack?"

"Of course not..."

"I thought..."

"But *you* could." He paused, as if for effect. "What I *can* say is, based on the tests we've carried out, the rucksack at some time contained a large quantity of cocaine *identical in constitution* to that found in Jack's wardrobe and under the floorboards in Copley Road. *Plus* I can confirm – or not, if you're wrong – that Kadawe wore those gloves at some time or other, *and* that they had been used to handle the material which was in the bag. That's what I can say; that's my job done.

"Then, of course," he continued, "it's down to *you* to put all that together and to link it to the other evidence – Kadawe admitting he took the sack into the party, claiming that the bag was empty except for some tools, finding the stuff but not putting any of it into the bag, etc. I think you could hypothesise convincingly that he took the stuff in with him and emptied the bag into the wardrobe bottom. Don't you?"

"Yes, I'm sure I could," Jo said.

"Just one question, Doc," Tina put in. "If this stuff was in sealed plastic bags, how come there's so much of it around on the inside of the sack and on the gloves?"

"Well, don't forget, Sergeant, when I say it's all over the inside of the bag, I mean minute traces of it. You couldn't see them with a magnifying glass even if you knew exactly where to look. We can pick up individual grains of the powder. And as for how the stuff gets there, well any number of ways. It gets on the outside of the bags when they're being filled, a faulty seal might allow a small amount to leak out, a bag could be dropped into the powder and wiped clean – that is 'clean' to the naked eye. Not anywhere near clean as far as we're concerned."

"But you say there's enough on the inside of the bag to be certain that it didn't just come off the gloves."

"Absolutely. Not a shadow of a doubt. No-one's going to challenge that, trust me. It's not the *amount* that points to that, it's the fact that it is *all over* the inside of the bag."

"And the tools in the side pocket," Jo said. "You were going to say something about them?"

"Oh yes. As I said, there is powder, but no prints, on the handles of the hammer, chisel and one of the screwdrivers, suggesting they were handled by the person who wore the gloves. Pretty obvious, I guess. It might also be possible to match some minute wood fragments on the chisel and the same screwdriver with the wood of the wardrobe or, more likely, the floorboard at the Midandas'. However, it might not be necessary."

Jo and Tina looked at each other with wide involuntary smiles. Jo turned back to the doctor.

"That's brilliant, Don; well worth staying up for. Could you do just one more thing? Would you write this up for us now, before you go, and post it on the case website? Then we can access it first thing in the morning."

"Sure, no problem. You can wait for it if you like."

"No thanks, it's beddy-byes for us, I think. Got a meeting in…" she checked her watch "… just under four hours, and quite a day with Mr Kadawe to look forward to. Thanks a million, Don."

★

By the time Jo arrived at the station a few minutes before seven, her team had already assembled and there was a buzz of anticipation in the MIT room. Waiting for her, in her office, was Harry Waters, clutching a type-written sheet of paper.

"Hi Harry. You don't need to come in for seven o'clock *every* day. I'll let you know when."

Harry snorted a laugh. "I just wanted to catch you before you got started. Tina's told me you've had a bit of a breakthrough with the rucksack."

"Well, possibly." She was careful not to sound too triumphant, given the vested interest of her audience. "But what's your news?"

"I just thought you might be interested in what nearly blew you to pieces. We've had the report on the explosives."

"Go on."

"Don't ask me how they know this after what was left of the building, but apparently it was PE-4 explosive, several quantities linked together in a circle with detonation cord. They can work it so all pieces explode simultaneously – more effective than one single charge using the same mass of explosive."

"So how did they do it? I thought PE-4 was very stable – you can't set it off remotely. You need a detonator, don't you?"

"Very good; you've been paying attention in class, haven't you?" He checked the sheet he was holding. "I'd better get this right. They tape a detonator to each end of the cord ring main – the circle of explosives – and the detonators are connected by wire to an exploder, which sets off the detonators using an electrical pulse. The pulse can be generated remotely – by a radio, say – or by a timer."

"Any clues yet as to who?"

"Well, that's the interesting bit. Classic Special Forces MO. Not exclusively them, but certain details of the main explosion point that way. Petrol was used in this case as an accelerant, which is why it fired the car so quickly. Special Forces are usually doing this sort of stuff on the hoof, so unlikely to be carrying quantities of petrol, but other than that…"

"So, dare I ask, where does that take us?" Jo said.

"Yet again, not where we want to go, I'm afraid. This sort of demolition is a basic Special Forces skill. Every member is trained to do it and there would be at least one expert in every unit. We're checking out whether Tom Brown was an expert in this field, although it's almost certain that information won't be released. And even if it was made available and we found that he wasn't a designated expert, he'd still be capable of doing this."

"Capable in theory, I suppose, but he'd have to get in and fix the charges. And before that, he'd have to *know* they were there – assuming they were the intended targets. It's the stuff of fantasy."

"Like your fantasy about Jack and Jason being innocent?"

"Yes, but that's looking like it might not be a fantasy, isn't it?"

"In which case, let's not be quick to dismiss this," Harry said. "One thing I think we've learned is that we should *all* keep open minds from now on."

*

Jo and Tina took their seats opposite the two men. The cut on Tina's head had been covered by as small a plaster as possible and hidden by a new hairstyle incorporating an eyebrow-length fringe.

"Interview started ten-twenty-three am; present, Mr Mickey Kadawe, Mr Chester Rockwell – representing Mr Kadawe, Detective Sergeant Christina Ramirez, Detective Inspector Joannita Cottrell; in attendance, Constable Geordie Carroll."

"I don't fancy yours much, Rocky. Come to think of it, I don't fancy mine either."

Jo looked up from her notes and across at Chester Rockwell.

"It might be wise, before we start, Mr Rockwell, to remind your client how he should behave; in his own best interest, of course."

The lawyer took a deep breath and stared back at her.

"What I *will* say, DI Cottrell, is that I object very strongly indeed to the way my client has been treated over the past five days. Mr Kadawe has been left for most of that time alone in his cell, with no attention paid to him at all except on three separate occasions when he has been questioned for no more than an hour each time. Subsequent sessions have been almost exact repeats of the previous ones, with nothing new presented in the way of evidence to support his being here under suspicion of this offence. I strongly urge you – in fact, I *demand* – that you either move this case rapidly forward with immediate effect or release my client. Either way, I will be making the strongest representation to the highest authority about the way this case has been handled. And I shall be making a complaint against you personally, Inspector."

"*Detective* Inspector," Jo corrected. "Thank you for making that very clear, Mr Rockwell. Can we now proceed with the interview?"

She turned back to Mickey, fixing his eyes with hers and feeling remarkably relaxed.

"Okay, Mickey, just to please Mr Rockwell, let's move this quickly on."

She turned to Tina.

"Detective Sergeant."

Tina pulled out the rucksack from behind her chair and placed it on the table.

"Do you recognise this, Mickey?" she said. "For the record, I am showing Mr Kadawe a blue-and-grey Karrimor rucksack."

Jo noted with satisfaction the brief moment of panic in Mickey's eyes. He half-turned to his lawyer before recovering himself.

"No, I haven't seen it before." The confidence and cockiness were missing from his voice.

"Are you sure?" Tina said. "*Absolutely* sure?"

"Why?" Mickey said. "Where did you find it?"

"Oh, just around, you know," she said. "Look at it again. You're sure you haven't seen it?"

Mickey turned to Rockwell, who raised his eyebrows, inviting him to answer.

"Yes," he said.

"You *have* seen it?" Tina said.

"No. I meant – yes, I'm sure I *haven't* seen it. Look, is this some sort of trick?"

"We wondered at first whether it belonged to someone in one of your bands," Jo said.

"No, it doesn't. I'm sure it doesn't."

"Is that part of what you have to do as a manager, Mickey? Be aware of every single item that each band member possesses. Must be the hardest part of the job, keeping track of all that stuff."

Mickey said nothing for a while.

"Oh, now I know where I've seen it…"

Rockwell leaned forward as if to speak – too late.

"You've just told us twice that you've never seen it before," Jo said.

Rockwell sat back again and sighed.

"Well… I've just remembered… It belonged to Jack."

"Jack who?"

"You know. Jack Tomlinson-Brown. The one who died… It belonged to him."

"Was he in one of your bands?"

"No, of course he wasn't, but he was…"

"Then we're pretty sure it didn't belong to him."

"Why? How can you be sure?"

"Because of where we found it."

Mickey did not respond right away. He turned again to his lawyer, then back to Jo and Tina.

"Can I have a word with Rocky – Mr Rockwell?"

"Certainly, but aren't you going to ask us first *where* we found it? It might give you more to talk about."

"Wherever you found it, it's definitely Jack's. I'm fairly sure of that."

"*Definitely* Jack's? *Fairly* sure? You're mixing up your adverbs, Mickey. Isn't that right, Mr Rockwell?"

"I would like to speak with my client, Detective Inspector. Please."

Jo spoke into the recorders. "Interview suspended at ten-forty am." She switched them off. "Constable Carroll, please find Mr Kadawe and Mr Rockwell a meeting room to use."

★

"Interview re-started at eleven-twenty am. Now…"

"DI Cottrell, before we go any further can I just clarify some of my client's previous comments."

"You can try, Mr Rockwell. Please go ahead."

"Just to say that Mr Kadawe did not initially recognise the rucksack, but then suddenly remembered where he might have seen it; that is, in the possession of Jack Tomlinson-Brown, who, as I know you are aware, spent a great deal of time with Mr Kadawe at his home in Woking. However, on reflection, my client cannot be certain of this and accepts that it may well belong to someone in one of his bands."

"Well, thank you for clarifying that."

"I mean, rucksacks are all pretty much the same, aren't they?"

Jo beamed back at him.

"Not this one, Mr Rockwell," she said. "Most definitely not this one." She turned to Mickey. "You still haven't asked me where we found the bag. Is that because you *know* where we found it?"

181

"Detective Inspector, I have just explained…"

"I know, Mr Rockwell, but you see I don't believe a word of what you just said. That's no reflection on you, of course; I'm sure you are just repeating what your client told you. So come on, Mickey, tell us where we found it."

"How the fuck would I know…"

"Well, because you put it there, of course."

"And I'm telling you, it's – not – my – fucking – rucksack!" Mickey was squirming on his chair.

"I didn't say it was," Jo said. "I don't care who it *belongs* to – you, Jack, one of your band members, Bob the Builder, whoever. What we care about is who used it last. And we're quite certain we know that. We just wanted to give you the chance to tell us."

Mickey slumped back and turned away, staring down at the floor next to his chair. Rockwell looked anxious and confused.

"DI Cottrell, would it be possible…"

"Not right now, sir," Jo said, her eyes fixed on Mickey. "We can't have a time-out after every question so that your client can invent what he believes is a suitable answer. Detective Sergeant, explain to our guests where we found the bag."

Tina held up the exhibit.

"This was found in the back of a van used by one of your bands. It was discovered by a sniffer dog during a routine security check at the SRH," she said.

"The what?" Rockwell asked.

"Sweet Rock Hall – it's a concert venue, at Portman Palace, just outside Woking. It was under the floor of the van's storage compartment. In it, we found – do you want to take up the story, Mickey?"

Mickey was silent.

"Okay; in it we found some hand-tools – in a side pocket, and in the main section of the bag, a pair of surgical gloves and very significant traces of a banned substance. It is certain – *forensically* certain, in fact – that at some time, recently we believe, this bag was filled with cocaine."

Mickey was doing his best to remain indifferent, but his breathing was noticeably louder and quicker. The signs were not lost on Mr Rockwell.

"DI Cottrell, can I please…"

"We are in the process of tracking down everybody who has used the vehicle within the past few months," Tina continued, "and we shall be taking DNA samples from each of them – to check against the skin residue found inside the gloves. However, that is just to eliminate them from our enquiries, because, as DI Cottrell said, we think we *know* who used the gloves and hid the rucksack in the van. We think it was you, Mickey."

"DI Cottrell, I insist…"

"I assume," Jo said, addressing the lawyer, "that your client won't object to our taking a swab for DNA testing?"

"Before this goes any further, Detective Inspector, I must speak to my client in private. I am sure you understand that it could be prejudicial to your own interests if you refuse me that opportunity."

"Interview suspended at eleven-thirty-nine. We'll reconvene at one o'clock after we've all eaten a hearty meal." She stopped the recording again. "Constable, could you arrange that for Messrs Kadawe and Rockwell, please?"

The two women left and walked back to the MIT room.

"Right," Jo said, when they were back in her office. "Let's up the ante." She looked at the sheets on her desk containing a long list of names. "I asked Jody to get me these."

★

"Interview restarted, one-oh-five pm. All present as before."

Mickey looked hard at Jo with the same intensity and menace which had unsettled her at the time of his arrest. For the moment she ignored him and addressed his lawyer.

"Do you wish to say anything before we resume, Mr Rockwell?"

"Yes; I most certainly do."

Jo and Tina sighed loudly enough to ensure it would be picked up on the recording.

"My client wishes to reiterate that he cannot say for certain whether or not he has seen this rucksack before. What he *can* say, however, is that he has certainly never used it, and if there is anything in the bag which appears to incriminate him, then it must have been placed there by someone for that specific purpose."

He leant back in his chair and folded his arms with an air of finality, as if he had just explained away everything.

"Is that it?" Jo asked.

"Yes, for now."

She turned to Mickey.

"Mr Kadawe, could you tell us where you were on the night of the party at Etherington Place?"

The same look crossed Mickey's face as when he had first been shown the rucksack; one of momentary panic.

"Why? I wasn't there. I told your people."

"Yes, I know you did. Would you like to change your story now?"

"Why should I? That's the truth?"

"Okay, so let me repeat the question. Where were you on the night of the party?"

"I told your people that as well. It's no secret. I was with a friend. A woman from South Africa, someone I knew from way back..."

"An ex-girlfriend?"

"I guess you could say that."

"How old were you when you left Johannesburg, Mickey? Ten? Eleven? Can't have been all that serious, then, this girlfriend."

"Look, does that matter? She came over to London; she'd got my address through Milton – that's my old man – and got in touch. She only had a few hours, so I gave her a lift to Heathrow so we could talk longer. Her plane was delayed so I stayed with her to keep her company. It was really late when I got back so I went straight home. Okay?"

Jo held his eyes. She didn't speak for a long time. It was Mickey who looked away first.

"What's her name?" Jo spoke, her voice little more than a whisper.

Mickey hesitated for just a moment. "Olivia," he said.

"Olivia who?"

"Don't know."

Jo laughed.

"Oh, come on, Mickey. Don't make it too easy for us."

"I don't know her last name. She's married now, and I can't even remember her name before. That's the truth. She just phoned and said 'it's Olivia' and asked if we could get together. I only know one Olivia."

Jo shook her head.

"You're losing it, Mickey. Where was she flying to?"

"Back to Jo'burg."

"Direct?"

"I think so."

"You must remember, surely? When it was delayed, there would have been announcements over the tannoy; information on the display screens. Was it a direct flight or not? Come on, Mickey, it wasn't that long ago. How many ex-childhood sweethearts from Jo'burg do you entertain at Heathrow in the course of a few months?"

Jo glanced across at Geordie who moved silently behind the two men.

"Look, you fucking bitch!" Mickey was suddenly leaning across the table, shouting. "I don't know, right! I have a life, you know. A *real* life. I can't be expected to remember precise fucking details of insignificant little things that happen to me like talking to an old friend. I don't care what her fucking last name is or how she was flying back. It's just not important!"

Jo looked calmly back at him though she could feel her heart beating faster. Rockwell put a hand on his shoulder to pull him away. Mickey shrugged it off, but subsided back in his chair.

"You're right, as it happens, Mr Kadawe," she said, dropping her eyes to look at the sheets of paper in front of her. "It's *not* important whether you remember or not. Because there were four flights that left Heathrow that evening for Jo'burg. Two direct, one via Amsterdam and one via Frankfurt. And not one of them was delayed. Not even for a few minutes."

She looked across at him and smiled.

"So what do you say to that? And while you're thinking of an answer, I'll check through these lists of passengers to see if I can find anyone called Olivia."

Suddenly, Mickey was on his feet and leaning across the table. Geordie was ready, grabbing him from behind and pinning his arms to his sides as Jo pressed the alarm button under the table. Even before she had released it, the door was flung open and two more officers raced in to grab the prisoner. Jo and Tina stepped back from the table as Mickey's face was forced down sideways onto it and the 'cuffs applied. He was wrestled from the room screaming obscenities and threats at Jo over his shoulder.

Rockwell had retreated to the corner of the room furthest away from the action.

"I think you should have a talk with your client, Mr Rockwell," Jo said, aware that her voice was shaking. "He's just suffered a bit of a setback."

She stepped up to the table.

"Interview ended at one-twenty-five pm."

She switched off the recorders.

★

The Lochshore cafeteria was large and airy with a long self-service counter separating it from the gleaming stainless steel of the kitchen at one end. At the other end, a small stage faced a double semicircle of around thirty chairs, serving as a lecture facility for meetings, announcements and training events.

Deputy Chief Prison Officer G. Alistair – Gally – McPherson's imposing presence dominated the stage and demanded attention. Over six feet tall, with powerful shoulders and barrel chest, his face was battered and scarred from his years of service working with the hardest criminals Scotland could offer.

"Okay, guys; change of plans. Departure has been brought forward and we've got to get the wee boat ready for six o'clock tomorrow evening. That gives us twenty-eight hours instead of forty-two."

Gally shouted above the chorus of groans which greeted the announcement.

"Hold on, it gets real exciting from here." He read from the screen of his hand-held iPad. "This is due to intelligence received about possible disruption to the journey by a third party organisation."

"You mean terrorists?" someone asked.

"A third party organisation," Gally repeated. "The new departure time must be kept to ourselves for obvious reasons.

Those of you who had plans for the end of the shift had better start inventing a suitable excuse as to why you'll be working a further four hours. The overlap will double our resources for half the next shift. And don't worry; they'll be working the extra four hours at the end of theirs. That will give us the equivalent of an additional shift's work before the new departure time. Just think of the extra money you'll earn, added to the amount you'll save tonight."

More groans and a few laughs.

"Big C will be back in just under three hours, so let's make sure we're at full speed by the time he gets here. We don't want him thinking we can't respond to a crisis without him, do we? And remember – no-one mentions the change of time. I don't want anyone contacting the next shift in advance either, or saying anything to them when they come in. I want to make sure they get the information from me. Okay? And if I find out anything else, I'll let you know straight away. Any questions? No? Okay, then let's get back to work."

★

Chester Rockwell tapped, almost apologetically, on DI Cottrell's half-open door, peering into the office as he did so.

"Come in, Mr Rockwell. Please sit down. Is your client ready yet to resume our discussion?"

"I believe he will be very soon," he replied, taking the seat offered. "In the meantime he has asked me to apologise on his behalf for his behaviour. And as a gesture of goodwill, he has consented to provide a sample of DNA. But he's someone who's used to having to fend for himself, you know, Detective Inspector, and when you back him into a corner like you did… Well, you can expect him to fight his way out of it. It's an instinctive reflex for someone like Mr Kadawe."

"I see, so it was my fault he attacked me?"

"Well, he didn't exactly attack you, did he? He certainly got very angry…"

"I would have thought you'd have got a pretty good view of what happened from where you were sitting – and standing. If Constable

Carroll hadn't reacted so quickly and effectively, your client would have been facing at least one additional charge right now."

"Well, perhaps so. And on the subject of charges, I'm getting confused. I'm not sure I understand the relevance of his whereabouts on the night of this party. What has that got to do with his being suspected of dealing banned substances? Are you suggesting that he was at the party selling drugs? My client has no idea what this is all about."

Jo chose not to respond for some time. When she did, it was with carefully chosen words.

"Mr Rockwell, this is somewhat out of order, isn't it – you coming in here, just the two of us, nothing recorded – trying to find out what we're going to say next to your client, so you can get him prepared with suitable responses. I don't believe that's how it's supposed to work. So instead of looking forward, just let's recap on what we've got. Firstly, Mr Kadawe felt the need to invent an alibi for the night of 3rd April – the night of the party at Etherington Place. Now why would he do that?"

"Well *you* say he invented the story, though I'm not sure where this reference to an alibi comes from. An alibi for what? And where does the rucksack come in to this?"

"Well, the rucksack has recently been used to store and/or transport a large quantity of cocaine. It also contained a pair of surgical gloves. DNA testing will certainly tell us who has worn these gloves, providing, of course, we can get – or already have – a sample from that person. As we have said, we believe that person is your client."

"But why? I just don't see how the two are linked."

"The rucksack was found under the boards in the back of a van containing equipment for use at small outdoor gigs. The last time the van was used was on the night of the party. The equipment was all taken out at the site and then replaced afterwards. No-one has used the van or the equipment in it since that night. It has just been parked up with all the stuff inside since then. We believe the rucksack had been placed there just before the equipment was put back in the van on 3rd April – in fact, on the morning of the fourth."

"But my client wasn't *at* the party, Detective Inspector. I think that's a given, isn't it?"

"It would have been if Mr Kadawe hadn't lied about where he was. He was invited to the party; he organised the music for the party; it was a surprise when he didn't turn up; and the reason he gave for not turning up was a lie."

"Is that it, Detective Inspector? I mean, you're making enormous assumptions here. Firstly, about when the rucksack was placed in the vehicle. Why *just* before the equipment was put back? Why couldn't the bag have been there a long time before the party? Since the previous time the equipment was used? In fact, any time someone wanted to hide it there, they'd just move the stuff and then put it back afterwards. And secondly, you assume my client *must* have been at the party just because *you* doubt he was where he says he was. Even if he didn't go to Heathrow he might have just changed his mind and made up the excuse. If you haven't tested the gloves yet, I don't see *anything* that links my client to the rucksack."

"Well, then let's just wait for the results…"

"And all this will prove beyond reasonable doubt, that my client is a drug dealer?"

"At the very least," Jo said.

"Really? What else did you have in mind?"

"Well, that's looking forward, Mr Rockwell. And we said we wouldn't do that."

Rockwell stood up.

"Anyway, my client still maintains he *did* go to Heathrow and feels he may have been mistaken about the delay at the airport, by the way. He may have just drawn that conclusion because of the long wait after checking-in. It's two-and-a-half hours before take-off on these long-distance flights, you know. And as far as the lady is concerned, it's not unusual for Black South Africans to change their names even now, in these post-apartheid times. I'm sure you, in particular, are aware of that."

"If that comment refers to the colour of my skin, Mr Rockwell, you should know I'm West Indian, not African," Jo said, "so, no, I wasn't aware of that. Oh, and as far as the aforementioned gesture of goodwill is concerned, I'm sure you reminded your client that we already have his DNA and fingerprints on file, anyway. So as far as gestures are concerned, not wishing to sound ungrateful, that's about as hollow as they come."

Rockwell walked out, closing the door behind him.

Jo reached for her desk phone and called O-SFS, asking to be put through to Doctor Menzies.

"We've got the okay to take a swab from our friend Kadawe, Don. Can you arrange? Tell whoever you send to take PC Geordie Carroll in with them."

"Okay, will do."

Jo ended the call then pressed the direct line button for John Mackey. It was a minute after 3.00 pm.

★

At 6.30 pm, Jo called Mags.

"Hi, Maggie, Jo Cottrell. I'm sorry but I don't think I'm going to make it tonight. I need to speak with John Mackay before I see you and he's not been available all day. So I have to wait here and hope he gets to me later."

"That's okay, Jo. Tomorrow then?"

"Yes, I guarantee to be there tomorrow. One other thing, Maggie. I think your husband should be there as well. I know you told me you're having problems, but… well, it's up to you."

Jo held on to the sound of a long pause then a loud sigh.

"Okay."

"Thanks, Maggie. See you tomorrow."

★

Tom glanced at the display on his mobile as the thumping rhythm of *Every Breath I Take* alerted him to an incoming call. He almost dropped the phone in his excitement.

"Katey! How are you? Is everything okay? It's been so long. Is your mum alright? Nothing's happened has it?"

"Hold on, Dad. Just one salvo of questions at a time, please."

He detected a lightness of tone – almost a hint of laughter – in his daughter's voice. Something he'd never expected to hear again.

"Sorry, Princess. This is such a lovely surprise." He could feel himself filling up with emotion, his voice wavering.

"Well," said Katey. "I'm fine – everything's okay – yes, it has

190

been a long time – mum's alright – and what's happened is your best pal, Mickey Kadawe, has been arrested."

"When? What for?"

"Last Thursday; for dealing – but that may not be all. I'm phoning to invite you to a meeting – tomorrow evening, here at the house. Detective Inspector Cottrell is coming round to give us some more information. We think you should be present."

"Does your mum know you're asking me along?"

"Yes, she's told me to phone you."

"Really! Are you sure? Look, perhaps it's not a good…"

"Just say *yes*, Dad. That's all you have to say. It's not difficult."

Tom allowed himself a smile. "In which case, yes," he said.

"There, that wasn't so bad, was it? I'll let you know what time later. We'll have a chance to catch up afterwards. Bye."

★

Jo's meeting with John Mackay did not start until just after 7.00 pm. John, it seemed to Jo, was a different person, hardly meeting her eyes throughout the session and using phrases and clichés which were completely foreign to the man she knew and respected.

"So just let me understand this," said Jo, her teeth clenched and jaw set in anger and disbelief. "Are you seriously asking me …"

"*Telling* you, Jo. Instructing, directing, ordering, demanding … but not asking. You do understand the difference, don't you?"

"You can tell me, instruct me, order me – whatever – all you like, sir, but you can't *make* me. So please bear with me while I go through this again and perhaps I might see the gaping hole you've spotted in what I thought was a water-tight case."

"Look, we've been through…"

"Please, sir. Just one more time."

"It won't make any difference, but…"

"Right – *one* – we have the loop established by David Gerrard – Mickey to Sammo to Laser to Jack, who was Mickey's close friend. *Two* – we have Mickey on the night of the party inventing an alibi to place him somewhere else. *Three* – we know for sure that he smuggled himself in to the grounds that evening carrying a rucksack, but left without it. *Four* – we have retrieved the same

191

rucksack – empty, but with enough traces of cocaine to show that it was at some time filled with the same stuff we found in Jack's room and at Jason's. *Five* – the gloves found in the rucksack, which had been used in handling the cocaine, may well have been worn by Mickey Kadawe – we'll know tomorrow with a bit of luck. *Six* – one of the users who originally phoned in and subsequently appeared as a key witness for the Prosecution, changed his story twice in as many minutes under questioning by me and Harry. And – *seven* – we have a motive. *C'est l'amour!* Mickey wants Katey Tomlinson-Brown. To get her, he has to get rid of Jason."

John sat impassively through Jo's animated pronouncement, making no reply.

"Is all that true, sir? Is there something I've missed – or something I've included that I shouldn't have done?"

He gave the slightest shake of his head.

"And all that is *new evidence*, right? None of it was available at the time of the trial," Jo said.

No response at all this time.

"Right! So, back to my question – why are you *asking* me to ignore all that and *ordering* me to charge him with dealing, when we may not have enough on him for the magistrate to commit; and when we know we've got more than enough to get him committed for perversion of justice? And if he gets released, then I cannot be held responsible for what happens to Catrina Thompson, when the kid has just about put her life on the line to help us see justice done."

John looked, unfocused, at the wall behind her, still saying nothing.

"I remember you telling me, sir, that the investigating team – and you – were desperate to find evidence that Jack and Jason were *not* guilty. Well this might be it. Do we ignore it because the timing's inconvenient?"

John got to his feet, taking Jo by surprise.

"Inconvenient! *Inconvenient!* Right, let me say something that I shouldn't – which is this: I agree with everything you've said. Okay? Not that it makes any material difference; I want you to charge Kadawe with dealing – for now. That will achieve three things. Firstly, there can be no comeback from Rockwell. He can't start claiming we've held his client too long for a charge of perversion, which technically we have. Secondly, we get the perversion case absolutely air-tight – never mind water-tight – so there's no wriggle room for him. And thirdly, it gives the police and Justice Department time to get their heads round what to say if – you'll say, 'when' – the case against Jack and Jason is shown to be flawed."

"So this is all about reputations; allocation of blame…!"

"Just leave it, Jo, okay!" John snapped back. "There really *is* an issue about public confidence at stake here. That's a *fact*. It's a matter of *opinion* as to how high a priority that is when stacked against a possible miscarriage of justice. That's all I'm going to say, and Eddie Mills would sack me on the spot if he ever found out what I've just told you. I said it out of respect for you, and now you show some for me and trust me. It's just as important to know your friends as it is your enemies. And you will find out that I am *definitely* your friend, Detective Inspector."

CHAPTER TWELVE

Wednesday; 23 September

Christina Ramirez was sitting across the desk from her boss wide-eyed with amazement.

"The fact is, we've got him, Tina," Jo said. "The big guys just want to make sure he doesn't slip away through some technicality, like taking too long to question him. This will give us the opportunity to seal him in good and proper," she added, borrowing from John Mackay's air-tight analogy.

Tina looked doubtful. "I can't see what else we can do, ma'am, Can you?"

"Only loose ends. The thing about his being mistaken regarding the delay at Heathrow, for instance, and about her possibly changing her name. We could use the time to show him passport photographs of all the passengers on the four flights and ask him to pick this woman out. That might be quite good fun, actually," she added. "He can't seriously claim he doesn't remember what she looks like. We have to get Mickey to admit he wasn't at Heathrow because we *promised* Catrina we would keep her out of the equation. So we can't use the recording at the SRH. As you said yourself, Tina, we *know* what happened, we just have to get Kadawe to trip up and confirm it."

"We could show him the pictures today, though. We've got until tomorrow lunchtime to charge him."

"I know, and we *will* charge him with perversion – very soon, I'm sure. In the meantime, once he's out of circulation, we've got until just prior to the trial itself before we need to change the charge."

"*If* the magistrate commits."

Tina left to gather the troops for the morning meeting. As Jo got up from her desk to join them, her mobile sounded.

"DI Cottrell here."

"Hi, Jo, it's Donovan Menzies. Good news. I can confirm that Kadawe definitely wore the gloves. Skin particles match with the DNA sample taken yesterday."

"Yesterday afternoon at two-forty-five wasn't it? This is somewhat less than the twenty-four hours you estimated. Must be a world record."

"It's not even *my* record. Just rushed it through for a friend."

"Well, thank you, Don. I really appreciate it – and we needed that, believe me."

"You're very welcome. Good hunting."

⋆

Tina stepped back into Jo's office after showing their visitor out and looked up to the ceiling, placing her hands together as if in prayer. She flopped down onto a chair and looked at her watch. It was 3.50 pm.

"Six hours with Laura Swindley," she said. "What did I do to deserve that?"

"Or anybody from the Office of the Crown Prosecutor for that matter," Jo added. "Actually, she's one of the best."

"I guess so, and we got Mr Kadawe as far as the magistrate."

"Yes, that went pretty well, considering," Jo said. "At least that's us over the first hurdle. I feel a lot better now. That data from Don tipped the balance, I reckon."

"If there was *one* good thing about the dealing charge," Tina said, "it's that Laura worked on the Prosecution's case with us against Jack and Jason, so supporting a case for perversion, would, by implication, have reflected on her role in bringing about the convictions. That would have been a test for her integrity."

Tina left the office and Jo sat for a long time, deep in thought, before picking up her mobile and scrolling through her contacts list to Maggie.

⋆

Katey's first day back at Bishop Adcock six-form college since Jack had died had gone as well as she had expected, helped, she realised, by the fact that her expectations were extremely low. She'd had no illusions as to how much work she would be capable of and, as such, she had arrived – just before lunch – with no books, no laptop and no knowledge of the timetable for the day. It was more of a flying visit to get over the inevitable hurdle of tearful reunions and outpourings of sympathy. That was as much as she was able to deal with, anyway, given all the other thoughts circulating in her head.

The text from her mother arrived as she was sitting in her car, a little after 4.00 pm, drained by the emotion of the past few hours. She made the onward call immediately.

"Hi, Dad. Seven-thirty. Is that okay?"

"Should I just arrive then, or should I come earlier? What do you think? I could come straight away."

"Well, I'm going to see Leila right now – I've been to *college*, can you believe? Aren't I a good little girl?"

"You certainly are. How did it go?"

"Okay. Didn't do much but talk. Starting properly tomorrow. But why not go round now. It'll give you and mum a chance to talk. You can pretend you expected to find me there, if that makes it easier."

"I'm not sure that's a good idea…"

Katey sighed like a frustrated parent.

"Oh, for God's sake, you're like a couple of kids. Well, I'll be back about six, so do what you want."

"Listen," Tom said. "Why don't I meet you at Leila's? I've been thinking I'd like to see her again. Got as far as Cobham station a couple of times, in fact – I just about remember. That's if you think it's a good idea. I guess she probably blames me for what's happened as well."

"No, I think that would be great. And she doesn't blame you, although she does keep a lot bottled up inside. I don't even know for certain if she believes Jay is guilty or not. I think sometimes it's just her way of dealing with it. It might be easier to come to terms with what's happened to him if she accepts that he is."

Neither spoke for a while before Katey continued. "So – are you coming or not?"

"Yes – definitely. See you there."

Tom watched the brake lights on the Porsche Boxter flash briefly before Katey swung the car out of Copley Road onto Redstone Avenue and roared away. He allowed himself a little smile, estimating that his daughter would be exceeding the speed limit within fifty yards of leaving the junction. Her aggressive driving, so often a cause of concern for him – and of friction between them – was today a welcome return to normality.

He leaned forward in the driver's seat of the Audi, his forearms resting on the wheel, thinking about the woman whose house he had just left. How she had hugged him when he arrived, like a long lost relative, the complete absence of any recriminations, her unqualified praise and affection for his daughter.

"As long as Katey's around, Jason will be as well, living through her," she had said, robbing Tom of his ability to speak for a while.

She seemed to accept what had happened to her son with a sad resignation but without bitterness. It was a reflection, he thought, of someone who expected very little from life and, as such, had the inner strength to take adversity as a matter of course. He compared that with his own situation; the first thing that had gone wrong in *his* life, and he'd fallen apart.

The sound of his mobile phone brought him out of his thoughts.

"Hi, John. This is a surprise."

"Hi, Tom," John Mackay said. "Just a quick one – Mickey Kadawe's appearing tomorrow at nine-thirty at Guildford Magistrate's Court. He's being charged with drug dealing."

"Okay, John. Thanks for that, though I'm not sure why I need to know."

"You don't, but you'll find out through Katey, no doubt, and I just wanted you to be clear about the circumstances."

"R-i-ght." Tom drew out the word, inviting John to elaborate.

There was a long silence. Tom could hear John's breathing.

"Is that it? What circumstances?"

"I really shouldn't tell you this, but it's possible that Kadawe could be linked to Jack's case. Something has come to light which puts a new complexion on it. That's all I can say right now and it's a lot more than I should have said. So please don't press me and *don't* repeat it. Okay?"

"Of course. Thank you, John."

"You're welcome. Bye, Tom."

He turned the key, pulled on his seat belt and eased away from the curb with a last, sad look across at the Midandas' home

★

Jo checked the time on the screen in front of her – 6.35 pm – time she was leaving for Etherington Place. She logged off and removed the laptop from its docking station, sliding it into its case and swinging the strap over her shoulder. She picked up her hand bag and stepped out into the team room just as DI Waters emerged from his office.

"Before you go, Jo…"

"Actually, I've got a meeting at seven-thirty."

"Won't take more than two minutes."

Jo followed him back into his office and perched on the edge of a chair. "I've really got to go, Harry."

"Literally, two minutes. You know we were looking into Tom Brown's record re explosives, and I said there was no way they would let us see it. Well, I was wrong. I got a contact of mine in Special Branch to ask the questions and, guess what; some senior admin guy from Special Forces actually *phones* me and tells me everything I want to know. I don't know what to make of it, to be honest."

"I guess you just know the right people – or your contact does. What did he say?"

"That Tom Brown *was* the designated expert in his unit. Not that he needed to be, I suppose, but it means there's absolutely no doubt that he was capable of the attack in Dorking."

"That *is* surprising – that they released the information, I mean."

"What I had to do, of course, was tell my contact *why* we needed the information, which means that our interest in Mr Brown is now sort of official. We can't guarantee to contain it any more."

"Right." Jo got to her feet. "Thanks, Harry. Now I must go."

★

Katey went right through the house looking for Mags before eventually finding her outside in the grounds, sitting at her easel in a heavy fleece, dabbing paint onto a canvas without enthusiasm or any apparent artistic purpose.

"Not much of a hiding place," Katey said. "Though I can't think why Dad would bother to look for you, anyway. Why can't you just make an effort? If not for me, for Jack. It was the last thing he asked you to do."

Mags said nothing. Katey sighed, then turned and walked away. Five minutes later, Mags followed her into the house. Tom had not arrived yet.

"Did he definitely say he was coming?" Mags asked.

"Yes, I left him at Leila's about half an hour ago. In fact, we left together. I thought he'd be here by now."

"Leila's? What was he doing there?"

At that moment, they heard the sound of tyres on gravel outside. Katey ran to the front door as Tom got out of the car.

"Hi, Dad! Forgot the way? I thought you were following me."

Tom smiled. "There's *no* way I could have kept up with you, young lady. All those lectures I gave you about speeding – like chaff to the wind."

"That's your fault for buying me a Porsche. What did you expect?"

They walked hand-in-hand to the porch where Mags was waiting inside with the faintest of smiles.

"Hi, come in," she said, turning away before he got close to her. "Did Katey tell you? DI Cottrell will be here at seven-thirty. I assume you'll want to eat with us?"

"That was an invitation to dinner, by the way, in case you didn't recognise it," Katey said, glaring at her mother.

"Yes, thank you," Tom said.

"I thought we'd eat before she comes. Just something light. Ready in about fifteen minutes."

Mags retreated to the kitchen, supposedly to help Millie McGovern finish preparing the meal. Tom and Katey looked at each other and shrugged.

"Small mercies," Tom said.

"What?"

"Let's be thankful for them. At least I'm getting fed. Although I wish I'd brought my food tester with me."

★

Jo finished the call on her Bluetooth as the huge gates swung slowly back. She pulled up alongside the silver Audi R8 and switched off the engine. Before getting out, she sat for a long time turning over in her mind Tom's new official status as a suspect, and wishing she'd insisted on leaving the station before Harry had had the chance to tell her.

Looking across at the porch, she noticed Mags was already there waiting for her. She got out and the two women exchanged a brief hug before Mags led her through to the sitting room. They were joined by Tom and Katey. Jo shook hands with them both, searching Tom's eyes for any sign of unease or discomfort.

"I'm sorry about last night," she said. "I had a meeting with my boss that didn't start until late. And as a result of that meeting, what I'm going to tell you tonight must go no further for the time being. I must have your promise in advance."

There was silence for a few moments before Tom spoke. "How can we promise if we don't know what you're going to tell us?"

"You have to, Mr Brown. There's no point in my asking you afterwards, is there? I'm taking a big risk with the information even under promise of secrecy. I wouldn't be saying anything at all except for the agreement I made with Katey on Monday."

"Agreement?" Tom said.

"What agreement was that?" Mags asked.

"There are certain things you should know which Katey is already aware of, but which I insisted I wanted to tell you myself. I am prepared to keep my commitment to Katey, but only if you'll make a commitment to me to keep silent."

"Oh, for God's sake, let's get on with it," Tom said.

Mags turned on him quickly.

"I think you should know that the Detective Inspector took an enormous risk on our behalf after the trial, by continuing to investigate Jack and Jason's case without the knowledge of John Mackay. And she did it as a personal favour for me. John is aware of that work now, of course, but he is *not* aware that it was at my request."

"A personal favour? Why wasn't I informed of this?" Tom asked.

Katey spoke to end a brief, uneasy silence.

"I suppose because you were officially still part of the justice system at the time, Dad. It could have put you in a very awkward position."

"That will do as the reason for now," Mags said, with a little smile. "The point is that Jo seems prepared to go out on a limb for us again. The least we can do is agree to protect her."

"Okay," Tom said. "My apologies, DI Cottrell; and my thanks, it seems. Of course you have our assurance."

Jo got up from her seat and paced up and down in front of them for the whole time she was speaking, as if she was delivering a lecture.

"Two hours ago we charged Mickey Kadawe with drug dealing. He will appear at Guildford Magistrate's Court tomorrow morning at nine-thirty and I am confident he will be committed and remanded in custody pending trial in a few weeks time. That is what I *can* tell you *officially*. However, it goes further than that and this is where I need your discretion.

"His arrest and this charge is a means of buying time to prepare for further action against him which directly involves Jack and Jason. We have reason to believe that he may have been complicit in planting the drugs in this house and at Jason's. If we can prove it, that alone would not establish their innocence given all the other evidence against them, but subsequent events point to the possibility that he organised that as well.

"It would mean, of course, that prior to the drugs being planted, he would have had to arrange for people to phone the police with reports of Jack and Jason supplying 'bad' drugs; for users to deliberately catch Jack on camera; and for people to make calls to the phones which were found with the drugs in the two houses. And, of course, for people to attend interviews with the police and submit evidence in court. It is an incredible series of events for anyone to even *attempt* to coordinate, let alone achieve.

"Our next step will be to go through the evidence collected and presented by the Crown and re-examine its sources." She looked at Tom. "Where possible," she added, her eyes fixing on his. He returned her gaze.

"I knew it had to be Kadawe," he said. "I instinctively believed that right at the start. But then the whole thing seemed so fantastic. That's when the doubts came in... But I knew; all the time I knew." He looked across at Mags and then back to Jo. "What I *don't* know is how a single individual can make so many people do so many bad things?"

"Fear I guess, Mr Brown. That young man can be the most charming or the most frightening of individuals at the flick of some internal switch. It seems he's as big a danger to his friends as he is to his enemies."

"But why?" Tom said. "Why would he go to all that trouble and take such a risk?"

Jo shot a glance at Katey, who gave a brief shake of her head.

"We don't know for certain yet, Mr Brown, but we have our theories."

Mags slumped forward, dropping her head into her hands, and began to cry, her shoulders shaking. Katey, sitting next to her on the sofa, turned and wrapped both arms around her, as her own tears trickled from her eyes. Tom stared into space.

"And Jason?" Katey turned to Jo. "What does this mean for Jason?"

"I can't say for certain at this stage, Katey, but it seems likely they'll take him off passage. It may come down to whether we can get a conviction, but... Well, let's say I believe there's cause for optimism."

Katey jumped to her feet, tears still flowing.

"Thank you, Jo. Oh, thank you so much," she said, embracing her, "I just can't believe it."

"Well, let's not get ahead of ourselves," Jo disentangled herself with some embarrassment. "I wouldn't say that if I didn't feel confident, but it's not a done deal, yet."

"So what's the big secret?" Tom asked.

"Well, up to now, there's been nothing officially released to the media about the investigation into Kadawe. There will be a low-key Press statement tomorrow, after the magistrate's hearing, about the dealing charge, but with no reference yet to Jack and Jason's case.

When anything does happen, of course, we'll let the Press know of any new charges, and… well, we'll take it from there."

No-one spoke for a long time; Mags finally recovered herself with a struggle.

"I am so sorry," Jo said, in a small voice choked with emotion. "For Jack," she added, in a barely audible whisper.

★

The flotilla of small boats bobbed and rocked as the bow wave from the huge vessel spread across the harbour. Prisoner Transfer Vessel Two set out on her maiden voyage, edging through the harbour entrance and turning fully to port to head for the open water of the Firth of Lorne.

The two men standing together on the bridge were starting their fifth journey together, this time with two hundred prisoners on board, fifty more than on each of their previous trips, and the last to be taken to Alpha. The men were similar in size and build, both in their early fifties with broad shoulders and slim waists. One had a full grey beard.

The other man checked his watch.

"Not bad, Skipper," said Calum Nicholson, Lochshore's Chief Prison Officer. "Seven past eight. Let's say twelve hours early rather than two late, although I'm not sure that's how the big guys will see it."

"Sod them, then," Douglas McLeod said, with feeling. "You couldn't have done it any quicker."

"You're right, sod them. Next stop, Tobermory."

CHAPTER THIRTEEN

Thursday; 24 September

It took Tom a few seconds to realise where he was when his alarm woke him at 7.00 am. It was a sound he had not heard for a long time. He swung his legs out of bed and looked round his room in Etherington Place, his eyes coming to rest on the unopened bottle of Jack Daniels on the dressing table. He remembered taking it from the drawer of his desk in the adjoining study last night, then thinking better of it.

Good decision, he thought, because he needed this early start.

He got out of bed, showered and picked out a set of clothes from his wardrobe, putting the ones he had worn the previous day into a small hold-all to take back to the apartment. He used one of his old electric shavers and then went down to the kitchen, pleased to find that he was alone. He left the house after toast and coffee at just before eight o'clock, with a note of 'thank you' for Mags – placed in the traditional spot on the kitchen workshop – which he ended with 'Love, Tom x'. He drove straight to his destination, arriving exactly an hour early for his planned encounter.

Parking in a side street close to the Guildford Centre of Justice, he waited near the gates through which Mickey Kadawe would be driven to make the quarter-mile journey to the magistrates' court. Opposite the gates across the huge courtyard, the site was dominated by Guildford New Station, the police headquarters for the South Thames Division and for the region's Flexible Response Teams. The rest of the complex comprised the Holding Centre, where Jack and Jason had been confined, the Crown Court building; the Police Academy, the Forensic Services Centre; and a large accommodation block boasting two penthouse suites. Tom recalled how he had spent a night there following a ceremony at which he had officially opened the Centre.

As the time approached 9.30 am, he walked down to the magistrate's court to wait with a small crowd of reporters hanging around on the off-chance of catching a familiar face entering the building. Mindful of his being recognised, he stayed well away from the group until he saw a police car approaching from the direction of the GCJ followed by a larger personnel carrier. The car stopped, and waited for the vehicle behind to discharge six police officers, heavy with body armour and each carrying a semi-automatic weapon. They formed a short corridor – three on each side – from the car to the base of the flight of steps up to the court entrance. Tom walked across to join the loose throng.

Jo Cottrell got out of the front passenger seat of the car, as a uniformed officer emerged from each of the rear doors. The one nearest the steps reached back into the vehicle to ease the prisoner out. Between them, the two officers escorted the handcuffed Mickey Kadawe up towards the front entrance of the building. Jo followed a couple of steps behind. At the top, Mickey stopped and half-turned, looking over his shoulder at the sea of faces. His eyes alighted on Tom. He stared and blinked in surprise before his expression twisted into a sneer.

"Well, look who's here!" he shouted, loud enough for the crowd to hear. "Come to hand yourself in for murdering your son, Mr Brown?"

Tom lunged forward, racing up the steps through the armed police escort. They hesitated, confused by the fact that he was instantly recognisable. Mickey shook himself free of the restraining hands of his escort to face the charge square on. Tom was within a few feet of the prisoner when Jo stepped in front of him, embracing him to halt his rush. Tom stopped, wrapped in her arms, and reached forward, pointing his finger and yelling over Jo's shoulder.

"Rot in hell, you fucking evil bastard!"

"*Mr Brown!*" Jo's mouth was so close to his ear that her scream of restraint made him wince.

The two officers dragged Mickey backwards up the last couple of steps when a distant muffled sound behind Tom resounded like thunder in his memory above the shouts of the crowd. His instant recall of its significance was confirmed the same second by the two explosions of blood and fabric on Mickey's chest. His eyes rolled upwards in their sockets as he shot backwards, with a force that sent all three men crashing to the ground just in front of the court entrance.

Taking Jo down with him, Tom dropped to the ground, shielding her with his body. The six men in the escort dropped into crouching positions with their weapons at their shoulders, looking around the scene in all directions. Reporters and photographers, slower to react, began shouting and screaming as they dived for cover.

Tom twisted his neck to look up at the three men lying prone ahead of him, and watched the trickle of blood descending the steps towards him. There was little force behind it, however; the heart had stopped pumping and the crimson meniscus came to rest on the step above where his chin was pressed to the concrete. He eased himself upwards, allowing Jo to roll out from under him with an embarrassed and trembling 'thank you'. She was already speaking into her police radio.

As Tom tried to get to his feet, he was forced back down again from above, his arms pulled round behind him.

"Stay perfectly still, sir."

Hands frisked him, feeling in his pockets and inside his jacket. He was half-dragged, half-helped to his feet. Jo was looking at him with something close to fright in her eyes. She glanced across at the armed officer who had searched him. The man shook his head.

"Nothing," he said.

She spoke again into her radio. Tom dusted himself down and looked at the still form in front of him, feeling nothing but satisfaction. The two officers had got to their feet, confused and looking across at him.

"It wasn't Mr Brown," Jo said.

"The shots came from over there," Tom said, turning and pointing high across the road in the direction where the armed group were now scanning the buildings.

"How do you know that?" Jo asked, with more than a hint of suspicion. "I didn't hear anything."

"I heard them. Believe me, Jo. I've heard the sound so many times before; it will always get through to me."

More police vehicles were arriving and armed officers jumping out. Jo ran down to the bottom of the steps to give all the information she had to their commander. They fanned out, running in twos and threes down the streets opposite the court trying to cover the arc from where the shots could have come.

The original six-man team were rounding up the Press and other members of the public close to the scene, many of whom were reluctant to emerge from their hiding places.

"No-one leaves until we have taken names, contact details and statements," Jo was telling people as they were corralled into an area near the bottom of the steps.

An ambulance screamed to a halt. Two paramedics jumped down from the cab clutching their medical packs and rushed up the steps to where Mickey lay. They crouched beside him, feeling for a pulse. One turned to Jo, shaking her head, just as another police car pulled up behind the emergency vehicle. John Mackay got out. He saw Tom straight away and went directly to him.

"What the hell are you doing here?" he demanded.

"I don't know, John, to be honest. But I wouldn't have missed it for the world."

"You actually confronted him, I hear." He led Tom off to one side. "You've let me down, Tom. I told you that stuff last night in confidence."

"Look, John, it wasn't my intention to let Kadawe even see me. And surely you can't believe that I had anything to do with what just happened?"

John did not reply but shouted across to DI Cottrell.

"Jo, can I remove Mr Brown from here. Do you need a statement right now, or will it wait?"

"Well, I…"

"We'll be in my office. I won't let him leave until you come to get him."

Jo looked at Tom, then she shrugged and turned back to appease the agitated melee of reporters. She could appreciate their frustration. They would probably have spent days, possibly weeks, just standing around outside the court, on the off chance of spotting someone significant. Right now, their natural instinct would be to rush off with what would undoubtedly be one of the biggest stories of the day, starring the former Home Secretary and a murdered drug dealing suspect. And she was stopping them doing it.

★

"What I told you last night was out of courtesy and for information only! If I'd thought you were going to do anything like this, then... Well, I'll know next time!"

From being mildly irritated when they had first arrived back at New Station, John Mackay's anger seemed to be growing by the minute as if some dark realisation was spreading through his mind.

Tom said nothing as he watched him storm around his office, suspecting that the cause of his anger was more sinister and fundamental than Tom's alleged breach of confidence. It appeared to him that something had spiralled out of his friend's control and now threatened to precipitate some sort a disaster. It was a lot to read in to the man's expression and demeanour, his darting eyes and laboured breathing, but Tom had never seen him in such a state of agitation before. Whatever was consuming his thoughts seemed to be draining him of his self-belief and composure.

He flopped into his chair, his eyes gazing at the wall behind Tom. As much as anything, he looked vulnerable. Tom waited out a long silence before speaking.

"What you said yesterday – about Mickey being linked to Jack and Jason. Does that mean they might be innocent?"

The directness of the question jolted John out of his trance.

"Well... no, I didn't say that exactly..."

"I know you didn't, John, that's why I'm asking you for clarification. Does it or doesn't it?"

"It's not as simple as that..."

"Oh, come on, John!" Tom said. "The question was *might* they be innocent. We've got a kid out there – Jason Midanda – going through God knows what. If there's even a *chance* he's not guilty, we should take him off passage; bring him back and hold him here. Let him see his family – and Katey. Now come on – answer the question, for Christ's sake."

John leant forward, elbows on desk, head in hands. He was silent for a long time then slowly looked up and across at Tom, dragging his hands down his face and resting his chin on them, as if his mind was too heavy to support itself.

"Yes," he said, in a quiet voice Tom would not have recognised had John not been there in front of him with his lips moving. It was a frightened, hesitant voice, alien to his character and position. "But even if there is a chance, there's nothing *I* can do to bring him back. That will be someone else, if it happens."

Tom looked hard into John's eyes, sensing guilt and sorrow, before the latter looked away.

"Just do one thing for me, please," Tom said. "Check that Jason's okay. Contact Bull Fort – or the admin centre there – and ask if he's alright. Say there's talk going round that he's ill or something and you just want to reassure his family. You can do that."

John didn't move or speak for a long time, still not looking at Tom. Then he reached for the phone.

"Janice," he said, making his voice sound as normal as possible, "you know how I love setting you these little challenges..." His secretary said something in reply. John went on. "Yes, I know you do, and that's why I keep on doing it. Well, could you get me through to Bull Sands Fort Holding Facility or – probably a better bet – its on-shore control centre?"

He listened as she read back the request.

"Thanks, Janice. And could you get past the security checks and questions before you put whoever it is through to me?"

Another comment prompted a genuine smile this time.

"Yes, I know you would have, Janice, but it makes me feel important when I get to ask."

His smile disappeared with the return of the receiver to its cradle.

"And that's all I can do, Tom." He seemed composed again. "Wheels will have to turn in their own good time – if they turn at all."

They sat in silence, waiting for Janice's call. It took almost five minutes. John grabbed the receiver, writing down a name on the pad in front of him as she put through the call. Tom could just about hear the deep male voice speaking a clipped greeting.

"Desmond Pritchard here."

He waved his arms to attract John's attention and mimed the words, "Can I listen?"

John nodded, putting his forefinger to his lips to indicate silence, before pressing the Speaker button.

"Mr Pritchard? John asked. "You're the Immingham Receiving Facility Manager?"

"Speaking," boomed the voice. "Chief Superintendent Mackay?"

"Yes, that's right. Sorry to bother you, but I wonder if you could help me…"

"If there's anything I can do, sir."

"Thank you, Mr Pritchard. It's about one of your prisoners on Bull Fort. Jason Midanda. There appears to be some information circulating that he…"

"Who, sir?"

"Jason Midanda. He arrived there on the 10th June with a group of prisoners on passage from Guildford. His family have heard that …"

"Excuse me, sir. I've only been here a couple of months, so that was before my time, but I do know we don't have anybody of that name on the Fort."

John and Tom looked at each other, wide-eyed with surprise.

"I'm sorry, there must be some mistake, Mr Pritchard. I watched him from my office window get into the transport vehicle with the rest of the group and leave for *your* facility."

"Well, he didn't arrive here, Chief Superintendent," Pritchard said, with palpable irritation. "I can check if you like," he added, with all the assurance of someone who knows for certain he is right.

"Yes, please," John said. "It seems unlikely that he just got off on the way without anyone noticing, don't you think?"

He drummed his fingers on the desk as Tom got up from his seat and paced around like a caged animal. It took just a couple of minutes for the records to be consulted. John repeated his signal for him not to speak.

"Not here," Pritchard said, with obvious satisfaction. "Never has been, either. So your theory seems to be correct, Chief Superintendent. He must have got off on the way. Anything else?"

"Listen, Pritchard!" John shouted. "Don't go all smug on me! Don't you understand just how serious this is? A high risk prisoner has disappeared whilst in transit between my holding centre and yours. Right now, I don't care who's to blame, but let me be absolutely clear, I certainly *will* care once we've got him back and found out what has happened. And you'd better hope that the fault doesn't lie at your end. So I want you to get back to me in less than an hour, having spoken to *everyone* who was employed on the transfer from Kirmington to Bull Fort. Right? I'll check at this end from Guildford to Kirmington. Are you absolutely clear on what you have to do, or shall I get the Minister of Justice to phone you personally with the request?"

"Yes, absolutely clear, Chief Superintendent," he said, sounding like a man who suddenly knew his place.

"One hour!"

John slammed down the phone.

"Jesus Christ! What the hell's going on?"

Tom had stopped listening and was already speaking to Kim Lacey on his mobile.

★

Tom was sitting in room 36A of the GCJ, waiting for Jo Cottrell, when the return call came through. In the meantime, John's conversation had made a few connections in his mind. The visit by the judicial advisor the day after Jack and Jason's trial had ended, with the shocking and unexpected news of the shortness of time before their transfer to Bull Sands Fort for the start of their passage to Alpha. Then his inability to contact anyone of any influence at Westminster in the following days, as if an invisible barrier had been placed around them. And now the news that Jason had failed to arrive at the first destination on his route.

"Tom? What on Earth is this all about?" The sound of Jonathan Latiffe's voice was strangely comforting. "Kim's just dragged me off the floor of the House. She says Jason Midanda has escaped."

"Sorry, Jonathan, but that piece of information was just to make sure I *got* you off the floor of the House."

"You mean it's not true? Then what, for God's sake?"

211

"Jason Midanda *is* missing – or should I say, he's not where he's supposed to be. But I don't believe he's escaped. I think I know what's going on, and for the sake of our friendship, Jonno, I really hope you don't!"

There was a brief pause.

"You've lost me, Tom. I have no idea what you mean by that, and I certainly know nothing about Midanda except that he's supposed to be at Bull Sands. Are you telling me he's not there?"

"He never arrived."

"How so?"

"We don't know, but Chief Superintendent Mackay, here at Guildford, has contacted Immingham and been told Jason never got there. They're checking what happened at both ends to see what went wrong."

He could hear Jonathan stabbing the keys of his laptop as he listened.

"Tom, I'll do you the courtesy of not asking why the hell you're involved in this, and I'll chase it up right away from this end. According to my information, he should be on Bull. Not that I expect to be made aware of every change of plan for every prisoner in the country, but the record should be up to date, and that's where it says he is. Obviously a different record from the one Immingham has access to. So tell me, what do you think has happened?"

"I think there are some very influential people who feel that Jason is a bit special."

There were a few moments of silence before Jonathan spoke.

"Let me know what Mackay turns up, Tom."

The phone went down abruptly, just as John burst into the room. He was breathing heavily and paced around as he spoke.

"Apparently Midanda got as far as Kirmington. That's for certain, because he definitely got on the plane at Heathrow and he must have got off it there because it came straight back again with just the crew and the security guys on board. That's all checked out one hundred percent. But our friend Pritchard has confirmed that he definitely *didn't* arrive at Immingham Wharf; he wasn't on either of the coaches. So…"

"Either he really *did* escape or someone got him off the plane and sent him – or took him – somewhere else. Do you fancy setting Janice another little task?"

The two men were back in John's office. Janice buzzed them on the intercom.

"Sir, would you mind listening to this?"

They both went through to the small reception area annexed to John's office, where Janice was sitting at her cluttered workstation holding the handset of her desk phone.

"I can't raise anyone at Lochshore. I'm getting a pre-recorded message asking me for a code – listen."

She pressed the speaker button then redialled. A digitised alien-sounding voice was activated.

"Security filter. Enter six-digit alpha-numerical code. Code will change in... thirty-six minutes."

John looked at Tom.

"Does that usually happen?"

"No. Unless the system has changed since..." His voice trailed off.

"I've tried three separate phone numbers," Janice said, "all listed on our system as alternatives." She showed them the short list on the screen in front of her. "Same thing every time."

Tom took out his mobile and entered the three numbers on his contacts list. Then he scrolled through to another entry.

"Gordon Sutherland," he explained. "He'll know what's going on."

His face screwed into a frown as he looked at the display on his phone.

"Not working," he said. He tried again, then held the phone out for John to listen to the continuous high pitched whistle.

"Do you think it's some sort of communications black-out?" Janice suggested.

Tom went to redial and clicked on Jonathan's number, with the same resulting sound. He held it for Janice to hear this time.

"That's the number I called half an hour ago," he said. "It was okay then."

The phone on Janice's desk rang.

"Chief Superintendent Mackay's office," she said, then looked at Tom in surprise. "Yes, he's here. Who... Yes, right away."

She handed over the phone.

"Tom, it's Jonathan. Not sure why but I can't get through on your mobile – keeps telling me it's an unobtainable number. Anyway, I've just spoken to Grace. It seems likely that Jason Midanda was taken straight to Lochshore. Grace says she can't be absolutely certain – which I'm not sure I believe – but she understood there was a plan to do that; for what reason she couldn't or wouldn't say."

Tom looked at his watch to check the date.

"The next group will be on their way to Alpha, won't they? They're the last ones for this platform, right? They'll have just left – a couple of hours…"

"That's the other thing. According to Grace they left at just after eight o'clock last night. The trip was brought forward because of intelligence about possible terrorist action. I've tried to check with Lochshore but there's a security filter in place. I'm trying to find someone here to explain what's going on. I can't get hold of Harding or Weller at the moment." He paused. "Look, Tom, I don't know whether Jason's still at Lochshore, on Alpha, or aboard PTV2, but it might be for the best, anyway. Getting it over with. Katey can put it behind her and move on…"

Tom wasn't listening. He thought he knew exactly where Jason was and why the vessel had left early.

"Okay, thanks, Jonno. Let me know when you find out anything else." He hung up and turned to John.

"We need to talk – right away."

John nodded. "Thanks, Janice," he said, following Tom into his office.

"We have to do something, John. I have a strong feeling that Jason Midanda is on that boat and that the change of schedule is somehow linked with Kadawe's arrest. Don't ask me what the connection is – I haven't a clue, only a feeling. But once he's on Alpha, there is no way of getting him off. If there's a possibility he's innocent, then he has to be stopped. If he's confirmed as guilty at some future date, I'll personally row him over there myself."

"I understand, Tom. I'll do what I can, make some calls. But I can't promise – in fact, I don't think… Just remember, Tom – and believe me, I don't like reminding you at a time like this – but you were prepared for this. In fact, you prepared everybody *else* for this.

Some innocent souls lost along the way – an acceptable risk, you said. And, anyway, we may never know, after what's happened with Kadawe today, whether Jason was innocent or not. What we know for certain is that right now – officially – he's still guilty as charged."

Tom had stopped listening.

"Can I use your phone?" he said. "In here, in private?"

"Yes, I guess so. But you won't be able to pull any strings, Tom. Leave that for me to try."

"It's a private call to someone who won't be interested in all this."

John left the room.

Tom finished the call ten minutes later, checking his watch; 12.20 pm. The PTV would be sixteen hours into its journey with another six to go at the most. That should just about be okay.

John was sitting on the corner of Janice's desk.

"DI Cottrell is ready to see you," he said. "Room 36A. Can you find your way back there?"

"Okay, I'll go straight away."

★

It was a few minutes after 1.00 pm when Tom turned into the Terminal 1 car park at Heathrow and made his way on foot to the secure private charter area. He wondered whether he would get much further. By now, they would realise at GCJ that he was not in the building. It was three-quarters of an hour since he had left John's office, supposedly en route to meet Jo Cottrell less than a minute's walk away. He could not imagine the DI's patience allowing more than ten minutes to elapse before chasing up her errant interviewee. The re-dial button on John Mackay's phone would reveal his current destination – something Tom hadn't thought about when he had contacted Josh Wilcox.

At the check-in lodge, he succeeded in convincing the guard to let him through using his Ministerial ID Card – albeit invalidated – along with a story about his continuing to work at tying up loose ends at the personal request of the Prime Minister. He was surprised and more than a little dismayed when it worked, especially in light of the recent publicity he had been attracting. He made a mental note, when all this was over, to email Ruby Weller, the Minister for Security and Counter Terrorism. But right now, it meant that the alarm had not yet been raised back in Guildford, or at least they had not worked out where he was heading.

Josh Wilcox was waiting for him at the departure gate. The pilot was in his late thirties; tall, tanned and muscular. The premature greying of his close cropped hair did nothing to detract from his good looks.

"Fuelled up; cleared for take-off at thirteen-fifty hours," he said, checking his watch. "You've cut it a bit fine; if we're not taxiing in about thirty seconds they'll cancel our spot. And what was all that about a parachute? Suddenly developed a fear of flying, have we?"

"No, just rediscovered a love of parachuting."

"In which case, you've chartered the wrong plane, buddy. You need to book 'Jump-for-Joy' through one of the Charity Event websites."

They climbed the five steps into the Cessna Citation Sovereign, Tom pulling them up behind him, and both settled into the cockpit. They were in the air in less than five minutes.

"Next stop North Connel," Josh said. "ETA in sixty-five minutes at fifteen-oh-six hours. Shame about Cheryl."

"What about Cheryl?" Tom asked.

"She's not here. And how come you only needed me as far as Glasgow last time?"

Tom thought back to their last flight together, heading north with Mags, ultimately to the rug and the peat fire in Farcuillin Lodge. It took him a while to compile a suitably flippant reply.

"Because you're not good enough to land this thing on the side of a mountain, so we had to pick up a chopper on the way. Anyway, Cheryl kept complaining that you were leering at her."

Josh laughed. "She was right. Every chance I had." He paused and turned to his passenger. "Listen, Tom. I'm really sorry about… You know…"

"Yes, I know. Thanks, Josh." He was still wondering how he had managed to get this far without the alarm being raised.

Once they had reached their optimum altitude and cruising speed, Tom took out his mobile, checking his contacts for the three new numbers.

"Am I going to be informed of the purpose of this trip?" Josh asked.

"Just some private loose ends to clear up," Tom replied. "Is it okay to use my phone?"

"So you're *not* going to tell me," Josh sighed. "In which case, no, you can't use your phone…" Tom shot him a surprised look "…but you can use one of the in-flight handsets in the arms of the seats back there."

Tom smiled and squeezed Josh's shoulder as he left the cockpit and went through to the passenger cabin. Five minutes later he returned.

"I don't know what's going on, but it seems Lochshore isn't taking any calls. How the hell can a major establishment like that just take the phone off the hook?"

"Did you try more than one phone? Perhaps that one…"

"No, I put a call in to my apartment – got straight through to the answer machine. The problem's at their end."

Josh thought for a moment.

"Look, I can contact Lochshore helipad control, if you like. If there's a wider problem with site communications, that might not work either, but…"

"Yes, do it, Josh. Thanks."

Josh entered the frequency for Lochshore on the radio keypad in front of him.

"K38-dash-C, Wilcox Sovereign calling Lochshore control. Please respond."

Half a minute elapsed with no reply.

"K38-dash-C calling…"

"Not recognised." A crackling neutral voice with no inflection interrupted. "Repeat!"

Josh looked across at Tom with large questioning eyes and shrugged.

"This is K38-dash-C, Pilot Joshua Wilcox, out of Heathrow, flying Cessna Citation Sovereign, calling Lochshore; destination North Connel, ETA…"

"Not recognised. What is your current position and course?"

Josh checked a screen.

"Position north fifty-five zero-nine-one; west zero-one one-zero-six; cruising twelve thousand feet, speed four-nine-five mph; just changed course to current bearing two-nine-six degrees. Do you copy?"

There was complete silence for almost two minutes, then the robotic voice again.

"Directive. Change course immediately through one-thirty-six to new bearing one-sixty degrees. Return to Heathrow. Do *you* copy?"

The emphasis on the word 'you' was the first indication that it was a human being on the other end of the link-up. Tom looked across at Josh and shook his head. Josh looked a little uneasy, but met the challenge head-on.

"Negative. Maintaining course. Have received no indication of contravening airspace regulations or restrictions. Please identify. Is this Lochshore control?"

Another silence, longer this time.

"You are designated call sign 'space invader'. Change course immediately. Return to Heathrow. Do you copy, space invader?"

"Copy but do not accept. This is routine charter flight to North Connel. Maintaining course and changing frequency. Out."

Josh punched a new set of data into the keypad.

"This is K38-dash-C, Pilot Joshua Wilcox, out of Heathrow, flying Cessna Citation Sovereign, destination North Connel airport, calling North Connel control, ETA in twenty-five minutes at fifteen-zero-eight hours. Request permission to..."

"Space invader, this is your final warning, change course; return to Heathrow."

Josh turned to Tom looking more than just a little uneasy now. Tom remained calm and focused. Neither spoke for a few moments. When he broke the silence, Josh's voice was unsteady. "I don't know about this, Tom. There must be something serious going on. I'm turning back..."

"No, you're not!" Tom's remark came out more aggressively than he had intended, betraying his own anxiety. "Look, Josh. They can't expect to push people around who are just going about their normal business without telling them why. Keep going – please."

Josh continued to look at him and then shrugged.

"Okay, we'll keep going for now until we get some sort of

explanation. But in the final say-so, *I'll* decide what we do. Okay?"

Tom did not reply but looked ahead leaving Josh to decide how to respond to their 'final warning'.

"By the way, I noticed back there that you do have a parachute?" Tom said.

"Two, in fact; one here as well." Josh pointed under his seat. "You're thinking in case we get shot down?" He gave a hollow little laugh.

"No, in case I need to get off before you turn back."

★

Over Moffat they turned due west to circumvent the air traffic around Glasgow and Prestwick airports. At the same time, 180 miles away, two Typhoon F2s from the Quick Reaction Alert Force at Lossiemouth in Morayshire screamed into the air. Climbing at a rate of 1,000 feet per second, it took just half a minute to reach their optimum cruising altitude of 30,000 feet, at which height they could achieve an airspeed of over 1,300 mph, taking them to Lochshore in less than six minutes. Each carried a payload of four ASRAAMs – advanced short-range air-to-air missiles. They wheeled south-westwards.

The tracking station on Benbecula picked up the Cessna as it reached the south end of Kilbrannan Sound, between Arran and Kintyre, and turned due north. Within a few seconds the station captured precise details of its position, bearing, altitude, speed and transmitting frequencies and fed them directly into the Typhoons' navigation system, locking the Eurofighters onto their prey to ensure they came together at the earliest possible moment. It also established a direct plane-to-plane radio link between the hunters and the hunted.

★

The now familiar voice informed them of their situation.

"Space invader, copy this. You are being tracked by two Eurofighters whose task it is to ensure you comply with this directive. They are already airborne and are due to intercept you in seven minutes. You are to alter course immediately and return to Heathrow. You have been identified as a threat to national security."

"National security!" Josh shouted, abandoning communication protocol for the moment. "Now I know this is a fucking wind-up!"

Tom was thinking hard, with his eyes fixed on their position in the centre of the downward-scrolling map on the display in front of him. They were leaving the Sound and passing over the tiny ferry terminal at Claonaig, heading towards Loch Fynne. He adjusted the image, zooming out so that he could see where they were in relation to the Western Isles and beyond.

"Okay," he said. "They've told us to change course, let's give them a bit of what they want. Take us nor'-west again, bearing... three-one-five. Go for it!"

"But that's..."

"Trust me, Josh, please. Just for a little while longer at least, until we find out what this is all about. You might want to change altitude as well; make it as confusing as possible for the chasing pack."

"Chasing pack?" Josh repeated. "That makes me feel really good!"

★

On the short drive back to the magistrates' court, Jo tried again to contact Tom Brown on the mobile number John Mackay had given her. And again with no success, the continuous note telling her for the second time that it was unobtainable. She wished she'd left a message for him with the receptionist apologising for having to postpone their interview.

Right now she was wondering whether she would live to regret the call she had made to Cat the previous evening, just as she was arriving at Etherington Place. It had simply been to reassure the singer with the news that Mickey would be appearing before the magistrate at 9.30 am the following morning. It had been harmless enough – except when she thought of what had just taken place on the steps of the magistrate's court and recalled Dagger's comments of three days ago; one remark in particular – 'She's only going to be safe if he's either exiled or dead.'

She got into the back seat of one of the police cars parked outside the court. Already in the car and waiting for her was the young woman whose statement had prompted the call she had received whilst waiting for Tom Brown in Room 36A.

"Mrs... Miss... Brennan?"

"Miss, but it's Alison – please call me Alison."

"Okay, Alison, I'm Detective Inspector Cottrell. You told Constable Medwin that you saw someone running from the scene of the shooting?"

"Yes, that's right. Well, I didn't know it was a shooting at the time. I was in Chapel Street – it runs parallel to Walcott Street – where the magistrates' court is – and I heard shouting and some people screaming. Then I saw two people – a man and a girl – running past the end of Chapel Street, away from where it was all happening. I went to see what was going on and got sort of rounded up along with all the other people and asked if I'd seen anything."

She paused and swallowed, looking away from Jo out of her passenger side window, as if she didn't want to say any more.

"And I understand from PC Medwin that you recognised the girl," Jo prompted.

Alison Brennan was silent for a few moments. Jo waited.

"Well, of course, I can't be absolutely sure..."

"You seemed very sure when you told the police officer."

Alison looked down at her hands, clasped together on her lap. She seemed to reach a painful decision.

"I *am* sure," she said, looking up at Jo. "In fact, I'm absolutely certain. It was Lilli Bo-Peep – you know – the singer..."

"Yes, I know who you mean," Jo said. "So she was running away from where you now know the shooting happened. Is that right?"

"Yes, that's right."

"And the man with her – did you recognise him?"

"No. I noticed she had someone with her, and then they were gone. I was just amazed at who it was. I'm a big fan, you know. I think she's brilliant. And she seems really nice as well. I hope I haven't got her into trouble."

"Could you see if they were carrying anything? Either one or both of them?"

"No, I didn't notice. As I said, I was just so amazed… I'm sorry I can't be…"

"That's alright, Alison. You've given your full statement to PC Medwin, I believe, along with your contact details. We may need to get in touch again. I'll just check but I think that will probably be all for now."

She got out of the car.

"Terry," she called across to Constable Medwin. "All yours."

She walked over to her own vehicle feeling sick.

★

Sixty miles due north-west of them, starkly visible against the abnormal clarity of the Atlantic horizon, the monstrous shape of Hotel St Kilda rose out of the sea, competing in its dramatic isolation with the vast cliffs of the island cluster of St Kilda itself twenty miles north-east of it. It had been over twelve minutes since the last contact from the mystery voice and Josh was about to take the Cessna around Berneray, at the southern tip of the Long Island, picking up the route of the transfer vessel somewhere ahead. Tom scanned the surface with the binoculars stored in the side pocket of the co-pilot's seat.

"There!" he shouted. "Ahead at one o'clock."

"Great," Josh said, without enthusiasm. He adjusted their bearing slightly to head directly towards the small shape in the middle distance.

★

The prisoner deck on PTV2 had been the vehicle deck of the *Long Island Princess*, before the vessel was modified for its new function as a key component of the government's plans for expulsion. The deck had an opening ramp at each end, previously for the 'roll-on, roll-off' of private and commercial vehicles; now for disembarking the prisoners in four lines of individual two-metre-square cabins, linked together like a giant flexible fairground ride, each line sitting, and moving, on a separate rail track. Down the centre of the deck were one hundred and ten cabins in two lines of fifty-five, back-to-back. Along each side, a line of forty-five, facing inwards. Each of the two hundred cabins had three solid metal sides and a fourth with steel bars and a sliding door. A walkway, two metres wide, ran between the lines of centre and outer cabins on each side.

The atmosphere on the deck was calm. The initial hysteria – fuelled by anger and despair as the prisoners were embarking and during the early part of the voyage – had long since subsided. Prison officers were in the process of collecting plates from the cabins after the passengers' final meal of the trip. Most were untouched, like the previous evening's meal, breakfast and the mid-morning snack.

In one of the forward-most cabins on the starboard side, the young man gripped the bars on the door of his cabin, paling the knuckles of his dark skin. He was tall and athletic, with broad shoulders and a slim waist. The expression of anxiety on his handsome features made him look older than his nineteen years. His normally bright eyes were glazed over in thought. He was thinking about a beautiful girl with long white-blonde hair. A girl he loved more then life, and who loved him with the same intensity. A girl he had made a promise to; a promise that someday they would be together again. It was a promise he was in the process of breaking.

He felt his stomach react as the vessel began to turn. It brought him out of his trance and he noticed an air of excitement among the guards coming and going onto the prisoner deck from above. He heard words exchanged in low voices; a few anxious expressions and darting eyes. The prisoner deck had become unnaturally silent as the others had sensed the tense atmosphere. Above the sound of the ship's engines, he thought he could hear those of an aircraft – getting louder.

★

The two men watched the huge vessel take shape in front of them as they closed in on it, unaware that twenty thousand feet above them the first Typhoon was rolling lazily on its axis and preparing to drop vertically into its deadly stoop.

There was no warning of its approach until the moment it plunged across the charter jet's flight path less than fifty yards in front of it. Its passing was so close that the sound of the plane reached them in the Cessna's cockpit as a deafening explosion at the same instant that it blotted out their view ahead.

A millisecond later they hit the fighter's jet-stream, rolling and bouncing as the waves of sound from above broke over them, smothering them in a blanket of noise. Both men cried out involuntarily in shock and momentary panic as Josh fought to steady the aircraft. As he brought it under control, the second fighter screeched past them even closer than the first and with the same thunderous, destabilising effect.

They scanned the airspace below and around them for the fighters' next move. Tom recovered quickly.

"It's okay, Josh. We'll be fine." He reached over and grabbed the pilot's shoulder to steady him, pointing ahead. "F2s," he said. "They're going away – look."

The Typhoons had climbed back to the same altitude as the Cessna and were racing away, one behind the other, half a mile apart and two miles south-west of them, on a bearing exactly the same as theirs. Tom and Josh watched them diminish in size until they had almost disappeared – the smallest of dots against the sky. Then they both veered right, still the same distance apart and with perfect synchronisation through a 180-degree arc, to bring them into a head-on approach with the charter jet.

"Jesus! Now what?" Josh's shaking voice was barely above a whisper.

Tom watched, fascinated by the tactical scenario unfolding in front of him and detached from its implications for his personal welfare. He was back with the military, appraising the enemy's performance.

The fighters were a single dot now, growing at an alarming rate directly in front of them. Tom looked down again at the vessel, no more than five miles away.

"I said – *now what?*" Josh was shouting this time. The dot had separated into two, a smaller one slightly below the other.

"Hold this exact bearing," Tom said. "They'll miss us."

The first Typhoon took shape, filled the cockpit windscreen and was gone, passing within a few feet over the top of the Cessna. The other passed below it, just as close, one second later. The fighters had crossed with the Cessna at a combined speed of around 1,600 miles an hour, and the noise was deafening as they flew through the rush of sound, accentuated by the shock of the turbulence.

As Josh stabilised the aircraft, Tom pointed down at the transfer vessel now within a couple of miles.

"Just hold this course and give me thirty seconds. Then you can do what you like."

He went through into the passenger compartment. Josh turned and watched in disbelief as Tom struggled into the parachute.

"What the fuck do you think…?"

The radio exploded into life.

"This is Seeker One to Space Invader. You have one minute to alter your course to return to Heathrow. If you do not comply, we will shoot you down. Do you copy? Over."

Josh hesitated for a split second only. "Copy. Will comply. Over."

"Timing from now, Space Invader. Staying in contact for countdown."

Josh turned his attention back to Tom.

"You're mad! What do you think you're doing?"

Tom was beside him again in the cock-pit looking down at the sea below as the Cessna was about to pass over the vessel.

"I'm getting off."

"The fuck you are! I'm turning back…"

"Forty seconds, Space Invader!"

"Hold it steady!"

Tom reached for the controls, grabbing Josh's hands and holding them in place to maintain their bearing. Bracing his feet against the floor, Josh pushed hard backwards, causing Tom to lose his grip and forcing him to back away from him. Tom lunged forward again, his forehead meeting Josh's elbow as he swung it at him with everything he had. Tom fell back out of the cockpit onto the cabin floor, momentarily dazed, and then scrambled to his feet, reaching for the exterior door on the left side of the plane. He grasped the locking wheel.

"Twenty seconds, Space Invader!"

"Tom, for pity's sake…"

Tom began to release the door, his face a mask of manic concentration.

225

"Ten seconds."

One of the F2s had taken up a position immediately behind them.

"Tom, please!"

"Five, four…"

Josh turned the Cessna to the right, diving as he did so. Tom fell away from the door, crashing against the spare seat behind him and catching the side of his head on the drinks cabinet. He struggled to his feet, but slumped down again onto the floor. He lay still for what seemed like a long time.

"Tom, are you okay?"

Josh's voice seemed to be coming from a mile away. He dragged himself into a sitting position, his legs stretched in front of him, leaning back against the folded seat. It was a full minute before he struggled to his feet and slipped off the parachute, before slumping into one of the passenger seats.

"Yes, I'm okay," he said, in a small voice shaking with both relief and disappointment.

"We've got company," Josh said.

Tom looked out of his window. On the left of the aircraft, one of the F2s was flying with its wing-tip almost touching that of the Cessna. He looked across to the right. The second fighter was in the same position on the other side.

"I thought only MiGs did this sort of thing," Josh said.

Tom leaned back in his seat. His head hurt where he had hit the cabinet. He closed his eyes.

★

Jo walked up the driveway of Dagger's apartment block where Tina was waiting for her near the entrance.

"Ready, ma-am?"

Jo nodded and Tina reached for the button on the panel beside the door. Jo's phone sounded.

"Hold on a second, Tina" She pressed the answer key. "Hello, DI Cottrell."

"Terry Medwin here, ma'am. Just thought you'd like to know, the bullets that killed Mickey Kadawe were fired from a high-powered rifle. Doc White reckons that from the angle of entry the killer was most likely on top of a high building around two hundred metres away from the court. That would possibly put him on the same street where Alison Brennan was when the hit took place."

Jo smiled and gave Tina a thumbs-up sign.

"Meaning, Terry?"

"Well, it's certain that neither of the two people she saw could have been involved."

"Thank you, Terry. You've made my day."

"One other thing, ma'am. The SOCOs found another bullet. Apparently three shots were fired."

★

Katey checked her mobile at the end of afternoon lectures at 4.00 pm and picked up the voice message from Catrina. She phoned her straight away.

"Cat! What the hell's happened?"

"Somebody shot him, Katey. Right there on the steps of the court. I think it might have been your dad!"

"Shot who? Mickey? My dad! Oh, please God, no! You mean you were there; you saw it?"

"Yes, me and Dags. We went along to watch him go in. You know to make sure he really was… Oh, I don't know why we went really, but…"

"Yes, but what actually happened, Cat? Did you see my dad shoot Mickey?"

She had slumped to a sitting position in the corridor, her back against the wall, both her posture and words attracting anxious glances from other students.

"Well, he was shouting at Mickey, right up close to him. That police woman, Jo, was holding him back. Then your dad's arm came up, like he was pointing at him and Mickey shot backwards. There was blood on his shirt and jacket. Then your dad and Jo sort of fell to the ground and… well, we turned and ran. I don't know why really."

"Was he dead – Mickey? Could you tell?"

"Not then, but we went back about ten minutes later and he

was still on the ground. There was no-one attending to him – I mean, like paramedics looking after him. Then some police started putting screens round him and we left again. I think he is, Katey. I think he's dead."

"Cat, I'll phone you back."

Katey was close to throwing up. She struggled to her feet and ran for the ladies' room, making it just in time and feeling a little more in control afterwards. Instead of calling Cat she phoned Guildford New Station, giving her name and asking to speak to John Mackay.

"Hi, Katey," he said, "how are you feeling? Look, I'm really sorry about everything that's happened. If there's anything I can do …"

His friendly greeting took her by surprise. Even so, her words came out in a torrent.

"I've just heard about Mickey Kadawe, about the shooting. I heard my dad was involved. Is he okay? I was so worried…"

"Slow down, Katey. He's fine."

"Oh, thank God! And Mickey?"

"Dead, I'm afraid. How did you find out about it so soon? We haven't released any details yet."

"Cat Thompson was there at the court. She saw what happened and phoned me; left a message. What was my dad doing there? She said it looked like *he'd* shot Mickey."

"Well he didn't. Long range shot from a high-powered rifle. I'm not sure exactly why he was there but he wasn't anything to do with the shooting. In fact, you've not long missed him. He left me a while ago to meet with Detective Inspector Cottrell. But tell me, Katey, did Miss Thompson say why she was there?"

"Morbid curiosity, I expect," she said.

"I suppose so," said John. "But I wonder how she knew he was going to be taken to court at that time. Ah well, I suppose there's some simple explanation. And remember, I meant what I said; if there is anything I can do, Katey, you only have to ask."

"Thank you, Mr Mackay."

She ended the call and phoned Cat.

★

Mags jumped up from her seat in surprise as the door to the front sitting room suddenly opened. She had been deep in thought and hadn't heard her daughter enter the house.

"God, Katey, you scared the life out of me." She checked her watch. "Has this stopped or have you? Don't you have a lecture this evening?"

"Listen, Mum. Something's happened. I don't know whether it's good or bad, but… Well, Mickey Kadawe's been killed. Shot dead outside the magistrate's court."

Mags flopped back down onto her chair, hand on heart. "How? Why?"

"Dad was there," Katey continued. "But he didn't do anything," she added, quickly, seeing the look of anxiety on Mags's face. "A sniper they think. But it's a wonder he didn't get shot as well – and Jo Cottrell. They were all close together when it happened."

"What on Earth was he doing, for God's sake?" Mags put her head in her hands. "What's going to happen next, Katey? When is all this going to end?"

"I don't know, Mum, but there's something else you need to know."

Mags looked up. "Something else?"

"Yes. It's about *why* – I mean, if Mickey *did* set up Jason and Jack – *why* he did it." She knelt down next to Mags and took her hands in hers. "It seems Mickey had an obsession – with me. I can see it now when I look back – all the little signs, the comments, the touching. Always when Jason wasn't there; when we were on our own. I thought he was just being – you know – mischievous, just having a joke. But I can see now that it was much more than that."

Mags looked at her, her brow creased in a frown.

"I'm not sure I see…"

"Well, when Dad said, right at the start, it was Mickey, I didn't even consider it, because there seemed no reason why he would do all that. He was best friends with all of us. But I can see it now. I've no idea *how* he did it, but I can understand why now. It all fits – he wanted me – so he had to get rid of Jason."

Mags was shaking her head

"Even if that's true, Katey, your father has to shoulder the responsibility for Jack's death. I don't know what Mickey Kadawe's original intentions were for Jack and Jason, but we *do* know they were *not* to send them into permanent exile. All his scheming and plotting – if it's true – must have started long before he knew they would be put away for good. If your father had not taken the – well, let's face it – unilateral stance on changing the sentencing laws for drug-dealers, Jack would be alive and serving a relatively short custodial sentence as a first offender. If he had listened to the public response to that change and climbed down off his bloody high horse…"

"I can't believe I'm hearing this," Katey shouted, springing to her feet. "That's absolutely irrelevant. The whole point, and the *only* relevant issue here, is that Jack wasn't the target – he was the collateral damage. It was Jason he wanted to get – to discredit him enough for me to ditch him or whatever. Jason – not Jack – and because of *me*. They were so close that Mickey would have had to involve both of them. No-one would believe that Jason could have been dealing without Jack knowing, so he needed to include Jack in the set-up. If anyone is responsible for what happened to my brother, it's me – and *you*, if you like. Not Dad – definitely not him! How many times did he tell us it was bound to end in trouble? 'Nothing but bad things will come out of this relationship.' Those were his exact words. He said them *over* and *over* again. And we just dismissed them – me, and Jack, and you! He couldn't have done more to avoid this. All he needed was for us – even just one of us – to listen to him!"

"Don't go all grown-up on me now, Katey," Mags said. "I have to blame somebody for all that's happened."

They were silent for a few moments, both breathing heavily with the emotion of the exchange.

"Okay, Mum, then make it me. Blame me – I can accept that. But think about your part in it as well. If you'd have supported Dad instead of taking the popular way out every time and siding with us no matter what, Jack would have been here with us right now, never mind serving a short custodial sentence."

Mags rose from her seat, eyes wide with hurt and anguish, tears welling, and rushed past her through the hall and up the stairs.

★

The Eurofighters disengaged as they crossed the border. One of the pilots saluted Josh just prior to his peeling away, grateful no doubt that they had not been required to take that terminal step. Tom came forward and slumped back into the seat next to Josh. He had remained silent in the passenger cabin since the F2s had settled on their wings, and it had suited both men not to speak following the drama of that critical moment.

It was the pilot who broke the silence.

"Would you mind telling me now what that was all about? What the hell were you hoping to achieve?"

Tom took his time to reply.

"There's someone on that vessel who shouldn't be there, I wanted to get him off."

"Get him off! How the hell were you going to do that?"

"Okay, then, keep him on. Make sure he stayed on and went back with the ship."

"Same question, Tom. How…"

"I just needed to get on board, that's all."

"That's *all!* Are you seriously suggesting that I could drop you by parachute onto that boat?"

"Not necessarily on – just near would have been okay. In the sea in front of it. They would have had to pick me up."

"Jesus, Tom. What is wrong with you? By the time they'd have got you – *if* they could get you – you could have frozen to death. Jesus Christ…!" He ran out of words.

"I just wanted to get to Lochshore, Josh. I thought I could get them to agree to it if I was there. You know, to contact the vessel and tell them to bring him back. I have friends… At least I *had* friends …" His voice tailed off. "The parachute was Plan B – I never really thought I'd need it, but we were so close."

He slumped forward, his head dropping in to his hands, feigning tiredness while trying to hold back tears. Josh looked across at him.

"Get some rest in the back, Tom, if you like. We'll be another twenty minutes or so. God knows what will be waiting for us when we get back. Police, army, both… What do you think?" Tom said nothing. "You can thank me when we get out of prison for doing you a favour. For saving your life."

Tom looked up.

"Better make it now, Josh, just in case it's a firing squad. Thanks for saving my life; I'm not sure about doing me a favour."

★

The young man was standing at the bars of his cabin door again. The sound of the aircraft engines was long gone and what passed for normality had returned to the prisoner deck. Whatever had been happening out there, it was over; lost to the past, like everything else. Even his identity.

He recalled his arrival at Lochshore three-and-a-half months ago, alone except for the driver and one guard seated beside him in the back of the armoured Land Rover. The two men had treated him with kindness and respect. They had even shaken his hand and wished him well before leaving him in the small anteroom attached to the Director of Operations' office.

Two minutes later he was standing in front of the Director himself.

"Name?" the man said.

"Jason Midanda."

Iain Campbell looked down at the sheet of paper in front of him on the desk.

"It says here you are Oliver Wangari."

"No, sir, I'm…"

"Oliver Wangari. Trust me; that's who you are now."

★

They landed as normal at Heathrow. Josh taxied to the holding area where the ground staff waited to manoeuvre the Cessna into its hanger. They passed through security with polite nods from all concerned, in spite of their eyes darting everywhere for a party of running officials bent on arresting them.

"Well, Josh," Tom said, as they reached the main concourse of the terminal. "From national security threat to a couple of nobodies in just over an hour. What do you make of that? Either something is seriously wrong with all this, or the knock on the door will come later."

232

The sound of *Every Breath I Take* told him his mobile was working again.

"Tom," Jonathan said. "You're reachable at last – good. Just to let you know, Jason *is* on PTV2 on its way to Alpha. Should be nearly there. Only he's not Jason Midanda any more, he's…"

Tom ended the call without speaking.

★

Robert Bogata glanced down at his computer then looked into the camera.

"We've just received a statement from the police about the incident earlier today outside the magistrate's court near the Guildford Centre of Justice."

He looked down again and read from the screen.

"Mr Mickey Kadawe, aged twenty, from Woking, was shot dead on the steps of Guildford Magistrate's Court on Walcott Street at nine-thirty am today. The weapon used was believed to have been a high-powered rifle fired from the roof of a building close by. Mr Kadawe was about to be charged under the Misuse of Drugs Act and police are not ruling out the possibility that the attack could have been related to this. However, investigations are at a very early stage. Mr Kadawe appeared recently as a character witness for the defendants in the trial of Jack Tomlinson-Brown and Jason Midanda who were both found guilty of dealing in banned substances at Guildford Crown Court on 26th May this year."

He looked up into the camera again.

"We'll keep you up to date with this story as and when we receive further information."

★

Jo Cottrell – along with all other interested parties – family and investigating officers – listened to the statement on the early evening news, noting the irony in the wording of the communication. The media release was absolutely true – in fact, it was the *whole* truth as far as it needed to go. However, the mention of Mickey Kadawe's testimony in Jack and Jason's case appeared to reinforce their

233

convictions rather than cast any doubt over them. His appearance on their behalf now seemed like a case of villains looking after each other, 'birds of a feather', a sort of honour among thieves – or dealers, in this case.

She also noted that there was no mention of Jack's death in custody or of his father's confrontation with Mickey on the steps of the building; nothing, in fact, that could lead to further questions about the event and a possible link to Tom or the fate of his son.

CHAPTER FOURTEEN

Friday; 25 September

Chief Superintendent Mackay sat silently in his chair, deep in thought, drumming his fingers on the desktop. Two deaths in custody in the space of four months; angry superiors and disenchanted subordinates; and the chilling echo of his Chief Constable's words on the day prior to Mickey Kadawe's arrest. 'Hold that thought,' Eddie Mills had said, when he, John, had suggested that getting rid of Kadawe would solve everything. Surely not in any way connected, but coincidental enough to make you think.

He checked his watch. Time to go, he thought – in every sense of the words. In a couple of hours he was due to take his wife, Andrea, for a celebratory meal – their thirtieth wedding anniversary. The table was booked for seven-fifteen. He'd never felt less like celebrating in his entire life.

He reached for the desk phone, buzzing through to his secretary, and starting in surprise when she answered.

"Hi, Janice, I didn't expect you'd still be here at this time."

"Well, I'm very hurt, sir. When have I ever left without saying 'goodnight' and, on Fridays, 'have a good weekend' as well?"

"You're absolutely right, Janice. I accept the admonishment with grovelling apologies."

"Well, I should think so, and you're forgiven. So, what can I do for you, Chief Superintendent?"

"Could you phone the Grand, please, and ask if they can put my dinner reservation back to eight o'clock, and then contact my wife and let her know. She'd shout at me but she'll be nice to you. I've just got a couple of things to do that won't wait."

"Very well, sir."

He replaced the receiver, opened Word on his PC and began typing on the blank page.

Wesley W Wallace
Chief Superintendent
Leicestershire Police

Dear Wes
I hope you are well. I appreciate that this is not how the new system of flexible resources is supposed to work, but I wonder if you would consider...

He stopped. He needed to think carefully about this. Putting it in writing might be unwise. He highlighted the text and pressed delete. But something else couldn't wait. He began to type again.

Edwin J Mills
Chief Constable
South Thames Region Police
Guildford

Dear Edwin
After much thought regarding recent events and my general feelings towards the position I have been so privileged to hold these many years, I have reached a painful, but inevitable decision...

★

Sunday; 27 September

Mags heard the faint tell-tale clang of the two heavy-duty bolts retracting on the main gates. She looked up from the newspaper, spread out on the breakfast bar in front of her, at the small monitor screen on the wall and watched as the camera followed the silver Audi R8 through onto the gravel drive and up to the house.

Tom let himself in and shouted from the hallway.

"Mags!"

"In here." She made her voice as light and friendly as she could manage, expecting to see that reflected in his face as he stepped through into the kitchen. Instead, she noted his sagging shoulders, lined features and an expression of something close to fear in his bloodshot, sleepless eyes. She slipped down from the bar stool and took a couple of steps towards him. He raised his hands to stop her.

"Tom, what?"

He rolled his eyes upwards and his lip trembled as he spoke.

"Mags, oh, Mags, what on Earth can happen next? What else can go bad?"

"For God's sake, tell me what's happened?"

"It's Jason." His voice was barely audible. "He's gone."

"Gone! Gone where?"

"To Alpha. They took him there three days ago; on Thursday."

She froze, then rushed forward, her arms raised, ready to beat him as hard as she could. But she was moving in slow motion. Tom's desperate attempts at comforting words were receding in a hollow distant echo, and then she was falling, into his safe arms, into a strong protective embrace, before the blackness overcame her.

It was over in a few seconds and she pushed him away, regretting the enforced intimacy of the moment, feeling he had somehow taken advantage of her. She turned and leaned against the breakfast bar, her shoulders hunched, her head hung forward.

"Please go," she said, in a whisper. "I'll tell Katey when she gets up. I'm not going to wake her, so there's no point in you staying."

"Mags, please. I'm so sorry." He stepped up behind her and she felt his hands gently gripping her shoulders. She shook herself free and moved quickly away from him.

"Just go!"

"She's my daughter as well, Mags. I want to be here when she hears the news. She will need both of us…"

"We don't need *you!*" she hissed. "I am asking you to leave because I *know* it will be best for Katey if you do. Don't you think you've done enough to destroy this family?"

She saw his eyes open wide in shock and pain. He turned and rushed from the house.

Jo followed David through the main bar to the restaurant as he ran the gauntlet of smiles, cheery greetings and a few clutching handshakes. They took their seats at what the waitress referred to as their 'usual table' and ordered drinks as she handed them a couple of menus.

"You seem to have a lot of admirers here, David." Jo gave him a mischievous smile.

"Yes, rugged good looks and perfect physiques seem to be very popular with the ladies of the village."

Jo smiled even wider. "But even so, they seem to like *you* as well."

David shook his head and rolled his eyes. "The things I have to put up with just to have lunch with a beautiful woman."

"Why, David…" Jo fluttered her eyelashes.

He looked at his watch. "In fact, she should be here any minute…"

Jo laughed. "Touché!"

The Dog and Duck in Meadow Village, where David now lived, was the venue for their frequent catch-up meetings. The pub dated back to when the village was first established around 250 years ago, although it had been extended a number of times since then, with the addition of a smaller bar at the rear and a large dining room to the right where Jo and David were now seated. There were open fireplaces in both bars and the dining room and the place retained its late eighteenth century feel throughout. It was friendly and lively and very much a 'local' for the four hundred or so residents of the village, a large proportion of whom, like David, had moved there in retirement. He leaned across the table as the waitress left with the menus and their food order.

"So how is Uncle Harry getting on with his hunt for the serial killer – or killers?"

Jo sighed and shook her head. "Hit a brick wall so far. He now accepts – *has* to accept – a connection between the shootings and the explosion, and the obvious link to Jack and Jason's case. And even the possibility that Kadawe was a key figure, which is a big climb down for him. But that completely destroys the focus of the search. We've no single MO to work with, and I can't think of a case on record where we have a murderer who takes out people with a neat head shot in lonely places on the one hand, and blows up buildings in rush hour on the other. Can you?"

"There must be good CCTV coverage at the place in Dorking – it being used by Witness Protection. Nothing from that?"

"Nothing helpful. They're all serviced apartments – the whole complex – so there are people going in and out all the time. Cleaners, wardens, maintenance workers and the like. Ironically, there was a routine inspection by someone from Witness Protection earlier that same day to review how the four guys were coping and to inspect their apartments – for drugs, weapons and such, I guess. He obviously wasn't looking for the right thing."

"And I'm sure you've got an explanation as to how Mickey could have blown up the place while he was in custody."

"By proxy – like the other killings. Set up before we picked him up. Catrina said he would never do stuff like that himself. That makes sense, doesn't it?"

"I guess so. What about the handsome stranger in the expensive suit?"

"Not shown up anywhere on camera. The only evidence we've got that he exists at all is one woman's description, based on a couple of glances. Harry's desperate enough to be checking his e-fit picture against known associates of Kadawe."

David shook his head. "So tell me about this insatiable desire of yours to get yourself killed."

Jo opened her eyes wide in surprise. "I don't know what you mean. Just an accident of timing..."

"I'm not just talking about the explosion. I mean the Kadawe thing, as well. Two narrow escapes in the space of a week."

Jo frowned. "You're not suggesting they're connected, are you?"

"Well, you're the conspiracy expert; you tell me. If they're not, then it's an unlikely coincidence. And explain how Mickey's death fits with your perversion theory?"

Jo took a long time to reply. "I can't. But from what Catrina told me about him, and from how scared you said Sammo was of him, *and* from what I saw in his eyes when I arrested him, I bet there's any number of people out there who would prefer him dead."

"There's a big difference between preferring him dead and actually killing him with a high-powered rifle from a few hundred yards."

"True, but if someone *did* want him dead, they might see that as their last opportunity. It could have been someone who was worried Mickey might do a deal for clemency by naming other dealers – that sort of thing. Desperate times call for desperate means and since the recent change, being caught dealing is as desperate as it gets."

"So you don't believe there is a direct link between Kadawe's death and the other killings?"

"Well, no. How could there be?"

David leaned further across the table so their faces were close together.

"I'm going to give you an alternative theory, which puts all the deaths together, including Kadawe's. Ready?"

Jo frowned. "This is the Tom Brown connection again, isn't it?"

"Yes, but actually it's only an extension of your own theory. Let's accept as a *fact* that Mickey Kadawe set up Jack and Jason. You say he set out to kill all the guys who helped him so they can never give him away, and his own death is just a coincidence. The alternative theory – based on the *same* fact – is that someone is looking to avenge Jack and Jason, in which case all those same guys would be on his hit list, *plus* Kadawe himself. In fact, he'd be top of it, wouldn't he?"

"I guess, but..."

"We now have *three* methods of execution. Close quarters head shot, explosive charge and long-range hit. So, Detective Inspector, who do we know who..." he counted on his fingers, "... believes Jack and Jason were victims of a set-up by Mickey Kadawe, has publicly promised to get *all* the people who were involved in it, was caught on camera close to the site of the murders in Cobham and Woking around the time they happened, *and* is capable of carrying out – or has the right connections to *arrange* to carry out – killings as diverse as the ones in this case?"

Jo remained silent with her thoughts for a long time before speaking.

"I probably shouldn't tell you this – although, God knows, I'm telling *everybody* things I shouldn't tell them at the moment – but

Mr Brown is formally a suspect in Harry's case. He now constitutes an official line of enquiry." She paused and shook her head. "Even so, I just can't see it. I mean, what you say makes sense, but I can't believe Tom Brown would do that. For a start, during the period of the killings he didn't seem to know *what* he was doing half the time."

"That's what he *says*. Nobody can be sure it's true."

"It's easy to believe, though, when you see some of the pictures and read the reports."

"Okay then, have you heard of dissociative amnesia?"

"Of course, but that's when people shut out part of their life after a traumatic event or experience. A defence mechanism when they can't cope with a memory – or something like that. It doesn't apply to someone conveniently forgetting bad things they're doing on a regular basis. He'd have to know what he'd done, wouldn't he, to remember who he'd ticked off his list and who was next?"

"Actually, recent research suggests that it *can* be relevant in such cases, where events are temporarily shut out and recalled later. I'm not saying it applies here but…"

"How do you know this?"

"I spoke to one of the other lecturers at the college."

The waitress arrived with their lunch plates.

"Anyway, time-out for now," David said, "in the interest of doing justice to the food, which I expect…" he beamed at the waitress "… will be as superb as always."

Jo gave an excellent impression of someone enjoying their meal, her mind all the time turning over David's comments in a failed attempt to dismiss them. As they sat with their coffees, he leaned forward again and patted her hand.

"Listen, young lady, going back to what I said about this desire to get yourself killed. Joking apart, I want you to promise me you'll be careful."

She smiled at him, touched, as always, by his concern. "That's very sweet, David, but I am *always* careful. That explosion thing – that was just bad timing, as I said – and it could have been much *worse* timing, in fact. That must have been set up before it was known Tina and I were going to be there. Don't you think?"

"Possibly, but it was the Kadawe death I was thinking of."

"Meaning I might have been hit?"

"Look, let me ask you this. Who do *you* think the third bullet was intended for?"

She blinked in surprise. "Well Kadawe, I assume, like the other two. What are you saying?"

"According to what you told me on the phone, the shots that killed him were about two inches apart in his chest. Is that right?" She nodded. "Pretty good shooting, I'd say. But the third shot hit the ground between his legs on the step where he was standing. So whoever it was couldn't have been aiming at Kadawe, could they? I'm surprised no-one has thought of that."

"Well, to be fair to Harry, he probably has. It's his case now. But you're not seriously suggesting someone was trying to kill *me*?" She found her voice was wavering slightly as she spoke. "Why would anyone do that?"

"Someone getting rid of everyone responsible for Jack's conviction."

"Oh, come on, David. You can't have it both ways. A minute ago, Tom Brown was the perp. But he was *there*, right next to me in the line of fire. He risked his life to shield me from any further shots. In fact, he might have actually *saved* my life, because I admit the third bullet must have passed very close to where we'd been standing. Surely if he'd set up the hit – whether it was just Kadawe – or Kadawe *and* me – he'd stay well out of the way."

David waited a few moments before replying.

"Here's a possible explanation. You met him the evening before, didn't you, and explained – or Maggie explained – that you'd been working to clear Jack's name at her request. He might have set up the hit before he knew that and then changed his mind about you as a target after hearing what you'd done; tried to call the hit man to tell him but couldn't get in touch with him. So he went along to the court, created a confrontation with Mickey so he could get to you and save you. You said yourself he seemed to know exactly where the shots came from even though you were there with him and didn't even hear them."

"But hold on; Tom didn't know when Mickey was appearing in court until I told him at that same meeting. So how could he have set it up beforehand?"

"Only if he already knew. If someone told him before you did."

Jo opened her eyes wide. "Jesus, David, don't ever accuse me again of being a conspiracy theorist. I'm just a beginner compared to you. How on earth can you imagine all that could be true?"

David smiled. "Quite simply because it fits the facts. *All* the facts."

★

Tom leaned forward in the leather armchair in the living room at Balmaha, elbows on his knees, hands supporting his chin, staring at the unopened bottle of malt whisky on the low table in front of him. His eyes stung with tears as he thought back to the moment a few hours ago when he had abandoned his family – again. Fleeing in a hurt rage, as if *he* was the injured party, and leaving them alone to face their horrendous disappointment.

He should have stayed, had the steel to face Mags down and comfort his daughter. It was his duty – and also his *right*. He had not even given himself a chance to tell them of his attempt to save Jason – ill-conceived and doomed to failure though it was. Surely knowing he had been prepared to take such a risk would have convinced them just how much he cared for them all – including Jason; showing them his willingness to put his own life in danger for their benefit. It was too late now; the opportunity had passed.

He reached forward and pulled the cork from the bottle.

CHAPTER FIFTEEN

Four weeks later

Saturday; 24 October

Tom awoke midway through the afternoon lying on his back on the floor of someone's bedroom. He was wearing only his boxer shorts. He knew he had never been in the room before, nor could he remember any of the circumstances that had led him there. Par for the course, he thought; standard routine for his latest descent into the abyss.

He tried to move, but his limbs would not react. He felt as though he was clamped in his current position.

"Hello!" he shouted, his voice barely carrying to the half-open door. He rolled onto his stomach, struggling into a crawling position as he felt the foul taste rising in his throat. He scuttled across the room on all fours to what he could see was a small en-suite, but failed to make it all the way and threw up on the tiled floor, sweating profusely and crying in his shame.

"Oh, God, Tom!" An angry voice behind him.

He tried to turn to see who had spoken but his neck was reluctant to respond, sending a searing pain up into the back of his head.

"Who…?"

"It's Grace. Here, let me help." He felt a hand on his shoulder.

"*No!*" Tom found his voice. It was loud and aggressive and Grace took a step back.

"Sorry," he said. "I didn't mean to shout. But just give me a few minutes, will you? Please."

"Okay. But don't go back to sleep. You need to start getting yourself together."

She turned and left the room.

He began a painstaking but unsuccessful effort to clean the en-suite and emptied a can of air freshener in an attempt to mask the evidence of his multiple visits. When, half-an-hour later, Grace returned and sat down in the wing chair near the window, he was half-sitting up in bed with the duvet pulled up to his waist.

Grace looked at him, shaking her head.

"The higher they fly…" she said.

"Where am I?" he asked. "What time is it?"

"You're in my spare bedroom, and it's…" she checked her watch, "… just after three-thirty."

"In the afternoon?"

"Well, yes." Grace looked over her shoulder at the window where the sun was streaming in through the thin curtains. "I haven't moved to Tromso, so it could hardly be the middle of the night, could it?"

"And what day is it?"

"Saturday. You haven't lost a full day yet, and you're not going to! I'm going to make sure of that."

"How did I get here? I don't remember anything."

"Probably a blessing. You were in the Penny Farthing last night, very much the worse for wear. Mouthing off as usual – the manager said – about your plans to free Jason. *Very* interesting – you must share them with me some time. Anyway, he asked you to leave and offered to call a taxi. Instead, you gave him my number and he called me." The memory of it seemed to further darken her mood. "No problem – it was only two-thirty in the morning, so naturally, I just jumped into my car – as you do when a really important fare comes along. By the time I arrived you had been moved outside and were sitting in a neat little pool of puke in the gutter."

"Grace, I'm so sorry…"

"And you should be," she snapped back, holding up her hand with thumb and forefinger a couple of millimetres apart. "I was that close to doing the fastest three-point turn in history and going straight back home."

"I wish you had," Tom had pulled the duvet up to his chin as Grace was relating the story, like the defensive action of a little boy being told off for doing something really naughty.

"Well, that's gratitude. You'd probably have died if…"

"Better that than you seeing me like this. Did you undress me?"

She sighed and rolled her eyes in exasperation.

"No, I phoned Oxfam and asked if they could come round and collect some clothes. I didn't tell them somebody was still wearing them, so they took them off you when they arrived. Saved a wasted journey."

"You're too bright for your own good – and certainly for mine," said Tom, trying to smile and managing a grimace instead.

"Yes, of course I undressed you. You were covered in sick, for a start…"

"Oh, please! Spare me the details. Hey, you didn't take advantage of me, did you?" It was his best stab at a joke.

"What do you think? I'm the ice-maiden, remember? And anyway, the only thing of any use to me certainly wouldn't have been working."

Tom tried another smile and was more successful this time. They remained silent for a while before Grace spoke again.

"Would you like a cup of coffee or something? A sandwich?"

Tom winced.

"Please don't mention food," he said, "but I'll take the coffee, thanks."

"Black?" Grace stood to leave the room.

"White, no sugar, please. Oh, and where are my clothes? Did you manage to save them?"

"All washed and dried. Ready when you are."

"What, my leather jacket as well? You didn't wash that?"

"Of course, and it was fine until I put it through the mangle and then … well, I'm sure you'll be able to claim on the insurance – *and* for the mobile phone."

"You *are* joking?"

"Look," said Grace over her shoulder as she left the room, "If you're going to continue asking me stupid questions then I'm not going to answer at all."

She closed the door behind her. Tom half-expected to hear the sound of a bolt sliding into position on the other side.

★

When Grace arrived with the coffee, Tom was in the shower. She put the tray down on the dressing table, noting that his clothes were still where she'd placed them – his jeans neatly folded on a small clothes maiden with his socks, and his shirt, clean and pressed, on a hanger on the back of the bedroom door. She sat down again in the wing chair to await his emergence from the en-suite.

In spite of herself, she found it impossible not to be impressed with his physique when he appeared, looking much fresher now and the well-defined muscles in his arms and shoulders flexing as he dried his hair with the hand towel. Even after months of neglect for his fitness and general condition, he remained well toned and with only the slightest hint of surplus weight around his waist.

She was aware also that Tom had recovered enough to notice what she was wearing – a low off-the-shoulder summer dress, short enough to reveal a great deal of bare flesh below as well as above it. His eyes seemed to be all over her and she noted that his boxer shorts were totally inadequate to hide the involuntary reaction to his appraisal. Lifting his jeans from the maiden, he turned away to step into them, hopping clumsily around before succeeding in pulling them on into place.

He sat, bare-chested, on the dressing table stool to drink his coffee, trying hard to look as though he was enjoying it. He managed half the cup, screwing up his face with every sip before standing up and reaching for his shirt.

"Thank you, Grace – for saving my life. I really *am* grateful, you know. And – of course – I'm sorry for all the inconvenience and... mess." He nodded towards the en-suite.

"Well, I won't say you're welcome in case you take that literally and do it again. And anyway, before you disappear, someone's got to clean my car – inside and out – and it ain't gonna be me, pal!"

"Oh, God!" He flopped back down onto the stool, his shirt still unbuttoned.

"It's okay," she said. "Only teasing. I had it valetted this morning, but you can pay for it at least. He charged me twenty and I gave him thirty. He deserved it, given the appalling working conditions."

Tom closed his eyes, as if trying to avoid picturing the scene.

"Look, I'd best be going," he said, fastening his shirt and tucking it into his jeans. "Can I have my un-mangled jacket, please? My wallet's in there – I'll give you the thirty – and the taxi fare, of course."

She gave him a long look while Tom sat down again and pulled on his socks, grimacing each time he leaned forward.

"Tell you what," she said, finally. "I know you can't face the thought right now, but you will need to eat something. Why don't you stay – relax – watch TV – whatever. I've got work to do this afternoon, so I'll be leaving you for a while, but I'll get something light we can share later when I get back. After your exertions last night and today, you can't have anything left in your stomach at all."

"No, really, I must…"

"I insist. The least you can do is be polite and accept. And anyway, you don't know where I've hidden your shoes."

Tom smiled.

"Okay, thank you, I accept. But only if you let me pay for whatever you force-feed me with. Deal?"

"Deal," she said. "Just stay out of my drinks cabinet while I'm out."

They engaged in an awkward smiling hand-shake and she left him to change her clothes before leaving for Marsham Street.

★

He sat for a long time in the chair she had vacated in the bedroom, trying to piece together snippets of memory from the previous evening. He remembered arguing with one of the barmen in the club – something to do with his annoying a young couple sitting next to him at the bar. Then a noisy confrontation – much later – with two doormen, leading to his being asked to leave, soon after which the request had been physically enforced. And, in between, meeting someone he knew – or thought he recognised – but whose identity escaped him for the moment. As the pieces fitted together, an excruciating picture of embarrassment and indignity emerged.

After a while, he moved through to the living area in an attempt to arrest the mental reconstruction, worried about what it might fully reveal. The room was large and rectangular, one end furnished with an expensive oak dining suite and bookcases in the same polished wood along the whole of the end wall. In the other half of the room, three easy chairs and a long sofa – of different styles but in the same fabric design – were positioned round a low rosewood coffee table. Two large floor-to-ceiling windows looked out onto the Thames and the London Eye directly opposite.

He wandered around, studying the collection of Peter Brook limited-edition prints on the walls and examining ornaments, with no real interest in them other than their ability to distract. Eventually he came to rest in a wing chair next to the coffee table on which was a selection of fashion magazines along with a single book; one he instantly recognised.

He picked it up.

"*The Meek's Inheritance* by George Holland," he read allowed. He turned it over to look at the author's picture on the back cover. And then it came to him. It had been George – last night – the person he hadn't been able to remember. He screwed up his face in a frown. George in the Penny Farthing! Surely not? He stared at the photograph, the sight of his friend's face reminding him of their penultimate meeting three weeks ago…

Jad's funeral had been a brief and unremarkable affair. It seemed ironic to Tom that a man who had once – and relatively recently – been just about the most famous person in the country should have so few in attendance at his final appointment in this world. It made sense to keep it quiet, of course, rather than prompting the Press to manufacture a wave of emotion to sell a few more papers. He was, after all – officially anyway – just a convicted murderer who had died in prison after a long illness. But even so, the occasion seemed inappropriately understated for the stature of the man to whom they were bidding goodbye.

It was also the last time he had seen his wife and daughter, although he remembered at the time he had not felt in any way that he was actually *with* them. They stood together – he, Mags and Katey – but they could have been on different planets. Tom was tearful and morose; Katey – understandably, perhaps – mostly indifferent; but Mags seemed to be in a world of her own, deep in thought and, it appeared, totally removed from the ceremony she was attending.

The service had taken place at the same chapel close to where, three years ago, Jad had been arrested when he was visiting his mother's grave. Others present at the small gathering included the brigadier who Tom had met on his first day as Home Secretary, a Captain Drake, and an attractive young woman accompanying a young man in a wheelchair – all associates of Jad in his professional role, he was informed. All four appeared unaffected by the occasion and Tom put this down to their attending through a sense of duty rather than a genuine feeling of bereavement. The only person there – other then himself – who appeared to be truly moved by the loss was George Holland.

A week to the day following the funeral, Tom and George had been the only mourners present when Jad's ashes were interred in Alma's grave.

Now he remembered. It *wasn't* George he'd seen last night – the man in the bar area standing on his own and watching him. Tom had picked his way through the crowd and greeted him loudly, only to be told he was mistaken.

"It's not George, it's Mike," the man had said, "but I know who you are and I'm very pleased to meet you."

"Have a drink, anyway," he'd said to Mike.

"Just going actually, but perhaps some other time." They'd shaken hands, and the man had turned and left before Tom could respond.

He looked at George's photograph on the back cover again. Then he turned the book over and opened it at the first page, which featured just the title. In the middle of the next page was the dedication:

'For, and in eternal memory of, my beloved Irene.'

He turned to the Foreword. The book was a copy of the first edition, and this section comprised, verbatim, Jad's speech from the dock at his trial at the Old Bailey three years ago.

He thought back to those early formative months of the New Justice Regime. Jad's killing of the Brady brothers – leaders of the brutal Cullen Field gang; the euphoria on the estate that followed their demise; the way that it had snowballed in the national Press; his own exploitation of the mood to further his ambitions for changes in the justice system. He recalled the passionate – albeit, one-sided – 'Justice or Law' debate at the council offices where 1,600 people had crammed into the three function rooms, and which had launched

George Holland on his national tour to engage people's support for radical change. Then, the tragedy of Irene's death, caught in the wrong place and accidentally gunned down outside the Dog and Duck in Meadow Village by the same Cullen Field gang, bent on revenge and targeting George for his outspoken condemnation of them and their kind.

He closed the book and turned it over again to the back cover, to the picture of the man he believed was the *real* hero of the NJR.

★

It was mid-evening when Grace returned, her noisy entrance jerking Tom out of a shallow sleep. He picked up George's book, which must have fallen onto the floor when he dozed off.

"I'm sorry for being so late," she said, heading straight for the kitchen and the task of preparing a stir-fry for their meal. "You must be starving. What have you been doing?"

Tom got up from his chair and followed her through.

"Reading Mr Holland's book," he said. "Well, dipping into it, anyway. Amazing that I have never read it before – I should be ashamed of myself – *am,* in fact. Especially when I'm mentioned in it so many times – and you, too, of course."

"Well, you're welcome to borrow it, if you want. I keep that copy out, but I've another one that I got George to sign for me."

"Okay, I will, thank you."

"If you've recovered enough to face a glass of wine, there's white in the fridge behind you and red in the rack next to it. I'll have a glass of Pinot Grigio, please."

"You really spoil me, don't you?"

She paused for just a second. "Make the most of it," she said, and then carried on stirring the mixed vegetables in the wok.

★

Grace had changed back into the dress she had been wearing earlier, and was seated on the sofa across the low table from him. She had kicked off her shoes and curled her legs underneath her. Tom was on the chair where he was sitting when she returned from work.

251

He felt recovered after his meal and was nursing his third glass of wine.

"You know what this reminds me off," he said. "That time at the Canoo restaurant in Düsseldorf. After the meeting. We were sitting like this with a Beck's each waiting to be served. Reggie had gone to the loo and…"

"Well, that's just kind of ruined it for me."

Tom laughed. "Not for me," he said. "We were just staring at each other. You looked fabulous – just like you do now."

"Why, thank you." Grace raised her glass to him. "Yes, I do remember. It was *really* freezing outside, wasn't it?"

"Yes, we must have been mad to walk there from the hotel."

They sat in silence for a while.

"Then later, back at the hotel," Tom said, "when Reggie had gone to bed, there were just the two of us again and I had the chance right then… Do you think I'll get another chance?"

"Where do you think this is going, Tom?" Grace's voice was full of steel.

"I was just thinking, that's all. Thing's could have been so different between us."

"How? Do you mean if Sir Joseph and Lady Winchester had never had a daughter?"

Tom frowned. "That's not what I meant at all."

Grace got to her feet and began to pace around.

"Okay, what *things* then?"

"Well, you know…If…"

"Yes, *things* could have been different, but opportunities to *make* them different couldn't have been more plentiful. Christ, all you ever did was talk about it!"

"But I thought we agreed…"

"We never *agreed* anything."

"Okay, *accepted,* then. I thought we accepted it couldn't go further. Our positions, our careers…"

"Your wife!"

"Come on, Grace. You knew I wanted to. I couldn't have made it more obvious."

"I'll tell you what was obvious, Tom. That we had a *real* relationship – not consummated – but real. You gave every

252

impression it was just a matter of time – you knew exactly what message you were sending out. And this against a background of your darling, hyphenated spouse trying her best to undermine you with every public opportunity – radio interviews, magazine articles, even vox-pops at international conferences – and no doubt during all that time giving you no sex. Then she clicks her fingers and two years of growing expectations are just wiped out. 'Guess what, Grace; Maggie doesn't think I'm so bad after all. Isn't that wonderful?' Well, no, it's not, actually. It's fucking pathetic!"

She was breathing heavily and still pacing, back and forth behind the sofa. Tom remained silent for a long time.

"Perhaps you're right, Grace," he said. "You probably did have every right to expect something more. In which case, I'm sorry. But let me ask you something that's none of anyone's business but yours. We've known each other for – what – five years – probably longer. In all that time, I have never asked you *anything* about your private life."

"But that's about to change."

"Yes, because you're making out to be a victim here; a vulnerable, lonely girl, looking for love…"

"I've never said that…"

"Who's been wronged by some frustrated married man, neglected by his wife, who has taken advantage of her, et cetera, et cetera. Well, I'm sorry, but you are *nothing* like that. You described yourself as the ice-maiden earlier. Now why is that? *I've* never called you that; I've never heard anyone *else* call you that. So it must be how you see yourself. You are a spectacularly gorgeous woman and you could have just about any man you want. So, tell me why you've never had a relationship for as far back as anyone can remember. Unless your partner is the most understanding person in the world, because I can't recall a single occasion when I – or Andrew or anybody else – needed you for something and you weren't available.

"And another thing. As I recall, this so called 'relationship' of ours wasn't exactly love at first sight. For a number of years, you didn't show any interest in me at all…"

"I'm not sure what's relevant in all this," Grace interrupted. "You asked me if there was any chance of shagging me and I was just pointing out that you've had more than enough chances already. Which raises the question – what's stopping you? Answer – you're listening out all the time for the next finger-click in the hope that Maggie's going to suddenly call you back."

Grace continued pacing and shaking her head. Then she stopped, as if she'd reached a decision, and leaned on the back of the sofa to look him in the eyes.

"I suppose there's no harm now in telling you this. I have not been in a relationship for over twenty years. On that occasion, it was someone I met attending a seminar in my last year at Cambridge. He was a young AV specialist talking to a group of students doing media studies as an optional extra. He was great-looking, a bit of a rebel, cool and dangerous, and every girl in the group fancied him like mad. We decided to have a competition to see who could be the first to lay him. Cut a long story short, it was no contest. I was the only one he was interested in and he invited me round to his apartment-cum-studio."

Grace walked round from behind the sofa, sitting down again and tucking her legs under as before.

"He was a *fantastic* lover. For over an hour on a thick fleece rug on his living room floor, I made it over and over again before he finally came himself, so far into me I thought I'd choke."

Her eyes had been burning into his. Now she dropped them to look lower and he became aware of his mounting excitement.

"I'm glad you're getting off on this, Tom, because now is where it gets a bit nasty. On the strength of that hour of frenzied sex, I knew I loved him; I wanted to be with him all the time. I had never felt like that before – or since for that matter." She paused, her face clouding over. "Then, just as he rolled away from me, the door leading through to his studio burst open and four guys – all with their dicks out – came rushing through, whooping and yelling. One of them was actually on the point of ejaculating, his eyes rolling in his head. My guy had set up a camera so they could watch everything as it happened on a TV screen in the next room."

"Jesus!" Tom was shocked, but Grace's revelation only fuelled his excitement. He could picture himself in that room, in front of the TV, watching this beautiful woman squirm and writhe, squeal and moan. He found his own eyes dropping now to her tanned legs, imagining them thrashing around in her throes of ecstasy. He looked up into her eyes again, finding it impossible to read her expression.

"The bastard! That's sick!" he said.

"Yes, you'd have hated having to watch that, wouldn't you?"

"Oh, come on, Grace…"

"It doesn't matter. I grabbed my clothes and rushed out. Pulled on my jeans and shirt more or less as I was running away, with all five of them out on the landing behind me shouting the most obscene stuff after me. And I've never been in a relationship since – never even *wanted* to be. Until I crossed the line with you – *wanting* to be, I mean. An unfortunate accident."

Tom didn't speak for a while.

"Christ, Grace. I'm so sorry. What did you do?"

"I went to see my friend and he sorted it out. He went round with six of his rugby chums in ski masks and smashed the place up, including his AV equipment, and bounced him off a few walls. Turns out – my lover revealed under torture – that he had a recording of our tryst, which he willingly handed over in exchange for the preservation of his kneecaps. He also very kindly agreed not to go to the police – still thinking about his kneecaps, no doubt."

"Useful friend to have."

"Yes, I met him when I was a fresher and he was completing a post-doc in politics. I started going along to his evening lectures and he sort of took me under his wing – to prepare me for great things, he said."

"*Only* his wing?" Tom smiled.

"Oh, yes. He was only interested in my mind – nothing else. Still is, in fact."

"Still is?"

"You know him, I think. His name's Andrew Donald."

Tom sucked in his breath. It was his turn to get to his feet and pace the room, his mind going back to his last meeting with Jackie Hewlett. Something she said had started him thinking at the time, but now her words crystallised into real meaning – 'I get the feeling that Andrew has some sort of hold over Grace and that everything you say to her goes straight back to him.' He stopped pacing and leaned on the back of his chair, staring into her eyes.

"So it's true. You *are* Andrew's spy. You tell him what people are thinking and saying and – no doubt – do whatever he tells you to do. It's a debt of gratitude; for saving your pride twenty years ago."

Grace laughed out loud. "A debt of gratitude! Oh, Tom, you are priceless – if that's another way of saying incredibly naïve. It has nothing to do with gratitude."

"What then?"

"Andrew kept the recording. He told me he'd destroyed it and was sure it was the only copy. Then years later, he wanted to recruit me at the start of his political career. I already had doubts about his integrity, so I said no thank you. He pointed out that I owed him; I said he had such a good time beating the shit out of the guy that I thought we were even. He said something like, 'I wasn't the only one who had a good time with him. You seemed to be really enjoying yourself.' I said what did he mean and he said, 'Well I'll check again tonight, but the last time I watched it you appeared to be having a great time.' So, guess what, I changed my mind about taking the job…"

"The bastard! And he's been blackmailing you ever since?"

"Not exactly. Subliminally, perhaps, but, I don't think it's ever been mentioned since then. I mean he's never demanded anything from me other than to apply myself to the ever more rewarding jobs he's given me. Right now – according to some people who know about these things – my position is probably the most powerful job in the government apart from the Prime Minister. If all blackmail victims suffered like I have, people would be placing full page notices in the dailies advertising for blackmailers. So, however it started, I've enjoyed the ride; no complaints."

"And has he still got the recording?"

Grace beamed across at him. "As far as I know. Would you like me to ask if you could borrow it? I'm sure you'd enjoy it more than George's book, if your reaction when I was telling you about it is anything to go by. Is it still there?" He stepped out from behind the chair and she lowered her eyes again. "I thought so."

Tom was breathing heavily now, the tightening in his trousers beyond his control. Grace looked up into his eyes.

"I could make that go away, if you like."

Tom strode across to the sofa; Grace swung her legs up and

lay down on it to receive him. Their bodies came together with a furious urgency, their clothes almost disappearing in the desperate frenzy. There was no struggling for early restraint, like his love-making with Mags, just a surging ambition to discharge his passion.

It was over quickly for him; he had hardly entered her, finding her surprisingly unreceptive to his thrust, as if choosing to resist him at the last moment. His hardness quickly receded after his release and he lay, breathing heavily, with Grace rigid beneath him, her arms by her sides. He pulled away from her looking down into eyes which glared back with a steely satisfaction and without a trace of tenderness.

"Grace, I..."

She pushed him away, grabbing her dress from the floor. Turning away from him, she pulled it on over her head before standing up and smoothing it down over her hips and thighs. Tom followed her lead, dressing quickly, his eyes on her all the time.

"Grace, I..." he repeated. She walked out of the room, returning a few seconds later carrying his jacket. She held it up for him to inspect.

"There you go," she said. "One un-mangled leather jacket." She held it out and he took it from her.

"My phone...?"

"In the jacket."

"Grace, for God's sake. Say *something*."

"You mean like, congratulations – you *did* get another chance and this time you took it. Oh, yes..." she held out her hand, palm upwards, "... thirty pounds for the valeting."

He fumbled with his wallet, not sure whether she was serious about the money. She took it from him, anyway, edging him to the door.

"Look, Grace, perhaps it was just the wrong time – you know. Perhaps..."

"No it was the right time – the *only* time, in fact." She opened the door and gestured for him to leave. He stepped through onto the outside landing. "Bye, Tom." She closed the door.

CHAPTER SIXTEEN

Sunday; 25 October

It was a quarter past midnight when he arrived back at Balmaha.

He picked up the phone on the table in the living room and heard the intermittent tone telling him he had messages. The first was from Daniel Hastings.

"Tom, not sure whether you've taken on a new lawyer. If so, I wish you'd told me. You've missed three meetings with me now – the last one on Friday. I can't represent you if you won't talk to me. If you *have* got another lawyer, then please ignore this call and wish him the best of luck from me – he's going to need it. Otherwise call me *right away.*"

The phone had been slammed down. The second message was from another close friend; one who had only recently been in his thoughts.

"Hi, Tom. This is Jackie. I guess you must have forgotten, but we had a date today – Saturday – at your apartment at two o'clock. If you remember I had Lucy with me in London and she'd asked if she could see you again. She's a big fan, like I told you. Don't worry about missing us – I know you've had a lot going on recently. But something really weird happened. When you get this message, can you phone me right away? It doesn't matter what time."

Tom looked at the wall clock. Nearly half past midnight, but she did say right away. He took out his mobile and scrolled through to Jackie, pressing the call key. The phone was answered on the third ring.

"Hi, Tom, thanks for getting back to me."

"Jackie, I'm *really* sorry – twice. First for not being here earlier and second for how late this is."

258

"That's okay. You're forgiven – *twice*," she said, with a little laugh. "I just needed to tell you this as soon as possible. When we went to see you today – well, yesterday – I buzzed you first from outside the building. But remember you gave me the security code for the outside door, so when you didn't answer, we let ourselves in and went up to your apartment. Just as we got there, this man came out of the other apartment. He said 'Hi' and then he sort of froze and shot off down the stairs."

"What did he look like?"

"Well, I guess you could say tall, dark and handsome. Heavy-rimmed glasses; well dressed…"

"That's my new neighbour, Oscar Strange. Strange by name and strange by…"

"Yes, but Lucy recognised him. She said he was the man who abducted her from school." He could detect a trembling in Jackie's voice.

"Is she sure? I mean, it was, what, three years ago?"

"That's what I said, but she says she's certain. She actually said, 'Now do you believe me when I told you he was dishy?' Do you remember her saying that at the time?"

"Yes, I do. But that would be an amazing coincidence, wouldn't it? I mean, particularly in central London."

"I've said all that and she still insists. I just wanted to check if you knew him – his background and such. Has he been there long?"

"Just a few weeks and I'd never seen him before then. What do you want me to do, Jackie?"

"I'm not sure; I'm still thinking about it. I have to say, it's put me on edge a bit. Because if it *is* the same person, then it might *not* be just a coincidence. The last time, when he took Lucy, it was to warn me off the NJR task force, and now he suddenly re-appears right after my appointment as Home Secretary. I know that's not logical because he couldn't have known I was coming to see you, so he could hardly have been lying in wait for me, could he? Even so…"

"And you say he *ran* away?"

"That's right – a sort of cheery 'Hi', then suddenly he was off."

"Okay, Jackie. I'll drop in on him and see what I can find out.

But I don't think you need to worry. You're right; there's no way this could be anything to do with you. And listen, we must fix up another meeting and I'll make sure I do better next time. Can't be standing up my fans these days. I haven't got that many left to lose."

Jackie gave another laugh, more relaxed this time. "Well, you'll always have two here – that's a promise. Night, Tom. Take care."

"Night, Jackie."

Tom put down the phone and walked back out of the apartment and across to his neighbour's, banging hard on the door with the flat of his hand.

"Oscar! I need a word with you, right away!"

At twenty minutes before one o'clock on a Sunday morning, there was no reason to suspect anything unusual about a young, good-looking man with – seemingly – plenty of money, not being home. It was arguably the norm rather than the exception. But, somehow, Tom thought otherwise – he had a feeling that there was nothing very normal about Oscar Strange.

He stepped back, looking at the keypad on the wall just to the left of the door handle. Four digits, like his own; ten thousand combinations – including four zeros. A piece of cake for the neat little memento in his bedroom from his Special Forces' days. If he could find it.

It took him less than five minutes; a small flat plastic rectangle the size and shape of an iPhone, with a screen on one side and a foil membrane on the other. Placing the membrane against the keypad he held down a button until a line of four digits appeared on the screen. He placed the device in his pocket and entered the numbers on the pad, hearing the lock release. He turned the handle and stepped into the hall.

The light came on automatically with the opening of the door. He looked along the corridor, seeing that all the doors off it were closed. There were no clothes on the hall stand and no shoes on the low shoe rack next to it. The apartment was a mirror image of his own so the main bedroom would be the first door on the left. He opened it and looked in. The room was bare, with not a single piece of furniture in it. The next door opened onto the guest bedroom – also empty. He walked along to the large living room at the end, knowing what to expect.

Tom retraced his steps across the landing to his own apartment. He took out his mobile to phone Jackie, and then thought better of it. Nearly one o'clock; she would almost certainly have gone to bed after she'd spoken to him. Tomorrow would do – or rather, later today. He went through to the master bedroom, placing his leather jacket on a hanger behind the door and emptying the pockets, as he did every night – at least when he was sober – before placing the contents – wallet, keys, and such – on the dressing table. In the side pocket, he felt something like a piece of card.

He took it out. A square beer-mat, with the same picture on both sides – the silhouette of a penny-farthing bicycle on a light background. Above the picture on one side were the words, *Jason – there is a way,* and below it, a mobile phone number.

★

He waited until early afternoon to make his first phone call, knowing that, unless something unusual happened, John Mackay never missed the morning service at his church.

"Tom, this is a surprise. How are you?"

"Sober, if that's what you mean."

"That's not what I meant, but I'm glad to hear it." There was a long pause.

"Is everything alright, John?"

"Yes, yes, of course. Just surprised to hear from you that's all. So, to what do I owe…?"

"A favour, please, John. Could you get someone to check out a gentleman called Oscar Strange – at least that's what he calls himself. Early thirties, I'd guess, about six-one, slim, dark hair, sometimes wears glasses. I've no idea what he does or what his background is, only that he's my new neighbour across the hall in SW1 and his behaviour is consistent with his surname."

"In what way?"

"Well it's difficult to pin it down. He seems to be spying on me – waiting for me virtually every time I arrive at or leave the apartment. But last night I went over to see him about something and found the place empty – and I mean *empty*. No furniture,

261

clothes, food, any sign at all that anyone has been there, except for a couple of chairs, a coat stand and a few pictures in the hall."

"How did you get in if he wasn't there?"

"Well... the main door hadn't closed properly. I just... sort of ... pushed it open."

"Yes, I'm sure you did. Look, couldn't he have just moved out while you weren't there? That's the obvious conclusion, isn't it?"

"But the other thing is, Jackie Hewlett and her daughter saw him coming out of his apartment yesterday when they were at Balmaha, and Lucy swears it's the same guy who abducted her three years ago. And Jackie said that when he saw them, he sort of ran away."

"But she was just a little kid when it happened. She's hardly likely to remember him."

"She was eleven, actually, and if it *was* him, that would explain why he ran away – you know – worried that Lucy would recognise him."

"Much more likely he was just doing a final check on the place, making sure he hadn't left anything behind. Probably had a taxi waiting downstairs or he'd parked on double yellows or something, and *that's* why he was in a hurry."

"But why would he leave the things in the hall? It's like he just put a few things there so if anyone came to the door it would look like the place was occupied."

"I don't know, perhaps they came with the apartment. I think you're getting paranoid, Tom. I'll look into it, but if he's using a different name then there's nothing to lead us to him. By the way, how's your defence coming along? You do remember I'm one of the chief witnesses for the prosecution, don't you? It's not what I want, but..."

"I know, John, and don't worry, you won't be called. I'll be pleading guilty, as I'm sure everyone will expect. I just want it out of the way – assuming I won't get a custodial sentence, of course."

There was no reply.

"John, are you still there?"

"Yes, yes, I do think that's best all round. Get it over with as quickly as possible as you say. It's going to be bad enough for you and Maggie – and Katey. By the way, you do know I'm working my notice at the moment?"

"*Really*? No I didn't know that. Unless I've been told and forgotten – which happens a lot."

"I told Maggie and just assumed…"

"I see. Well, we've not been in touch lately. You've not resigned because of what happened with Jack, have you?"

"I guess that came into it, but…"

"That was hardly your fault, John. I'm so sorry."

"Not *just* that. A lot of other stuff as well. I planned to leave with immediate effect but Eddie Mills asked me to work a couple of months longer so I'd still be in post for your trial. He thought it would look a bit untidy otherwise – and I agree with him on that. But it's about the only thing we have agreed on for a long time, so I'm ready to go."

"Well I hope everything goes well."

"And with you, too. In the meantime, I'll look into the strange Mr Strange."

"Thanks, John."

He put the phone down and picked up the beer mat again.

*

The 800 or so acres of Hampstead Heath sit astride a sandy ridge which is one of the highest points in London. Designated a Site of Metropolitan Importance for Nature Conservancy, it is a magnet for city dwellers keen to sample a taste of the outdoors. It had been an adventure playground for Tom, his sister and two brothers; and he and Mags, with their own children, had been regular visitors.

As always, he enjoyed the walk from Hampstead Heath station past the wide diversity of properties on Parliament Hill Road – all of which seemed to complement each other – before making the small step through the gap at the road end into a completely different world of meadows, trees, and ponds, culminating at the top of the Hill itself with the wonderful vista of the capital. Tom looked across at Canary Wharf, the Gherkin, the Shard and St Paul's, their angles and curves picked out by the late afternoon sun; and his old place of work, the Houses of Parliament, albeit somewhat obscured by the surrounding buildings.

The bench that was the terminus of his journey was over to his right and although he now knew the identity of the man waiting for him, he felt himself wanting to call out George's name in greeting. Mike Needham, chief designer of Platform Alpha, got up from the seat to receive him with a warm handshake.

"I get asked all the time," Mike said. "'Aren't you the guy who did those speeches and wrote the book?' I even had someone recently telling me how sorry they were about Irene. I just said thank you – I thought it would be too embarrassing for him to find out I wasn't Mr Holland."

"I'm surprised we haven't met before," Tom said. "Amazing our paths haven't crossed."

"Well they did cross, actually, but that was all, shortly after the platform was in position. I was leaving Alpha on the chopper you arrived in. The weather was closing in so it was a quick turn around – no time for introductions."

"So tell me, what's a prominent engineer doing mixing with the riff-raff in the Penny Farthing – me included."

"As I said on the phone, I went there looking for you."

There were a few moments of uneasy silence.

"Let's sit down," Mike said. "I see you came prepared." He nodded at the small hold-all Tom was carrying.

"As instructed," Tom said. "Where exactly are we going?"

"Before I tell you, let me start with a confession." Mike paused, as if choosing his words carefully. "I didn't follow orders exactly with the design of Alpha. That is, I didn't follow *official* orders, which were to ensure there was no way off the platform. The facility was intended as a one-way trip, with no possibility of retrieving anyone once they were on there. Then someone decided otherwise. Don't ask me why. I don't know who made the decision and I can't reveal who it was who told me about it. So no point in asking. Okay?"

He glanced at Tom, who was looking straight ahead, eyes staring. "Okay," he said. "For now, anyway."

"The new directive was to create a means of entry which could only be accessed from *outside* – leaving it open for egress, but *not* capable of being accessed from within the structure. Fairly simple, but because as few as possible had to know about it, the hardest part was getting it done involving only two people other than myself. We

had to pretend we were strengthening part of one of the columns –
anyway, you don't need to know that – yet."

"Yet?"

"Until you decide."

"Until I decide what?" Tom said. "Can you get to the point,
please? What's this about?"

Mike frowned back at him. "Let me ask *you* a question. You said
you read my note about twenty times. In light of what I've just told
you, what do you think it means?"

Tom thought for a moment, then repeated the words on the
beer mat. "'Jason – there is a way.' You're telling me we can get
Jason off Alpha."

"Bravo," Mike said, with a smile. "So you have to decide
whether you want to try. Not now..." He held up his hands as Tom
opened his mouth to speak. "Not until you've spoken to the man
who can help you achieve that. So, do you want to meet him?"

Tom didn't speak for a long time.

"Tell me, Mike. How did you know where to find me to give
me the message?"

"My nephew – a regular member of the Penny Farthing riff-
raff. He mentioned a week or so ago that you'd been in there a
few times telling everyone you were going to get Jason off Alpha. I
asked him to let me know when you were next in and on Friday I
got a text from him saying..."

"Next question – why? Why do you want to help me get Jason
back? You're taking one hell of a risk telling *anyone* about this secret
way in, let alone a drunk who doesn't know what he's doing or
saying half the time. I'm sure you're aware of my recent record of
instability."

Mike breathed out and leaned back on the bench before
replying.

"The reason for deciding to contact you *initially* was to find out
if you knew about the entry point. Because if you did – and *because*
of your recent record of instability, as you put it – there was every
chance you'd be telling everybody in the Penny Farthing about
it sooner or later. And that would blow up in the government's
face, wouldn't it? One of the NJR's cornerstone principles – that
expulsion is an irreversible step – turns out to be a lie; and revealed

265

as a lie by the man who, six months ago, went on television and forcefully restated that principle to the nation at the time of the changes to drug dealer sentencing laws."

"So you were concerned that I might be mouthing off about saving Jason because I knew I could?"

"Yes."

"That would make sense, Mike, if you hadn't just told me yourself. In fact, I didn't know about the entry site, so there would have been nothing to worry about. But I do now, so what next? I can't promise not to get drunk again and next time I talk about rescuing Jason, who knows what I might say? *I* certainly don't."

"I said that was *initially* the reason, and this is where it all gets a bit – well – mushy, I'm afraid. Because I found myself wanting to help you. I've followed your political career from the time you left the military, through your first campaign for a seat in parliament and every step along the way. And I've since been back through your record in the Forces as well – shunning a commission to start at the bottom, time in Ulster, transfer to the Marines, then the SBS, youngest ever appointment to the full rank of colonel. Hero of Sierra Leone, Shah-e-Kot, the Al Faw peninsula. A shining example of courage, loyalty and integrity. It appears there's not a single thing wrong with you, Mr Brown. Somebody like that *deserves* helping, and I felt privileged to be in a position to oblige. There you go, I said it was mushy."

Tom said nothing.

"And if all that is too over-sentimental for you, then think of it as *you* doing *me* a favour. It's an opportunity to test the system. To gain entry, find Jason and get out again. To make sure the provision I made can actually work before we do the same on Beta."

"And what do we do with Jason if we get him back?"

"*We* don't do anything. Jason would be *your* responsibility – one hundred percent. And remember, he's tagged, so there aren't many places you can go where they can't find him. In fact, somewhere in the northern half of Scotland is probably your only bet. But you need to know the answer to that question before you decide to go ahead, because my man will want nothing to do with him afterwards."

The two men sat in silence.

"When exactly did you have this change of heart?" Tom said. "You know, from finding out what I knew to offering to help."

Mike smiled. "About five seconds before I wrote the message on the beer mat and slipped it into your coat pocket."

Tom snorted a laugh and they fell silent again.

"So tell me," Tom said. "Who knows we're having this conversation?"

"So far, just three people. You, me and the man I just mentioned; the one who can help you. Help us both, you might say."

Tom got to his feet, picking up the hold-all. "Okay, let's go and talk to him."

Mike stood up and reached into his pocket, taking out a mobile phone. He held it out to Tom. "A present from me. Put your old one in there." He pointed to a rubbish bin next to the bench.

"Hey, just a minute…"

"Where we're going you won't need it, but more to the point, they can find you if you hold on to it. That's the deal."

Tom took out his mobile and looked at it for a long time before pitching it into the bin. He took the replacement from Mike and put it in his pocket as they set off back down the hill.

★

The jogger in tracksuit bottoms, running vest and trainers crested the rise and stopped at the bench. He was of average height, slim and muscular, with dark hair and a full, stubbly beard half-covering a hard, battered face. Over his right eye was a thin, horizontal scar, which showed up white against his tanned skin. He placed each foot alternately on the seat, leaning forward to stretch his other leg, repeating the exercise ten times. Then he checked his watch and sat down. After a couple of minutes he took a casual look round, and removed a cereal bar from his pocket. He ate it slowly, before placing the wrapper in the waste bin and picking up the discarded mobile phone. Then he set off jogging back the way he had come.

CHAPTER SEVENTEEN

Monday; 26 October

The slight change in the engine tone was enough to stir Tom from his sleep. He looked out of the passenger side window at rolling hills and clusters of trees in neat plantations, illuminated by a brilliant full moon in a cloudless night sky. The Range Rover swept round the large roundabout and swung left in a wide curve towards the low brightly-lit building.

"Where are we?"

"Abington Services," Mike said, pulling the car to a halt away from the other vehicles so it faced a grassy slope rising in front of them to a summit half a mile away. "Welcome to Bonnie Scotland."

"Scotland! What time is it?"

"Just after three o'clock."

"Last thing I remember was pulling out of a service station somewhere near Birmingham."

"Stafford – that was more than two hundred miles ago. You've been sleeping like a baby since then. I bet that's the longest proper sleep you've had for quite a while."

"Well, you're wrong there – I've had no trouble at all sleeping."

"I said *proper* sleep, as opposed to a drink-induced coma."

Tom shot him a glance. "Oh, I see. So you're my carer now."

He opened the door and slipped out, stretching and yawning, then walked across to the slope, looking up the hill. Mike got out of the car and joined him.

"Where the hell is Abingdon, anyway?" Tom said.

"Abington; south of Glasgow on the M74. Shall we grab a coffee and a sandwich?"

Tom turned and looked across at the welcoming lights. "Good idea." He set off towards the building; Mike grabbed his arm.

"You stay here. I'll get them. Can't have you being recognised. What would you like?"

Tom sighed. "Coffee, white, no sugar. Anything in the sandwich."

Tom got back in the car and Mike joined him within five minutes carrying a paper bag and two Styrofoam cups in a cardboard holder.

"Tuna mayo or ham and tomato?"

"You choose."

"Okay," Mike said. "I'll take the ham." He handed Tom the other sandwich.

"So where are we going? Or are we already there?" Tom asked.

"Ardnamurchan. And from there – well, that depends on you."

★

Mags picked up the house phone in front of her on the breakfast bar, checking the name on the display.

"Hello, Dan." She glanced at the time on the wall clock – 8.45 am. "You're bright and early"

"Hi, Maggie, I hope I didn't disturb you."

"Not at all. Is it about the case against Jack? Have you found out anything?"

"No and no, I'm afraid. No, it's not about that, because, no, I haven't found out anything. I am trying hard, though. Actually, it's about Tom. I know you and he are not... well... together right now, but I wondered if you knew where he was."

"I assume he's still in SW1, but I haven't seen or spoken to him for weeks now – three or four, I guess. Why, has he gone missing?"

"I'm not sure, but I need to contact him. We are eight days away from his trial and we haven't even talked about it yet, let alone prepared his case. I saw him six weeks ago and since then I've phoned him God knows how many times, and turned up three times at the apartment for pre-arranged meetings. He either wasn't there or he just wasn't conscious. I don't know what to do. Sorry to put this on you, Maggie. It can't be easy for you."

"Look, I'll make a few phone calls and get back to you. And

please keep pushing with the other thing. They can't just ignore what they found out about Kadawe just because the little shit got himself killed."

"I will, Maggie – I *am*, in fact – but there's a strong message of 'case closed' coming from all directions. And to save you time with the phone calls, I already spoke with Tony Dobson and George Holland over the weekend. Dobson hasn't seen him for six or seven weeks, and the last time George was with him was at the interment of John Deverall's ashes. That was about three weeks ago, wasn't it? From what I hear Jack's girlfriend might be a good starting point. He seems to be a regular visitor at her local in Woking. Sorry to involve you, Maggie. I just don't know what to do."

"That's okay, Dan. I'll do what I can."

★

George Street was teaming with the day's first wave of late-season tourists disembarking from a line of three coaches parked half on the pavement and causing chaos for the local traffic and pedestrians. Horns were sounding and people shouting, the whole scene in stark contrast to the tranquillity of the water and the stillness of the boats anchored in Oban Bay.

Mike picked their way through the melee to the roundabout and onto the one-way system leading to the ferry terminal. They continued past the large Calmac vessel taking on cars to their right, and out of town by the side of Kerrera Sound. A mile further on, they pulled off the road onto an area of hard standing and stopped at the shoreline facing a small inlet with a slipway in front of them and a stone jetty to their left. A fishing boat with a rust-painted cabin was moored against the jetty.

Tom got out of the Range Rover and stood looking at the hills behind them, aware that he was within a couple of miles of Lochshore. He thought again about his visit there earlier in the year, the helicopter ride to Hotel St Kilda; the bodies impaled on the wire and, later, his departure for Knoydart and three perfect days with Mags. Mike watched him and waited, as if reading his thoughts. Tom turned back and looked across at the boat.

"Your transport for the next lap," Mike said. "The cabin's

cramped and filthy; you can't see out of the windows, there's no heating, TV, phone, wifi, galley or cocktail cabinet – just a kettle. Other than that, it's not much different to any other executive launch."

Tom smiled. "I've travelled in worse; *and* with people shooting at me."

"Okay, let's go then."

Mike opened the rear door, taking out a small battered suitcase, and passing Tom his hold-all. After locking the car, he led the way along the jetty to the boat. The two men already on board, in hi-vis waterproof coats and black working trousers, were carrying out final checks on the deck-mounted fittings. Neither spoke or even acknowledged their presence. Mike leaned across to Tom.

"Don't expect any exhilarating conversation. We'll be lucky if they tell us where they keep the coffee and milk."

They climbed down the metal ladder attached to the side of the jetty and dropped onto the boat. Mike said a cheery "Hi" to their hosts and was rewarded with a muted grunt from one, who even extended them the courtesy of glancing in their direction. They slipped down the five steps into the cabin and sat on the hard benches across from each other.

"Well, there's the kettle," Mike said, nodding towards a shelf at the forward end. "Let's see if we can find the rest of the essentials."

★

Mags moved the easel round a little to capture more light from the window. She had started the painting of Farcuillin Lodge immediately after their return from Scotland and it had been standing untouched in her studio-cum-office at Etherington Place since the police raid. That was long enough, she thought. Now she was going to finish it.

The extension phone rang on her desk just as she placed her pallet and brush down on the work table. She checked the name on the display and grabbed the receiver, smearing it with paint.

"Hi, Dan."

"Hi, Maggie. Got your message. First chance to call back. Any luck so far?"

"Well, it appears he's still alive and still at the apartment, or at least he was yesterday."

"Not today, though, Maggie. He wasn't answering again, either the phone or the doorbell, and his mobile's going straight through to voicemail. Who have you spoken to?"

"Chief Superintendent Mackay and Jackie Hewlett both talked to him yesterday and Jackie's sure he was at Balmaha very early on Sunday morning. Well, he must have been because he was calling her back after picking up a message she'd left on the phone there. And he phoned John Mackay from the landline in the afternoon."

"You didn't tell Mackay he was missing?"

"No, just that he wasn't picking up my messages."

"I just don't know what to do. That's the trouble with representing friends. Anyone else, I'd just tell the court I'd done everything reasonable to contact my client. The police would then start looking for him. But I don't feel I can do that."

"Well, your loyalty does you credit, Dan, but you need to be fair to yourself as well. You have to make the court aware of a possible no-show before it happens. You can't just turn up a week tomorrow without your client."

"No, I suppose not. Can you think of anyone else? What about Megan?"

"Katey reckons Megan hasn't seen him for a good few weeks. He's not been to see Leila Midanda again either – he went there the day before Kadawe was shot. I could check out Jenny, his PA – ex-PA. She might still be in touch, I guess – doubt it, though. I'll get back to you."

Mags wiped her hands on a cloth and searched through the battered notebook on the desk next to the phone for Jenny Britani's mobile number. There was no reply, so she left a message asking her to phone back. Five minutes later, Jenny obliged.

"Hi, Mrs Tomlinson-Brown," she said, with obvious pleasure. "How are you?"

"Fine, Jenny. And you – what are you doing with yourself these days? Who's your lucky boss now?"

"I'm fine and keeping my fingers crossed at the moment. I've applied for my old job – PA to Mrs Hewlett. Been through all the tests and just waiting to hear."

"You mean you have to be tested to see if you can do the job you've been doing brilliantly for two years! That's ridiculous."

"Well, thank you," Jenny laughed. "You're very kind. But it's policy when there's more than one applicant – and there are *loads* for this position. But I'm hopeful." There was a pause. "Even though it won't be the same. No disrespect to Mrs Hewlett."

"It will be great, Jenny. She's a lovely person and I know the *ex*-Home Secretary would be delighted if you got the job."

"Thank you."

"And speaking of the ex-Home Secretary – it's a bit embarrassing this – I don't suppose you know where I could contact him. Things between us have not been all that good recently."

"I know and I'm really sorry about that, Mrs Tomlinson-Brown. I do hope it works out. But I'm afraid I can't help you. In fact, I've tried to contact him myself a few times. Just before he resigned, he said he'd be happy to be a referee for me. Perhaps he was just having a joke."

"I'm sure he meant it, Jenny. He's just been difficult to pin down recently. Can you remember when you last saw or heard from him?"

"It was a long time ago. Just hold on, please." Mags could hear the sound of fingers on a keyboard. "It was on 12th June, the day he was charged with… you know. He came along to the office in Marlburgh. Sorry I can't help."

"Thanks anyway, Jenny, and if you do hear from him, please let me know."

"I will – oh, I just remembered. I was talking to Josh Wilcox last week and he mentioned he'd seen Mr Brown on the day that drug dealer was killed. He said he'd taken him somewhere – didn't say where. I guess that was a long time ago as well, though, wasn't it?"

"It was, but it's worth a phone call to Josh. Thanks, Jenny – and keep me posted about the job."

"I will. Great to talk to you."

"You too. Bye."

Mags picked up the notebook again.

★

DI Cottrell jumped to her feet as John Mackay entered his office.

"Jo, please." He waved for her to sit down again. "Janice is following close behind with coffee and toasted teacakes." He beamed across the desk at her as he sank into his chair. "Might as well fuel my addiction before I have to give it up."

She gave him a sad smile.

"Don't look like that," John said. "My decision, remember." He sighed and shook his head, his face clouding over. "To be honest, Jo, I'm ready to go right *now* – today. I should be pulling out all the stops to help put this case of Harry's to bed before I leave. It does bother me that there's no push from any direction to get a result – certainly not from above. A multi-skilled serial killer on the loose and apparently no urgency to catch him. No progress at all for four weeks. Having said that, you're aware who's emerging as a prime suspect?" He took a deep breath and swallowed hard. "We've been checking his movements over the period of the killings from police and press reports but, to be frank, I've no stomach at all to take up the chase. Not after my role in what happened to Jack."

"You were only doing your job, sir," Jo said. "Anyway, I find it impossible to get my head round the fact that Mr Brown could be involved. There's no evidence other than circumstantial. No *material* links to any of the deaths."

"I agree, but as Arthur Conan Doyle said – through his great detective – 'when you've eliminated the impossible, what remains, however improbable, must be the truth'. I know we're not at the stage yet where we've eliminated everything else, but I have no desire to be around if and when we get there." He looked across at Jo. "Does that sound cowardly?"

"Not at all, sir. You've had a lot to deal with."

"Yes, but I'm paid to deal with a lot, Jo. I'm a big boy." He leaned back, forcing a smile and patting his stomach with both hands. "*Too* big, in fact... And this isn't going to help. Come in, Janice!"

The door opened and Janice backed through it, pulling a small trolley bearing a cafetiere, two cups and saucers, a milk jug, sugar bowl and a large plate covered in foil, which she removed to reveal the teacakes. John's secretary was in her mid fifties, petite, and with a pretty face under a neat bob of greying hair. She put the plate on the desk.

"Is this instead of lunch or will you be ordering that later?" she said, with a stern look which demanded the right answer.

"That rather depends on how many of these I get to eat myself."

Janice looked at Jo. "Please do him a favour and eat *all* of them."

The two officers laughed as Janice left the room. John poured the coffee and they each helped themselves to a teacake.

"Anyway," he said, "the reason for my wanting to see you is to let you know that your next assignment will be the same as your last one. Chief Superintendent Wallace has requested you back as soon as possible, and I have told him that you are available with immediate effect."

"But, sir, I've been working with Brighton…"

"I know, and I've cleared that with them. I feel we owe it to CS Wallace given that we reclaimed you almost immediately after you'd started there. It would look bad if we sent you somewhere other than back to him – look bad for the whole principle of flexible resources, in fact. I'm afraid, as much as we all like having you around, your job, for the most part, is to be somewhere else."

He leaned forward and smiled, his eyes twinkling and his whole body seeming to become lighter.

"And if you tell me you don't want to go, I'll have a quiet word with a certain detective sergeant in Leicester and then you'll have some explaining to do. Now do me that favour and eat a few more of these."

He pushed the plate over towards her.

★

It was late afternoon and the light was fading when the boat nudged up against the stone jetty next to the ramp at the Kilchoan ferry terminal on Ardnamurchan. One of the crew climbed up the four iron rungs on the jetty wall and secured the boat forward and aft with ropes thrown to him by his companion. Neither had spoken a word to their passengers throughout the trip, spending all five hours on deck, leaving Tom and Mike below with their coffee and their thoughts.

"There's our man." Mike nodded towards the figure in jeans and a light bomber jacket standing at the end of the narrow concrete walkway in front of them. As they set off towards him, he turned away, heading past the miniature grey-stone ticket office with its slated roof to the small car park beyond it on the left. They followed him to where he was waiting next to a battered dark-green Land Rover Defender.

The man was the same height as Tom and of a similar age and build. He had thick dark hair and the classic features associated with Hollywood movie stars in the nineteen-fifties and sixties. But most notable of all about his appearance were his eyes – ice-blue and unsettlingly intense. His greeting, nevertheless, was warm enough.

"Colonel Brown." He spoke with a refined American accent and held out his hand which Tom shook. "Welcome to the middle of nowhere. Please, climb aboard."

Mike had already got into the back of the vehicle and Tom climbed into the front passenger seat, placing the hold-all on the floor behind his feet. The man got in next to him, started the engine and turned the car left onto the road to the village.

"Excuse me," Tom said. "You are?"

"Kade."

Tom waited. "Well, that's a start, I guess. Kade who or who Kade?"

"Just Kade."

Tom gave a little laugh. "A bit John Wayne, isn't it?"

The man didn't reply, focussing on the road ahead.

They drove through Kilchoan – "the most westerly village on the mainland," Mike informed them – continuing for about five miles in the descending gloom along a single-track road, lined for much of the way by shrubs and trees which the headlights seemed to ignite, creating a blaze of brilliant early-autumn colours. A mile before reaching Ardnamurchan lighthouse they turned off north along a road which was little more than a track and which deteriorated rapidly from that point. It was a relief when they finally stopped at a wooden cabin a few yards off the road overlooking a white sandy beach. Tom could just about make out the shape of an Archer Class launch anchored fifty yards off shore in the small bay.

"Okay," Kade said, nodding towards the cabin and opening the driver's door. "Let's eat – then talk."

"Just a minute." Tom grabbed his arm. "Have we met before?"

"Definitely not."

"It's just that… Kade…It rings a bell."

276

"I see. Then he must still talk about me." He smiled at Tom's puzzled expression. "You'll work it out, Colonel."

★

Mags lifted the phone to the familiar voice.

"Maggie! What a surprise. Just got your message. How are you?"

"I'm okay thanks – and you?"

"All the better for hearing your voice. To what do I owe the pleasure?"

Mags gave a little laugh. "Well, it's about Tom actually."

"Awww! And I thought you were phoning to ask me to take you off somewhere. I'm devastated."

"Just behave yourself, Josh Wilcox! I'm a happily married woman." She paused, surprised at the words that had come out so naturally.

"Well, I'm *very* glad to hear it," Josh said. "How can I help?"

"I just wondered whether you'd seen him recently."

"How recently?"

"Well… today, preferably."

"No, not seen him for a while. Not sure I want to either after last time. Call me Mr Wimpy, but I'd just as sooner stay alive."

"I don't follow. What do you mean 'after last time'?"

"Well, you know – the strange case of the nearly-getting-shot-down-over-the-Atlantic."

"I'm sorry, Josh, but I haven't a clue what you're talking about."

There was a long pause.

"Oh dear, I hope I haven't spoken out of turn. You mean he didn't tell you about…" His voice tailed off.

"No he didn't – whatever it was! But *you're* going to tell me, *right now!* So fire away."

Another long pause.

"Josh! I'm waiting!"

"Okay… about a month ago, I got this urgent call from him, around lunchtime. Could I take him somewhere, right away – right *then*, in fact? He was lucky; I was free; so we set off, heading up to North Connel."

277

"North Connel? What for?"

"That's what I asked, but he wouldn't tell me at first, fobbed me off with some stuff about loose ends. Then as we got further north we were told to turn back because – get this – we were a threat to national security. Tom insisted we carried on but got me to change course and follow the prisoner vessel heading out to Alpha. Anyway, we spotted it and just at that moment we were attacked by a couple of F2s."

"Is this a wind-up, Josh? Because if it is…!"

"Pilot's honour, Maggie. I have never been so shit scared in my life. But wait for the big finish. They threatened to shoot us down and were within seconds of doing it just as we got over the vessel, and Tom – you won't believe this – gets a parachute from the back and starts to open the *fucking door* – sorry, Maggie – I'm shaking here just thinking about it. Anyway, just at that moment I tipped the plane over, he fell away from the door and then… Well, he'd missed his chance and he sort of calmed down."

Mags could hear him breathing heavily as if the effort of recalling it had exhausted him. She found herself lost for words.

"Maggie, are you still there?"

"Yes, Josh. I'm just… What was he trying to do, for God's sake?"

"He said there was somebody on the vessel who shouldn't be there and he wanted to get him off. I said how the hell did he think he was going to do that, and he said if he could get onto the ship, he could make sure this person stayed on when they disembarked the rest of the prisoners and bring him back."

"How could he possibly get onto the boat?" Her voice was now small and shaky. She could feel a wave of emotion rising inside her.

"Well, he knew he couldn't – not directly. He said if I could drop him into the sea just ahead of the vessel, they'd have to pick him up."

The wave broke, the phone fell to the floor, and she held her face in her hands, tears leaking through her fingers.

A long way off, she could hear Josh's voice, shouting in panic.

"Maggie! Maggie!"

★

On the shore side of the cabin, out of sight of the road, was a compact generator, which Kade started up as Tom and Mike went inside. The interior was well appointed, with two strip-lights on a flat boarded ceiling, a couple of convector heaters mounted on the end walls and a work top running the full length of the room on which were a two-ring camping stove, kettle and small microwave oven. A fridge under one end of the work top started purring as the power came on. The lights flickered into brightness above them. In the centre of the floor was a rectangular wooden table with four ancient dining chairs around it – one at each side. A door at the far end led through to what Tom assumed would be a store room and toilet.

Mike hooked up the stove to a Calorgas canister under the work top and filled the kettle from one of two large bottles of water sitting on a sturdy shelf next to the single window, which looked out onto the bay. He opened the gas tap, sparked the ignition, and within a couple of minutes the kettle was singing on the hob. The high-pitched sound of a small engine began to intrude on the generator noise from outside and Tom could see a medium-sized inflatable heading towards them across the still water from the direction of the Archer.

Kade stepped in through the door carrying a large cool box, which he placed on the table. He took off the lid and removed packs of sausages and bacon, eggs, two loaves of bread, butter, milk, cartons of juice and a clear plastic bag containing mushrooms and tomatoes.

"I don't know about anyone else, but I'm ready for my full Scottish breakfast." He glanced at his watch which told him it was 6.25 pm. "Ten hours late is better than never."

The engine noise outside sputtered into silence and the muted sound of footsteps on sand approached the door. The man in camouflage trousers and combat jacket who entered was huge – two metres high, with a barrel chest and immense shoulders and upper arms. His black hair was thick and tousled and his full bushy beard showed just a hint of grey. His close-set piggy eyes seemed disproportionately small for such a vast frame.

"This is Sergei," Kade said, "ex-FSB and your chef for the evening." He looked across at his companion and nodded towards the pile of food on the table. Sergei smiled and rolled his eyes in mock frustration; then, after shaking Tom's hand, he set to work.

＊

David pressed the pause button, temporarily sparing the two outlaws the precipitous plunge into the roaring river. He placed his recently-emptied shot glass on the table beside his chair and juggled his mobile out of his pocket just in time to answer it after checking the caller's name.

"Why do you always phone at the most exciting bits?"

"Not Liberty Vallance *again*?"

"No actually it's…"

"Butch and Sundance?"

"Got it in two. How do you do that?"

"I've no idea. I mean, it's not like you're predictable or anything, is it?"

"Not in the least. So, what news?"

"It's just to let you know, I'm going back to Leicester; with immediate effect, which means I start on Thursday; driving there the day after tomorrow. I thought we might get together on my way up. As it's a Wednesday you won't have to bunk off college. So, what do you think?"

"I think it's a great idea. Where shall we…"

"No, I mean what do you think about me going to Leicester?"

"Well, it's good, isn't it? When a FART's gotta go… and I would have thought that's where you'd want to be – not that I'm allowed to say *why*, of course."

Jo made no reply.

"Nothing's wrong between you and Seb, is there?"

"No, not yet."

"Not *yet*? He's going to be over the moon, isn't he? I thought you would be as well."

"Whether we are or not, I can't help feeling this is the beginning of the end for us. That's what I'm dreading most, to be honest."

"Sorry, I…"

"Well, I can't see us having a meaningful – let's say – romantic attachment if we're working together all day, *every* day, can you? That's hard enough to come to terms with because I *really* like him. But to not have that relationship, we're going to have to formally end it, and what is *that* going to be like when we're with each other all the time? I can't get my head round it at all."

"Well, speaking as someone who has a proven record of cocking up relationships, I suggest you learn from my mistakes and stick with him. No point in dumping him before you *try* and make it work. Then if it doesn't … Anyway, you're only there on assignment; you'll be somewhere else soon, no doubt, then you'll be moaning about not being with him."

Jo laughed. "Thanks, David. As always, you've said exactly what I wanted to hear. There's something else, though."

"Oh, God, really? I've got Paul Newman and Robert Redford hanging in mid-air over a waterfall here. Go on, then."

"It's what Johnny Mac said when he told me I was going back to Leicester – that Wes Wallace had asked for me again and he felt he couldn't say no – that sort of thing. But when I spoke to Seb an hour or so ago, he said Wallace had told *him* that Mackay had *requested* – a few weeks ago, actually – that he take me back as soon as possible."

"And?"

"Well… that's it really. But I've been working with the police and customs in Brighton for the last couple of months, and I thought – and I'm pretty sure Brighton thought – that that's where I'd be going next. In fact, it's been mentioned a couple of times – just sort of off-hand. You know – 'it will be easier once you're down here' – that sort of thing."

"My advice to you, young lady, is to rejoice in what has happened and stop looking for hidden agendas everywhere. In a couple of days you'll be back with Mr Carter, which is what you both want. What *exactly* passed between a brace of Chief Supers in order to achieve that doesn't really matter, does it?"

Jo took a few moments to consider before she answered.

"No, I guess not. Anyway, what about this nosh on Wednesday?"

"Well, I assume you'll go clockwise M25 to the M1, so I'm not sure what's – quote – 'on my way up'."

"I was thinking I'd go *anti*clockwise and drop off in Meadow Village. What do you think?"

"You'd do that for *me*? I'm filling up…"

"*Only* for you. Shall we say midday? I'll come to the Fold."

★

Kade's imposed protocol of not discussing business during the meal had been admirably observed and the plates and mugs were now piled in the stainless steel sink in the worktop. The quartet faced each other across the table which now supported four non-matching whisky glasses – each containing about a triple measure – and a half-emptied bottle of Glenfiddich.

"Okay," Tom said, leaning forward, elbows on the table. "My thanks to the chef…" he nodded to Sergei, "… for an excellent and timely meal. And now, can we *please*…"

Kade held up a hand to stop him.

"The *only* item on this evening's agenda is a decision on whether we go ahead, and yours is the only name against that item, Colonel. You can assume, as Mike has already told you, that the mission is achievable, although, of course, with no guarantee of success. The subject of *how* is not a topic for discussion tonight. Any information as to who we are, Mike's role and involvement, methods, tactics, will flow from that decision; that is assuming you say yes. You'll be told *what* you need to know *when* you need to know it and not an iota more or a second before. The only thing I *will* tell you now is that you will be part of the mission which *I* shall command. Is that understood?"

Tom looked back into the piercing pale eyes, neither man moving a muscle or blinking for a long time.

"I *understand* what you're saying," Tom said. "However, understanding is not necessarily the same as accepting. But one thing I am entitled to ask, I think, is about the funding required and the source of that funding. Put another way, how much will this cost me?"

Kade smiled. "How much do you think Jason's life is worth?"

"Look, let's not play games," Tom said, leaning further across the table. "You know there's no answer to that."

"Okay, in relative terms then."

Kade half rose from his chair to remove a piece of paper from the back pocket of his jeans and then sat down again. It was a sheet of A4, folded twice, which he opened out and placed on the table in front of him. The sheet contained a hand-written list of items with a cash value against each. Kade continued to speak without looking at it.

"You own outright three properties with an overall value in excess of six million pounds. That's Balmaha at just under a million, Villa Margarita in Marbella at two-and-a-quarter and Etherington Place at just over three. Three million is a conservative valuation, in fact, ignoring the opportunity for developing one acre of the property for a small estate of four five-bed executive homes with a profit potential of a further two million on sale completion; a scheme for which a business plan and outline planning permission already exist.

"You have off-shore investments to the value of seven million – we're still talking pounds – all of which are locked in for periods varying between one and six years. Your *on*-shore investments total a further sixteen million of which half is in growth bonds, global equities and property. All the above are in joint names with your wife. The other half of the sixteen million is split into individual instant-access savings accounts, four million in each name."

Tom continued to stare into Kade's eyes. Kade smiled, seeming completely relaxed.

"The sum of these readily accessible and readily disposable assets amounts to – round numbers – thirty million pounds. And then, of course, there's Wolverine Holdings – the Winchester-Tomlinson-Brown business empire, comprising a prestigious art gallery in Kensington, the eco-property development company GreenHouses, and the building merchants, Wolverine Supplies. The companies are managed by your wife but jointly owned by the two of you and your father-in-law, Sir Joseph Winchester. Last year Fairbanks International – the largest construction company in Europe – made an offer of one hundred and seventy million pounds for GreenHouses and Wolverine Supplies. An offer which you turned down – presumably because you didn't need the money."

Tom banged his fist down on the table, causing the glasses to jump and prompting Sergei to leap to his feet.

"None of that is any of your fucking business!" Tom shouted. "What has it got to do with anything?"

Kade leant back in his chair and shrugged, smiling sweetly across the table. He signalled for Sergei to sit down again.

"I'd really like to hear what value you place on Jason's life. I was just reminding you of a few comparators. But you haven't got the first idea about the value of money, have you? Because you haven't contributed *anything* to that fortune. It was just handed to you while you went off to play soldiers and, since then, by your in-laws? So you wouldn't have a clue about pricing a life, would you? Perhaps you should phone your wife and ask her?"

Tom was silent for a long time.

"Major Marty Kade," he said. "*Now* I remember. John Deverall told me about you. You're the guy who helped Abu el Taqha escape from John's patrol. Right?"

Kade did not move but Tom saw the smile disappear from his eyes and the muscles in his jaw tighten.

"You know how it is, Colonel," he said. "You are trusted – and *paid* – to follow orders. You should know; you decided that you'd much rather *follow* orders than give them when you gave up the chance of leadership to start at the bottom in the ranks. Why did you do that, by the way?"

"Perhaps because I was tired of getting things given to me, like you said." Tom was calmer now, sensing Kade's partial retreat onto the defensive. "I wanted a chance to show I could do it on my own, without all the advantages my family gave me."

"Very noble – heroic, some would say. But it's all part of the same picture, isn't it? You could only make that choice – become plain old Private Brown, instead of Lieutenant Tomlinson-Brown – because you didn't have to worry about your future. Daddy would make it okay whatever happened. I can't think of any other rationale for someone giving up the chance of a commission with all its rewards – financial and the rest – in order to spend five years working up to it."

It was Tom's turn to smile across the table.

"Let's be clear, Major – or is it General now? – I'm not ashamed of coming from a rich background…"

"I'm not suggesting…"

"Nor am I proud of it. As you pointed out, none of those riches had anything to do with me. Just an accident of birth. Waiving a commission was just my way of dealing with that. And, just in case your research hasn't gone this far, *Daddy* didn't get me from private to full colonel faster than anyone else in British military history. I did that myself."

Kade nodded. "That you did, Colonel. No-one is saying…"

"But what of you, Major. How quickly did *you* get promoted after 'following orders' in the Hindu Kush?"

Kade sighed and looked down at his hands clasped together in front of him on the table.

"Barely a week passes without me thinking back to that day." He looked across at Tom. "You know the story from Deverall?"

"His side of it."

"Then you'll know we were part of Operation Ptarmigan, ostensibly flushing Taliban out of the mountains. In reality, they were impossible to find; too dispersed and not that many of them left there after Anaconda. There were two groups that day forming one patrol – SEALS and Royal Marines – Major John was with your lot and I was in overall command. We hadn't seen anything all day so we split into our national teams and went on separately. I guess you know all this, right?"

"Go on."

"I'd had my orders from above that we must report in before engaging in any action and I'd passed that on to the Brit leading your group – can't remember his name now. I got a call through from base about half an hour after we split to say that Abu el Taqha had been located in the area – I passed this on to the Brits and we both headed for the coordinates of the sighting. They got there well ahead of us and their guy contacted me. They'd got el Taq in the cross-hairs and could they shoot?" Kade paused and looked down at his hands again. "This is where it gets painful."

"If it eases the pain at all, Major, John Deverall had nothing but good things to say about you."

Kade looked up at Tom and smiled. "Well, yes it does, but I'm not sure I deserve it. I told them 'no, we need VTI' – verification of target identity. I just made it up, to give me time to check back with High Command. They said get there quick and make sure it's us and not the Brits that take him down. So we can tell the folks back home – 'we got him!'" Kade snorted a laugh. "It's easy to sneer at it now, but it was less than a year after 9/11 and that sort of hands-on retribution seemed real important."

He shrugged and reached for his untouched glass, throwing half of its contents down his throat before placing it back on the table.

"And the rest is history, as they say," he went on. "Thankfully, little-known history. When we got there the target was already about a mile away in a speeding jeep, disappearing in a cloud of dust. In my worst dreams I still see the expression on Major John's face. I thought he was going to shoot *me*."

"He told me it did cross his mind."

All four men laughed before Kade's face clouded over again.

"The other thing I have nightmares about is the carnage that came afterwards in Bali, Madrid, London, Istanbul – all supposedly involving Abu el Taqha. If I could go back, I'd just say kill him, and take the consequences. I bet Major John had his own demons to deal with. Right?"

They sat in silence for a while.

"Hindsight, Major," Tom said. "Not worth thinking about. There are one or two things I'd do differently if I could go back just six months."

He reached for his drink, a prompt for the others to do the same. Four empty glasses went down in unison on the table and Sergei reached for the bottle and replenished them.

"The answer to your question about the price of Jason's life is 'whatever it takes'," Tom said, "and the answer to 'do we go ahead?' is 'yes'. And I guess that's meeting closed. Here's to success."

He raised his drink, reaching across the table. The four glasses came together with a dull, non-crystal clunk and a chorus of "to success".

CHAPTER EIGHTEEN

Tuesday; 27 October

Mags let the phone ring five times before ending the call. She didn't leave a message, knowing the person always picked up the missed call and phoned back, usually straight away. Less than two minutes later she was proved right.

"Hi, Maggie. Sorry, couldn't find the phone."

"That's okay. Where was it?"

Jo laughed. "Usual place – right in front of me on the desk, but buried under half a rain forest. I don't know about this legendary entity 'the paperless office', but there's more paper than office visible here right now."

"This is to do with your move, I guess. I got your text."

"That's right. Most of this is for the shredder – just cross checking everything's on e-file. Anyway, what can I do for you? I was going to phone later."

"Well... actually, I'm worried about Tom."

"I'm pleased to hear it, Maggie, if you don't mind me saying."

"The thing is, I don't know where he is. I'm at the apartment in SW1 – came yesterday and stayed overnight. Only he really should be around right now because a week today he's due in court, but his lawyer's not been able to contact him. He was here on Sunday – definitely – but his car's gone and it looks like he might have packed a bag recently – you know, drawers pulled out and such – and there's no sign of keys, wallet, mobile."

"Could he be with his family do you think?"

"No, I've spoken to them. Wish I hadn't; I've got them worried now. I know this is a massive imposition, Jo, but I wondered if it would be possible for you to come to the apartment and go through it with me again. You'd know what to look for in terms of clues as to what he might be doing, where he might have gone. If it's not possible, then I fully understand, but…"

"No, it's okay. I'm sure we can arrange something. I'm moving up to Leicester tomorrow, actually. I won't be able to make it into London today and I've got an appointment with someone at midday tomorrow, but I could fit it in after that."

"Are you sure you don't mind?"

"Not at all, Maggie, but I have to say, the police should know by now that he's not contacted his lawyer. Perhaps it's time to make it official. You could always speak to John Mackay first."

Mags paused.

"I probably will, but not yet. I know you're walking on eggshells, Jo. John still doesn't know about you and me – you know, being friends. You must feel a bit uncomfortable."

"Well, not so much now. We did meet legitimately when I was preparing to search your home for the rucksack, so we could say we struck up a rapport from there if it ever came out that we kept in touch. I'm not as concerned about that as with how little I can help compared to official police channels. I'm happy to meet up tomorrow, but if anything does surface that was a cause for concern, then it might need to be referred to them anyway."

"Yes, I understand that. I do appreciate this, you know. Hold on, though. You'll be *driving* to Leicester, won't you? This is going to put you way out."

"No, if we make it, say, mid-afternoon, I'll leave the car somewhere near the start of the M1 – Romford, perhaps – and go in by train. That's no problem."

"Three o'clock, then? I'll meet you off the tube at Pimlico."

"Okay, see you then. And try not to worry too much. If he's packed a bag and taken the car, he must have planned this. It's not as if he just hasn't made it back home."

"You're right. Thanks, Jo. See you tomorrow."

Mags got up from the bench seat on the triangular balcony off the main bedroom. This had been her and Tom's favourite spot at Balmaha, overlooking the Thames. She remembered the many evenings when the temperature had been totally unsuitable for sitting outside, but they had steadfastly huddled together clutching their drinks, each kitted out in a down jacket over a fleece, determined to beat the cold.

Right now, at 10.30 in the morning, in just a light jacket and sheltered from a gentle breeze, it was the pain of those memories that drove her back inside. As she closed the balcony door, the phone in the living room rang and she went quickly through to answer it. The name on the display was someone Jo had mentioned a few minutes ago and, for a moment, she wondered whether the call was more than just a coincidence.

"Hello, John."

A pause; then, "Maggie! Is that you?"

"Of course. Which other woman would be answering my husband's phone?"

John Mackay laughed. "None that I can think of. It's just that… you didn't say anything yesterday. Are you and Tom… you know … together?"

"Not in any sense of the word, I'm afraid." She hesitated. "He's not here at the moment; I'm just waiting for him to sort out a couple of things. Can I give him a message?"

"Yes, please. When he phoned me on Sunday it was to ask for information about his new neighbour – across the landing. A gentleman who calls himself Oscar Strange. Can you tell Tom we have no record of him at all, and not only that, we can't find anything relating to the sale or letting of that apartment either. The people who own it are not aware that anyone has been living there."

"Sounds very exciting, John. What has this person supposed to have done?"

"Tom got the feeling he was spying on him – that could have been his imagination, of course. But Jackie Hewlett went to see Tom with her daughter, Lucy on Saturday and – can you remember when Lucy was abducted for a few hours?"

"I certainly can. I feared for Katey at the time."

"Well, they bumped into this man and Lucy thought she recognised him as the same one."

"Really? That's a bit creepy, isn't it?"

"Anyway, it seems Mr Strange – or whoever he is – has left. My guess is that Lucy is wrong. It was three years ago and she was only eleven at the time. Well, I'd best go. I hope you and Tom do get together *and* very soon."

"Thanks, John. Bye."

"Bye, Maggie. See you in court next week, no doubt."

Mags replaced the phone. "Not the way things are looking at the moment," she said to herself.

★

The man with the beard and the white scar over his right eye got out of the front passenger seat of the ancient Volvo 940 estate and slapped the roof a couple of times as 'goodbye'. He watched the driver do a rapid three-point turn in front of the garage set into the hillside at the edge of the road before speeding away north along the narrow B-road back towards Oban.

The rusted hinges squealed in complaint as he pulled open the wooden double doors, dragging a couple of small boulders into place with his feet to stop them swinging back. The decrepit condition of its hiding place was totally at odds with the gleaming Audi sports car it concealed. There was just enough clearance for the man to squeeze along the side of the vehicle. With no room to open the door, the hood had been left down and he swung his legs over into the driver's seat. After pulling the car out onto the road and closing the hood, he shut up the garage again and set off in the same direction as the Volvo.

Four hours and one hundred and fifty miles later, he parked the car close to the jetty in Ullapool, having run a gauntlet of admiring glances and double-takes as he entered the town and crept along the main thoroughfare in the sleek silver vehicle. He pulled a mobile phone from his pocket, removed the back cover and checked inside it one last time. Replacing the cover, he slipped it into the drop-down glove compartment on the passenger side.

He got out of the car, locked it and walked away along the quayside. After fifty yards he stopped and leaned on the rail above the harbour. He looked back at the R8 and, with a sigh of regret, dropped the keys into the brown, gently-rocking water below.

★

Wednesday; 28 October

Jo checked her watch again. It was 1.50 pm.

"And now I really *must* go. Thanks for meeting me here. It goes without saying I would have much preferred your fan club HQ, but..."

"That's quite alright," David said. "I thought the meal was excellent – *and* the company, of course."

They left the Ciao Bella Italian restaurant on South Street for the short walk of 150 yards or so to Romford rail station where they had parked their cars.

"Look," Jo said, "I don't suppose you want to come along with me, do you? It will make it even less official if you were there as well. You know, we were having a meal together, Maggie phoned, asked if I could meet her, so, as it wasn't actual police business, we both went along. Another pair of eyes, another brilliant mind – that sort of thing."

David snorted a laugh. "And what if you *did* find something and it *did* have to become official, how are you going to square my being there with DI Waters? I seem to recall the last time we met he more than just put me on hold."

"Yes, you're right. To be honest, I'm getting tired of telling lies – to Johnny Mac, to Harry – to Maggie now that Tom's a suspect. I feel like I'm trapped in a giant porkie."

They walked under the railway bridge and turned right towards the station.

"When is your train?" David asked.

"They're every ten minutes; takes about half an hour into Liverpool Street. Then Central Line to Oxford Circus and Victoria from there. Plenty of time."

They turned to face each other at the entrance to the station, slipping naturally into an embrace.

"Hope it goes well with Maggie," David said. "And safe journey to Leicester. You'll be staying at the same B&B as last time, I suppose," he added, with a serious face.

Jo laughed. "No vacancies, I'm afraid. But I know the owner of this other place..."

"Well, you take care."

Jo walked through the station entrance, turning once to give him a little wave.

★

The living room at Balmaha was luxuriously furnished in a modern style with squared black leather chairs and sofas on a polished oak floor, and glass and chrome dining furniture and cabinets. The walls were plain white and hung with a selection of Mags's paintings. The artist herself was sitting on one of the armchairs and Jo on the end of the sofa closest to her.

"So, where are we up to?" Jo said.

"Well..." Mags placed her cup on the coffee table in front of her and leaned forward "... I've been through the post, nothing much there except the final summons asking him to acknowledge his intention to attend court next week – that was unopened, by the way. Checked incoming calls and messages – no clues at all, although I know he responded to at least one recently – Jackie Hewlett. He also phoned John Mackay on Sunday asking for some information about our new neighbour across the landing – now our *ex*-neighbour it seems. The other outgoing calls over the past couple of weeks have been mainly for taxis."

"Going anywhere in particular – I mean regularly to any one place?"

"Well I'd need to check with the taxi companies, I guess."

"Yes, of course..."

"There were only a few anyway. Tom actually *enjoys* the tube and the train."

"Right. Anything else?"

"A lot of unread emails on his PC but nothing of any real significance; from Jackie Hewlett and his lawyer mainly. A few from Katey but she stopped trying a couple of weeks ago. As far as emails *sent*, none at all for five or six weeks." Her voice faltered a little and she paused to recover. "Except for one to Josh Wilcox – a pilot we know – three weeks ago. An apology for something."

"Are you okay, Maggie?" Jo frowned, placing her cup on the table and reaching across to take her hand.

"Yes, just being silly and thinking of the last time Tom and I were together with Josh." She smiled at Jo, her eyes moist. "Anyway, as you can see, I'm no good at this detective game."

"I wouldn't say that. You've checked all the right things – not your fault if there's nothing to find. You said car keys, wallet and mobile phone are missing?"

"That's right, and the car's gone from the basement. So, where do we look next?"

"Just to get one silly question out of the way, you have tried his mobile – I mean, a number of times?"

"Yes, the last time was when I was waiting for you at the tube station. Straight through to voicemail every time."

"I did say it was a silly question. And you said that drawers were open and clothes had been taken out?"

"Well, I assume so. There's a bag – a hold-all – missing that he took from the house some weeks ago. But there was stuff everywhere in the bedroom..." she looked round, "... and this room as well. I've tidied it up and I'm thinking now perhaps I shouldn't have. You know, it might have been better if you'd seen it as it was."

"I don't think so, Maggie." Jo smiled. "It's not a crime scene, is it? What about Tom's passport? Did you find that?"

Mags opened her eyes wide. "God, I didn't think of that. I do know he took it when he moved here, because it's not with mine at home."

"Would he usually carry it with him?"

"No, he never did, except when he specifically needed it, of course. He always kept both of them – mine and his – in a drawer buried under some clothes, for whatever reason. I don't think he knew himself." She gave a little laugh.

"Well, that's something else we can look for. Can you tell what clothes he took – whether they were summer clothes, outdoor clothes, whatever?"

"Difficult to tell. He moved here in June and he hasn't taken anything from home since then – oh, except a change of clothes when he stayed the night after you came to tell us about Mickey Kadawe. That's when he took the hold-all. He has a full wardrobe here but I'm not sure I could tell you what's missing. I don't come very often."

"Okay, let's start with the hunt for the passport. Turn out all the drawers and cupboards, pockets in his jackets, coats, trousers. If you do that, I'll have a look at his PC and check out any websites he's accessed recently. There may be a clue there. Did you check the Trash folder for any emails he might have deleted?"

"Yes, but it's set to automatically empty every seven days; there wasn't anything in it at all. Nothing in Spam of any use either – shows that's working, anyway."

Jo smiled. "Okay, let's get started."

★

She had just abandoned her fruitless search for clues on the internet and was logging off when she heard the cry from Mags. It was more of a squeal, in fact. A squeal of surprise bordering on fright.

"Jo! In here!"

She hurried through to the guest bedroom and found Mags staring at the open bottom drawer of the tall-boy. Clothes from the drawer were piled on the floor leaving it empty except for one thing. Jo's stomach gave a little flip.

"Is that Tom's?" Jo asked.

"It must be I suppose, but I've never seen it before. What is it?"

Jo knelt down to get a closer look.

"It's a SIG P-two-two-something semi-automatic pistol. Did you know Tom kept a gun?"

"No – in fact, I was sure he *didn't*. Well, not at the house, anyway, and he swore to me that he didn't own one at all." She looked at Jo, still wide-eyed with shock. "Am I being naïve? Do senior politicians keep weapons – you know – for their own protection?"

"I don't believe so. Not as a general rule, although if they have a license and a legitimate reason, like being a collector or member of a gun club. I really don't know."

Jo continued to study the gun, then she stood up again and turned to Mags.

"Maggie, we need to inform the police about this."

Mags screwed her face into a frown. "The police, but why? It's just a gun stuck right at the back of a draw in the ex-Home Secretary's apartment. What we *need* to do is what we're trying to do – find Tom. And then we can ask him why it's there."

"It's not as simple as that, Maggie." Jo sighed. "Let's go back through there and I'll tell you everything."

★

"Just before we go any further, Jo, can you tell me why you were searching Tom Brown's apartment in SW1? Just so I don't look like a complete bozo when I talk to his wife."

Harry was speaking on the hands-free en route to Balmaha. Jo had stepped out onto the balcony to take the call.

"Didn't Craig explain?"

"Craig's here in the car with me – driving it. He told me you were there trying to help Mrs T find out where her husband was. Am I to assume that Leicester Constabulary have taken over my case, because otherwise... Oh, for Christ's sake!"

"What's wrong?"

"We've stopped again! This bloody satnav has been programmed to seek out traffic jams and drop you right into them!"

"Just calm down, Harry. This has nothing to do with your case. Tom Brown is supposed to appear in court next week, as I'm sure you know, but he hasn't been in touch with his lawyer yet and no-one seems to know where he is. His wife asked me if I would have a look round the apartment to see if there were any clues as to where he might be. In seeking the aforementioned clues, we came across the gun and I phoned you straight away."

"But why *you*? That's what I don't get."

"I'll explain later, because right now it doesn't really matter, does it? I would have thought the priority is to get a team here ASAP – which I am sure you have arranged. How far away are you?"

"About half a mile – say three hours at this rate. They could be there before us unless they're using the same satnav. How is she – Mrs Tomlinson-Brown? I assume you've told her about our interest in her husband and the reasons why."

"Yes I have. Punch-drunk I'd say. She must be wondering what's going to hit her next. And she's mad as hell at me."

"And the gun?"

"SIG P-226."

"And you haven't moved it?"

"Only to shoot out a few light-bulbs. Oh, and I killed a couple of pigeons with it that were crapping on the balcony chairs." Jo could hear Craig laughing in the seat beside Harry. "But I've put it back exactly where we found it."

"It's lucky Belmont is driving or I might have crashed the car, I'm laughing so much. The 226 is a 40-cal, isn't it?"

"The standard model is, but – if I'm reading your mind correctly – it's easy to convert to 9mm with an exchange kit. You just swap over the slide assembly and mag."

"You are such a *swot*, Cottrell! Anyway, we're here now, just turning into the driveway. Can you let us in?"

★

Mags and Jo were seated on the armchairs at either end of the long coffee table in the living room with Harry and Craig on the sofa. The small search team of just four officers had arrived shortly after the two detectives along with someone from the Armed Response Unit who checked that the firearm was safe to handle. At Harry's request they were in plain clothes and an unmarked car so as not to attract attention outside or add any more to the tension within. Mags had agreed to the search although they did not yet have a warrant. She could hardly refuse, Jo thought, having asked her round specifically to do that exact same thing.

"This is extremely painful for us, Mrs Tomlinson-Brown," Harry said, "so I can't even begin to imagine what you must be feeling. We hope very much that we will be able to eliminate your husband from our enquiries into the deaths DI Cottrell has told you about. But we are duty-bound to follow all avenues of investigation and, by coincidence or otherwise, Mr Brown seems to tick all the right boxes in terms of motive – which he has publicly stated; opportunity – we know he was in the vicinity of at least some of the killings at the right time; and means – he certainly has the skills, background and contacts to carry out the crimes."

Mags said nothing.

"We are aware," Harry went on, "that you and Mr Brown have not been living together for some time now." He paused and Mags gave the slightest of nods. "In which case, we accept that you may not be able to help us in any material way. But if you can think of *anything* that will move us forward and, hopefully, enable us to put an end to this line of enquiry, then…"

"*Why* would he kill these people?" Mags interrupted. "Tell me that."

Harry shrugged. "If he believed they were complicit in getting Jack convicted, then an act of revenge…"

"*Wrongly* convicted. *That's* what he believes – as I do. So why would he kill the very people who could clear Jack's name? It makes no sense at all."

"A lot doesn't make sense, Mrs Tomlinson-Brown, which is why, as I said, as soon as we can eliminate him from our enquiries …"

"Well I can help you with that, Detective Inspector, because I can tell you for *certain* that he didn't carry out those killings. The barbaric acts that DI Cottrell described are the work of a coward – or cowards. And my husband, based on recent evidence, is the bravest man in the world."

Harry sighed.

"I could accept that without question, Mrs Tomlinson-Brown, if the man we are talking about is the *same* man who existed six months ago. But *we* have recent evidence, that I'm sure you are familiar with, which shows that is not the case."

★

It was almost midnight when Jo came to the roundabout on the ring road just a hundred yards from her new place of work. She took the third exit, which took her directly away from Leicester Constabulary headquarters, along Kenwick Lane for the three-mile drive into the open countryside to the village of Kenwick itself – population circa 120 and the home of Detective Sergeant Sebastian Carter.

She reflected on her parting with Mags, shortly after Harry had left with the gun and two spare magazines found in the second-to-bottom drawer of the same cabinet. She was sure they were still friends; they had embraced as she left, although Mags's face still retained some of the anger which had exploded when Jo had told her about the police's investigation into her husband. Better that, Jo thought, than a look of abject despair to fuel her guilt at leaving her alone at Balmaha.

She pulled to a halt behind the Toyota Celica in front of the small terraced cottage with its long front garden, picket fence and gate. Her spirits were lifted by the appearance of a figure in the window, who waved briefly and disappeared from sight. The front door opened seconds later, just as her mobile phone sounded.

"Hi, Harry."

"Hi, Jo, sorry to call so late but you asked me to keep you informed."

"Am I going to like this?"

"I'm afraid not. The gun from Tom Brown's apartment is the one that killed Sammo Sampson and his four clients."

"There's no doubt?"

"None at all."

"Okay, thanks, Harry."

She ended the call as her eyes filled with tears. Seb was waiting in the doorway, his large, muscular frame silhouetted against the light from inside. She got out of the car, taking her suitcase from the back seat. Seb was walking towards her down the path. She dropped the case and ran into his arms.

★

Thursday; 29 October

"Good afternoon, I'm Jocelyn Knox, and our main story this Thursday lunchtime. Police are keen to contact the former Home Secretary, Mr Tom Brown, as part of their investigation into the recent deaths of a number of drug users in the Woking, Cobham and Dorking areas. Detective Inspector Harry Waters, the officer leading the investigation, told reporters in a statement today at twelve o'clock that he believed Mr Brown could provide valuable information relating to the case. He appealed for him to contact the police immediately.

"Mr Brown, who is due to appear in court next week following the alleged assisted death of his son whilst in custody earlier this year, has not been seen at or near his home on Vauxhall Bridge Road, SW1, since last Friday – 23ʳᵈ October – and his current whereabouts are unknown. DI Waters said that he may be staying with someone because an overnight bag has been taken from the apartment and his car is missing from its underground garage. The vehicle is a silver Audi R8 soft-top sports car, registration TB 75. Anyone seeing Mr Brown or his car should contact the police on one of the three numbers shown below, or at their local police station.

"Obviously, we will keep you updated with this story as it develops."

★

Mags activated the main gates as John Mackay's voice crackled over the intercom. She met him at the front porch door and they embraced awkwardly.

"Coffee… or something?" Mags asked.

"Not for me, thanks."

She led the way through to the back of the house. "Katey's here."

Katey was sitting in the middle of the four-seater sofa which faced the floor-to-ceiling windows overlooking the rear garden and large pond, currently illuminated with solar lighting. She got to her feet when they entered and she and John hugged.

"Katey, I'm so sorry…"

She nodded as he ran out of words.

"Please, John." Mags waved him to the armchair at the end of the coffee table, and sat down close to her daughter, pressing up against her and clasping both her hands with hers in a four-handed fist, their knuckles showing white through the skin. She suddenly felt a wave of sympathy for her visitor. His face was a mask of sadness and anxiety, as if he was reflecting their own despair.

John checked his watch before speaking.

"Well, as you probably know by now, we found Tom's car earlier today in Ullapool, north-west Scotland. In about twenty minutes, at nine o'clock, we'll be putting out a further statement about the search for Tom. It will include details of what was found in the car and, as a result of *that*, we shall be mentioning the discovery of the gun at the apartment."

Katey gave a loud sob. Mags's expression stayed neutral.

"I wanted to tell you both," he went on, "before the rest of the country hears about it; and to give you the opportunity to ask me any questions. I don't have to say, do I, how absolutely sick I feel about the whole thing? I'm sure you know that already."

"We know," Katey said. "Please go on."

"In the back of the Audi, behind the seats, we found some wire along with a couple of detonators. It's impossible to be certain, but we believe it to be the same type of equipment used in the bombing of the apartments in Dorking. This is part-circumstantial based on what we already know, but it fits an emerging picture; because this links Tom to those killings just as the gun links him to the others. And *all* the victims can be linked back to Jack and Jason."

"Well, I'm glad they're dead!" Katey's shout took them both by surprise. "But if Dad had decided to kill them, no way would he do it like that. He'd confront them; make sure they knew why it was happening to them. Not sneak up behind them…"

"We don't know he did that," John said, "or whoever killed them did that. He might have confronted them, then made them turn round."

"I think he's run away so he doesn't have to go through with the court case about Jack's death. That will be why."

"I don't think so, Katey." John said. "He seemed pretty relaxed – as much as he could be – about that. He said he was pleading guilty and was keen to get it out of the way. He told me *and* Mr Hastings."

"Well I'll *never* believe he did it. Innocent people could have been killed in that explosion – it's a miracle they weren't. You know him better than that."

John sighed. "Who knows anything anymore?"

"What John means, Katey, is what DI Waters said yesterday at the apartment. We're talking about the man we knew six months ago. I know part of that man still exists – know it for a fact – but I'm not sure I could vouch for him all the time now like I could then." She turned to John. "So what else will they say in the statement?"

"Apart from the information about the detonators and the gun, we'll ask anyone to contact us if they see him, like we did earlier.

And we'll say not to approach him. I don't believe for a second he's a danger to the general public, but we *have* to say that."

They sat in silence for a long time before John spoke again.

"The Ullapool connection just doesn't make any sense to me. There's nowhere to go from there, except the Outer Isles – and the Atlantic. It's just about the end of the world. There's no bag in the car, so he must have his clothes, wallet and stuff with him. But why would he leave his phone behind?"

"Possibly because he might be traced through it," Mags said. "You can do that, can't you?"

"Yes, of course," John said. He paused to think for a moment. "Which means he's probably moved on from there. The police have checked all the B&Bs, guest-houses, hotels – and campsites and hostels – within five miles of the town. No sign of him at all. They've also been checking passenger lists on the ferries between Ullapool and Stornoway. Nothing there either. Where could he be going? Have *you* any idea, Maggie"

Mags shook her head, disguising the glimmer of understanding that had just come to her.

CHAPTER NINETEEN

Sunday; 1 November

In the pale light of morning with a hazy sun rising behind them below the canopy of cloud, the five men stood in a tight group on the towering cliffs of Mingulay, looking out to sea into the teeth of the westerly gale. Four of the men were trying to carry on a conversation, shouting to make themselves heard above the howling wind. The fifth member and leader of the group looked with ice-blue eyes and calm dismay at the pitching seascape in front of them.

This storm had not been forecast until a few days ago but was hardly out of character for the time of year. He had known from the beginning the problems in managing small craft to and from this particular island in anything other than near-perfect weather conditions. That was the reason it was uninhabited, which was why he had chosen it for their purpose. So having taken the decision – and hence the risk – to use it as their starting point, he could hardly complain. He wondered, not for the first time in the last few days, whether they had left it too late.

"No chance!" he shouted above the roar. "Pray for tomorrow!"

The men turned away from the cliffs and began the walk of just over half a mile back to their base. With the gale at their backs, they could breathe more easily and were able to cover the ground quickly.

When they arrived at the beach they looked eastward beyond the dunes at the two Archer Class boats anchored a hundred yards out in the bay, lurching violently in the swell. They each bore the initials BOSV on their sides and superstructures. A smaller craft was secured with chains to the deck of one of the boats, under a winch near the stern. This strange-looking vessel had the appearance of a large casserole dish, flat-bottomed and oval-shaped, with a transparent domed 'lid'.

"I'm sure the Oceanographic Society will wait one day more for such important work," said one of the men. They all laughed and turned to enter the prefabricated building, which was to be their home for a sixth day, and to join the other three members of the party.

One man hesitated in the doorway then turned and walked back to where they had been watching the boats.

"You coming in, Colonel?" the leader shouted across to him.

"In a minute."

"Briefing starts in ten."

He went inside and closed the door.

★

The square wooden table in the centre of the main room in the building was for now – according to Kade – *not* a table but a replica of Alpha, which was why each leg was supported by an upturned metal crate which lifted it off the floor so the full height of its legs could represent the extent of the columns above sea-level. Around the edges of the table top, cardboard boxes had been placed to symbolise the lower floors of the ten-storey accommodation blocks, which surrounded and enclosed the main deck of the platform.

The six men and two women were seated round the perimeter of the room, two at each side. The walls were covered with charts and technical drawings, along with hand-written lists of bullet-points and diagrams on sheets of A1 taken from the two flip-chart pads, one at each end of the room, clipped to their easels.

The whole display represented four days of planning, each subsequent day more or less identical to the previous one, as the group went through the minutiae of the assault on the platform, each time on the basis that this could be their last opportunity before the action. They were all aware that one day very soon, it *would* be, and that the details needed to be at the forefront of their minds.

303

The group – Tom had been told as they made their way across The Minch five days ago – was a privately-owned concern, specialising in hostage rescue and with some very high-profile successes to their name. Not that they had a name, as such; their 'shop-window' was a mobile phone number – the one Tom still had somewhere, written on a beer-mat. Their main customers were governments – very large to very small – and occasionally revolutionary groups whose ascendancy suited the ambitions of the West. The owner was an anonymous international business magnate, rumoured to be Dutch, who – according to Kade – creamed off a third of their earnings. Even so, there was very little to pay out in terms of expenses; all equipment, weaponry and ammunition normally being sanctioned and provided by the client from an inventory presented prior to the contract being agreed. Kade said, with a wry smile, that he was the 'Operations Director'. He had taken over from his predecessor eighteen months ago following the latter's death on a mission in the Gulf of Aden rescuing three hundred American tourists from a cruise liner taken by Somali pirates.

Tom looked around the room at his new comrades, his eyes stopping on Kade who was looking – and smiling – right back at him.

"Colonel, perhaps you'd like to start by reminding us who we are and why we're here. Let's hear again how much you have learnt about us."

Tom returned his smile and got to his feet. He turned to the man seated on his left.

"Michael Needham," he said. "Engineer supreme and designer of the greatest off-shore hotel in the world. Mike's role is to provide details of the structure and in particular his entry-exit route which this group will use to access the platform. Also – critically – he will provide the assault team with vital, live information during the course of the mission. In spite of his now being recognised widely as a designer, Mike saw early active service with the British Royal Engineers and has been involved with Special Forces in the recent past on a number of critical field activities requiring on-the-ground innovation."

He looked across to his left at the tall, woman in loose-fitting DPM fatigues. She was around forty years old, slim and athletic with blonde hair pulled back in a short pony-tail. Her face seemed to Tom a little too hard to be genuinely pretty, although her features were sharp and even.

"Lydia van Roden, doctor of psychology, born in the Netherlands but educated in the US, acquiring American citizenship before working as advisor for police, CIA, FBI and Special Forces, majoring on hostage situations involving domestic, criminal, religious and terrorist incidents. Now a full-time member of this action team and, I'm led to believe…" Tom gave her a wide smile "… a very competent dancer – of sorts."

There was gentle laughter round the table. Lydia glared back at Tom before her expression melted into a smile.

"Sergei Rouschek," Tom went on, looking at the giant seated next to Lydia. "Native Russian, ex-FSB Alpha team, world famous hostage rescue expert and one of the biggest guys I've ever seen. His role will be off-location support to the assault team because he won't fit through the narrow places Mike has engineered for our smooth entry. A shame, because I would really like to have him on my side – and *at* my side – in anything I'm likely to do in the future."

This time the muted laughter was accompanied by nods of agreement.

"Ex-Major Shirley-Ann Donnelly," he smiled at the woman to his right, seated next to Kade. She wore the same fatigues as Lydia, but that was the only similarity between the two women. Shirley-Ann was early-thirties, no more than average height and sturdy, with muscular shoulders and thick limbs. Her face was round and pleasant under a bob of short dark hair.

"One of the first women Navy SEALS and the *very first* woman to serve in action in an infantry unit. Already with missions around the globe in three continents, and decorated twice before falling foul of bureaucracy after disobeying orders on a covert operation in Syria early this year. This breach of discipline meant that around twenty civilians were saved who would otherwise have died. But, hey, Uncle Sam knows best and Shirley-Ann was discharged – albeit honourably. Her joining this team means that the US's loss is the world's gain. Shirley-Ann will be Cassie's pilot for this mission."

Tom looked across to the two men sitting opposite him.

"Two of the very best," he said.

The man on the left was black, mid-forties, tall and slim with short-cropped hair, sharp handsome features and intense green eyes. Tom nodded towards him.

"Commander Jules Cartier, ex-GIGN, the elite French counter-terrorism unit. French Senegalese, whose family moved to Paris over half a century ago, following independence. A quarter of a century's experience in hostage rescue, and the youngest member – by far – of the team involved in the freeing of hostages from the hijack of the Air France flight in Algeria back in 1994. Jules was one of the first to board the plane, under intense fire from the terrorists, after it landed in Marseilles, and was one of nine GIGN operators wounded in freeing all the hostages unhurt. And since then, missions too numerous to mention. Jules will be one of the assault team on Alpha."

Jules nodded in acknowledgement as Tom turned to the much smaller, stockier man with the Latin skin tone and hair colour at his side. His mild expression and rimless glasses gave him the look of an academic and belied his record as a front-line warrior.

"Enrico Santana, born and educated in Peru, best-selling author on his favourite subject of group dynamics among underprivileged and ostracised minorities, and world-class hostage rescue expert and negotiator. Many defining moments, but none so spectacular as his first assignment with the Peruvian commandos in an assault on the Japanese Ambassador's residence twenty years ago in Lima where seventy-four hostages had been held for several months. The rescue was so well planned and executed that it was over in just forty-one seconds. All fourteen terrorists were killed. Rico will also be part of the assault team."

Tom nodded to him then pointed to himself with both index fingers against his chest.

"Tom Brown, born Jacob Simon Tomlinson-Brown, a rich, spoilt kid, who wanted for nothing and did whatever he liked. More recently, disgraced ex-Home Secretary. But now, right back where he belongs. Ex-SBS with hostage rescue experience, including the Nigerian Oil Rig incident in 2003, as a covert adviser to a contract rescue team preparing to release hostages on four off-shore rigs seized by striking workers. I will be part of the assault team on Alpha, ostensibly to ID Jason and to ensure he will leave without resistance. However, may I say what a privilege it is to be part of this group and I guarantee I will *not* be a passenger, but a fully contributing member."

He turned to Kade.

"And finally, our leader. Former Navy SEAL, operating throughout the conflicts in Iraq, Afghanistan plus other covert – and overt – assignments in Central Africa and Indonesia. Put simply, it is his job to take four people onto Alpha and bring five back."

★

He was much closer to them than he had been yesterday, and today he was certain that his lungs and heart were *not* going to give out, which was a definite improvement. Another good indicator was that he had stopped envying Mike his exemption from the daily training routine. 'Routine' was perhaps an overstatement for a mid-morning two-mile run and heaving at a few weights in the afternoon, even though the run was a there-and-back ascent of Carnan, the highest hill on the island, rising ever more steeply from sea-level to a trig point at around 900 feet.

He recalled the embarrassment of the first day, the first run. Standing – just about – hands on knees, gasping for breath and looking up towards the modest summit as the rest of the gang streamed past him on their way down, glancing at him with expressions of disdain. But he had won them over – to a degree, at least – by going out again, alone, that same day and repeating the challenge. And he'd put in the extra run on the second and third day, too, and now, as he entered the building to smiles all round and a burst of applause, he was already breathing normally again.

"Mis-timed my sprint finish," he said. "I'll get you tomorrow."

They laughed as he took his place next to Mike.

"Okay, time out over," Kade said. "Mr Needham."

Mike rose from his chair to address the group, holding a telescopic pointer, which he extended as he stepped across to a nautical chart on the wall.

"This is the island group of St Kilda," he said, pointing at the chart, "and here, twenty-two miles to the south west, its off-shore hotel, Platform Alpha. From above, as shown on the map, the main

307

structure is a square, tilted slightly so the *corners* of the square – where the columns are – point approximately north, east, south and west."

He circled the table, tapping the bottom of each leg in turn.

"On the inside of each column, three metres above sea-level, facing in towards the centre, is a plate measuring two metres high by one metre wide. From the outside, all four plates look identical, but this one…" he stopped and tapped the bottom of the last leg "… at the base of the east column, is the access door."

Glancing round the room, Tom couldn't fail to be impressed by the focus of his comrades, all leaning forward in rapt attention as if they were hearing this for the first time.

"The other three plates are dummies, just a panel fastened to the column by ten hexagonal-head bolts. The east column plate looks exactly the same, with the same configuration of bolts." He pointed to a hand-drawn diagram on the wall. "But their only purpose is to disguise this as a door. The plate is hinged on the inside, and opens inwards. I'll say this a few times during the course of the day, but please be aware that this is the *only* door you will pass through, until you reach the living accommodation, which can be opened *from the inside*."

He looked round the room to ensure that all seven heads had nodded their understanding.

"Access is achieved by turning the centre bolt-head on the left-hand-side of the plate anti-clockwise and pushing the door open. Once inside the column, you will be ninety-two metres below the main deck – that's about three hundred rungs of a ladder to climb." Mike stepped over to a schematic diagram on the wall showing a vertical section of the column. "The diameter of the column itself is twenty-five metres. The shaft you will be climbing up is two-and-a-half metres square and has three equally-spaced landings, which split the climb into four stages. Each landing is accessed from below by releasing a bolt on a hatch which allows it to be raised and held open – repeat, *held* open – enough to enable you to pass through. The hatches are designed to fall back into position once they are released." He moved the pointer to another diagram. "The bolt is on a return spring, which will automatically lock the hatch when it closes. The hatches cannot be opened from above, so they *must be wedged open*; otherwise you won't be coming back.

"Be aware that this is a free climb with no safety-harness facility, which means that if you fall, it will be onto the landing below you. That could be over twenty metres, in which case – again – you won't be coming back. There is a solar-powered strip light under each landing, which will illuminate the section below it and make the climb a little more comfortable. Even so, you will each take a head-torch in case the lighting fails."

Mike paused and made a silent circuit of the room before continuing.

"Alpha has eight hundred identical apartments completely surrounding the main deck to a height of ten storeys, eighty on each level, twenty along each side. So the whole encloses the deck like the sides of a box. Suspended nine metres below the main deck is the receiving floor." He tapped the edge of the table with the pointer. "Around three sides of this is an observation-stroke-recreational corridor, forming a sort of squared-off horseshoe, accessed only via stairwells at each corner from the main deck above. This corridor is made entirely of glass – the outer walls around the whole of the horseshoe, the inner walls which separate the corridor itself from the rooms off it, and the partitions between the rooms. It is designed to create a light and airy environment, a wrap-around window onto the wider world. The fourth side, by the way, is open to accept the prisoner cages onto the receiving floor via the satellite platform.

"The fourth hatch you encounter, at the top of the climb, will take you out of the shaft and onto an enclosed sub-floor, which runs under the full length of the corridor – along all three sides and two metres below it. This floor carries power lines, communication cables and water pipes linked to the control hub on the satellite platform for the wind farm, solar panels and wave power modules.

"Immediately above you on the sub-floor is another hatch – one of four situated directly above the columns at each corner. These hatches operate like the others – open only from below – and give access to the corridor itself and direct contact with the Exiles. This is where it gets a little complicated and where you're going to need me again."

Mike looked across at Kade, who held up his hand for him to stop.

"Thank you, Mike." He tuned to Shirley-Ann. "Major."

Shirley-Ann stood up and took the pointer from Mike. Her voice was soft and gentle with the hint of a southern drawl.

"We will take two boats. Why two? Well, as much for insurance as anything – who can tell when, for example, a mechanical fault will happen and…" she smiled "… it could be embarrassing calling the coastguard. But it will also give us some flexibility if we need to split up on our return, though this is not part of the plan. Archer-One will have six people on board – Kade, Mike, Jules, Rico, Tom and me. Mike's job is to drive the boat and watch TV, mine is to deliver the other four to the base of the east column. How difficult that will be depends on the weather, but the first challenge is to get to the door.

"Both boats will travel together as far as St Kilda. From there, Archer-One will head south and then west so we make our approach directly from the east. We will lay up five miles short of – and facing – Alpha, while we drop Cassie off the stern, out of sight of the platform – here." She pointed at a red dot on the chart. "I'll take her down ten metres and then Archer-One will continue and enter the turbine ring before passing south of the platform and laying up again to the west of it." She moved the pointer across the chart from the red dot to the tilted square of Alpha. "I'll follow on the same course at constant depth towards the east column. It will take Cassie around forty minutes to get there. At five fathoms down in anything but a mirror-flat sea, our approach will not be observed either by the inmates or by Lochshore through the sea-facing cameras that surround the platform at main deck level. Even so, from that point Mike and Archer-Two will be deployed as distractions."

"Thanks, Major." Kade interrupted and turned to Lydia. "Diversionary tactics?"

Lydia walked over to the chart, taking the pointer from Shirley-Ann on the way.

"Sergei and I, in A-2, will stay with A-1 until we reach St Kilda then take a wide arc to approach Alpha from the north." She traced the route on the chart. "We will head south directly towards the platform, timing our approach to coincide with Mike's arrival, before veering off to link up with him. At this point the boats will be in close proximity, inside the turbine ring near the west column"

"Rationale for this?" Kade asked.

"Two-fold. Firstly, to attract the attention of the Exiles away from Cassie's approach. Secondly, to draw the majority of the Exiles in the corridor together in an attempt to clear at least two of the hatches to allow the assault group to access the corridor safely. That will depend on whether we can generate enough interest for them to want to watch the boats."

"And this where Lydia's dance – *of sorts* – will help." Sergei added.

A burst of laughter greeted the comment.

"But you won't see it, Colonel." Lydia smiled at Tom. "You'll be busy somewhere else."

★

The wind had dropped significantly and the earlier angry sky had given way to white cloud with a promise of the sun breaking through. Tom could feel the familiar sensation in his stomach that came with the anticipation of action, because, unless the weather changed dramatically again, he knew they would go tomorrow; for certain. And yet he realised that, by any standards, he was content, and that such a feeling was nothing short of miraculous given his recent despair and decline.

He turned to look at the beautiful woman at his side. He had decided that Lydia van Roden *was* beautiful when she smiled, the hardness morphing into an almost angelic face framed by her golden-blonde hair. In fact, she reminded him very much of someone else. They sat together, watching the lapping of the waves and the gentle swaying of tomorrow's transport out in the bay. Tom had managed to separate her from the rest of the group at their second break of the day and they had walked through the ruins of the ancient settlement and down to the shoreline. There was something he had wanted to say to her.

"Listen, I'm sorry for the remark about the dancing. It was a tactless thing to say to someone I hardly know. It wasn't intended to be sexist or suggestive or…"

"Forget it, Colonel. I'm used to a lot worse and with no apology forthcoming. This is a man's world – they keep telling me. By which they mean, if you don't like it you know what you can do."

"I guess you don't like this part?"

"It gets the job done. But if you can think of a better way of distracting a bunch of horny males so someone can sneak up on them, please let me know and I'll go tell Kade. Until then... And they don't see any more of me than you're seeing right now. The body-suit makes sure of that. It's all in their imagination – they just don't *know* that."

Tom laughed. "Well, I'm sorry anyway."

"About saying what you did or about not seeing the show?"

She gave him a wide smile.

"Both, I guess," he said, smiling back.

Since clearing the air they had been sitting in silence for a long time, content with each other's company.

"Is it right you know Kade?" Lydia said.

"Not until a week ago. What makes you think that?"

"Just seeing you together. You seem connected somehow."

"That's very perceptive."

"I'm a psychologist, remember. I can just about read people's minds."

"Then I'd best be careful what I'm thinking," Tom said. "Kade and I have – *had* – a mutual friend – well, *my* friend, *his* acquaintance."

"John Deverall."

Tom turned to her, eyes wide in surprise.

"It's a small world at this end of the business," Lydia said, smiling at him. "Anyway, we'd best be getting back." She stood up and reached out her hand to him. "Come on, let's go." He took her hand and she pulled him to his feet.

★

Shirley-Ann had the pointer again, indicating a close-up drawing of the bottom of east column.

"When Cassie arrives at the column, Lydia will be the only one on deck on either of the Archers. She will have a tactical radio *somehow* concealed on her and will advise me if and when it is okay to surface. We have no idea, of course, how calm or otherwise the sea will be when we arrive in position below the door. We have ten feet to climb to the door from a craft with no keel. Here's how we'll try…"

She pointed to another diagram showing a plan of the column cross-section and the submersible from above.

"I'll pull Cassie in sideways so her port beam will be hard up against the column before we flip the lid. We'll then secure her with two powerful magnetic discs on the end of telescopic poles. These we'll attach to the column hull with the poles fully extended, fore and aft from the submersible at just above sea level. Once the magnets are secure, the other ends of the poles will be clamped into brackets in the bow and stern and then retracted to pull us in as tightly against the column as possible – like shortening a guy-rope on a tent or awning. That should hold us long and steady enough for the team to get out of their wet-suits while I fix the magnetic ladder up to the door.

"Once you're safely in the shaft, I will remove the ladder and the magnetic poles and lay off the column. This will enable me to take Cassie down if we get any prying air or surface craft – again, Lydia will be in the best position to advise. But it means when you exit the column, you will have to jump into the water and I'll pick you up. Because of that, you'll store five lifejackets at the base of the column for your return. And you need to close the door behind you on your way out – in whatever way you can."

"Do we all understand that?" Kade put in. "It takes more than one person to handle the poles, so the Major can't re-attach on her own. On the other hand, we must leave Alpha the way we found it – with the door closed and the ladder removed. Okay?"

All heads nodded.

"Thanks, Major. Commander, *s'il vous plait*."

Jules Cartier got to his feet and spoke with a soft voice and a beautiful accent.

"When we are inside the shaft, I will lead the climb to the top." He had in his hand what looked like a wide metal g-clamp which he held up high and regarded with a puzzled expression. "This, I believe, is what English-speaking people call a wedge." He beamed as a ripple of laughter went round the group.

"At each hatch, we do the same. Three of us go through and make tight a wedge to the rim of the hatch in such a way that it will stop it closing and also keep back the spring bolt." He opened his eyes wide and gave a quintessential Gallic shrug. "I don't know why it needs to do both. *Eh, bien!* We do this each time, leaving one person beneath for safety until we know the hatch does not close. Then he comes through to join us. When we get to the top, we wait for Colonel Tom to catch up, then…" He paused as the laughter came again. "*Je suis desolé*" he said, nodding to Tom, who mimicked his shrug with a smile and, "*C'est d'accord!*"

"After the hatch number four, we tell Mike we are here and wait on the sub floor for him to advise the access point to the corridor. This will depend on where the Exiles are mostly together, and where our target is on the platform."

He bowed to the four sides of the room and sat down.

"*Merci*, Commander," Kade said.

"*Je vous en prie.*"

"Mr Needham."

Mike turned his chair round to face a laptop on a narrow table against the wall behind him. He entered a password and ID and the screen filled with the digital lattice which represented the populated areas of the platform – the apartments, main deck and lower corridor. Tiny points of light were scattered throughout the network and as Mike moved the mouse, the flat image rotated and tilted slightly into a three-dimensional diagram, causing clusters of lights to separate. He clicked on an icon and the image was projected onto a large screen on the wall above the laptop. Chairs were shuffled round so that all of the group were facing the screen.

"Let's just recap on positional terminology so we don't need to describe in detail where we are on the day." He used the cursor as a pointer on the screen. "This, near the bottom of the lattice, around three sides of the platform, is the recreational corridor, which we will refer to as 'the corridor'. Below this is the sub-floor, which we will call 'the sub-floor'. You will be climbing the east column, so the hatch at the top of the climb which gives you access from the sub-floor to the corridor is 'east hatch'. Going clockwise around the structure we have south hatch, west hatch and north hatch. Starting at north hatch and coming back around the corridor – or sub-floor

– the three sides of the horseshoe are Section A, Section B, Section C.

"Each pinpoint of light represents a lost soul on Alpha. There should be seven hundred and ninety-eight lights if they are all alive, which, thankfully, they are."

He moved the cursor to point to a display showing various data on the right side of the screen, stopping on a cell which displayed the number he had just quoted.

"You are looking at a live picture – this is the distribution of Exiles on the platform at..." he checked his watch "... two-fifteen this afternoon, and is what they will be seeing in the monitoring suite at the Lochshore Exile Monitoring Centre. This is a simultaneous stream from that system and I will have the same set up on Archer One. It is the only full picture we have of activity on Alpha. All but eight of the three hundred and twenty cameras that initially provided CCTV images have been found and wrecked by the inmates. Not a very clever move on their part because they existed for *their* benefit, but a conditioned reflex to a symbol of authority, no doubt.

"The information on this system reaches us from a tiny transmitter surgically implanted close to the heart of each inmate, which sends information in a continuous flow, so the monitoring team can check a range of health indicators and respond accordingly. *Our* interest in the transmission, of course, is because it also tells us the person's exact location on the platform. Our target is Oliver Wangari – formerly, Jason Midanda. Let's see where he usually hangs out."

He clicked on another icon, which brought up a blank box at the top of the screen into which he typed the name.

"Let's see where he's been over the past seven days," Mike said,

He worked his way through a couple of menus and hit Enter. The image of Alpha which had faded into a muted background while Mike was entering the data, sprang forward again, this time with an animated picture showing a single spot of light moving around the lattice and a changing number at the bottom of the screen displaying time and date. Eventually the light stopped moving when the current time showed.

"Thank you, Mike," Kade said. "Sergei, comments, observations?"

The Russian got to his feet and walked across to where Mike was sitting, leaning over him to point at the screen. "Again, please, Mike," he said, in a voice whose strength and timbre perfectly suited his huge frame and filled the room. Mike clicked on the screen again to start the same sequence.

"We can see our friend lives on floor five of south block," Sergei said. "He rise early and leave apartment each day at half-morning – about ten-thirty. He spend much time in computer suite on main deck; but *most* time in radio room in Section C corridor on receiving deck level. He is, it seem, communication enthusiast – and, probably, genius. We wish him to be in radio room when team arrive on platform. This we help by radio link with Alpha as team climbs column, wishing target to receive messages I send from A-2 and hope to get him to talk to me. If most are interested in Lydia's dance more than my message, target should be easy to pick from small number."

Lydia smiled across at Tom as Sergei continued.

"Climbing team will know where he is by Mike telling through radio contact. When target alone or with small number, then team opens correct hatch and takes him. However, if..." Sergei counted on his fingers, "... target goes with others to watch Lydia; if many people are in radio room to listen to message; if he is somewhere not on corridor – perhaps main deck or in apartment, then we have the *big* problem."

Sergei went back to his seat while the group shifted their chairs back to face the table then looked towards Kade for his next prompt. The leader remained silent for a long time then got to his feet. He nodded towards the last speaker.

"Thank you, Sergei, for your comments and your closing statement – the *big* problem. For the moment, let's think of our target as a hostage, though, of course, that isn't really true. In all this group's operations together, we have always been fairly clear in advance where the hostages were. They may have been split up and spread out to make it more difficult for a rescue attempt, but we knew where we had to go to get them. We wouldn't attempt to rescue them until we *did* know, in fact. Tomorrow – because it *will be* tomorrow – we have no idea where the target will be when we get there. Although Mike has shown us his movements over the past seven days – and, as Sergei says, we can identify some places of his preference from those – no two of those days have been the same.

"Once we reach the sub floor, we rely completely on Mike to guide us. And I mean guide in the sense of directional and positional data. He can tell us where Jason is and how many people are with him, where – and in what numbers – the rest of the Exiles are and their proximity to the target. Mike's is a vital – a *critical* – role, but *I* will be the one to decide how we proceed in the light of that information." He fixed his piercing pale eyes on Tom. "As the Colonel said earlier today, my job is to take four people on to Alpha and bring five back. That's Plan A. Plan B is for the four to return safely."

The group remained silent for a long time. Kade eventually turned to the man across to his right.

"Rico – weapons."

Enrico Santana got to his feet and turned to pick up a gun from a shelf behind him. He held it up in his right hand and turned it back and forth to show the group.

"Our good friend Heckler Koch MP5 – SMG – favourite weapon of hostage rescue teams across world. Assault team will carry these, but these ones are special. They will not have live bullets, for two reasons. First we must not kill anyone; a light suddenly becoming still with no life output will be flagged quick on screen at Monitoring Centre and they will see someone dies. Not good for secret mission." He opened his eyes wide to emphasise the point. "Second, if someone loses his weapon to one of the Exiles we have enemy armed with live ammo. So no live bullets. Okay?"

Everyone nodded their understanding.

"But this gun is special in another way. It is adapted for use with blanks so, when fired, this special chamber on barrel produces sound like ricochets – like bullets bouncing off wall. This will help make it real to Exiles." He smiled. "I hope so, anyway."

He looked across at Kade and sat down. Kade got to his feet.

"One change," he said. From the side pocket of his gilet, he took out a second gun, holding it out to the group on the flat of his hand.

"Glock 18 select fire pistol. Can be used as a standard Glock 17 or flicked to full-auto mode. Along with the Heckler, I will be carrying this, loaded with *live* ammo."

The group exchanged surprised glances; Tom rose from his seat.

"This is *not* what we decided. We have been through this four, five times and you have never mentioned…"

"I've been keeping it for this moment, Colonel – just before we go – because I knew this would be your reaction. I have no intention of using the gun; it will be there as a last resort. You have to decide whether you know enough about us to trust me on this, because I am not going without it."

Tom remained standing for a few more seconds then nodded and sat down. Kade waited a while before speaking again.

"One last – *huge* – piece of the puzzle. What happens to the target if – let's say *when* – we get him back. Colonel?"

Tom got to his feet again as Kade sat down. "Jason is electronically tagged like the rest. The chip is surgically implanted close to the heart, powered by the heartbeat itself, and cannot be removed except by further surgery. So, *as things stand*, when we drop him through one of the corridor hatches onto the sub-floor, Lochshore will see him move out-of-bounds of his permitted area of access. When we start to descend east column, his light will show for about twenty feet until it goes out of range of the digital lattice. At that point they can – and no doubt will – switch to the national tracking system – NTS – which we use across the UK to monitor the location of Deferred Life Exiles who all carry a similar tag, and track him from there.

"That, as I said, is *as things stand*. What we need is a window in time, during which he is effectively off the scanner, from just before he drops through the first hatch to when we can get him to a place where NTS can't pick up his signal. Mike has explained how this window will be achieved and…" he turned to the engineer, "… he will go through it again in a few minutes.

"So let's take it from when we get him into the submersible. When Cassie has cleared the area on a direct heading back to here, Archer-One will pick her up around five miles outside the ring and continue on the same course. As soon after that as it can get to us, a chopper will lift Jason and me off the boat and take us to a place called Farcuillin Lodge tucked away in Knoydart, which is as remote as it gets anywhere in the UK. We are sure NTS can't pick up a signal from there. The lodge is owned by a close friend of my wife's family.

Access to the property is by a keypad and, conveniently, there's a helipad close by. I just hope this person's not taking a late holiday. The chopper will have a stack of food to deliver along with the two of us, but I'm also banking on the lodge being well stocked because we sure as hell won't be going shopping from there.

"After that, then I'm not sure. New evidence points to a possible mistake with Jason's – and my son's – convictions. It's too late for Jack, but I'm confident – well, hopeful – that we might be able to … If things work out, I mean…"

He ran out of words and there was a long awkward silence before Kade spoke. "Well," he said, "we wish you luck, Colonel, and hope things *do* work out. After all you'll have been through, I don't like to think of you both starving to death on a Scottish hillside."

Tom smiled. "Thank you," he said.

"And now, Mr Needham, tell us how you're going to create this window in time."

The group relaxed and Mike got to his feet.

"With some help from our number nine."

★

Katey dropped her fork onto her half-empty dinner plate and stared wide-eyed at her mother.

"He did *what*?"

Mags remained silent, looking down at her hands, clasped together on her lap.

"And you've known about this since Dad told you – what – over a month ago?"

"No, he didn't say anything about it at the time he told me about Jason. I only found out from Josh Wilcox…"

"When?"

"Monday – six days ago."

"So you've known for nearly a week. Well, thank you for telling me. Why *didn't* you tell me?"

"What was the point? Nothing came of it."

"Then why are you telling me now?"

Mags sighed and leaned back on her chair.

"Look, Katey, I've been agonising all week about whether to say something to you or not. Whether to let you share in yet *another* disappointment. If I did the wrong thing, then I'm sorry. But how am I supposed to know what the right or wrong thing is anymore? I've taken just about as much as I can!"

Katey reached across and took her hand.

"I'm sorry, Mum. That was completely out of order. It's just another shock to have to deal with. But I'm glad you told me, really I am. It's good to know that he's still the dad I've always been so proud of. But isn't that a clue as to why he might be up there? Shouldn't we tell Mr Mackay?"

Mags shrugged. "I don't know. That's what I thought on Thursday when John told us where they'd found his car. I nearly told him then. But I thought, if he is planning to get Jason, why don't we let him go ahead and try? If we tell the police, they'll make it impossible for him to succeed. They'll swamp the area with boats and helicopters – they'll have the jets back again. No-one will get anywhere near the place."

Katey was wide-eyed again.

"*Succeed!* Mum, this 'place' you're talking about is Platform Alpha. There is no way off it – Dad made sure of that. There is no way he can... *succeed!* We don't need the police to make it impossible for him."

"You don't know your father when he sets his mind to something."

"I *do* know my father. Not as well as you, but enough to know he can't work miracles – well, not the impossible, anyway."

"Okay, so if that *is* what he's trying to do, he'll fail and then he'll come back, won't he? But it's best that he comes to terms with that himself rather than someone stopping him trying."

They sat in silence for a while before Katey spoke. "And what if something happens to him? What if he doesn't come back?"

"Then that's something else we'll have to live with. But let's not forget that right now he's being sought by the police as a prime suspect for eight murders. Whether he's guilty of them or not, don't you think that helping them find him would be an act of betrayal?"

CHAPTER TWENTY

Tom opened his eyes to complete silence, quickly realising that it was the absence of sound that had woken him up. He pushed aside the down duvet, rolled over and swung his legs off the top bunk, dropping lightly onto the wooden floor. He pulled on his jeans and grabbed the heavy fleece from its hook by the door. After wriggling his feet into his still-laced-up trainers, he slipped out of the bunk-room into the open plan area and out through the door into the cool morning.

In the clear sky above, the stars sparkled in their millions with no artificial lights to dampen their brilliance. He checked his watch – 6.25 am. Five minutes before the mechanical timer kicked in to start the generator. But it wasn't the absence of the engine noise that made the difference. There was no sound at all – no wind blowing, waves lapping, birds calling.

He decided to walk to the top of Carnan rather than run. It wouldn't look very sensible if he sprained an ankle – or worse – jogging along the rocky path in the near-darkness just a couple of hours before they were due to set off. As he descended, he noticed that the lights were now on in the building and the concrete yard outside was illuminated by the circle of arc lamps. The hum of the generator permeated the silence. Against the background glow, he noticed a figure climbing up the path towards him.

"Good morning, Colonel."

"Good morning, Doctor. Are you a search party?"

"Well, we did wonder if you'd left without us, which worried us a little – until we counted the boats, of course."

Tom gave a little laugh. "No, just woke early to the deafening silence and came out to check if it was the end of the world."

"It just about qualifies, I think, this island."

Lydia turned as Tom drew level with her and they walked back side by side in silence until they reached the flat ground in front of the dunes.

"How do you feel?" she asked.

Tom looked at her. "Is this a psychotherapy session, or just small talk?"

"Just interested. Must be strange going into action to save a family member – well, *nearly* a family member."

Tom sighed and shook his head.

"To be honest, Lydia, I'm not sure what counts as strange any more. Six months ago… Well, let's just say *everything* is different, so I've no normality to measure anything new against."

She gave him a nudge in the ribs with her elbow. "Hey, that's what *I* should be saying to *you*. Do we have a demarcation issue here?"

He gave a little laugh, grateful for the humour, but Lydia continued.

"Have you decided what your *preferred* normality would be?"

He looked at her with a puzzled frown. "Why do you ask that?"

"Just watching you over the last six days, you seem to fit in so easily with the rest of the group. It makes me think perhaps this is what you like best." They had reached the door of the building and turned to face each other. "Not that it's any of my business," she added.

Tom smiled. "And here's me thinking you were offering me a job. But you're right; the stakes, for me, are higher than any other mission I've been on, but there's nowhere I'd rather be right now; nothing I'd rather be doing." He shook his head. "Don't you ever get tired of being right?"

★

The boats picked up speed heading out of the bay before swinging south and then west through the Straits of Berneray between the two southern-most members of the Long Island group. Once into the open Atlantic, the mirror-flat water became white-flecked with small wave-tops and they could feel the boats swing in a low swell.

Clear of the Straits, they turned north towards their initial destination eighty miles away, from where the boats would go their separate ways. The Archer Class patrol boat, at just under seventy feet long, was the smallest commissioned vessel in the Royal Navy, used extensively to patrol the British coastline and inland waterways. Its design top speed was twenty-five knots, but with a moulded glass-reinforced plastic hull capable of taking up to nearly twice that, the 2000 bhp replacement engines in Kade's small flotilla would get them to the archipelago in less than two hours.

Kade, standing at the bow of the leading boat, checked his watch – 9.07 am – and calculated the timescale. Arrive St Kilda, say, 11.00; thirty minutes for collecting samples – 11.30; eighteen miles – around twenty-five minutes – from there to Cassie's drop-off point – 11.55; minimum ten minutes for the off-load – 12.05 pm; then forty minutes in Cassie to the door at the base of east column. Even with a little slack in the system, they should arrive around 1.00 pm, when – based on their observed activity over the past few days – virtually all Exiles should be up and active.

He unclipped the radio from his belt.

"Survey vessel Archer-Two, radio check."

"Archer-Two receiving."

"Stay on channel eight; one-five-six point four hundred megahertz. Confirm."

"Copy and confirm. Out."

"Out."

An unnecessary exchange, he knew, but his way of managing his impatience and... yes... nerves. The natural fear of the unknown. He looked ahead at the empty sea with its abnormally clear horizon, then turned to go aft just as a figure appeared beside him.

"Colonel. Sea-legs okay?"

"Fine," Tom said, "but I'm grateful for the calm conditions."

"I'm sure that goes for all of us – Lydia in particular. Can't have her falling overboard halfway through her routine."

They laughed.

"How long before we see Alpha, do you think?" Tom asked.

"I'd say about an hour. I guess we'll see the turbines first, then the platform a few minutes later. Now – I'd best go say 'Hi' to Cassie."

He left Tom at the bow and made his way to the stern where Shirley-Ann was already seated at the controls with the dome of the submersible open and clamped safely against the winch.

"Everything okay, Major?"

"All systems a-okay, sir. Radio-checked with Archer-Two; de-floatation controls tested and passed this morning; magnets fully charged. No probs, can't wait to get going."

Kade smiled and nodded. "Great stuff, Major."

★

Seventy minutes into their journey, their final destination made its appearance on their port bow. First, as Kade had predicted, the turbines closest to them – but still nearly fifty miles away – came into view, as the tip of each huge blade cleared the horizon at the top of its arc and dropped back out of sight again. Then the gigantic bulk of Hotel St Kilda appeared behind the circling blades, and seemed to rise out of the sea, like the Kraken suddenly aware of an approaching threat.

All eight people were on deck, the boats fifty yards apart and guided by the onboard satnav system. They stared in wonder at the monstrous structure.

"Times like this I feel a bit like Professor Frankenstein," Mike said, "wondering what I've unleashed on the world."

It was said without humour and received with sombre silence.

With the top half of the accommodation block showing, it stopped rising from behind the horizon as it slipped behind to their left and they turned their attention to the massive cliffs of the island group racing towards them.

Jules turned to Kade. "A shame we can't just go west from here directly to Alpha; instead we go to St Kilda."

"We have to go through the motions of taking water samples from close to the islands to compare with samples collected near Alpha. The BOS need to know the platform's impact on sea-life at the bottom of the food chain. That's the story that gave us clearance in these waters and gets us inside the ring. Confirmed by the Society itself, in fact – at least that's what Lochshore believes. So they're expecting us on Hirta. We don't want to disappoint them."

★

By the time the police helicopter was crossing the border on its way north, Harry Waters' initial nervousness had passed beyond severe anxiety and had reached a silent state of white-knuckle panic. If he was honest with himself, he'd put off making the trip as long as possible in the hope it wouldn't be necessary, but he'd run out of reasons for delaying it further. Air travel – of any kind – was his most hated form of transport and he swore to himself he would never again complain about gridlock in central London.

He recalled one of his favourite quotes – attributed to a Jewish philosopher – 'If God had intended us to fly, he would have given us tickets.' It never failed to make him laugh – except at times like this when he was putting the underlying message to the test. Had he been heading for a holiday destination on a 737, by now he would be on his third or fourth whisky and ready to take over in the cockpit should the need arise.

Beside him was DC Natalie Crusoe, relaxed and pointing things out as she looked out of the window with the enthusiasm of an excited child, seemingly oblivious to his discomfort.

The approach and landing were smooth and uneventful and by the time the door was opened, most of the colour had returned to Harry's face. They climbed down the steps from the chopper, ducking instinctively underneath the slowing rotor blades as they made their way, with their overnight bags, to the person waving to them from the edge of the field. The tall, well-built man with a craggy, weather-beaten face and short-cropped red hair stepped forward and reached out his hand.

"Detective Inspector Stuart, Highlands and Islands Police. Very pleased to meet you, DI Waters."

Harry shook his hand. "You too, Inspector. Please, call me Harry. This is Detective Constable Crusoe, part of my major incident team."

She smiled and reached forward to shake his hand. "It's Natalie – Nat," she said.

"I'm Charlie. They call me BP behind my back, short for Bonnie Prince." He rubbed his hand over his face. "I think it's what they call irony – or sarcasm, perhaps."

They laughed.

"Let's get away from these rotors and meet the rest of the team," Charlie said.

In the relative quiet of the small receiving lounge with all-round windows, Charlie introduced Detective Sergeant Isabel Macken and Rob Cameron, the senior officer from the area Crime Scene Investigation Unit whose team had been responsible for examining the car.

"This is some patch you have here," Harry said, turning a full circle to take in the spectacular mountains and the gleaming water of Loch Broom behind the town, whose white buildings dazzled in the bright sunlight. "A bit different to Guildford. I don't suppose you have any vacancies?"

Charlie snorted a laugh. "You're right; it's a beautiful part of the world. But Isabel's the lucky one." He nodded to his colleague. "She's based here in Ullapool, and covers Wester Ross down to Lochalsh. Rob and I work from Inverness – more like Guildford, I imagine."

"Not a whole lot more," Natalie said. "I'll take Inverness any day."

★

The Archers completed nearly a full circuit of Hirta, the main island of the archipelago, periodically lowering containers into the water for effect, to avoid raising any suspicion in the observation tower on the site of the old radar station, before laying off the island on the western side under the mighty escarpment of Mullach Bi. Kade looked across at the spectacular cliffs and sea stacs, host to thousands of perching and circling sea-birds.

"What an amazing place. And this is part of Scotland?"

"The farthest outpost of the UK," Tom said, "forty miles west of anything else. And one of only twenty-four places on the planet designated as a Dual World Heritage Site."

"And people actually lived here and managed to survive on their own?" Kade asked.

"For about four millennia until less than a hundred years ago, then so many people had left as to make it unsustainable. The military set up a missile tracking station in the fifties, and we now use it as a base for servicing Alpha – and for any further platforms. But it's pretty much like it's always been; all our facilities have been installed underground to preserve it as it should be."

They edged the boats close together to avoid having to use the radios as they ran through their final checklist, and at 11.35 am, Archer-One pulled away south, retracing its route to align itself due east of Alpha and begin its approach.

A couple of minutes before noon it stopped again, directly facing the platform just five miles away. Tom stood at the bow, trying to take in the vastness of the structure and its ring of wind turbines. He'd never seen it before from sea level. Approaching it from the air, as he had done on a number of occasions, it had taken his breath away. Right now, it was threatening to stop his heart.

For the first time, he wondered if what they were attempting was even remotely possible.

"Colonel. Wetsuit."

Kade's voice interrupted his thoughts. He turned to see the submersible already off the deck and hanging over the stern. Kade, Jules and Rico were half into their suits as Mike operated the winch to lower Cassie, with Shirley-Ann on board, into the gently rocking sea.

Tom removed his black combat trousers and jacket, stuffing them into his waterproof bag along with his weapon, head-torch and tactical radio set. He pulled on the wetsuit, stretching the hood over his head, then picked up the full facemask, testing it in position before taking it off again. With Cassie now stable in the water, the four-man assault team climbed down the short ladder fixed to the stern of the boat and stepped into it, taking their seats, two-abreast behind Shirley-Ann. The craft was designed for a maximum of seven people – one driver and six passengers.

Once aboard, the men placed their bags in the watertight compartments next to their seats, Jules's along with the small rucksack containing the lockable wedges. They all put on their face masks, each attaching a tube to the mouthpiece from an air tank under their seat. After they had tested the supply and nodded to Shirley-Ann, she activated the reinforced Perspex dome which closed slowly over them and sealed itself into position with a hiss of compressed air. After giving the thumbs-up sign to Mike, who was leaning over the stern of the Archer, she pulled a lever to her right, flooding the passenger compartment with cold Atlantic water. Powerful heaters beneath their feet kicked in to compensate for the drop in temperature.

The image of Archer-One began to twist and shimmer as they sank below the surface to their cruising depth of thirty feet. Shirley-Ann held it suspended there for a few moments until she was satisfied each member's breathing had stabilised.

"Okay to go, Mike."

They could hear her voice as she gave the signal and Mike's muffled reply sounded in the submersible.

"Okay, Cassie. Good luck."

The water above began to churn as the twin shafts of the Archer started up and the boat receded from sight ahead of them. Cassie set off, due west, building up to her top speed of eight knots.

★

Fifteen minutes after her sister craft's departure from Hirta, Archer-Two set off heading west, passing south of the lofty heights of Soay, to prepare for her own approach from the north.

At 12.15 pm, half a mile from the platform, it entered the ring of fifty-five massive wind turbines circling the platform at 100-yard intervals, each 350 feet high from the surface of the sea to the top of their towers and 500 feet to the tip of a vertical blade. Along with the solar panels and wave energy converters, they supplied more than enough power for the platform and the support facility on Hirta.

At that same moment, Archer-One, already inside the ring, was passing south of the platform, heading for their pre-arranged rendezvous point due west of Alpha. At 12.23 pm the two boats came to a stop, twenty yards apart, facing each other and beam-on to the platform.

On Archer-Two, Lydia appeared from below in her flesh-coloured, insulated body suit and small bikini, and climbed the short ladder onto the top of the cabin.

On Archer-One, Mike went below, entered the co-ordinates into the onboard computer and activated the automatic stabilising mode to hold the boat's position. He turned to the monitoring system and watched the pin-pricks of light on the screen swarming over to the west side of the platform.

★

The four police officers and Rob Cameron stood together outside the circle of crime-scene tape, which still surrounded the now vacant space where the Audi had been found at the side of the harbour.

"How long do we think it had been here?" Harry asked Charlie.

"Well, as soon as the appeal for information went out on Thursday we had thirty or so people get in touch right away. Apparently, it had been a focus of public interest for a while. We reckon it must have been parked here for at least twenty-four, more likely forty-eight, hours before we got to see it. So that would be from last Tuesday, or, latest, Wednesday."

Harry nodded. "And you don't think it had been touched during the time before you got to it?"

"No new fingerprints on the door handles, which, as you know, is usually the first contact. The gulls had peppered it a bit. We needed the bomb disposal lads to check it out, of course. The detonators and wire were visible behind the seats; it was just possible it could have been booby trapped. Then CSIU photographed it and forensically recovered it the same day – Thursday.

"We've removed a couple of things for examination since then, which you know about. The mobile – it was in the glove box. I assume he's got himself a replacement so we can't trace him – that's the only reason I can think of why he'd leave it. Anyway, the last call he made from it was to Jackie Hewlett, the Home Secretary, very early last Sunday morning – around half past midnight. At least that was the last one on the outgoing calls list – unless he's erased some. The techies are checking it out. He's had a dozen or so missed calls since then, mostly from his wife, a couple from someone called Dan. And the detonators and wire – we removed them to compare with the stuff used in the Dorking bombing, like you asked."

"Did the satnav tell us anything?"

"Only that he didn't use it to find his way here. Not that you'd expect him to. It's the only town up here and there's only one way to it from the south – the A835."

Charlie's mobile sounded. He took it from his coat pocket. "Excuse me," he said, and stepped a few paces away. After a brief exchange and a few questions, he ended the call and turned back to the group.

"That was Chief Superintendent Stevenson – my boss. She's just had a call from Donny McClure, no less. Apparently, Mr Brown and his wife spent a few days at a place called Farcuillin Lodge on Knoydart earlier this year. She said it might be worth checking to see if he's gone there."

DS Macken frowned. "He'd hardly come to Ullapool on his way to Knoydart…"

"Unless he was trying to throw people off the scent," Charlie said, "which he'd want to do, of course. And he'd have to hire a boat from *somewhere*…"

"Or steal one, I suppose," Isabel said. "There's one missing from further along the loch at Morefield, but they think that's just come off its mooring. It's a wee, crappy thing – not something you'd want to take out into The Minch. I guess we could check for anyone landing at Inverie."

Harry and Natalie exchanged a brief glance, not lost on Charlie.

"Sorry," he said. "Knoydart is much further south and only accessible by boat. Although…" he turned back to Isabel, "… if that's where he was going I'm not sure how he'd get around once he arrived. He's bound to be recognised, for a start."

"Who's Donny McClure, by the way?" Harry asked.

"Donald McClure, Head of Grampian Police. He remembered Mr Brown saying he was going to Knoydart directly after a meeting they both attended at Lochshore in April. Anyway, Cath Stevenson's sending a chopper to check it out – apparently there's a helipad next to the Lodge. She wants to know if we'd like to go along. It's a long shot. What do you think? I said I'd phone her back."

The colour drained from Harry's face. "I'll pass on that, if you don't mind."

"Don't mind at all," Charlie said, looking relieved. "Hate those bloody things. I'll just let her know to go ahead without us, then I'll take you to where we've got the car so you can see it for yourselves."

He turned away again to make the call. When he'd finished, Harry was staring out across the loch, deep in thought.

"When you think about it," he said, "we don't really know why he's up here. I guess we're assuming – *I* was assuming – he's gone on the run or into hiding, but the timing doesn't fit, does it? He's not been seen since a week last Friday – that's ten days ago. Well, half-two in the morning on the Saturday, to be exact, when he was – shall we say – 'helped' to leave a club on the Embankment in London. The manager, at Brown's request, phoned someone to pick him up on a number given to him by Brown. A woman answered, wouldn't give her name, but agreed to come and get him, which we assume she did, because he'd gone when the doorman went to check about twenty minutes later."

He was silent for a moment, counting off the days in his mind before continuing.

"We're ninety-nine percent certain he was at his apartment when he made that last call from his mobile to Jackie Hewlett at twelve-thirty on Sunday morning, and later that day he was *definitely* there because he phoned John Mackay – that's *my* boss – from the land-line. That appears to be the last contact anyone's had with him. His lawyer called at the apartment on Monday and got no answer, and you're saying he hasn't answered his mobile since before then."

He paused again, deep in thought.

"Where's this going, sir?" Natalie asked. "Am I being thick or something?"

"Sorry, I'm rambling a bit; just bear with me. His wife goes to the apartment later on Monday and finds he'd already left – no car, holdall and clothes missing, wallet and keys gone. DI Cottrell searches the place on Wednesday with Mrs T and they find the gun. We put out an appeal for info on his whereabouts on Thursday lunchtime. Are you with me?"

They all nodded.

"So the first time he'd know we were looking for him – and that's *if* he had access to TV, newspapers, Internet, whatever – would be then, Thursday lunchtime. Right?"

"And by then he was already up here," Charlie said. "So he must have had another reason for coming. Unless it's just a coincidence that he went on the run just before we put out the appeal."

"I'm afraid…" Harry began.

"DI Waters doesn't believe in coincidences," Natalie interrupted.

"That makes two of us," Charlie said. "So perhaps it's not a hiding place we should be looking for."

★

"Cassie to Archer-Two. All clear to surface?"

"All clear, Cassie." Lydia's voice. "Come on up."

Tom pulled back the tight cuff of his wetsuit and checked his watch – 13.07. Cassie nudged against the column as Shirley-Ann evacuated the water until the craft came to rest on the surface ten feet below the door. The column climbed away upwards to the five-and-a-half acres of the main deck with the receiving floor suspended below it. Around 200 yards across from them, through the gap between the north and west columns, the satellite platform – a 120-foot-square lift shaft, designed to raise the prisoner cages from the transfer vessels to the receiving floor – towered to the same height.

Below the surface, the four main columns extended down a further hundred feet and were joined together by a huge pontoon – like an enormous square doughnut – to create the semi-submersible design, providing a low centre of gravity and optimum stability. The whole structure, anchored by sixteen deep-water chains and a network of wire mooring lines, had been originally designed to survive a once-in-a-lifetime storm in the merciless waters and wind systems of the Gulf of Mexico.

"Cassie to Archer-One and Archer-Two. In position. Flipping the lid now and changing to tactical radios in… ninety seconds."

The Perspex dome hissed open and over, coming to rest on the water at the side away from the column. They removed their masks and breathing tubes, and unclipped the extendable poles from their brackets at the sides of the hull. After using the magnets to secure Cassie against the column, the four men wriggled out of their wetsuits and back into their trousers, close-fitting jackets and light-weight boots. They took out the MP5s, each slipping the strap over his head and shoulder, and pulled on the black beanie hats, strapping the head-torches against their foreheads. They clipped the lightweight digital radios in place around their necks, adjusting ear and mouthpieces to leave their hands free, and checking frequencies. Finally, they pulled on fingerless gloves with toughened rubber palms to assist with gripping the rungs of the ladder and checked the karabiner on the leather waistband of their trousers, which could be hooked onto a rung to free their hands at any point of the climb.

Shirley-Ann had secured the magnetic ladder against the hull, extending it upwards to just below the door. Jules pulled on the rucksack, tightening it in place against his chest to give easy access to the wedges.

Kade looked round, checking readiness. "Okay to go?"

"Okay to go." All replied.

He checked his watch. "Team to Archers; entering shaft at thirteen-twenty-one. Out."

He turned to his comrades.

"Right, let's do it."

Jules climbed the ladder, turned the bolt-head, pushed in the door and slipped through the opening. He leaned out again, while Kade threw the five lifejackets up to him, then the rest of the team followed him into the shaft, closing the door behind them.

★

Oblivious to the shouts and whoops of the crushing mass around him, Jason Midanda watched the woman swinging her body around the mast on the bridge of the boat. It wasn't a unique experience seeing a female in a bikini close to his new home. Even in the short time he'd been there, there had been several cruise ships passing by – Alpha now seemed an essential part of all island tours – providing lots of opportunity to watch sunbathers on their heated decks through the telescopes and binoculars mounted on the continuous shelf which ran along all three sides of the corridor. But this display seemed to be entirely for their benefit. So either this woman was the world champion prick-teaser or something else was going on.

He turned his bins onto the other boat. Nothing moved on deck; no sign of any activity. BOSV on the sides and cabins – 'British Oceanographic Society' or 'Survey' he guessed – 'Vessel' probably. He wondered what possible value a pole dancer could bring to a scientific mission.

★

One hundred and fifty miles away a much smaller group was watching the spectacle unfold on the digital lattice on the huge wall screen in front of them and on the smaller screens showing images from the sea-facing cameras. The four-man Lochshore monitoring team covering the afternoon shift saw the same rush of Exiles to the west side of the platform, and the same exotic dance on the survey boat.

"She'll be in deep shit if this gets back to the BOS," said one man.

"Well they won't find out from me," said another. "Just in case she's planning to do it every week."

They laughed, then seemed to remember the tall, striking-looking man with the mane of grey hair and the expensive suit standing behind them watching the same screens. There were a few moments of uncomfortable silence.

"What do you think, sir?" The first man broke the tension with his question.

The tall man smiled. "No comment," he said, "except that they won't find out from me, either."

They laughed again.

★

The woman on the boat had stopped dancing and was waving to her audience. Jason felt someone grab his arm frosm behind.

"Ollie!"

He turned. A small, stocky young man with a pock-marked face and prematurely-thinning brown hair dragged him through the crowd away from the floor-to-ceiling windows.

"What's the panic, Razor?"

Ryan Azinger held on to his arm, pulling him along the corridor, not looking back.

"Come on, you need to hear this," he said.

★

Tom was already suffering as they approached the first landing. Not only could he feel the exertion of the climb but the dim, flickering light on the ceiling above them along with the darting beams of the head torches had brought on a feeling of nausea.

Jules stopped his climb with his head touching the first hatch cover, reached for the karabiner on his belt and clipped it to the ladder. Pulling back the sprung bolt, he stepped up another rung, using his neck and shoulder muscles to ease open the hatch. Holding it in place, he removed the first spring-locking wedge from the sack and snapped it around the rim. He unclipped the karabiner and climbed through, holding back the hatch for Kade and Rico to follow. Tom waited below as Jules let the hatch fall back. The wedge did its job, the hatch remained ajar, and Tom followed them through to the next stage.

The light above them shone with a bright and steady glow.

"Right, let's dip the headlights," Kade said, switching off his torch. They all complied, and Jules set off again up the ladder.

"Completed stage one," Kade said into his radio.

★

"What is he saying?"

"How would I know?" Jason said. "I don't even know what language he's speaking."

A group of twelve had gathered in the radio room to listen to the chanting voice; more were arriving.

"Sounds like east European, possibly Russian," Razor said.

"How the fuck would you know that?" The speaker was Kenny Morrison, a large well-built man in his early twenties with a shaved head and scarred features.

"Roscoe would know – *might* know, anyway," Razor muttered. "I'll go get him." He hurried from the room.

They listened in silence as the deep voice filled the room with short, rhythmic sentences.

"Sounds like poetry," Jason said.

Five minutes later Razor returned accompanied by a tall, thin young man with an untidy beard and uneven teeth.

"Do you know what this is, Rosk?" Jason asked.

Roscoe screwed up his face in concentration for a few moments.

"It's Russian," he said. "Poetry – kid's poetry – you know, like nursery rhymes."

"What the fuck's going on?" Kenny asked.

Jason frowned and shook his head. "No idea, but it's a bit of a coincidence, isn't it? We get someone spouting Russian poetry at the same time that a pole-dancer turns up to entertain us."

"You're right," Kenny said. "What *is* this, some sort of fucking arts festival?"

★

At the third hatch, Jules fumbled the wedge as he took it from the rucksack. It slipped out of his hand. Rico, third in line, took a spectacular one-handed catch and the crisis passed. Pulling himself through onto the final landing, Tom lay exhausted on the floor, his lungs and heart pumping and his legs feeling like jelly. Kade glanced at him. "We'll take ten this time. Last climb, then it's easy from there." He smiled. "Except for the eight hundred or so guys waiting for us."

Tom recovered quickly, exercising his legs with a few punishing squats until they felt like his own again.

"Everyone okay to go?" Kade asked. "Right." He turned his head to speak into the radio. "Completed level three."

Tom stopped several times on the last stretch, aware that he needed to be in good shape when they passed through the next hatch. From there they had to be prepared to move decisively at short notice once an opportunity presented itself.

They secured the wedge on the final hatch and climbed through to the sub-floor, which was dark apart from the area briefly lit by the strip light below as they passed through the opening. They switched their head torches on again and looked around them. At one side of the hatch, a few yards away, the floor ended in a solid,

336

featureless wall. At the other side, it stretched away from them into blackness beyond the effective range of the torches. Above them was the entrance to the corridor, their access to the hatch made easier by a vertical, metal ladder the ends of which were bolted to the floor and ceiling.

"Completed stage four; on sub floor now. Lighting?"

"Sensors will activate lights as you move past them." Mike's voice. "Target has arrived in radio room on corridor Section C. That's the section above you, but closer to the far end. So he's around one-twenty metres away from east hatch above you and thirty metres from south hatch. In attendance are around fifteen inmates, some starting to leave. Suggest you wait to see how the picture develops. Archer-Two, are you receiving?"

"Archer-Two receiving." Sergei's voice. "Copy target's position."

"Time for the second act. Out."

Kade reached up and switched off his head torch. "Let's save the batteries." They all followed his example and the darkness returned.

★

The group of eight remaining in a cluster around the receiver heard the voice change to a more conversational tone, speaking clipped English in a quiet and relaxed way, with little more than a trace of a Russian accent.

"Good afternoon, boys. I hope you enjoyed little trip back to my childhood. Those were poems my mother used to read to me when I was little boy in Kazan."

Jason leaned forward and threw a switch on the panel in front of him.

"Who is this? Please identify yourself and state your business."

"I am Sergei Rouschek. Who is asking?"

"What the fuck do you want?" Kenny's voice was hard and challenging.

"That was not the person who spoke before. I wish to speak to him."

Jason held up his hand for Kenny to remain silent.

"My name is Oliver Wangari. The other person you heard is Kenny Morrison. Tell us what you want."

"Just to talk. I'd like to know what it's like on there, how you are all getting along together. Things like that."

"Why?"

"Like to hear. We have some Russian people would benefit from your type of holiday."

"Fuck off, you snide bastard!" Kenny shouted. Jason held up his hand again.

"What my friend means," Jason said, "is that we are not here for *our* benefit, so we don't appreciate your comments."

"Okay, let me say then we have many million Russian people would benefit from *other* Russian people being in your place."

"Are you a reporter?"

"Would you like I was?"

"We wouldn't give a fuck!" Kenny shouted again. "But if you're calling just to take the piss…"

"How did you find this frequency?" Jason interrupted.

"Just by chance."

"I don't believe you. Where are you?"

"That's good thing about talking on the radio, Oliver? You can be *anywhere*."

Fast-running footsteps sounded in the corridor outside the room. A gangly youth, with eyes wide and shining, and breathing heavily from his sprint, appeared in the doorway.

"You should get back there. She's stripped off. Great tits. Come on!"

★

Mike's voice seemed to be amplified by the darkness around them.

"Four people including target still in radio room. Suggest move along to south hatch."

"Copy that." Kade thought for a few moments before continuing. "How many people in the actual corridor above us right now?"

"None, Section C corridor empty; just four in radio room."

More silence. "Am opening east hatch above us before proceeding to south hatch. This will be our best point of egress."

Mike hesitated. "In which case, ensure south hatch is closed

immediately after access. You can't leave two hatches open."
Another pause. "Apologies for stating the obvious."

Kade gave a little laugh. "No apology needed, Archer-One. You are correct and we will comply. Stay connected."

Kade and Jules switched on their torches, directing the beams onto the hatch above them. "Right, Commander, open and secure."

Jules stepped on to the ladder, extracted the bolt and pushed open the hatch just enough to attach the wedge.

"Archer-One. Wedge in place. Any movement in Section C."

"None; still empty."

"Okay. Proceeding to south hatch. Out." He turned to his companions. "Right. Let's test these sensors."

He led the way and within a few yards a strip light high on the left side wall flickered into life illuminating the first part of their route. The ceiling was around two metres high and clear of any pipes and cables, all of which ran along the walls. Even so, it was low enough to make them instinctively stoop as they made their way. More lights came on as they moved forward so the whole length of the sub-floor was bathed in a pale yellow glow by the time they reached the south hatch.

★

Jason's instincts were telling him that something else was happening other than the two seemingly unconnected but coincidental intrusions on their routine. A pole-dancing stripper keeping everyone occupied on one side of the platform; someone holding him in a seemingly pointless dialogue while this was going on. The Russian appeared to have no objective other than to perpetuate the conversation; to keep him talking.

"Hey, what?" Kenny started as Jason flicked off the transmission switch and clicked on an icon on the computer screen next to the receiver, cutting off radio contact in mid sentence.

"Let's try somewhere else," Jason said.

A column of numbers representing working frequencies appeared on the monitor, rising from the bottom of the screen and highlighted in turn as the system checked each for five seconds for any current activity. Jason kept his eyes on the moving set of figures, interrupting the trawl a few times when a transmission was heard, until he found something which struck a chord.

"Arrived at south hatch. Awaiting information on position of target and others."

"Target still in place with same three others."

Then a familiar accented voice. "Archer-Two to Archer-One. Lost contact with target."

"Copy, but confirm target still in place."

Kenny screwed up his face in a frown.

"What does that mean, Oll? What the fuck's going on?"

"Let's try to find out." Jason's voice betrayed his feeling of unease. He turned to Razor. "Go and get as many back here as you can tear away from the cabaret. Tell them something really big is going down."

Razor set off at a run. There was half a minute's silence before the last voice on the radio spoke again.

"One person has left, heading for west side along Section B. Three only now in radio room, including target."

"Do you have names for the other two?" Kade.

A brief pause. "Kenny Morrison; Ross Kowalski."

"Thank you, Archer-One. Watch closely from now. Going up. Out."

The three men looked at each other wide-eyed. Jason broke the tense silence.

"What did he say – 'the other two'? If you're 'the *other* two', then that means I'm the target. Shit, what the fuck do they want?"

He checked the frequency – 156.400 megahertz. He locked on to it and waited.

★

A similar vertical ladder bridged the gap between the floor and the south hatch. Kade, Tom and Rico unslung their Hecklers as Jules climbed it and gripped the bolt. This time he pulled it back in a slow motion, producing no noise, opening the hatch only a fraction, just enough to attach the wedge. He eased it back down again to check it didn't close then stepped down the ladder to the floor and slipped off his own SMG.

"Okay," Kade said, speaking quickly. "Just three guys. We'll try to do this without them seeing who you are, Colonel. So stay outside the room; near the hatch, ready to close it if we have company or if we call you in. If we can get back down the same way, we can close the east hatch as we leave. Okay, all?"

"Okay." All replied.

Kade darted up the ladder and through the hatch, the others following and crouching down round the opening to take in the scene. From where they emerged they could see along two sides of the corridor. Ahead of them was Section C, running 160 yards to where they could make out a small irregularity in the floor, which was the hatch they had opened and secured at the top of east column. The radio room, according to Mike's directions, was about a fifth of the way along on the left.

At right-angles to Section C, running the same length to their left, was Section B, which formed the base of the squared-off horseshoe and the way to Section A on the west side where the majority of the Exiles on that level were watching Lydia's performance. They could make out the whoops of delight; the shrieks of appreciation and raw excitement.

The four men paused before Kade led the sprint for the radio room. Tom stayed crouched near the hatch just round the corner from Section B and out of sight of anyone who might return from the show.

★

Through the glass-panelled walls, Jason, Kenny and Roscoe saw the men approaching well before they reached the radio room. They looked round the room for anything resembling a weapon. Kenny picked up one of the computer chairs, holding it up like a shield in front of him, its four castors aimed towards the door. Jason and Roscoe followed his example. As the three men in assault gear burst into the room, they charged at them, line abreast, yelling loudly.

Kade moved quickly to his left and Jules to the right, splitting the point of attack and deflecting the impetus the charge. Grasping the guns tightly in one hand, they reached forward with the other to grab the cross-pieces which held the castors. Rico missed and took a hard blow to the head from Kenny's. He went down, rolling to avoid the follow-up kick from his attacker and continuing his roll, clamping Kenny's legs with his own and taking him down as well. The other two managed to parry the attack, each clutching hold of the chair with their free hand and forcing their assailants back, Kade punch-kicked Roscoe, karate-style, high on his thigh causing him to release his grip on the chair enough for Kade to wrench it from his grasp. He hurled it aside and raised the Heckler.

"Stop – now!" Kade's voice filled the room, the barrel of his gun under Roscoe's chin forcing his head back.

Jason looked across at them, letting go of his chair, and Jules pressed his Heckler hard against his chest. Rico had Kenny pinned face-down, his forearm pressed against the back of his neck. He got up, pulling Kenny to his feet.

There was silence for a few seconds, all breathless from the action.

"Jason Midanda," Kade said, "you're coming with us."

"What the fuck's going on?" Kenny shouted. "There's no-one here called…"

"Do you want to tell him?" Kade looked at Jason.

"My name is Oliver Wangari. You've got the wrong man."

Kade smiled. "Okay, I'll tell them."

The next voice echoed around the room and into the team's ear pieces, creating a weird stereo effect. "Large number of inmates making their way from Section A; twenty to thirty, more starting to follow."

The six men turned to look at the receiver on the long table next to the wall. Kade turned back to Jason with a smile.

"You're even better than we thought, Mr Midanda."

★

Tom heard the message from Mike over the radio at the same time he became aware of the sound of running feet a long way off. He sneaked a glance around the corner. At the far end of Section B, a crowd of people were running towards him, filling the whole width of the corridor. He removed the wedge from the hatch and let it fall, irreversibly, into place. Along the corridor, Kade stepped out of the radio room.

"How far away, Colonel?"

"Twenty seconds, max."

"Time to show your face. All under control here."

Tom watched him duck back inside then stepped out to face the oncoming horde.

★

Kade waved the Heckler towards the door.

"Move, Jason. *Now!*"

"My name is Oliver Wangari. Whatever you want, you've got the wrong person."

"That's right," Kenny said. "He's…"

"Jason Midanda." Kade said. He turned to Jason. "Are you coming with us or would you rather stay behind and explain to Kenny and Ross – *and* the rest – why they changed your name?"

"You're *wrong!*" Jason didn't flinch.

"They changed his name because he is the boyfriend of Katey Tomlinson-Brown, whose father is the guy who put you here – Tom Brown, former Home Secretary. Understandably, they didn't want any of you to know that. Right, Jason?"

"*I am Oliver Wangari.*"

"Twenty eight inmates approaching corner of Sections B and C." The disembodied voice again, this time tinged with anxiety.

They could hear shouting now and, suddenly, a burst of gunfire. Kade raised the Heckler to his shoulder and took aim at Jason's head. "You can die now or later when they beat you to death – or you can come with us. Now fucking *move!*"

Jason didn't move. Kenny spoke without looking at him.

"Is that true about Tom Brown, Jason?"

"No, of course it's not."

There was a moment's silence as Jason realised his mistake. He looked wide-eyed at Kenny and Roscoe. "Makes no difference. I'm one of you now."

The expressions on their faces told him otherwise.

Jason glanced across at Kade. "Okay, I'll go," he said, heading towards the door.

Kade spoke into his radio. "Team to Archer-One; freeze the signal."

★

Ahead of Tom, halfway along the corridor, the crowd were scrambling to their feet, looking around and behind them in bewilderment, their reflections in the glass walls at either side making the whole scene a confused mass of bodies. They started forward again. Beyond them, Tom could see more appearing from the west side, running to join the others.

Kade appeared at his shoulder. Tom glanced to his right to see Jason and Rico running for the east hatch. Jules was standing in the doorway of the radio room, his Heckler held waist-high, covering Kenny and Roscoe.

"Stop where you are!" Kade yelled at the advancing group. "We are not here to hurt anyone. We have what we came for and we are leaving."

The ones at the front stopped at the appearance of the second man and the shouted command, allowing those behind to catch them up, swelling the numbers and forming a solid wall of people, pressed together across the width of the corridor. Then they began to creep forward again, around fifty of them now, silently and in slow motion, behaving like a single entity, seemingly with one mind, like a scene from a zombie movie. They were no more than fifteen yards away.

"Okay!" Kade shouted. "Straight through them this time!"

They aimed directly at the crowd. Those in the front stopped; some raised their arms, eyes wide now with horrified anticipation; others dropped to the floor or flattened themselves against the walls, scrambling and falling over each other, even before the Hecklers thundered and echoed along the corridor.

Kade turned to Tom. "Okay, *go!*"

They set off towards the east hatch with Jules ahead of them and Kade removing the Glock from his jacket as they ran. At the radio room, Kade stopped, aiming carefully through the doorway and loosing off an extended burst. The transmitter disintegrated

344

in a spectacular eruption of sparks and flying metal as Kenny and Roscoe dropped to their knees and covered their heads.

Twenty seconds later they reached the hatch, with a hundred feet pounding along the corridor behind them. By that time, Jason and Rico were already through and Jules was lowering himself onto the ladder. Kade was ahead of Tom. He turned as they reached the opening and handed Tom the Glock.

"Take this and hold them off while I get the wedge." Tom spun round to face the charge as Kade dropped down through the hatchway. He held out both guns towards the advancing crowd, loosing off a burst from the Heckler again.

"Stop there! Don't make me shoot anyone! We are leaving…"

Tom heard the sound of the hatch closing behind him.

★

Mags's mobile trilled on the side table in the family lounge next to the armchair where she was trying her best to read a magazine. She checked the caller's name and the time on the display. John M; 14.45.

"Hi, John. Any news?"

"None I'm afraid, Maggie. DI Waters and one of his team are up there right now but the local guys had done a really thorough job already, so nothing new. Just a question to you, though. You and Tom stayed up there earlier this year, didn't you? Out in the wilds."

"That's right. Farcuillin Lodge on Knoydart." Mags choked a little on the words.

"Right. Well they checked it out today to see if that's where he might be – though I understand it's a long way from Ullapool. Anyway, he's not there but I just wondered if you thought there was any chance that's where he might be heading."

"It's possible I suppose. He could certainly get in. The lock's on a keypad, and he knows the combination. Not that you need to lock your door up there because there's no way to the lodge except by chopper or a twenty mile walk through the mountains. So *just* possible, but very unlikely."

"Okay. We'll keep watching anyway. It's just hard to know where he could be hiding up there. And *why* up there? That's what I don't understand."

Mags didn't reply.

"Maggie, are you still there?"

"Listen, John. There's something I should perhaps have told you last Thursday when you were here. About why he might be up there. Although this is even more unlikely than him walking to Knoydart."

★

Tom had his back against the end wall when he heard the faint sound of the bolt being retracted. The fifty or so inmates were crowded within a few yards of him, some staring at him with puzzled and increasingly hostile looks, but most with their eyes fixed on the floor where the hatch had closed. Suddenly, with a metallic squeak, it opened again, slightly, towards where he was standing. Kade's eyes glinted through the gap. Tom raised both guns, aiming into the group, and squeezed the trigger on the Heckler, hoping it still had some credibility as a weapon.

Kade swung the hatch up as far as it would go and leaned round it to face the crowd, firing at them with his own weapon. The Exiles dropped back instinctively, wheeling away to the sides of the corridor, but this time no-one dropped to the floor.

Tom grabbed the rim of the hatchback and Kade dropped down to the sub-floor, freeing the ladder for Tom to slip through the opening. He swung the hatch back over and grabbed the handle on the underside to close it as fingers from above wrapped around the edge, trying to pull it open; angry voices shouted, hurling abuse and obscenities at them. Tom let his legs swing free, giving all his weight to the task. For a long moment the hatch was suspended in dynamic equilibrium as more fingers gripped and pulled on the rim before Kade climbed past Tom to club at the restraining hands with the stock of his gun. There were yells – of pain this time – and more screamed obscenities as the hatch fell shut, the bolt springing back into position.

Tom swung his feet down to the floor and released his hold on the hatch. The strip lights along the sub–floor had switched off automatically and they were in total darkness, except for the sliver of light coming up through the wedged hatch at their feet.

"What the hell happened there?" Tom's voice was shaking with anger. Rico lifted the hatch open, flooding the area above it with light and showing Jason looking wide-eyed in disbelief at Tom.

"Accident," Kade said. "Hatch fell shut and the bolt jammed. Inquest later. Let's go."

"Mr Brown." Jason hadn't moved since Tom spoke except to open his eyes even wider.

"That's for later, too," Kade said. "Right now, Jason, you need to concentrate really hard. Jules!"

He turned to the Senegalese who took a leather belt and an extra pair of the rubberised gloves from the rucksack and handed them to Jason.

"Put on these and use karabiner'clip on the belt when you take a rest on the way down. We stay at your pace, so no need to go faster than you can with safety."

Jason took the belt and gloves.

"Thanks. Where now?"

"Down there," Kade said, pointing through the hatch to the landing eighty feet below. "Let's go, Colonel."

Tom led the way down, Kade second, then Jason and Rico with Jules last, collecting the wedges on the way. With three stages behind them, they stopped on the lowest landing.

"Team to Archers One, Two and Cassie. One stage to go. Will reach outer door in five minutes. Cassie, are you ready to receive?"

"Ready and waiting to welcome you aboard, sir."

"Thanks, Major. Archer-One, estimated time until they discover problem with target's data."

"Earliest eight minutes from now at fifteen-twenty."

"Assume you copy that, Lochshore," Kade said. "Confirm when you can and keep all informed. Archers One and Two, disengage; Archer–One rendezvous with Cassie in approx one hour. All out."

Kade reached for the final hatch. "Let's go catch our ride."

★

The four police officers sat round a table in the new cafeteria annexe to the police station, the floor to ceiling windows around three sides letting in the low afternoon sun, which cast a whole new pattern of shadows on the heights beyond the loch and on the town itself.

Four mugs of coffee steamed in front of them. Rob Cameron had returned to Inverness after they had carried out a further examination of the Audi R8.

"I'm not sure what the Super expects us to do with this information – if anything," Harry said. "You really do wonder about Mr Brown's state of mind when he tries something as lunatic as that. But surely he must have abandoned any idea of saving Jason now he's *on* the platform. So what *can* we do?"

Charlie shrugged. "Apart from checking the area around the platform."

"Which we've done," Harry put in.

"Which we're *doing*," Charlie corrected. His mobile sounded. "This could be it." He remained seated to take the call. "Right... Right... all cleared with Lochshore? ... Good... *Did* she now?" he smiled. "Right... But nothing out of the ordinary? ... I mean nothing *else* out of the ordinary? ... Okay, thanks, Colin." He ended the call and pocketed the mobile. "Nothing except a couple of boats from the British Oceanographic Society, taking water samples around St Kilda and the platform. Trying to save the planet, no doubt."

"And the smile, sir," Isabel said. "What was that about?"

"Apparently a woman on one of the boats did a striptease for the lads. Perhaps we should bring her in for questioning."

"Or an encore," Harry suggested.

Natalie shook her head and sighed. "Can't take you anywhere." She turned to Charlie. "And what wasn't anything out of the ordinary, if you don't mind me asking?"

"Oh, just a bit of excitement on Alpha – other than the stripper, I mean. People charging about. They think a fight or something. All calmed down now, he said."

They sat in silence for a while, sipping their coffee.

"Pretty weird behaviour for someone who's part of a scientific study, don't you think?" Natalie said. "Doing a striptease in the middle of the Atlantic in November. Without dropping this young lady in it, would it be worth a phone-call to the BOS to check the survey was legit."

"Lochshore confirmed it was when my guy asked just now. They'd okayed all the clearances and such."

Natalie shrugged.

"Right. I don't want to step on anyone's toes. I just thought, in the absence of anything else we can do right now…"

★

They pulled open the door at the base of the column and looked out onto a different world from the one they had left two hours ago. A weather front was driving in from the west and a significant swell was heaving Cassie up and down twenty or so yards away, with Shirley-Ann working hard to keep her in position. A fine rain was blowing across the water, reducing visibility to around half a mile, poor enough to make Tom wonder about the link-up with the chopper.

They pulled on the life jackets and Tom, Jason, Rico and Jules dropped into the water, striking out hard for the submersible. Shirley-Ann edged it towards them, opening the dome just enough for them to squeeze aboard but avoiding the wind catching it and destabilising them further.

Kade backed half-out of the opening until he was standing on the threshold, with the door partly closed. In a single movement, he grabbed the handle and jumped up and out, placing his feet at either side of the opening and leaning back, almost horizontally. The door slammed close and he twisted the handle to secure it before dropping into the water. He scrambled aboard, where the others had removed their life-jackets and over-clothes and were pulling on the wetsuits. Five minutes later they were ready to leave.

"Cassie to Archers One and Two." Shirley-Ann spoke into the on-board radio, "Leaving Alpha. Changed back to main communications from tactical radios."

"Archer-One here." Mike's voice. "System has just flagged Jason's data as anomaly. Await further details from Lochshore."

"This is Archer-Two." Lydia's voice. "Copy all that."

"Kade here; we can rendezvous closer with poor visibility. Same heading, two miles instead of five. On borrowed time now. All copy?"

349

Archers One and Two responded.

Shirley-Ann again. "New ETA with Archer-One, eighteen minutes. Please advise exact co-ordinates. Flooding cabin now. Out."

★

The shift supervisor at Lochshore screwed up his eyes at the screen on the wall.

"What's the meddling little bastard done now?" He moved the curser on his PC monitor and clicked on the highlighted number, bringing up the last three readings from Jason's chip.

"Well we don't know for certain that he's done anything. Could be a malfunction," one of the other men said.

"If it was anyone else but Wangari..."

"What has he done, exactly?"

The question came from the fifth man in the room. To this point he'd been a silent observer.

"I'm not sure exactly what he's done *this* time, sir, but he's a bloody pain in the ass, hacking into programs and files. And he's built himself a transmitter and been talking with God knows who in the past few weeks. You'd know more about that than us, I guess, sir. We just get to hear rumours, but one is that he's made contact with terrorists colonising disused rigs in the North Sea. Don't know if it's true. They jam his broadcasts whenever they intercept them but he manages to jam the jamming somehow."

"Well, you're right," the man said. "He *has* been in touch with some dodgy characters recently, and it *is* a concern of ours what his end objectives are. But what's happened right now?"

The supervisor moved the cursor to one of the pin-pricks of light on the screen.

"That's the signal from Wangari's chip – or supposed to be. It's showing him to be in the lower corridor just outside the radio room. He's been there, in that position, for over half an hour – according to the signal. That in itself would be unusual, though not significant. But the system scans the medical data for every Exile every fifteen minutes; it's designed to pick up incidents such as death and heart failure, but it also highlights other anomalies; and

350

it's just flagged that Wangari's readings have been exactly the same for the last three scans."

"And that *is* significant? I mean, is he unconscious or what?"

"It's significant in that it shows there's something wrong with the *signal* – not necessarily with Wangari. All his indicator levels are normal."

"So, couldn't it mean he's just stable – you know, relaxed?"

"Even in its most static condition – say, a deep sleep – the human body experiences slight changes in heart rate, breathing patterns and blood pressure. Two identical sets of readings, fifteen minutes apart, could just possibly be a coincidence; three is definitely a system anomaly. You can see on the live monitor, there…" he pointed to a panel at the bottom of the screen, "… there's no movement, no fluctuations in the data lines at all."

"So how could that happen?"

"Well, someone's got to *make* it happen. We can do it…" he waved his arm to include his colleagues, "… but no-one else should be able to – other than the techies, of course. But our friend Wangari is always screwing with stuff."

"And what does it mean, exactly?"

"It means he's not where it says he is and his health readings are not what they are showing. Put simply, his signal is frozen for the time being."

"Couldn't you just *un*freeze it?"

"Not us; we're not allowed to touch it. There might be a knock-on effect if we do the wrong thing. It's a form of sabotage, in effect, and we need the really clever boys and girls to unpick it."

"But what would he have to gain by freezing his own signal?"

"My guess is he's just messing about – making a nuisance of himself for the sake of it."

"So what happens now?" the man asked.

The supervisor considered before answering. He checked the time on the screen in front of him. "Three-thirty-four. We'll give it until four o'clock to see what happens. He's nothing to gain by disconnecting with us, other than a bit of recreation. It's *his* health we're monitoring, for *his* benefit, so I'm sure he'll come back on-line at some point."

"And if nothing's happened by then?"

"Then we'll get the techies in. I'll alert them now."

He reached for one of the phones on the table in front of them.

"Okay, twenty-five minutes," the man said, turning to leave the room. "I'll be back in time to see. Please excuse me for now."

As he entered the small office he had been allocated further down the corridor, he slipped the miniature microphone out from behind his silk tie and checked that the carbon fibre in his ear was still in position.

★

The weather had closed in further and visibility was down to a few hundred yards. The rain was heavier and the wind and sea more hostile. Mike breathed a sigh of relief as Cassie rose out of the water behind Archer-One. He checked his watch. The new ETA had been spot on; 3.44 pm.

Archer-One was holding her position facing due west into the wind and Shirley-Ann manoeuvred the submersible under the relative shelter of her stern. After a few anxious moments as the wind whipped at the open dome, Jules and Rico attached the chains from the winch, the dome was closed again and the craft lifted onto its station at the rear of the bridge. As the pilot and her five passengers went below to change out of their wetsuits, Mike's radio sounded.

"Lochshore to Archer-One."

"Receiving. Go ahead, Lochshore."

"They've established what you did with the signal, though they believe the target was responsible. On that assumption, they're waiting until four o'clock to see if he reverses what he did, then they plan to refer it to technical support. I'll suggest they might want to leave it longer, but we should assume this timeframe. Will advise going forward. Is target on board yet?"

"Target just on board. Thanks for the information. Out."

Mike wiped a hand over his face, working out the time. Fifteen minutes before they call the techies; ten more for them to get there and start looking; fifteen max to find what's wrong and switch to NTS to check where he is.

At best they had forty minutes.

For the first time, Tom and Jason were alone – relatively – on deck in the bows of Archer-One. Jason was still as wide-eyed with astonishment as in that first moment of realisation and Tom gave a little laugh as he waited for him to find the words.

"Why is this happening, Mr Brown? What have I done? Why me?"

"This isn't official, Jason. It's you because *I'm* doing it. *I* decided to get you back."

"Yes but why? And who are these guys? They look official enough."

"They're a professional hostage rescue outfit, hired privately by me to take you back to Katey – eventually. I don't know when – I haven't thought that far ahead. In the meantime, you and I will be holidaying in the Highlands."

"But how will you do that – I mean, take me back? Surely you can't go back yourself."

They had been standing shoulder to shoulder, looking ahead. Tom took a step to one side and turned to face Jason.

"What do you mean, can't go back? What's to stop me? Not straight away, I admit – not with you, anyway. Stuff needs sorting first. New evidence has come to light in your case. Mickey Kadawe …"

"But he's dead." Jason interrupted. "He was shot, wasn't he?"

"How did you know that?"

"It was on the news. We've got TV, radio, Internet."

"Yes, of course you have. But what you don't know…"

"That's how I know about you – why you can't go back."

Tom furrowed his bow and shrugged.

"Sorry, Jason, you've lost me. *Why* can't I go back? Can't go back *where*?"

"Well, the whole country is looking for you. They say you've killed eight people."

Tom staggered and clutched the rail.

"You must know that, surely," Jason went on. "It's been the number one story on the news for the past five days."

Tom was unable to speak, his eyes glazing over.

"Mr Brown, are you okay?"

"I haven't seen the news," Tom said. "Not for ages. Who am I supposed to have killed?"

"You mean you really don't know?"

"Who am I supposed to have killed?" Tom shouted the question this time.

Before Jason could respond they heard the sound of engines coming across the water at surface level; the deep sound of large engines; much larger than a helicopter's. They could see nothing yet; the engines seemed far off, but getting closer. After a few minutes, a second sound competed for their attention; a higher pitched noise, the source of which lifted into the air. After a couple of minutes, an intense beam of light penetrated the haze. A Sea King helicopter took shape behind the glare, descending diagonally towards the boat, losing height as it approached out of the east.

The rest of the team were suddenly all around them, shaking their hands and wishing them luck. Shirley-Ann gave Tom a brief hug and he found himself wishing that Lydia was there to do the same. But what was missing, he realised, was the sense of triumph and euphoria which traditionally – *automatically* – comes with success. They seemed tense and wary; uncomfortable.

The chopper was hovering overhead now and the winch-man was descending towards the boat. Jules was guiding him down. He called across.

"Jason first. *Allons-y!*"

They fastened him into the spare harness and lifted him, swaying in the wind, into the Sea King, returning for Tom in less than two minutes.

Kade was the last to speak to him. His eyes were full of sadness and he held on to the handshake for a long time.

"It's been a privilege, Tom. After this, while there's time, please try to think of me as someone who doesn't *always* blindly follow orders; not when I'm sure they're wrong."

The harness tightened against Tom as it took the weight of his body, and his feet lifted from the deck. A thought came to him from nowhere and he shouted down to Kade.

"How did you know they'd changed Jason's name?"

★

Within a few minutes, they began to lose height, and Tom peered through the mist at the shape below them, which became clearer as they descended. He recognised a River-class patrol boat, 250-plus feet long with a displacement of 2,000 tonnes – many times larger than the Archers.

The Sea King came to rest on the flight deck at the rear of the vessel and the rotors slowed as the boat crew secured the wheels to the heavy metal rings set in the deck panels. The door was opened and two of the air crew dropped down, turning to signal for Tom and Jason to follow.

They were taken, single file, through a door and down a few steps – one man leading, the other bringing up the rear – to a comfortable, carpeted cabin and waved to a pair of armchairs at one side. The men took up what Tom assumed were pre-arranged positions, one standing behind each chair. Tom half-turned to look at them and saw they were both staring at a second door leading from the room.

It opened; someone stepped through it; Tom gasped.

At that moment, he felt the slightest pin-prick on the back of his neck. He rose to his feet, eyes wide and mouth open. The figure in the doorway seemed to sway; the edges of his field of vision glowed brightly with a light which spread to engulf everything in front of him. He barely had time to speak the person's name before the light dimmed and he felt himself lurching into blackness.

CHAPTER TWENTY-ONE

Tuesday; 3 November

Tom opened his eyes. He was on a bed, lying on his back, his head propped up on a pillow. His limbs seemed heavy when he tried to move them and his neck barely responded to his attempt at taking in his surroundings, limiting his field of vision to how far he could move his eyes. The ceiling above him was white, as were the plain blank walls around the room. Six spotlights, set into the ceiling, cast a cheerful yellowish light. He felt calm and relaxed.

Then he felt the room rocking gently, and his recent memory began to assert itself through the soft barrier of his apathy. He looked ahead of him past the end of the bed and saw that the apparition had returned. The same figure, framed in a doorway as before, but this time the image was clear and steady.

"Grace," he said. His voice was hoarse and it was an effort to speak. "Is that you?"

She walked to the side of the room, picked up a chair and placed it beside the bed. She was wearing DPM fatigues and her hair was pulled back in a tight bun behind her head. She had on her thick-rimmed glasses. She leant on the back of the chair to look down at him before easing herself onto it.

"Yes, it's me."

Tom gave a painful chuckle. "I always seem to be waking up in your bedroom."

Grace looked at him but did not reply. Tom could feel himself coming round and the inertia of his limbs and neck suddenly mattered. He felt a point of soreness on the left side of his chest. He bent his arm to touch it – a raised lump, like local bruising or an insect bite; but harder, and it seemed to move under his skin. He strained his neck to look down at it and noticed he was wearing the same clothes as when he had met Mike on Hampstead Heath.

"What's happened to me?" It was as much of a demand as he could manage. "Help me sit up."

"You don't need to sit up, Tom. You're fine where you are."

"Where's Jason?" he snapped.

"He's fine where he is, as well. Recovering from a minor op he had yesterday to remove something from his chest."

Tom was breathing heavily now from the effort of being angry. He lay still and silent for a while, gathering his thoughts. "Where are we?"

"We're on HMS *Jura*; River-class patrol vessel, converted into a hospital ship, specifically for covert operations. Right now we are about fifty-seven degrees north and seven degrees west, anchored in the lee of Beinn Mhor off South Uist. And to save you asking when, it's zero-two–hundred hours; Tuesday; 3rd November."

"And why are *you* here?"

"Because *you're* here, Tom, and I wouldn't want you to go without my saying goodbye."

"Goodbye? Am I under arrest? Jason said the police think I killed people. Is that right?"

"No and yes." Grace's voice was flat and neutral. "No, you're not under arrest, although…" she glanced at her watch, "…you're supposed to be in court in around eight hours' time. And yes, it's true the police think you killed people."

Tom screwed up his face in a frown and made another attempt to move, this time managing to raise himself up a little further on the pillow.

"Which people? Who would I want to kill?"

Grace opened her eyes wide and shrugged.

"You should know. You'd been *threatening* to kill them for some time."

"Who? Tell me *who.*"

"Quote – 'I promise that the people involved are going to pay for what happened to Jack and Jason. Not one single person is going to get away with what they did' – unquote. Possibly not verbatim, but clear enough. You set out to avenge your son and Katey's boyfriend."

"I don't recall ever saying that…"

"Oh, but you did. On many occasions. Almost as many times as you threatened to rescue Jason. It seems you keep your promises, Mr Brown."

"If I did say those things, it was just words, angry words…"

"So who is that young man in the next cabin, and how did he get there?"

"I mean about the killing. I didn't…"

Grace raised a hand to silence him. "It's alright, Tom. As it happens, I know you didn't kill anyone. But the fact is, they died. Eight of them – nine including Kadawe – all people who helped, directly or indirectly, to convict Jack and Jason. Died in the sort of rampage that would be well within the capability of an ex-Special Forces hero, with all his skills and connections, bent on revenge. So you can understand why the police came to that conclusion."

"So how come you know I didn't kill them?"

"Because I know who did, and why."

Tom closed his eyes. He breathed deeply and felt himself drifting off before rallying in an attempt to concentrate.

"You're talking in riddles. Are you going to explain?"

"Let me ask you something first. Do you believe Jack was guilty of dealing?"

"No, of course not, I never…"

"Well, I'm glad to hear it, because at one point I really wondered. You see, I never doubted his innocence for a second. Not a fraction of one. They were set up; *must* have been. Collateral victims – to use one of your favourite phrases – lost souls in a cruel world."

"So what has that got to do with my being here right now?"

"Just about everything."

She paused; Tom closed his eyes again and sighed.

"More riddles."

"When you changed the rules for expulsion, Tom – when you made it mandatory for drug dealers to be banished into exile – you introduced – for the first time – the possibility of innocent people being sent away for ever. Before then it was nice and neat – people with a known record of repeatedly and cynically rejecting this society get to experience a different one, more suited to their attitudes."

"You sound like Sylvie Hanker – when she interviewed me…"

"Ah, yes, the lovely, *flirtatious* Ms Hanker. How you used to enjoy her... probing – if I can put it that way."

"Not on that occasion, if you remember."

"I *do* remember, because she was right. She got you to admit what everyone was thinking and worrying about; that there really *could* be 'innocents caught in the crossfire' – I think were your exact words – and that this was an acceptable risk. And when I say 'everyone', that included me, Andrew, Jonathan and any number of front and back benchers on both sides of the House. It was a testament to your popularity and the trust you had earned that the drug dealer thing was accepted. And – wouldn't you know – just two months after the Hanker interview we had two of those very innocents convicted of a crime which would send them into exile."

"I still don't follow. Look I'm tired. Can we leave it for now?"

"There isn't time, Tom. I want you to understand this before it's too late."

"Too late for what?"

Grace ignored the question. "Right now, for most people, it's a done deal. As far as they're concerned, Jack and Jason *were* guilty; Jack, sadly, died and Jason has gone to where he deserves to go. Nobody cares any more; it's water under the bridge. *Except...* for one very tenacious little madam who was determined to join all the dots. Detective Inspector Jo Cottrell would not leave this alone. I can't criticise her for that – she believes exactly what I believe – that somebody set them up. The big difference between Cottrell and me is that she was hell-bent on *un*covering the miscarriage of justice and I was just as determined to cover it up."

Tom struggled up further on his pillow.

"Think of the bigger picture, Tom," Grace went on. "Something you were never any good at. Our party was elected for *one* reason. It promised people a New Justice Regime, where we would be harder on criminals and, particularly, on the indiscriminating little bastards who set out to disrupt ordinary people's everyday lives. And expulsion to Alpha was the cornerstone – king-pin, flagship, call it what you like – of the NJR. The bold, decisive, uncompromising means of separating the tormentors from their serial victims. The symbol of a new beginning.

"But so *much* of our credibility rides on the success and integrity of the NJR that if people start to think we screwed up by going too far, there's a real possibility that this government will implode. And that will happen if it gets out that we really *have* put innocent people – or an innocent *person* – onto Alpha. From where there is no return – at least that's what they think, and must go on thinking. So I will do everything I can to ensure that doesn't happen – that it *doesn't* get out. And 'everything' includes making certain that there is no-one around to reverse – or even cast any doubt on – the jury's decision to convict Jack and Jason."

Tom pushed himself up on one elbow and turned towards her. "Am I hearing things? You're fucking mad!"

From his elevated position, he noticed that the room was like a small operating theatre, with a stainless steel worktop at one side and a metal trolley next to it with several surgical instruments laid out neatly on its two shelves. He flopped down again onto his back, breathing heavily from the exertion.

"Right from the beginning, I thought it had to be Kadawe," Grace said. "He was the only player in the picture with the wit and nerve to do anything as big as that – set up all those people to lie, with the confidence that they were so shit-scared of him they wouldn't give him away; then actually *plant* some goods in both houses. I mean, you have to say, it was *brilliant* what that guy did. So when Cottrell – actually, it was her ex-boss – established the link between him and one of the guys who'd approached Jack on Delaware, it sealed it for me.

"I figured Kadawe himself wasn't a risk. He wasn't the type to fold. Much more likely that one or more of these other toe-tags would make a mistake. It helped that Mackay and Waters had their pride and reputations to think about. Denial was a better option for them than doubt. How would they look if they'd got it wrong and a rather special – and innocent – young man had died because of their mistake, and another one was lost forever? Mackay managed to reign in Cottrell at first, but he was never going to hold her off for long."

Grace shrugged and got to her feet, moving to stand at the foot of the bed, leaning on the end frame and looking directly into his eyes.

"So who had to die, Grace? Who do the police think I killed

– and why would I get rid of people who might have proved Jack wasn't guilty?"

"As I said before, Tom, revenge – for their conspiring to convict him – or at least playing a part. But you asked who. Well, four of the guys who approached Jack on Delaware. David Gerrard – Cottrell's pet rottweiler – found out that at least one of them was instructed by his regular trader to ask Jack for drugs. It was quite possible, then, that others were put up to it by the same person – that would look very suspicious if it ever came to light. So they had to go."

"Jesus Christ. And who…?"

"Who killed them? Well it seems this same trader – Sammo Sampson – wasn't making such a great profit that twenty grand in used fifties for discharging four bullets was unattractive to him. We even lent him the gun, which we got back – along with the money – when he died suddenly of unnatural causes. The same gun, in fact, that was found in your apartment in SW1."

"*What?*"

"But the list is longer than that. There were the guys who phoned the police complaining about the stuff they claimed Jack and Jason were supplying. Seven of them. So far, three down – out of the four who came in for questioning – blown to bits in a so-called safe house in Dorking using the same type of explosive as the police have just found in your car. It should have been all four – in fact, with a bit of luck, it could have been six if Cottrell and her colleague hadn't got delayed in traffic.

"And then there was Mr Kadawe himself, of course. As I said, he was the one I didn't think would be an issue until Little Bo-bloody-Peep put her delicate oar in and revealed he'd been at Jack's party with a rucksack and an unlikely story about *looking* for drugs. And that let Cottrell back in with a vengeance, so he had to go. It's obvious *you* didn't kill him – you were right there when he died – but it would have been easy for you to arrange for one of your ex-buddies to do it. Or so people will be encouraged to believe. Shame about Kadawe; I was thinking of offering him a job…"

"How far?" Tom interrupted.

"Sorry?"

"How far do you go? Who's next? Jo Cottrell?"

"Very astute question. We had the perfect opportunity to do just that along with Kadawe. It would have looked like an unfortunate accident – a stray bullet – until you stepped in like double-o-seven and took her down out of the line of fire. Still I can hardly complain, you've made life very simple for us in terms of wrapping everything up. People will find it easy to believe the revenge scenario. Ex-Special Forces guy goes off the rails – riddled with guilt because of his involvement in his son's death – lashing out by taking down everybody who helped convict him."

Tom managed a sneer.

"You're out of your tiny mind, Grace. There is no way a court will believe that. It's my word against yours. You wouldn't even dare…"

"A court, you say? And you think *I'm* out of my mind. It won't go to court. Waste of taxpayers' money. If you add up the gun, the explosives, the threats you've made in public, the fact that you've been caught on CCTV several times near where the shootings took place – albeit a fortunate coincidence – there's more than enough to convince people even *without* the circumstantial evidence of your training with the Special Forces. Motive; opportunity; means – *fait accompli*. No point in confusing the issue by giving you the chance to deny it."

"What do you…?"

"So, in the spirit of the NJR – taking out of the system all time-wasting admin – this is an easy decision. You will be one of those collateral victims you said were an acceptable risk in achieving our ends. Think of it as setting an example."

Tom stared at her wide-eyed, searching for a softening in her look; a change of tone in her voice; *anything* to indicate that he was wrong in what he had shockingly concluded from her words. There was nothing to cast a particle of doubt.

"So, what happens, Grace?" He could feel his voice trembling. "I disappear, leaving my blood on your hands. Is that it? Not that you're not up to your elbows in the stuff already."

Grace held up her palms towards him.

"Look, squeaky clean. No need to mess them up when you have a trained psychopath straining on a leash. Friend of yours, I believe. A freelance sadist called Jamie Walcott – a.k.a. Oscar Strange; long time associate of Andrew Donald and eager to please him at all times – even before he was in office. Remember Andrew wanting to get rid of Hewlett from the shadow cabinet and the NJR project team, and you did your Boy Scout impersonation – let's all be friends and work together, ging-gang-goolie-goolie. It was Walcott who snatched Lucy and made mummy see the light. But you know that, don't you? Hewlett phoned you and said she'd seen him at Balmaha, and you asked John Mackay to check him out."

"That little shit! And how do you know that?"

"Hey, he's not so little – *anywhere* as it happens – and he did you a few favours. Stopped you choking on your vomit a couple of times. And he returned your lost phone, remember. Well, I say 'lost' – what I really mean is 'stolen'. And before he returned it, he did make one little modification. The smallest transmitter-receiver in the world, inserted next to the SIM card; so from that moment on we were able to hear every word you spoke or heard within five metres of the phone *and* disable the phone if necessary. Talk about multi-skilled; our Jamie's got the lot."

"The fucking slimy bastard!"

"Well, I'm right with you there. If things were different I'd give you the co-ordinates of his unmarked grave so you could dance on it. But I'm afraid your dancing days are over."

Tom watched Grace as she turned away from the bed and began to pace the room. Eventually she sat down again.

"This thing with Jason," Tom said. "What was all that about? I assume the raid was your idea – or at least you authorised it."

"No, it was *your* idea. Well, in the sense that you told a lot of people you were going to do it – though I'm not sure what you had in mind until Needham came along. But it got me thinking. During the few short weeks he'd been on Alpha, Jason had become a fucking nuisance. A *brilliant* fucking nuisance, but a fucking nuisance all the same. Interfering with systems and programs, hacking into files, talking with God knows who – possibly God himself – on his DIY transmitter. So getting him off the platform did seem like a good idea – a necessity, in fact. If he could do so much in such a short time – what would he be like after he'd really got to know his way around the software?

"And after all I'd done for him, that's how he repays me. Andrew wanted him shipped out straight after the trial. That's why I had him

363

lifted at Kirmington and taken straight to Lochshore – so Andrew would think that's what was happening. But I'd already decided to delay his exile to Alpha for as long as I could – to make sure he'd be out of the news – and to change his name in case anyone recognised it. At least then he'd have a chance out there.

"With the benefit of hindsight, it would have been better to let you succeed in getting him off – or keeping him on – PTV2 on the day we sent him there. I have to say, I was pretty impressed with that – just how far you were prepared to go to save him. The idea of jumping into the sea – that was quite something."

"You won't get away with a fake security operation like that? Someone will challenge you about what was going on."

"Oh, they did. Ruby Weller was *furious*. We had a blistering row. But by then I had Lawrence Harding in my pocket – although I don't think it's my *pocket* he wants to get into. I got him to position it as an exercise to test how quickly we could respond to a security threat. You know – had to do it without telling people in advance or it would be meaningless – that kind of thing.

"Jonathan sort of mediated – I have an *excellent* relationship with him by the way – and we're all friends again, to a point. It doesn't take much to create a temporary communications shutdown. That was just to get Jason shipped out as quickly as possible with the Kadawe thing coming to a head. Couldn't risk somebody requesting that we take him off passage, not with Andrew thinking he'd already gone. Then you turned it into a *real* emergency with your little pilot chum. Actually, it's surprisingly easy scrambling a couple of jets."

"And they'd have shot us down?"

"I'm really glad they didn't, because, as I said, within a few weeks it became clear we needed to get him off. We had the means, we had the access, *and* we had a volunteer who knew Jason and, if necessary, could easily persuade him to leave with the promise of his being reunited with the lovely Katey. So it was two birds with one stone."

Tom felt himself tiring again as he struggled with the meaning of Grace's words. His own voice seemed distant and faint when he spoke.

"Two birds?"

Grace shifted her chair a little so she was facing him more directly.

"An exchange, Tom – you for Jason. That's how it was planned.

Kade was supposed to leave you there. So we get Jason off the platform and destroy the transmitter – that's bird number one; we leave you where you'd *never* be found and the south London serial killer disappears without trace, assumed drowned – bird number two. You're the only person the police are looking for and if they can't find you then everyone else is safe."

"You… really… are… mad…" Every word was a major effort now.

"Oh, there are a few loose ends." Grace continued as if Tom hadn't spoken. "The other four guys who approached Jack on Delaware and the three who phoned in but didn't agree to be interviewed – we think those three are part of the same four, anyway. But they seem to have disappeared off the face of the Earth of their own accord, and with Kadawe out of the way, and Jack and Jason now consigned to history – well, I'll take my chances. There's the guy who survived the Dorking bomb, but I think that will prove a temporary reprieve once he comes out of Witness Protection. We'll be monitoring Cottrell, of course – she's with her toy boy in Leicester and she'd do herself a big favour if she kept her mind on him in her spare time. It was a good move of Mackay's to send her back there; it might just save her life. And we'll be watching Gerrard, as well. Then there's the singer and her guitarist friend – I hope nothing has to happen to them because I think she's really good, don't you?"

She paused and he noticed just a hint of compassion in her eyes.

"To be honest, Tom, this is not about setting you up for murder. You've been a big concern for us for some time, which is why Walcott bugged your phone. We needed to know exactly what you were mouthing off about in your drunken revelries. If you continued expressing concerns about Alpha and the NJR, like you had been doing, you still have a big enough following out there to take a majority of people along with you. It was never initially planned to link you with the killings. You just played into our hands saying all the right things and being in all the right places."

Tom felt as though he was sinking into the mattress of his bed. The lights seemed less bright now.

"You said assumed drowned?"

"Your car was found abandoned in Ullapool about a week ago; parked near the harbour. A boat is missing from a mooring just north of the town. That boat will be found empty, except for a few of your personal effects, grounded on the Shiant Islands in The Minch some time soon, close to where you'll be dropping in very shortly. Eventually the story about your previous attempt to rescue Jason will come out. Then people will draw their own conclusions – an attempt to escape a murder wrap; another ludicrous stab at saving Jason Midanda; suicide; whatever. Your most optimistic fans will hope that it's a successful attempt to fake your own death and you'll be living on a desert island somewhere in luxury. No matter – it will be over. If Kade hadn't screwed up, of course, you would never have been found. But even if you are, then an autopsy will show you died from drowning, which will just confirm what most people had assumed."

Tom was silent for a long time, gathering his strength to speak.

"Who on the mission knew about this?" Grace had to lean forward to hear his whispered question.

"They all knew we were getting Jason off the platform because his transmissions were a genuine risk to the security of Alpha. So they knew that you wouldn't be taking him to Knoydart and believed you were there in case Jason resisted leaving with them. Only Kade, Jules and Rico knew that you weren't supposed to come back. And Jules and Rico were only told just prior to your leaving Mingulay. Of course, Harding didn't know that part either – he was your number nine on the mission, by the way. Useful to have someone who can just walk around Lochshore asking questions whenever he likes, without anyone wondering what he's up to; but a bit of a risk when it comes to sharing something like that."

"So Mike...?"

"Needham believed that the *only* purpose of the mission was to get Jason. He didn't even know we planned to pick up your phone from the Heath."

Tom managed a little smile.

"He nearly left me, you know."

Grace frowned. "What do you mean?"

"Kade. I understand now. He must have given me the Glock to use on myself. He closed the hatch and left me behind in the corridor. Then he opened it again."

Grace raised her eyebrows. "Really? He told me he didn't have an opportunity to leave you behind. Well, he's lucky he'll have the chance to redeem himself."

Tom moved his hand to take hold of Grace's. It felt like he was pushing a heavy weight.

"Please, Grace, for God's sake. We made love…"

"*Love*. That wasn't love, Tom; it wasn't even lust. It was more like … *masturbation* on your part. And for me, it was just for the satisfaction of knowing I could make you unfaithful to Maggie." Her voice softened a little. "I didn't want it to be like this, Tom. But it has to happen. Everything fits. And it makes it a little easier when your personal pride has been trampled on, and your loyalty rewarded with humiliation and rejection."

She pulled her hand away and got to her feet. Tom turned his head to her, using up all his remaining strength, every word now a test of willpower.

"Jason? What… happens… to…?"

"Well he can't go back, can he – to Alpha *or* Cobham?"

"So?"

"Use your imagination, Tom – but you'll need to be quick."

"And me? What…?"

"That's already happened."

She walked to the door, her image fading as he passed into unconsciousness.

★

The stretcher with the prone figure zipped into the thermal bag was pushed across the lounge on its trolley to the steps leading up to the flight deck – the ones down which Tom and Jason had been escorted twelve hours earlier. The trolley was raised on its telescopic legs and the stretcher slid out onto the deck. Four crew members grabbed the canvas handles at the corners and carried it the short distance to the helicopter, angling it up to be pulled into the cabin by Kade and his pilot. They secured it in place against the bulk head and Kade dropped down onto the deck. He was still wearing his combat gear and beanie hat. He went down into the lounge where Grace was waiting for him, seated on one of the armchairs.

"All set?" Her voice was clipped and strained. "If you'd done what you were supposed to do – what you're *paid* to do…"

"Then you wouldn't have had to face this moment." Kade completed the sentence for her. "It would all have happened conveniently somewhere else. Right?"

"Just remember your place, Kade, and who you're talking to. We all have our parts to play. When we've a little more time, you can explain why you decided to disobey a simple order."

"I'll tell you now; it takes no time at all. I *rescue* people, *save* people; I don't murder them – at least not good people who deserve to live. Which is why I'll need to consider my future with this group going forward. I'll complete this mission because the guys deserve their pay-check. That's the only reason."

Grace smiled. "That would sound very noble if you hadn't accepted the mission in the first place. But it wouldn't have been murder, anyway, would it? Our Mr Brown is a brave and natural leader – and if anyone could talk himself out of a tight corner, it's our Tom. Who knows, he may well have survived to lead a mass break-out or something."

"So what's this – now – if it isn't murder?" Kade said.

"Death by drowning. He'll be alive and sleeping peacefully when you leave him – natural causes. And please don't screw up this time, Kade. We've arranged an escort for you and I'll be tracking him on NTS, *and* watching his heartbeat. Just do your job."

She held out her hand for him to shake. He looked at it for a long time then shook his head.

"Sorry, ma'am, daren't risk it. Whatever it is you've got, it might be contagious."

He turned and went up the steps and across to the Sea King.

★

Ten minutes after take-off – twenty miles into their journey – Kade saw a light approaching from over to the west and Grace's 'escort' – a Lynx helicopter from the station on Benbecula – tucked in behind them to track them to their destination a further thirty-five miles away.

"Nice of them to care so much," Kade said to the pilot. "Let's give them what they want to see."

★

"Lynx to *Jura*, in position tracking Sea King."

"Copy, Lynx."

The two men in the cockpit of the Lynx remained silent from that point until they reached their objective twenty minutes later. The wind and rain had abated and breaks in the clouds allowed an occasional moonlit glimpse of the island group as they approached. They passed over the two largest islands, stretching north to south and joined by a narrow isthmus, across to Eilean Mhuire to the east.

They saw the Sea King hover a few feet above the waves near the island's northern tip and the cabin door slide open. The man beside the pilot focussed his binoculars on the two men in the opening. One, in casual clothing, lay horizontal and still on the cabin floor. He watched as the other man, in black combat trousers and jacket, wearing a beanie hat, knelt behind him and rolled him out of the helicopter into the waters of The Minch.

"Done." The man with the binoculars spoke in a hushed voice.

"Lynx to *Jura*; visual confirmation. Object entered water at fifty-seven degrees fifty north; six degrees twenty-five west. Sea King leaving site and heading north east. Should we maintain surveillance? Over."

"Copy, Lynx." A woman's voice now. "Let them go. Return to base. Out."

The contact was broken.

"Right, let's get the fuck out of here."

His companion's strong Ulster accent took the pilot by surprise. He glanced at him, noting that his eyes under the peak of his black baseball cap were shining with tears. The man twisted round to place the rifle he'd been holding behind his seat.

"Won't be needing this," he said, his voice now soft and refined again. "A Barrett M82," he added, speaking to himself, "the most powerful sniper rifle in the world; capable of bringing down a helicopter with a single shot."

369

In the small IT suite on HMS *Jura*, the two people present checked the NTS monitor to confirm the co-ordinates of the drop. Their attention switched to the panel at the side of the screen showing the five life indicators, their signals weakening from a succession of vigorous peaks to gentle undulations and finally to a series of flat lines.

They sat in silence for five long minutes before Mike rose to his feet.

"I'm going on deck," he said, his voice steady and calm.

Grace nodded, saying nothing.

The door closed behind him; and the ice around her finally melted and ran down her face as tears.

THE SHIANT ISLANDS

The group of islands known as the Shiants (pronounced 'Shants') lies five miles off the east coast of Lewis. In addition to the three main islands, a line of Galtachean rocks stretch out to the west, like the tail of a gigantic sea monster. The highest cliffs reach a height of five hundred feet, dropping vertically to the cold waters of The Minch. The islands are home to seals, sea-birds and black rats.

And sheep.

Crofters from Lewis graze small flocks on all three islands, particularly on the most fertile of the group, Eilean Mhuire. The shepherd's house – now a bothy – is on the south island of Eilean an Taighe, and until the beginning of the twentieth century supported a family of seven. The islands are now uninhabited and visitors are rare, confined mainly to wildlife study groups and crofters checking their animals. From late summer to spring, the group is deserted by humans.

So for someone to be on Eilean Mhuire in November – at 4.00 am on the very day that a low flying helicopter dropped something into The Minch just a hundred yards off its northern tip – was an incredible coincidence.

ACKNOWLEDGEMENTS

Once again thanks are due to the many people who contributed in different ways to the production of this book.

To Alan Isherwood – again – who gave up his time on a number of occasions to provide me with information and answer questions relating to police procedure and policy. A great example of the police helping the public with *their* enquiries!

To all the people – friends, acquaintances and strangers – who have purchased *Catalyst* and *Heaven's Door,* and pursued me for the date of the next book in the series. Their encouragement and generous feedback made it an easier task to complete the final instalment of the *Hotel St Kilda* trilogy.

To those who have helped in a practical way to promote my work through meetings with reader groups and other organisations, in particular the Bury group of libraries who have provided me with opportunities to reach a wider reader population. And, on an individual basis, sincere thanks to my good friend, Leonie Fitton, for arranging a number of events through her own circle of social groups, and for her constant interest and support.

To my publisher, Matador, for making the whole experience of creating these books such an enjoyable one; and to Gary Smailes of Bubblecow – again – for his detailed editorial critique and invaluable advice following on from this.

To my family for their continuing encouragement; and especially to my wife, Carol, for both her wise counsel and her amazing achievement in converting my ethereal thoughts about book cover design into such excellent final images.

Thank you all.

MICHAEL KNAGGS was born in Hull in 1944. He moved to Thurso, Caithness, in 1966 to work as an Experimental Officer at Dounreay Atomic Power Station, and relocated to Salford in 1968 to complete a degree in Chemistry. From 1970 up to his retirement in 2005, Michael worked for Kellogg Company – the global breakfast cereal manufacturer – latterly as Human Resources Director with responsibility for pay and benefit policy across the company's European organisation.

He lives in Prestwich, Manchester, with his wife, Carol. Their passion is hill-walking and they undertake at least one long distance walk each year. They have two children and two grand-children.